Praise for *Getting Hot with the Scot*

"A fun, sexy, and delightful read!"
　　　　—*New York Times* bestselling author Julie James

"*Getting Hot with the Scot* is a wild romp, a ton of fun, and a new addition to my favorites shelf!"
　　　　　　　—*New York Times* bestselling author
　　　　　　　　　　　　　　　　Christina Lauren

"Unabashedly sexy and romantic, Melonie Johnson's debut is a fabulous read!"
　　　　—*USA Today* bestselling author Kate Meader

"*Getting Hot with the Scot* is compulsively readable and entirely satisfying."
　　　　　　　—*New York Times* and *USA Today*
　　　　　　　　　bestselling author Julie Ann Walker

GETTING *HOT* WITH THE *SCOT*

Melonie Johnson

St. Martin's Paperbacks

This is a work of fiction. All of the characters, organizations, and events portrayed in this novel are either products of the author's imagination or are used fictitiously.

GETTING HOT WITH THE SCOT

For information address St. Martin's Press, 175 Fifth Avenue, New York, NY 10010.

ISBN: 978-1-250-19309-4

Our books may be purchased in bulk for promotional, educational, or business use. Please contact your local bookseller or the Macmillan Corporate and Premium Sales Department at 1-800-221-7945, ext. 5442, or by e-mail at MacmillanSpecialMarkets@macmillan.com.

Printed in the United States of America

St. Martin's Paperbacks edition / May 2019

St. Martin's Paperbacks are published by St. Martin's Press, 175 Fifth Avenue, New York, NY 10010.

10 9 8 7 6 5 4 3 2 1

Dad.
This first one is for you.
Love, Mouse

CHAPTER 1

THREE WEEKS AGO, Cassie Crow left Chicago armed with a naked charm bracelet and a full box of condoms. Now, she sat alongside her traveling companions and dearest friends, crammed together on a wooden bench of indeterminate age in the great hall of an ancient Scottish castle. Cassie shifted and glanced down; the silver chain at her wrist sparkled in the late morning sun streaming in from a row of arched windows high overhead. She tilted her arm, enjoying the soft tinkle of charms that marked her travels through Italy, Spain, France, the Netherlands, and most recently, Scotland. No longer bare, her bracelet was loaded with tiny keepsakes she'd found in shops all over Europe.

The condom box, however, was still full.

Nearing the last leg of her vacation of a lifetime, Cassie still had not gotten the one souvenir she'd been looking forward to ever since she and her friends had first started planning this dream trip ages ago——a fabulous, wanton fling. A heart-pounding memory she couldn't stick in a photo album, plop on a shelf, or wear on her wrist.

This trip was supposed to be her chance to let go, to be impulsive, to take the risks she refused to even consider back home. Opportunities had come her way, sure, but something always seemed to stop her from sealing the deal. There had been that one guy in Monte Carlo, panty-dropping sexy, but he'd been looking for something more, um, *adventurous* than what she'd had in mind. Even if she spoke perfect French, how was she supposed to know "Wanna play with my monkey?" was not just a euphemism?

Oh, who was she kidding? Cassie knew what the problem really was—her. Even though she'd promised herself that once she was on vacation, she would finally let loose, the truth of the matter was, she wasn't the type to talk a perfect stranger into a one-night stand. Maybe that had been the flaw in her plan all along. In all her years of dreaming about steamy foreign encounters, she'd never envisioned how she'd actually hook up with her fantasy fling. Her brain simply skipped to the good stuff.

"This place could be on the cover of one of those romance novels you're always reading, Cass." Cassie's best friend, Bonnie, pushed the tumble of red curls away from her face and stared up at the wide wooden beams bracketing the ceiling.

"Yeah," Cassie agreed. She wasn't going to admit she'd already been thinking the same thing—had been, in fact, since the moment they'd arrived at Edinburgh Castle and she got her first up-close glimpse of the towering turrets. As she and her friends climbed the stone steps, Cassie had imagined a hulking warhorse, hooves drumming across the courtyard, kilted rider yelling something appropriately battle worthy, eyes flashing in his fierce yet handsome face.

She took in the rows of ancient battle axes and claymores lining the walls, picturing a broad-shouldered Scotsman wrapping a brawny fist around the hilt of one these weapons, muscles bulging and kilt swinging. Cassie sighed. "Sadie and Ana are going to be so sad they missed out on this."

"Don't worry about those two," Delaney muttered from Cassie's other side, tossing her long, strawberry-blond ponytail over her shoulder. "I think it's safe to say they had more than their fair share of whisky last night."

"What time did they get back to the hotel?" Cassie asked.

"No idea." Delaney shrugged. "But when I left our room this morning, they were still in bed, nursing authentic Scottish hangovers."

"Well, I'm not going for a hangover today . . . just a nice buzz." Cassie nodded toward a stout little man with jowls like a bulldog who was walking between trestle tables laden with rows of empty shot glasses, checking the IDs of the crowd gathered for the castle's whisky tasting. Bulldog paused at their table and ran a jaundiced eye over their passports before handing each of them a plastic bracelet.

Though they were all in their late twenties and well past Scotland's legal drinking age, Bonnie's sweet, freckled face looked much younger. "I think he growled at me," she whispered, sliding the bracelet on her wrist.

"Be glad he didn't bark." Delaney grinned and put her own bracelet on. "He looks like he bites." Another stout little man appeared, this one with a frothy, white beard bristling beneath a cherry-red nose. Delaney's grin widened. "And *he* looks like Santa Claus."

"Makes sense." Cassie chuckled in agreement. "He is bearing gifts, isn't he?"

Santa proceeded to pour each of them a measure of amber liquid.

"'O thou, my Muse! Good old Scotch drink!'" Bonnie recited as she lifted her glass.

Cassie turned to her best friend and blinked. "What was that?"

"Burns."

"You haven't even tried a sip yet," Delaney argued.

"No, *Robert Burns*. Famous Scottish poet," Bonnie explained and raised her glass higher, striking a dramatic pose. "'Inspire me, till I lisp and wink, To sing thy name!'"

"Um, if you say so," Delaney muttered, unimpressed as she lifted her own glass. Bonnie had been spouting literary passages all over Europe, ever since the start of their trip. Delaney took a whiff of her drink and coughed. "Hel-*lo*." She held the whisky at arm's length. "I think I'm getting drunk off the fumes."

"Oh, come on," Cassie teased. "I know you preschool teachers hit the hard stuff on a regular basis." Cassie downed her own shot. "Whoa," she wheezed, eyes watering.

"Told ya." Delaney smirked.

Cassie chugged a glass of water and refilled her tumbler from the pitcher on the table. While waiting for Santa to pour their next round, she pulled out her phone.

"Ugh, are you on that thing again?" Bonnie's usually smiling rosebud mouth dropped into a pout.

"Excuse me, but some of us can't completely disconnect from our jobs." As teachers, both Bonnie and Delaney had the summer off to do as they pleased. Even Sadie was on hiatus, having recently wrapped up her role on a daytime soap opera. Of her traveling companions, Ana was the only other one doing anything resembling work, and that was mostly checking out restaurants in the name of "research" for her catering company. "It's just a quick check of my email, okay?"

"I thought you were still on break from taping the show,

anyway." Delaney downed the last of her first shot and gagged.

"I am." Cassie squinted at her phone. It was taking more effort than normal to log into her work account. Fingers sliding clumsily over the keys, she realized it wasn't a Wi-Fi issue. Delaney was right, the drink *was* potent. Or maybe she wasn't used to hitting the bottle before noon. One shot in and she was getting tipsy.

"*ChiChat* is in rerun rotation until September, but I asked Therese about scheduling a meeting when I get back next week, before the new season starts." Cassie had been working up the courage to discuss her idea for a new position with the executive producer of the morning Chicago talk show for months, and decided to bite the bullet right before she left town, hoping being on vacation would help keep her from fretting. Of course, she couldn't stop thinking about it. Bonnie was right, she'd been obsessively checking her phone the entire trip. "If Therese gets back to me, I don't want her to think I'm ignoring her."

"Well, *I* think you're ignoring *us*." Bonnie grabbed Cassie's phone and dropped it into her purse.

"Hey!" Cassie yelped as she watched her phone get swallowed into her best friend's cavernous bag. "You better not squash my phone," she warned.

Bonnie patted the side of her purse, which was big enough to hold the *Complete Works of William Shakespeare*, and probably did—the unabridged version. "Your phone will be fine." She paused while Santa poured the next round. "And soon enough, you'll be home, selling Therese on how you plan to change lives with serious news stories."

Once all their glasses had been refilled, Bonnie raised her fresh whisky in a toast. "To old friends and new beginnings."

Cassie clinked glasses with Bonnie and hoped her friend was right. She had a lot riding on that meeting. With a prayer for her future, Cassie downed her drink, gasping for breath as the alcohol singed her vocal chords. "How many rounds are in this tasting?" she croaked.

"Check the list." Bonnie held up the tasting brochure.

Cassie glanced at the names of whiskies and their descriptions. As she tried to do the number-of-shots-to-speed-of-getting-wasted math, she heard a squeak from Bonnie. Or maybe that was a hiccup. Cassie eyed Bonnie over the top of the paper. "You okay?"

Bonnie shook her head, blue eyes wide, mouth opening and closing like a fish out of water. Cassie set the brochure down and frowned at her best friend. If Cassie was a drinking lightweight, Bonnie was a featherweight. "What's wrong? You're not going to puke, are you?"

"Puke?" From the other side of Bonnie, Delaney leaned to the side with ninja-like reflexes, her long, strawberry-blond ponytail whipping out of harm's way. "Who's puking?"

"Nobody's puking." Bonnie sucked in a breath and flipped the tasting menu over. "Look!"

Still poised for escape, Delaney read the section Bonnie was pointing at. "Some local author is visiting the castle today." She relaxed and eyed Bonnie, who was practically vibrating in her seat. "So? Why are you so excited? All your favorite authors have been dead for eons."

"Nice." Over Bonnie's head, Cassie slapped Delaney a high-five.

"Very funny." Bonnie waved the paper in Cassie's face. "It says the author is giving a lecture today, and it's open to the public. And it's in the *castle library*."

Cassie and Delaney groaned in unison. Bonnie was a library whore. The mere glimpse of an old book got her more worked up than a boy-band fangirl with a front-row seat and a backstage pass. Country after country, Bonnie had dragged them into every historical library and used bookstore in every city they'd visited so far. Rome had been the worst. Prior to this trip, Cassie didn't know the Italian city was home to some of the most gorgeous libraries in the world. But she knew now. She'd been in them. *All* of them.

To be fair, Bonnie had returned the favor and indulged Cassie's desire to visit as many museums as possible. As the bearded whisky-bearer approached with the next bottle, Cassie consulted Delaney. "Well? Do we let her go fondle some books?"

Bonnie's gaze darted between them, feet tapping, knees bobbing, rattling the bench they were sitting on.

"Why not?" Delaney hopped up and adjusted her pony-tail. "That first shot was more than enough for me, any-way." She waved a hand over her barely touched second drink. "No more for me, Santa. Thanks."

Cassie held out her glass. "I'll take one more. For the road."

Santa pulled back the decanter and frowned, the corners of his mouth disappearing into his beard.

"I'm kidding!" Cassie giggled. "We took a tour bus."

Santa poured her third shot, eyes narrowed beneath his bushy brows. "The whisky doesna leave this room," he warned, "you ken?"

"I ken." She giggled again. A sucker for that accent, she could eat him and his Scottish brogue up.

"You're getting rather giggly there, missy." Delaney observed in her teacher voice.

"Come on, Cass!" Bonnie wriggled off the bench.

"Okay, okay." Cassie quickly tossed back her third whisky and stood. The liquid burned a path from throat to belly as she got to her feet, which were less steady than she'd have liked. "All right." She turned to Bonnie. "I'm ready. Lead the way."

Ecstatic, Bonnie did an impromptu jig as she maneuvered them around tables and benches, auburn curls bouncing.

Once outside the great hall, Cassie held up a hand. The three whiskies, on top of the water she'd chugged, not to mention the monster-size latte she'd had this morning, had suddenly caught up. "You two go on ahead. I'll meet you in a minute."

"This goes against the buddy system." Delaney frowned. "You sure?"

"Yes, Miss Delaney. As long as you're sure this place has modern plumbing somewhere."

"I think the bathroom is that way." Bonnie pointed and then gestured in the opposite direction. "The library's this way."

"See? No problem." Cassie shooed them off.

Before Delaney could argue further, Bonnie yanked her down the hall. Cassie turned and headed the other way, keeping an eye out for signs for the bathroom. She grinned, recalling the funny restroom sign she saw while at a pub last night. It had the usual image for women of a stick figure wearing a triangle as a dress. But on this sign, the stick person for the men's room also wore a triangle—indicating a kilt. Too bad there hadn't been any men at the pub dressed in one. Contrary to her fantasy version of Scotland, hunky, shirtless guys in kilts weren't sprinkled liberally across the country.

Ah well, Cassie bet when people came to America they expected everyone to be dressed like cowboys. She wouldn't mind a cowboy either—or maybe a cowboy wearing a kilt—she'd throw money at a romance novel with that cover.

An impromptu fantasy of Fergus McCoy, the Scottish Highland Cowboy, kept her happily occupied until she finally encountered a sign for the WC.

After locating the restroom, with flushing toilets and running water—thank goodness for anachronistic modern plumbing in ancient castles—Cassie took her time retracing her steps. Bonnie loved old books, but Cassie was fascinated with old places and adored touring castles and estates. She had started out as a cultural anthropology major in college, and if not for a stint she'd done sophomore year on the university cable access news show, she'd probably be teaching classes on culture and society, working alongside Bonnie, who was an English professor at a small liberal arts college in the city.

That had been the original plan, but Cassie didn't regret the shift her career path had taken. She loved her job on *ChiChat*—well, liked it, anyway—she'd love it once she convinced Therese to let her take on more meaty topics, stories with the potential to change people's lives. And while her current role on the show had more to do with social media than social history, Cassie still enjoyed studying cultures and examining the day-to-day details of how people lived.

As she made her way back toward the library, Cassie paused in front of the rooms open for viewing. Like a life-sized dollhouse, each room was decorated in painstaking detail, filled with historical props and dramatic touches so realistic the castle felt alive, as if the inhabitants had just stepped out and would be back any moment. An antique sewing basket rested at the foot of one wing-backed chair. A secretary desk stood open, revealing a stack of letters tied with a ribbon piled next to a stationary kit, complete with feathers and a brass quill knife.

Plush, red velvet ropes blocked most of the doorways,

forbidding as giant stop signs, but if she leaned forward and craned her neck around the threshold, the view was worth the risk of landing on her slightly tipsy face. *Maybe a little more than tipsy.* Cassie blinked, looking around the empty, unfamiliar corridor. *Where am I?*

A woman wearing a headset rushed around the corner, almost knocking Cassie over as she scurried past.

"Excuse me!" Cassie called out. "Do you know where the library is?"

The women stopped short and turned around. "Hmm?"

Cassie raised her voice. "The li-bra-ry?" she overenunciated and mimed opening and closing a book.

"Oh, right." The woman pressed a button on a black box clipped at her waist. "Hold on," she barked into the microphone connected to her headset, "I think we've got one more." She returned her attention to Cassie. "Sorry about that." She shifted the microphone away from her mouth and tapped her chin. "The library. Yes. Um, I believe it is . . . er . . . let me think now . . ."

Doubt curled in Cassie's stomach mixing with the alcohol. "You do work here, don't you?"

"What's that?" The woman smiled and nodded. "Aye, I'm working here today, sure enough. Now, the library. You'll be wanting to go down that way." She pointed to the end of the hallway where another corridor broke off on the right.

Cassie squinted down the deserted hall, uncertain. "Are you sure?"

The woman nodded again. "Och, quite sure." She waved her hand in brisk dismissal. "Now, if you'll excuse me."

"Thank you!" Cassie called after the woman, who was already zipping away in the other direction. Cassie thought she heard the woman say something about getting ready because she's on her way, but couldn't be sure.

With a shrug, Cassie turned down the corridor on the right as instructed. It didn't seem familiar, but maybe she'd roamed so far off course this was a shortcut back. About halfway down the hall, an odd croaking stopped her in her tracks. Worried she'd upset a loose floorboard, Cassie went up on her tiptoes and took a careful step forward.

The wooden floor remained silent beneath her, but as she neared a doorway, the croaking came again, louder and more distinct this time—a moan, long and low. *What the hell?*

The door stood slightly ajar, a sliver of light peeking through the crack and kissing her toes. Cassie dropped to her heels and glanced around the hall. She was completely alone. Since there wasn't any of the dreaded velvet rope blocking her way, she pushed the door all the way open and cautiously entered the room.

Golden August sunlight sparkled on floating dust motes, filtering across the wooden planks of the floor in shadowy patterns made by the beveled lead dividing the glass of the tall windows. An ancient four-poster bed stood in the center of the room, shrouded with thick, hunter-green curtains. *All right, Cassie promised herself, if the noises are coming from that bed, you have permission to haul ass out of here.* As if on cue, another groan filled the room, hollow and haunting.

The good news? The sound was definitely not coming from the bed. She shivered with a freaky combination of relief and apprehension. The groan had come from the other side of the room, where a massive bookcase filled most of one wall.

On a hunch, she crossed the room and ran her fingers slowly over the bookshelves. Nothing happened. "What did you expect, Nancy Drew?" she chided herself. "A hidden spring revealing a secret passage?"

"Who goes there?" A hoarse Scottish burr rolled from behind the wall.

Still gripping one of the shelves, Cassie stumbled sideways and the entire bookcase moved with her, sliding open like a closet door. "Holy shit!"

"For shame, lass. What a tongue ye have," a husky voice growled.

She peered around the edge of the bookcase. A man sat in the recessed space, one shoulder propped against the inner wall of what appeared to be a passageway. His legs were sprawled in front of him—his bare legs.

Would you look at that? The man is wearing a kilt.

Note to self: Cassie Crow—be careful what you wish for.

The man groaned again and raised a hand to shield his eyes from the sunlight now cutting across the hidden alcove.

"Are you all right?"

"I will be fine once ye douse that blasted light." He squinted up at her. "Be ye a new chambermaid?"

Chambermaid? She eyed the wide sleeves and open neck of the old-fashioned piratey shirt he wore. "Not sure what kind of weird-ass stuff you're into buddy, but I don't do RPG."

"Weird . . . ass?" His dark red brows drew together as he shaped his mouth around the letters. "Are pee gee?"

"Role playing games. You know, like cosplay or whatever." She pointed at him. "Look, you're the one wearing that get-up and talking like a reject from *Macbeth*."

He narrowed his eyes at her finger. "Be ye a witch?"

"What did you call me?"

With another groan, he lurched forward. Oh God, what if he was hurt? For all she knew he was a member of some historic castle tour who got lost in a back passageway and hit his head. She leaned down to inspect him for bruises.

He threw a hand out, palm up, warding her off. "Back away, sorceress," he hissed.

"Seriously?" She slapped his hand out of the way. "Here, let me help you out of there." Cassie tugged gently on his shoulder. The voluminous shirt was loose, but she could feel—and appreciate—the thick spread of muscle beneath the soft fabric.

Just my luck, I finally run into a hot Highlander, and he's delusional.

The man waved off her assistance and struggled to his feet, shaking a wild tousle of thick, red hair out of his eyes. Cassie never fancied herself to be a ginger girl, but it worked on him . . . or maybe that was the kilt talking. She eyed the swath of plaid fabric wrapped around his hips and wondered, like any female in her position would, what might or might not be under there. Reluctantly, she raised her gaze and caught him scrutinizing her in return.

"What be these strange breeks ye wear?" he asked, moving in a circle around her.

Cassie swore she could feel the weight of each of his eyeballs resting on her denim-clad backside. *Fair enough.* After a prolonged moment, she glanced over her shoulder. "Get a good look?"

"Aye." He swallowed. "'Tis most unseemly, lass." He shook his head, gaze still glued to her ass.

"They're called jeans." She pivoted to face him. "Are you for real?"

He met her gaze, his answer falling from his lips in a deep, rich brogue with trilling *r's* that curled her toes, "Aye, lass, I'm real."

Cassie's heart hiccupped. *Of course he's real. Unless*

those shots were stronger than I thought. "Were you at the whisky tasting?"

"Whisky?" His green-gold eyes lit with interest. "Do ye have whisky for me, then? I could use a wee dram. Be a good lass and fetch it for me."

"Ha! I think you've had enough, mister. Is that how you ended up stuck in there?" Even as she said this, Cassie doubted it. She didn't smell a hint of alcohol on him, though she did pick up other pleasant smells. Mint and clove and man and . . . *Stop being ridiculous.*

His broad shoulders lifted and dropped. "I dinna ken."

"How long were you in there?"

Another shrug.

Cassie dragged her attention away from the wide curve of his shoulders and leaned past him, inspecting the dark, narrow space behind the bookshelf.

He grabbed her wrist and pulled her back, panic edging his voice. "Nay, lass. Doona be going in there."

"Why not?" She inched forward and tried to get a better look.

"It canna be safe." He tugged on her wrist again, his fingers warm and firm.

Tiny butterflies danced along the path where his skin touched hers. She brushed away the tingling sensation and slipped out of his grip, careful not to snag her bracelet. "Well, you were in there, and you appear to have managed."

"Are ye daft, wench? I was trapped!"

She sniffed, not sure she liked being referred to as a wench, and frowned up at him. "What's the last thing you remember?"

He closed his eyes and slumped against the shelf. "I canna recall anything afore the moment I woke to find my-

self crammed within yonder wall." He blinked and focused intently on her. "The moment I found you, lass."

Cassie decided she liked being called lass much better
than wench, especially when he was looking at her like
that. Gazes locked, her other senses sharpened, heighten-
ing her awareness of his body and its proximity to hers.
She cleared her throat. "Hm. I think it'd be more accurate
to say *I'm* the one who found *you*." Telling herself she was
only searching for injuries, she reached up and tentatively
skimmed her palms along his temples, her fingers trailing
his scalp.

"Looking for devil's horns?" The man cocked one
wicked brow at her as he raised his arms to mirror her
movements, running his hands over her head and shoulders before brushing his palms down her back. "Ye've
naught got any fairy wings, so I'd say we're even. In fact,"
he whispered against her hair, standing so close the low
burr of his voice became a purr in her own chest, "ye feel
perfect to me."

Like the migrating monarchs her dad studied, the butterflies made a return trip, enveloping her in a fluttery
haze. She shivered. Whether it was the Scot or the scotch
or both, Cassie didn't care. He was here and she was here,
and damn it all, it was about time she skipped to the good
stuff. With a forceful mental click, Cassie turned off her
brain, tilted her chin up, and caught his mouth with hers.

He made a low sound in the back of his throat, of protest or surprise, she wasn't sure. But then his hands settled
at her waist, and he returned the kiss. His mouth was
somehow soft and hard at the same time, and when he
slipped his tongue between her lips, she felt more light-
headed than if she'd downed every shot of whisky that
had been on that tasting list.

Cassie rolled her tongue against his, savoring the delicious contact. He met her thrust for thrust, deepening the kiss until she was swept away on a tidal wave of desire. *This. This is what I've been waiting for.* She clung to him, hands gripping his shoulders, swimming in sensation, drowning in it.

In response, he gripped her tighter, clenching the waistband of her jeans in his fingers. Shifting his hips, invading her space. The possessive move sent a jolt of heat between her legs, which in turn jostled her brain enough to send a random scrap of common sense bobbing to the surface.

"Time out," she breathed. She stepped back and shook her head. But when she looked up, Mr. Sexy Kilt was still standing there, still staring at her with those green-gold eyes. For a moment, Cassie indulged in the fantasy that had been building in the back of her mind ever since she'd first discovered him. Looking at his big, kilted body, it was all too easy to cast him as a warrior from long ago. A Highland hero sent forward in time to find his true love.

But that was the plot of her favorite romance novels. Unfortunately, this was real life, and brawny, beautiful men in kilts did not magically appear from behind hidden walls. And Cassie did not plant her lips on said brawny, beautiful men—not in real life, anyway.

In fantasy land . . . hell yeah, she did.

Cassie laughed at the utter absurdity of the situation. He grinned in response, white teeth flashing. Something about his smile snagged her thoughts. "Who are you?"

"I dinna ken that either." He closed the gap she'd created between them. "But perhaps," his gaze dropped to her mouth, "if you kiss me again, I might remember."

"Ah, not happening." She took another step back.

"Willna you help me?"

"Help you do what?"

"Figure out who I am." He placed both his hands over his heart. "The Fates sent you to me, lass. Mayhap you know the answer." His words were spoken with sincerity, but she caught a hint of mischief hiding in the corner of his mouth, making him look like a naughty frat boy.

Why does he seem so familiar? She narrowed her eyes, tossing up the niggling sense of recognition to the fact he looked like he stepped right off the cover of one of the many Celtic time-travel romances on her keeper shelf. "Well, I know what you're not." She crossed her arms over her chest. "I know you are *not* some time-traveling Highlander."

"Time travel? So ye *are* a witch, then? A sorceress?" He closed the gap again. "Aye, that must be it, for surely I've been bespelled."

He licked his lips. Yes, she stared. Yes, she noticed he had a very nice mouth, the upper lip chiseled and quick to quirk into a naughty grin, the lower lip full and begging to be caught between her teeth. *Focus.* She ordered her lady parts to stand down. She needed to think.

It didn't take a genius to figure out something weird was going on. Even three sheets to the wind, or at least three shots, the man's archaic outfit still had Cassie wondering if he was part of a castle tour or dramatic reenactment or something—but why the hell would he be hiding in a wall?

And that accent. She'd be the first to admit her weakness for Celtic brogue, but his speech pattern bordered on the absurd. The whole thing seemed like some kind of joke, a stunt the staff might pull on random tourists, or a prank . . .

Shit.

She glared at him, 100 percent annoyed for not recognizing him sooner. It was that smile of his that first tipped her off, the look of mischief she *knew* she'd seen before. The encounter with the woman in a headset from the hall swam through Cassie's rapidly sobering brain. She wanted to kick herself. Better yet, she wanted to kick him. "I don't believe it."

He leaned closer and brushed a finger across her cheek. "Doona believe what, lass? Ye can tell me."

Oh, he was good. But he seemed oblivious to her shift in mood. Fine with her. She peeked up at him and fluttered her eyelashes, hoping she looked demure as she lifted her hand and placed it over his. "You're right. I do know who you are."

"Aye?"

"Aye" she mimicked and squeezed his hand tightly, quelling the urge to knock his wicked frat-boy grin sideways. "You're Logan fucking Reid."

His face fell as her words registered, but he recovered in seconds. Barely missing a beat, he pulled his hand out of her grip and pounded a fist against the wall, shouting, "Cut!"

CHAPTER 2

THE ROOM ERUPTED in controlled chaos. The moment Logan pulled the plug on the scene, a crowd of people poured through the door. Janet, his sister and coproducer, led the hustle, shouting orders over her headset. Two lads pulled mics from strategic hiding places while another worked on dismantling the stationary cameras.

One of the crew ripped a cord too hard, and it clipped some fancy wee table. Logan frowned, but before he could ream the man out, Janet was on him. Logan almost felt sorry for the bloke. His sister was a tyrant. However, the last thing Logan needed was someone from the historical society coming after him for a ding in one of their antiques.

Not to mention the hefty damage deposit on the line. Filming in a real castle had its risks, but for this prank to work, he and Janet had agreed it needed to be shot on location. He'd called in a few favors to book this site for his latest escapade. It had been a close call when the mark had poked her head into the passageway and nearly saw the crew, but he'd managed to distract her.

And Christ, what a distraction.

Not that he was complaining. The lass could kiss. She had to be from the States. Everything about her shouted American, from the rounded accent in her direct way of speaking, to the rounded curve of her ass, and the cut and color of her "breeks."

Logan turned to catch another look at the girl's fine backside, grinning as he replayed how she'd glanced over her shoulder, a challenge in her dark eyes when she called him out for eyeballing her bum. Now she stood across the room, trying to exit, her path blocked by Janet, who hovered in the doorway, clipboard in hand. All business, Janet was. His sister made an excellent coproducer, her militant attention to detail the perfect counterpoint to what she liked to call Logan's creative lunacy.

"Abso-freaking-lutley not." Over the din of his crew he could hear the lass clearly as she shoved Janet's clipboard away. "There is no way in hell I am signing any waivers."

She's going to be prickly about it. He grimaced. Many of his marks were reluctant at first, but they always came around. If Janet couldn't bully the lass into signing the release, he'd have to charm her into it. Because there was no way Logan was giving up. Though the prank had tanked at the last minute when she'd recognized him, the rest of the sketch had played out perfectly. Better than any of the other takes that day. They'd caught a lucky break when Janet had run across the lass in the hall.

Logan crossed the room, watching the girl's body tense as Janet continued to natter on about releases and permissions and would "Miss" please look at the contract?

"No, Miss will *not* look at the contract," the lass snarled.

Before his sister ended up taking a clipboard to the head, he stepped between the women. The lass turned her dagger glare on him. Her dark eyes, smoky sexy only a little while ago, now burned with fury. Logan swore he felt his eyebrows singe. Time to defuse this wee firecracker. He smiled. "My apologies. Janet can be relentless."

"Well, she can stop wasting her time. I'm not signing anything."

"I heard you before." He glanced around the room. "I think we all did, aye?" The activity was starting to die down. Most of the equipment had been bundled and the crew was now loading the bulky crates onto a dolly.

Logan tried another smile, the lopsided one that always seemed to charm even the testiest mark. "I'd introduce myself, but seems you already know who I am."

She made a face like she'd caught a whiff of something foul. Logan had the unpleasant sensation it was him.

"Yeah, I know who you are." She crossed her arms and pinned him with a few more daggers. "Logan Reid, devil-may-care internet host and notorious hooligan."

"Hooligan? That's a wee harsh." He chuckled. "I take it you've seen some of my work?" Pride and pleasure washed over him. He was thrilled this lovely woman had heard of him. Maybe Janet was right—maybe *Shenanigans* could generate the kind of interest they needed from the female demographic to land that telly deal.

"I've seen enough." She shrugged. "Snarky interviews with B-list celebrities, karaoke with bands desperate for promo spots, and a *lot* of juvenile pranks in silly costumes." Her dark eyes narrowed, scrutinizing him again, though sadly her gaze held none of the flirty interest it had the first time she'd taken him in. "Is that a wig?"

"What?"

She made a grab for his head, and he backed up.

"Hey!" He ran his fingers through his hair, distracted by the punch of lust to his gut when she'd touched him the same way earlier. "This red mess is all me, I assure you. But you're right, I usually have a more, ah, elaborate costume for my sketches." He leaned toward her and widened his smile. She couldn't resist his charm forever. "How'd you know it was me?"

She tapped him on the chin. "Your snarky, shit-eating grin gave you away."

Logan felt his mouth go slack. She slipped her finger under his chin and flicked, closing his mouth for him. "Sorry if I blew your cover."

The saccharine tone of her voice told him she was anything but. He decided to change tactics. "It's no problem. You did a lovely job." He glanced at his sister for confirmation. "Aye, Janet?"

"Can't say the same for you, loon." His sister stuck a finger in her mouth and made a gagging sound. "That was some of the most god-awful brogue I've ever had the misfortune to hear." She shifted her attention to the girl. "But you? You were fabulous. We got some great footage." Janet turned back to Logan. "This is the one. I know it." His sister buzzed with excitement. "The kilt. That kiss! Gold. The 18–49 demo is ours."

Logan could almost see the streams of data flowing through Janet's brain as she crunched web analytics. He fist-bumped his sister and whooped in triumph.

"Keep your kilt on." The girl shook her head and tossed her hair, a lovely dark brown almost the same shade as the chestnuts his family roasted at Hogmanay. "I wouldn't celebrate yet." She put her hands on her hips.

"Why not?" Logan asked dumbly, his thoughts stuttering to a halt as he remembered how it felt to have his own hands there, tightening on her waist, his tongue in her mouth as his fingers learned the dips and swells of her body. *Easy, mate.*

"It doesn't matter what kind of footage you got, you can't use it. I'm not signing those papers." She chucked a thumb at the clipboard in Janet's hands. "I know how this works. Without my permission, you can't post any of that *great footage*"—she made sassy little quotation marks with her fingers—"on your wee website."

"Wee?" Janet puffed up like a bantam rooster. "Do you know how many millions of hits we get a month?" she asked, her body stiff with indignation. "And I'm talking unique visitors here, not spambot rubbish."

If Janet had thought to console this girl by bragging about their stats, she'd missed the mark. Time to switch tactics again. "What I think Janet is trying to say is, we offer significant compensation. If you'll look at the details of the agreement—"

"And what *I'm* trying to say is, I'm not interested."

"But you haven't even heard the terms of the offer." Janet turned the clipboard toward the girl.

"I don't care." She shoved the clipboard back at Janet and turned her scowl on Logan. "For the last time. I. Am. Not. Interested." With that, the lass spun on her toe, tossed her dark, delicious mane over a sassy shoulder, and stalked out of the room.

"I'd say someone knows how to make a dramatic exit," his sister drawled.

"Ease off, Nettie. I'll handle this." He snatched the clipboard and headed for the door.

"She was looking for the library when I hooked her," Janet called after him, and Logan nodded, the floorplan he'd studied while planning the prank unfolding in his mind.

"Don't come back until she signs that waiver!" His sister's voice followed him out to the hallway, echoing off the castle's stone walls. "And don't call me Nettie!"

Janet might drive him batty with her big sister bossiness, but Logan knew without her, he'd probably still be uploading his half-baked stunts to YouTube on the weekends. Sometimes, he wondered how his sister felt about putting her graphic arts degree to use as coproducer and web designer for his "wee sketch show," but it had been Nettie's idea in the first place to create the *Shenanigans* site.

If Da was still around, he'd probably have kicked both their arses to see his children wasting their education. Then again, if Da was still around, Logan probably never would have started *Shenanigans* at all. Metal bit into the skin of his palm as he tightened his grip on the clipboard. He wasn't going to think about that now.

An American producer was debating between *Shenanigans* and another internet clip show for a new late-night talk show they were developing. Logan was thrilled with the success of *Shenanigans*, but this was his chance to do more, to be more. Not just a series of sketches viewed on the web, but an actual show on the telly—in the States— an international career. The producers had indicated they were inclined to sign him as the show's host, but their sponsors would feel more comfortable if Logan first proved he could draw in better numbers from the vaunted female viewership.

All Logan needed was something to tip the odds in his favor. He'd found that something. If Nettie was right, this prank could be their ace in the hole. As much as his sister despised being called by her childhood nickname, it'd be nothing compared to her wrath if he didn't track that girl down and get the bloody release papers signed.

Logan turned another corner and growled at the empty hall ahead. How fast could she move those curvy legs? He quickened his pace, determined to catch his winning hand before she escaped the castle—and him.

* * *

Cassie made her way around another corner before pausing to catch her breath. She hadn't exactly raced through the castle halls, but she'd given her aunt Eleanor, Queen of the Minnesota Mall Walkers, a run—er, fast walk—for her money. She sneaked a peek back, but the hallway was deserted. There didn't seem to be any tourists in this part of the castle. Exhaling heavily, she leaned against a door and reached for her phone.

And remembered it was still in Bonnie's purse.

Shit.

Cassie risked another peek around the corner and groaned. Her luck was not improving. Mr. Sexy Scot was stalking down the hall toward her, which wouldn't be the worst thing in the world, save for that damn clipboard in his hand.

He could shove that clipboard up his kilted ass. She hadn't spent the last three years of her life busting her own ass to prove herself, only to have one lusty little lapse in judgment destroy everything. She wanted to be taken seriously, respected. And that wasn't going to happen if a video of her swapping spit with Scottie the Hottie became the latest internet clickbait.

She knew better than most how one wrong move on social media could spiral out of control. After all, as Chicago's morning pop-culture princess, she covered such stories on a regular basis. That was how she'd recognized Logan fucking Reid in the first place.

It had been an interview on *ChiChat* with a local rapper promoting his latest album. While on tour in the UK, he'd made an appearance on *Shenanigans*. The prank went down in a pet store with her kilted Highlander playing the role of a clumsy employee who'd "accidentally" left a cage open. Leading to an encounter with a snake, and the rapper freaking out and screaming hysterically.

At first, Cassie had found the clip amusing too, but midway through her interview, the rapper broke down, crying about how mean people could be—not exactly good for the tough-as-nails image he was cultivating—and blaming the whole situation on "Logan fucking Reid." As the interview with the rapper spiraled, Cassie had pressed for details, and he explained he'd signed off on appearing in the show without realizing how the prank would impact his image. It was all "Logan fucking Reid's fault." That, she remembered clearly. He'd repeated the phrase often, keeping the show's engineers busy in the sound booth with the edit button. Thank goodness for broadcast's seven-second profanity delay.

Screw the speed walking. Cassie picked up the pace. She could use a seven-second delay now, she'd barely had a seven-second head start. The rapper may have been foolish enough to sign off on appearing in one of Logan fucking Reid's videos, but she refused to make the same mistake. On the verge of finally being taken seriously as a broadcast journalist, she wasn't going to let anything—or anyone—ruin her credibility.

Flying around the next corner, she was relieved to see this corridor filled with tourists lingering in small groups. Even better, up ahead, near the entrance to the great hall, stood Santa and Bulldog. "Hey!" she called out, dodging clusters of people and charging toward them.

Bulldog tapped his wrist and shook his head, jowls quivering. "No reentries allowed."

"Oh!" Cassie glanced at her plastic bracelet. "Um, no, I don't want to get back in to the tasting room."

"Poor lass." Santa's fuzzy white mustache twitched

beneath his cherry nose. "I wager the whisky was more potent than you'd expected, aye?"

"Ah, you could say that." Cassie's insides heated, thinking of a certain Scot, whose kiss was way more potent than she'd expected—a certain Scot who was currently on her tail. "Um, look, my friends went to the library. Can you tell me which way that is?"

Bulldog turned to point the way, but a shout from the corridor made him pause. He glanced behind Cassie, bushy brows crawling up his forehead and blending into his hairline.

Cassie groaned, knowing exactly what he was looking at—*who* he was looking at. She could make a break for it, but she'd probably end up with more men chasing after her, which did not promise to be as fun as it sounded. She swiveled and watched Logan fucking Reid march toward them.

The few tourists loitering in the hall scurried out of his path, gawking after him as he passed. Not that Cassie blamed them. She'd stare too. His broad shoulders took up more than their fair share of space, and his messy, ginger mane glowed like burnished copper under the recessed lights.

And then of course, there was that damn kilt.

"Logan Reid. We meet again." Did she sound cool? She hoped she sounded cool.

Logan stepped closer to her. "Can we talk for a moment?"

"Isn't that what we were just doing?" Cassie didn't want to talk to him, and she sure as hell didn't want to look at him. She avoided his eyes, avoided his smile, avoided his face altogether. She trained her gaze straight ahead but decided that was no good either. Their difference in height meant her line of sight landed a smidge north of pec-land.

His puffy pirate shirt was loose and open at the collar, revealing the strong lines of his neck and the masculine thrust of his Adam's apple.

She watched that apple bob as he asked, "I was hoping you'd be interested in going out for a drink."

Rather than interrupting her thoughts, his invitation invaded them, her mind filling with images of pouring a shot of whisky in the tempting hollow at the base of his throat and lapping it up.

"On me," he added, a knowing smirk in his voice.

Oh God, am I that obvious? Her gaze snapped back up to meet his. "I've had enough for one day, thank you."

"You know," he began, and this time his smile wasn't the confident frat-boy smile, but a gentler curve of lips and cheek that Cassie, to her great frustration, found irresistible, "I just realized I don't even know your name."

"There you are, Cassie!"

Cassie stiffened at the sound of Bonnie's and Delaney's voices carrying across the hall. She froze, pretending not to hear her friends call her name again, closer this time. Was it too late to play dumb?

"So," Logan murmured, his wicked brows curved in a mocking question, "*Cassie*, is it?"

Yep, definitely too late.

Delaney strode forward, shaking her finger. "Cassie Crow, I am going to kill you. Where the hell have you b—" Delaney swallowed the rest of her sentence as she took in the scene in front of her.

"*Cassie Crow*," Logan drawled, gleeful triumph expanding the vowels in her name, the gold shards in his green eyes glittering.

He'd dropped the ridiculous accent, but the brogue was still there, softer than his thick trills from earlier. Still, the way he faintly rolled the *r* in her last name was enough to make all sorts of things quiver inside her. She smiled weakly.

Her legs much shorter than Delaney's, Bonnie finally caught up. "Oooh," she breathed, grabbing Cassie's arm for support as her wide blue eyes snagged on Logan's kilt. "Oh my."

"Deep breaths, kiddo." Delaney fanned Bonnie with a hand while giving Logan the once-over, from leather boots to copper crown. "What's your story? Do you come with the castle or something?"

At least Cassie hadn't been the only one to assume he was part of a tour. The thought made her feel a little better, a little less foolish . . . but only a little.

"I don't remember seeing anything about this—about him—in the brochure." Bonnie's eyebrows furrowed, and Cassie knew her friend was mentally reviewing the castle guidebook.

"Me neither." Delaney grinned. "If I had, you can bet I would have suggested we start with him rather than the booze."

"Ah, the whisky tasting?" Logan's question was full of congenial understanding.

As if he knew all about her friends. As if he had a right to be so familiar. Cassie glared at him.

He ignored her. "I was just asking *Miss Crow* here if she'd meet me for a drink this evening."

"And I was just telling him no." She turned toward her friends. "Come on, we better get moving or we'll miss the bus."

"Our hotel is just down the street," Delaney pointed out. "We can walk back."

Not helping. "Yeah, but what about our lunch reservation?"

"We still have twenty minutes," Bonnie said automatically. Cassie wished, just this once, her best bud didn't have the ability to recall every detail of their itinerary with such swift efficiency.

"See, Cass," Delaney agreed, blinking with the wide-eyed innocence of one of her rugrats. "What's your rush?"

"I'm afraid it's me that has her in a hurry," Logan apologized, appearing remarkably contrite. "She kissed me and then ran away from me." He heaved a sigh, so dramatically forlorn that for a moment even Cassie felt sorry for him. "And what was a besotted fool like me to do but chase after my heart?"

"You kissed him?" Delaney looked impressed.

"No!" Cassie shook her head. "I mean, yes, I kissed him, but that's not why I ran away." She glanced around. Their little party was starting to gather quite an audience. "Look"—she gritted her teeth and lowered her voice—"I'll tell you about it later. Can we just get out of here?"

Logan clasped the clipboard to his chest with one hand and reached out to her with the other. "And wilt thou leave me so unsatisfied?"

Bonnie clutched Cassie's arm and squeezed. "Shakespeare, Cass. He's quoting Shakespeare!" Good thing her best friend had an on-the-brink-of-setting-a-date fiancé back home, otherwise Cassie was pretty sure Bonnie would have climbed Logan like a tree and made him her personal Scottish jungle gym.

Even Delaney was eyeing the man like he was a particularly yummy piece of cake. And Delaney *loved* cake. With both her friends devouring the eye candy on display, Cassie decided to play along for a moment. She clasped a hand to her own chest, copying Logan's melodramatic pose. "What satisfaction dost thou wish tonight?"

When Bonnie's eyes almost popped out of her head,

Cassie shrugged defensively. "What? I lived through your *Romeo and Juliet* phase, remember?" She turned back to Logan. "And don't say the exchange of thou love's vows for mine, or some such shit," she warned.

Bonnie gasped in outrage, and Delaney snorted. Her friends were not being very helpful.

"Nay, lass," Logan said. He'd upped the brogue again. Bastard wasn't going to play fair. "All I ask is to bide a'while in your company."

His overblown accent was absurd. Unfortunately, that didn't make it any less effective. "Can the blarney, bud."

"As you wish." He looked straight at her, green-gold eyes intense, a hint of the bad-boy grin crooking his mouth. "Have a drink with me tonight."

Free of the outlandishly thick brogue, his husky voice was dark and smoky. She hadn't thought it possible, but he'd managed to turn the charm factor up *another* notch. The man was one hundred proof. If he got any more potent, he'd be lethal.

"Please," he purred.

Yep. Lethal.

"Go for it, Cass." Delaney didn't even bother to whisper.

Cassie was tempted. Oh, how she was tempted. That kiss, foolish as it had been, had lived up to all her fantasies, and then some. "Are you asking me out on a date?"

"Absolutely." Even toned down, the subdued lilt of his brogue tumbled over the sounds and syllables on his tongue, making that one simple word sound downright seductive.

"If I agree, *that*"—she pointed at the clipboard in his hand—"doesn't come with us."

He glanced down and appeared to debate it for a moment. Cassie's heart dropped. She knew it. The man wasn't really interested in her, just her signature. She sighed.

"Never mind." Cassie turned her back on him and faced her friends. "Let's go, girls," she said, urging them to start walking. "We still haven't seen the gift shop."

"Deal." Logan's response carried across the hall.

Cassie heard him, but kept moving. Bonnie tugged on her elbow. "Come on. Give him a chance, Cass."

Delaney tugged on Cassie's other elbow. "Yeah. We both know you're not going to find a better souvenir than *that*"—she tilted her head, ponytail flicking in the direction of the kilted slab of sexy Scot waiting behind them— "in the gift shop."

At the mention of souvenirs, Cassie fiddled with her bracelet. The condom box was waiting, still unopened, in her suitcase. But even for the sole purpose of fulfilling the fantasy fling she'd been dreaming about forever, getting involved with Logan fucking Reid, the man who made a tough-guy rapper cry from embarrassment, was a bad idea. A terrible idea. All risk and no reward.

The memory of his hands reflexively gripping her hips and pulling her closer flashed through her. *Okay, fine, some reward . . .*

Cassie turned back and looked at Logan. Eyes never leaving her face, he yanked the papers from the clipboard and crumpled them in his fist. She'd had have liked it better if he'd ripped the form to shreds, but she supposed the message was the same.

She glanced at her friends. They stood on either side of her, the proverbial devil and angel on her shoulders—except in this case good and evil adamantly agreed with each other, chins nodding in tandem like a pair of demented bobbleheads.

"What the hell," Cassie said, pursing her lips to fight off the grin threatening to break across her face. She raised her gaze to meet Logan's. "One drink."

CHAPTER 3

SEVERAL HOURS LATER, after lunch with the tour group and a leisurely stroll along the Royal Mile back to their hotel in downtown Edinburgh, Cassie sorted through her outfits, examining and discarding various pieces of clothing. "How about this one?"

Delaney glanced up from the travel guide she was reading and shook her head. "Nope. Not sexy enough."

"Who said I was going for sexy?" Cassie countered, but tossed the clothes aside. She was meeting a hot Scot for a drink. Damn right she wanted to look sexy.

"I can't believe you kissed him." Bonnie was lying on her stomach, feet propped on the pillows of her bed, staring dreamily out their hotel room window, where the castle they'd visited this morning hovered on the hillside, stone walls glowing in the late afternoon sun.

Sprawled across a leather armchair, Delaney twirled a finger in her ponytail. "I can. That man was f-i-n-e *fine*."

Before Cassie could thank her for the impromptu spelling lesson, a quick series of knocks sounded at the door. "At last," Delaney cried, popping up from the chair. "My roomies have risen from the dead!" She whipped the door open, and Sadie and Ana stumbled in. With a groan, Sadie flopped onto Cassie's bed while Ana collapsed into the chair Delaney had just vacated.

"Hey!" Delaney smacked Ana with the travel guide. "You stole my spot."

"You snooze, you lose." Ana tightened the tie on her bathrobe and scooted her generous bottom deeper into the leather chair.

"Says the girl who slept half the day away," Delaney scoffed, lying down next to Bonnie.

"What time *is* it?" Sadie mumbled, face buried in the clothes piled on Cassie's bed.

"After three." Cassie nudged Sadie. "Get off my stuff."

"Ugh," Sadie groaned and shifted to her side, allowing Cassie to pull the pile of clothes out from underneath her. "I am *never* drinking again."

"I've heard that before." Ana chuckled with disbelief.

Like Bonnie and Cassie, Ana and Sadie had been best friends since childhood, no doubt making mischief since the day they met. Yin to the other's yang, in looks, they were polar opposites. Ana was tall, with striking long, black hair and ample curves, the antithesis of Sadie's short stature, playful cap of blond waves, and petite frame. Cassie often thought of the two of them as the duo from the classic movie *Gentlemen Prefer Blondes*, with Sadie as a pixie-sized version of Marilyn Monroe and Ana as an even bustier Jane Russell, if such a thing were possible.

"And both of you *are* going out with us tonight. Cass has a date."

"What?" Sadie rolled over so fast she almost fell right off the bed. She blinked up at them from beneath a halo of tousled golden tresses. "What's this about a date?"

"It's not a date," Cassie argued. Amazing how fast her

friends seemed to recover when her love life was up for discussion. Wait, no, not her love life. What she'd said was true, this was *not* a date. She was simply meeting a man she found equal parts attractive and irritating for a drink. That was all.

Besides, it's not like she and Logan were going to be having a romantic evening alone, her friends were coming along—Cassie had insisted on it. She didn't think Logan was planning to take advantage of her, but better safe than sorry. The Monte Carlo monkey boy had taught her that lesson.

Though to be honest, she wouldn't mind being taken advantage of . . . a bit . . . on her own terms, of course. Cassie tugged a few more pieces of clothing out of her suitcase, and the box of condoms, which had been wrapped inside a rolled pair of jeans (the airport security people checking her luggage didn't need to see *everything*) tumbled to the floor.

Ana eyed the box pointedly and chuckled, her throaty voice even huskier than usual, still scratchy from sleep and an abundance of whisky. "Not a date, huh?" She scanned the discarded outfits strewn about the room. "That one." Ana pointed to a blue dress draped over the desk. "Wear that for your non-date."

Cassie dropped the box of condoms on the desk and picked up the dress. It was a sweater dress, soft fabric and a simple cut. She'd packed it because it traveled well and was easy to accessorize. Plus, she loved the color—a pretty shade of indigo that walked the line between blue and violet.

"Nice call," Delaney agreed. "She's right, Cass. That's the one. Your tushy looks amazing in that dress."

Cassie held the dress up in front of herself. "We're going to be sitting at a pub, he's not even going to see my tushy."

Sadie collapsed back down on the bed and blew a tangle of unruly blond curls out of her eyes. "Who is this *he*? And can we stop saying 'tushy,' please? You sound like my nana."

"Sorry. Habit." Delaney shrugged. "For some reason, parents tend to complain when you ask their four-year-olds if they remembered to wipe their ass."

Bonnie cleared her throat. "Well, this conversation has quickly gone south."

"Agreed." Sadie looked over at Cassie again. "The point is, Ana's right. Your ass *does* look amazing in that dress. Just be sure to get up and go to the bathroom or something so your mystery man gets the opportunity to appreciate the view."

"Yes, Ana is right. Ana is always right," Ana agreed, leaning her head back against the chair and rubbing her temples. "Now then, if Sadie and I are going to have to pull our wretched selves together and go out tonight, I want details. Who is this mystery man?"

"Oh my God, he is so cute!" Bonnie squealed. "He quoted Shakespeare and he was wearing a kilt—"

"Hold up, you saw a cute guy in a kilt without me!" Sadie rolled over again, and this time she *did* fall off the bed. "Ugh," she grumbled into the hotel rug before propping herself up. "Ana and I stayed out all night looking for guys in kilts and found nothing."

"It's true." Ana yawned.

"Hey, where *did* you find him, Cass?" Bonnie asked. "In the bathroom?"

"Ah, no." Cassie focused on the contents of her travel jewelry case. "On the way back from the bathroom. I got lost." She took out a pair of earrings and held them up.

Ana shook her head. "Not those. Something longer, dangly—sexy."

"Dangly is sexy?" Bonnie asked.

"Depends what's dangling," Delaney quipped, patting Bonnie on the head. "Sorry, you walked right into that one."

"Yeah, well *I* walked right into Mr. Sexy Kilt." Cassie offered the jewelry case to Ana. "Here, you pick."

"Sit down so I can do your hair first. You can't choose a pair of earrings until your hair is done." Ana tsked. "Haven't I taught you anything?"

Cassie sat on the floor at Ana's feet, jewelry case in her lap. While her hair was brushed and pulled, twisted and braided, she shared the entire embarrassing encounter, from start to finish.

"Logan Reid . . . why does that name sound familiar?" Sadie didn't bother to get up from the floor, but instead rolled over to lie next to Cassie and monitor Ana's handiwork.

"I told you, he runs that web show *Shenanigans.*" Cassie rummaged in her jewelry case again.

"Oh, I've seen him before!" Sadie propped herself up on an elbow. "He does those funny clips with bands, like that carpool karaoke guy," Sadie said, pointing out tendrils of hair Ana missed, "except he makes the bands perform in an elevator . . . 'Live in a Lift,' is that it?"

"That's the one." Cassie stood and crossed to the mirror over the desk, slipping the hooks of the earrings she'd settled on into her ears. "He also films stupid prank videos."

"Good. That means he has a sense of humor." Sadie's pretty pixie face dimpled. "And he's cute, right?"

"Right," Bonnie agreed. "Very cute." She wiggled into Cassie's spot in front of Ana. "Do me next."

Ana sighed and ran her hands over Bonnie's auburn curls. "I should start charging you people."

"You probably should." Cassie tilted her chin and admired the fruits of Ana's labor. She'd done a great job, pulling the top half of Cassie's thick, chestnut waves into two braids that twisted elegantly over her ears before sweeping into a single braid that draped down her back. "But I probably wouldn't be able to afford you."

Delaney, who only did her hair in one of two ways, up in a ponytail or straight down, laughed. "Go ahead. Wouldn't be a problem for me." She joined Cassie at the desk mirror and pulled her ponytail out, letting her straight, smooth, strawberry-blond hair drift over her shoulders. Then she picked up the condom box and shook it. "This Logan guy, do you think he could be your long-awaited foreign fling, Cass?"

"I told you, it's *not* a date." Cassie grabbed the box out of Delaney's hands and shoved it in the desk drawer.

"R-i-i-ght." Delaney winked at the other girls. "I guess we'll find out tonight, won't we?"

That evening, Sadie halted at the entrance of the pub and braced her hands on the brightly painted doorframe. "Someone pinch me."

"If it will get you to move, sure." Directly behind Sadie, Ana reached two fingers out and nipped her friend in the arm.

"Ow!" Sadie let go of the doorframe, rubbing her elbow.

Ana maneuvered her bosom around Sadie and grinned. "Don't say I never did anything for you." A step later she came to an abrupt stop. "Oh. My. God." The girls stumbled in after her, the heavy wooden door of the pub swinging shut behind them, the sound buried beneath an eruption of male cheers.

Suddenly Cassie understood what had frozen Sadie and Ana in place. This morning at the castle, she had mourned the fact Scotland didn't seem to be overrun with hot kilted men. Apparently, she hadn't been looking in the right place. From wall to wall, back bar to front door, the pub was packed with guys, and almost every single one of them was wearing a kilt.

"Praise Jesus," Sadie exhaled, raising her palms to the rafters.

Bonnie's forehead puckered. "I thought you were Jewish."

"She is." Ana smirked. "But she goes all holy roller when she's horny."

Sadie smacked Ana with her purse.

"Ow!"

"You had it coming for that pinch." Sadie waggled her fingers toward a kilted duo standing at a high pub table, one fair-haired and the other dark, a matching pair to her and Ana's coloring. "Now, what do you say we find out what religion those two are?"

Delaney shook her head. "While I'm all for a bit of package handling, we came here as backup for Cassie's date, remember?"

"It's not a date," Cassie couldn't help repeating, bristling. *Why was she being defensive?*

The rumble of male voices drifted on warm air pungent with the scent of ale and what could only be described as eau de fried tavern food. Bonnie glanced around the kilt-bedecked room. "How are we ever going to find him? It will be like looking for a needle in a haystack!"

"Now that sounds like a fun game." Sadie tossed back her short blond curls, grinning as she rubbed her hands together.

Cassie swept a glance over the line of men at the bar and stiffened. In the far corner, a tall redhead stood in profile, nursing a long-necked bottle. Cassie swallowed convulsively, sending the butterflies on a return trip to her stomach as she followed the line of the man's broad shoulders down his back to his—*oh my God, he had a fine ass.*

No question, the novelty of a kilt was alluring, but something had to be said for the view provided by a good ol' pair of tight blue jeans. Cassie let her gaze linger on Logan's backside, appreciating how the faded denim clung to his firm butt and equally firm thighs. She'd had a good look at his muscular calves this morning and was not disappointed to see the rest of him seemed to match. Heat crept up her neck, and Cassie turned away before one of her friends caught her staring.

Too late. Ana looked from Cassie to Logan and back again. "Is that him?"

In a move so synchronized it was almost comical, the other girls followed Ana's glance to where Logan stood at the bar, his ginger mane a beacon. Maybe it was the weight of ten feminine eyeballs boring into him, but he seemed to sense their presence and turned to face them. He caught sight of Cassie and smiled, and if the collective gasp from her friends was any indication, Cassie wasn't the only one to feel the impact of that sexy grin.

"Yeah, that's him," she muttered, annoyed at the sense of possessiveness flashing through her.

Logan took his time turning his attention to Cassie and her friends. He had known the second the girls entered the pub—of course he'd known, for the last twenty minutes he'd kept his gaze trained on the pub's entrance, wondering if she would show up. And then she'd appeared in the doorway, sandwiched between her four mates. At the sight of them, Logan chugged his beer, wishing for a whisky himself right now. He wasn't feeling quite so brave at the moment and could use a shot of liquid courage.

What was his problem? Women didn't make him nervous. Logan couldn't think of much that made him nervous. So why did it feel like a spring salmon had gotten loose in his gut?

Suddenly glad he'd kept his promise to the lass and left the consent form at home, Logan decided he would not try to convince Miss Cassie Crow to sign anything . . . not tonight, anyway. There would be no mention of media releases or websites or contracts or anything of the kind. Tonight, he was going to enjoy a drink with a pretty girl and her pretty friends, and the only thing he might try to do was convince the lass to kiss him again like she had this morning.

She'd noticed him. Logan couldn't say how he knew for sure, facing away from the door as he'd been doing since the second she'd entered the pub, but he knew without a doubt the moment her glance landed on him. His entire body sizzled with an electric current. Knocking back the last of his beer, he screwed his courage to the sticking place—what was that crack she had made earlier about him and *Macbeth* rejects?—and turned to face her.

On the telly a kick went awry, and the crowd exploded in a flurry of half-drunken curses. Cassie and her friends jumped at the outburst, but didn't seem intimidated. Most of the lads were too focused on the match to pay the girls much mind, but Logan knew with the way these lasses looked, that wouldn't be the case for long.

"You came," he said, barely able to hear himself over the roars of outrage as the opposing team scored.

"I did." She nodded toward her gaggle of girlfriends. "And I brought my friends."

Logan smiled at the girls, the two redheads he remembered from this morning, the tall leggy strawberry-blonde and the petite lass with frizzy auburn curls, and two more, a raven-haired vixen with an impressive rack and a tiny blonde with violet eyes who made him think of the wee folk from the stories Gran used to tell.

None of them, however, could hold a candle to Cassie. Her hair was pulled back, and the thick rope of her chestnut waves gleamed in the dim pub light. The dress she wore hugged her curves in a subtle, sexy way. She looked warm and soft and oh so touchable. The snug fabric was a deep blue, almost purple, reminding him of the sky over the loch at gloaming back home.

Logan made the round of cordial formalities and leaned in close to catch each girl's name as she shouted over the din. The last girl had to repeat herself three times, finally jumping up to yell in his ear. A foul play on the telly had the pub exploding with expletives, and he barely heard what she said.

This wasn't going to work. How the hell was he supposed to charm the lass if he could barely hold a conversation with her? He slid in next to Cassie. "I think this was a mistake."

"Oh?" Her brow crumpled.

"No, not seeing you again." Logan backpedaled as he realized how that had sounded. Christ, he was such a bumbler. "I meant coming here." He waved a hand at the shouting crowd. "It's too loud."

"Huh?"

"Exactly." He tried again, bending low, her soft braid brushing his cheek. "Why don't we go somewhere with a wee less craic?"

"Crack?" she repeated.

He nodded. "Somewhere quieter." She hesitated, and he hurried to reassure her, nodding at her friends. "They are welcome too, of course." He'd rather spend the evening alone with the dark-eyed beauty, but any time with her was better than nothing.

"Bonnie." Cassie shifted on her bar stool and tapped her friend on the shoulder. "You okay if we go somewhere else?"

"Where?" Bonnie asked.

"Where?" Cassie repeated, looking back at him.

Logan shrugged. "I doona care, you pick."

The little redhead glanced over at the other girls in their party. They ignored her, engaged in a game of eye tag with some lads across the room. She shook her head and turned her attention back to Cassie. "I'm up for it, but I don't think we could drag those three out of here right now." She scrunched up her face in thought. "How about the hotel bar?"

Cassie nodded and smiled at Logan. "Do you know where the Caledonian is?"

"Aye." He returned her smile. *They were going back to her hotel? Better and better.*

As Cassie and her friend gathered their things and made their farewells to the other three, Logan settled his bill and passed the barman a few extra quid. He was sure her friends could handle themselves, but no harm asking the lad if he'd keep an eye out for the trio.

Soon enough, he was escorting Cassie and Bonnie back to their hotel for a drink at the much quieter bar there. A quarter hour later found them settling in on luxurious low-backed leather stools. "If I'd known you were staying at the Caldy, I would have suggested we meet here in the first place," Logan said.

"Oh?" Cassie glanced up at him suspiciously. "Why's that?"

Logan winked. "The Caledonian is pretty ritzy digs. You ladies are having quite the holiday."

Bonnie shrugged. "Sadie's dad hooked us up. He's a big shot with Waldorf-Astoria and booked us rooms in their hotels for every stop on our trip." She flipped through the cocktail menu with fierce concentration. "Anyway, it's definitely quieter here."

"Is that pub always like that?" Cassie asked. She leaned back and cast an admiring glance up at the ceiling, where the brass-plated lighting ran parallel above the entire length of the bar.

Logan tried not to stare at the creamy expanse of throat her movement exposed. "Ah, well, I forgot there was a match on tonight."

She dropped her gaze back to his and laughed. "And here I'd started to worry a Scotland full of men in kilts was only a fantasy."

"Oh, aye?" He let the brogue slip in; he couldn't help it. He wanted to hear more about her fantasies.

Her eyes went smoky. "Oh, aye," she echoed.

In an instant Logan was rock hard and damn glad he wasn't wearing a kilt, or he'd be pitching a plaid tent right now.

"Oooh, how about this one, Cass? It's called *Edinburgh's Bramble*."

God bless her friend for the timely distraction.

Cassie swiveled away from him and eyed the menu Bonnie held out to her.

Logan shifted on his stool and gestured for the barmaid, ordering a St. Mungo for himself and Brambles for the ladies. No hard liquor for him. He'd stick to lager and hopefully keep his wits—and his cock—under control.

Two Brambles later, Cassie was feeling mellow and as fuzzy around the edges as her comfy sweater dress. Relaxed. As the evening wore on, Logan continued to be nothing but a perfect gentleman, and gradually, she'd let her guard down. Not once had he mentioned his internet show or that contract he'd wanted her to sign.

Instead, he regaled them with tales of his childhood growing up in a place called Lochalsh. Cassie adored the fact Logan really was a Highlander after all. She'd actually kissed a Highlander. Mid-Bramble number one, Cassie had started to mentally relive their kiss in her mind, and by Bramble number two she had moved on to imagining what it might be like to kiss him again. The ice clinked in her empty glass, and she looked over at Bonnie. "One more?"

Bonnie shook her head and hopped off the stool. "Not for me, thanks." She blinked owlishly. "I think I'm going to head up to the room."

Logan stood when Bonnie did. Cassie found his Old-World response adorable. He looked at her over the top of Bonnie's mass of curls. "Should we walk her up?"

"Not necessary," Bonnie answered for herself and yawned—a big, ridiculous monster of a yawn. Cassie felt a tug of affection for her best friend; she knew exactly what Bon was up to. Over the years they had spent countless sleepovers together, and Bonnie was always the *last* one to fall asleep.

"At least let us walk you up," Cassie said as Logan settled the bill, another gallant gesture she both noted and appreciated. Unless, of course, this was all meant to be some big setup. Despite how much she'd enjoyed herself, a part of her still couldn't help wondering when he'd turn the conversation back to that stupid prank for his show, but so far he'd been on his best behavior.

Her back to Logan, Bonnie winked at Cassie. "If you insist."

Cassie took her friend's arm, Logan following behind, acting as escort as they made their way to the elevator. When they passed the hotel's other bar, a more open lounge area with low tables and plush chairs, Bonnie stopped and squeezed Cassie's hand. "You two should stay here and have another drink. I'll be fine on my own."

Logan raised a questioning brow to Cassie. "I'm game if you are?"

Ignoring the cartwheels her insides were performing, Cassie shrugged and agreed. "Sure, just give me a minute." She walked the few remaining steps to the elevator with Bonnie. "I know what you're doing."

With her big blue eyes, Bonnie already looked innocent by nature and could appear downright guileless when she wanted to. "I have no idea what you're talking about." She leaned closer to Cassie and grinned. "But I do know he's been staring at your ass ever since we got off those bar stools. Ana was right about the dress."

More than a little pleased, Cassie matched Bonnie's grin with one of her own. "Ana's always right."

Bonnie laughed. "She really is. Before we left the pub she slipped me a key to their room. You know, in case I wanted to wait up for them in there." The elevator dinged. The doors slid open and Bonnie glanced sideways at Cassie. "I think I might just do that." She stepped into the elevator and raised a hand, fingers making the "okay" sign.

As the elevator doors closed on her best friend, a happy glow that had nothing to do with alcohol seeped through

Cassie's chest. Bonnie had sat with Logan, talked with him, got to know him a little. And her best friend approved.

Glancing back to where Logan stood waiting for her, Cassie felt a shiver of anticipation. She adjusted the charm bracelet on her wrist. Ana had been right about the dress. Perhaps Delaney would be right too.

Logan handed Cassie the drink he'd ordered for her while she'd seen her friend to the lift.

Her gaze traveled around the room as she let out a giddy sigh. "It's beautiful, isn't it? Peacock Alley, they call it."

"Aye." Logan nodded. The lass was rambling. Alone with him now, perhaps she was feeling nervous. "Loud buggers, peacocks." He glanced around the lounge, recalling how he'd once released a brace of peacocks in this very room for one of his earlier pranks for *Shenanigans*. Not very original, he'd be the first to admit, but blasted funny—turns out peacocks are extremely fond of cocktail cherries.

"Really? I didn't know." She sipped her drink and watched him from beneath lowered lashes, a very feminine gesture that had his body responding in very masculine ways. Every part leapt to attention, especially the one between his thighs.

Logan took a long pull on the double of Glenlivet he'd ordered instead of another beer. Who had he been fooling? He needed a round of something stronger. "I have an idea," he said, easing back in the chair as liquid heat curled through him. "Let's play a game."

"A game?" Cassie dropped the straw she'd been twirling and peered up at him.

He took another sip of his drink and flashed Cassie another smile. "Yes, a game."

She eyed him with a hint of suspicion before taking

another sip of her drink. He liked the way she looked at him, a stubborn quirk to her mouth. An admitted flirt, Logan enjoyed the chase, and he loved a challenge. And Miss Cassie Crow, with her hot-as-hell curves in her snug soft dress and her chestnut waves and smoky dark eyes and her kiss-you-and-then-tell-you-to-go-fuck-yourself attitude . . . she was a challenge.

"Well?" Logan quirked a brow, hoping she enjoyed a challenge too. "You up for it?" He shifted on his chair. *Christ knew he was.*

Cassie poked at the orange rind curled in the bottom of her glass. Her fingers and toes felt pleasantly tingly, and her nose had started to go numb, her unofficial cue to cut off the booze. She wasn't drunk—not yet—but another round of whatever was in these Edinburgh Brambles (tasty devil of a drink that it was) and she'd be approaching dance-naked-on-tabletop levels.

She wouldn't mind some naked dancing. Just not on a tabletop. Maybe in her hotel room—with Logan. That, she wouldn't mind at all. He'd switched to scotch when they'd moved to the lounge, and she liked the way he handled his drink. Liked the smooth way he sipped it, savoring the rich liquor in his mouth for a moment before swallowing, his sexy Adam's apple bobbing. She liked the way he held the glass in his hand, his long, strong fingers encircling the tumbler in a firm yet easy grip.

He set his drink down and laced his fingers together. She lifted her gaze from his hands to catch him watching her, a smile curling the corner of his mouth.

"Okay, a game," she agreed, returning the smile.

"Twenty questions," he suggested.

Cassie narrowed her eyes. "If one of them starts with, will you sign this form—"

"No, nothing like that." Logan leaned forward in his chair, shoulder muscles bunching beneath the thin linen of his shirt. "Come now, give me a wee bit of credit."

Hard to trust a man who had the devil's own grin, but to be fair, he *had* been a perfect gentleman all night. "Fine. Twenty questions."

"Favorite color?"

"Purple."

"Favorite flower?"

"Irises."

"Ah, because of the purple."

Cassie nodded and took a tiny sip of her drink. Very tiny—she had to make this one last.

"Virgin?" he asked.

She sputtered. *He wasn't wasting any time, was he?* "No."

"Oh?" He quirked his satyr's brow. "How many men have you slept with?"

"Pass." This time she didn't sputter, but she didn't answer him either.

"Fearty cat."

"Did you just call me a farty cat?" Despite herself, Cassie giggled. *Damn alcohol.*

Logan's face twisted in confusion for a second, then cleared. "No. A fearty cat, chickenhearted."

"I'm not a chicken. It's just none of your business." She jabbed at the orange rind again.

"Fine, I'll guess." He took a slow sip of scotch and eyed her over the rim. "Ten?"

"Excuse me!?" The few other couples lounging in the chairs nearby glanced her way.

"What, a dozen then?" he asked innocently.

"Three! Only three," Cassie answered in a furious whisper. She knew he'd been goading her into answering him and was annoyed he'd been successful. "How about you?" she challenged him. "How many?"

"I'm asking the questions." He settled back in his chair, long legs sprawling. "Okay, three." Logan held the tumbler in front of him and traced a lazy circle around the rim of his glass. "When?"

Distracted by a vision of his finger moving in the same gentle motion on her breast and possibly other places, Cassie didn't think before replying, "One in high school, and two in college." Eyes still trained on his circling finger, Cassie took another sip of her drink and tried to ignore how her nipples were poking through the barely there satin of her bra.

"Oh, *boys* then." He shook the ice in his glass, dismissive. He was baiting her, had tossed the line out, and was waiting for her to bite.

Cassie couldn't help herself. She bit. "What's that supposed to mean?"

He shrugged. "Nothing."

His response was a tease. A non-answer that left the ball in her court. But she knew exactly what he was hinting at. "And with you?" she prodded, playing along. "I suppose *that* would count as being with a man?"

With calculated casualness Logan set his empty glass on the table between them, all confident male grace. Electricity pulsed, zinging along an invisible current connecting her to him. "I dinna ken, lass." He leaned closer and smiled. The line tightened, bait bobbing on the surface of his tempting grin. "Why don't you tell me?"

And just like that Cassie was caught—hook, line, and sinker.

Logan stood back as Cassie pressed the button for her floor. While she'd finished her drink, all he'd been able to think about was getting her mouth on his again, of getting his hands on her ass. He'd offered to escort Cassie upstairs, not with any hopes of staying, her friend had already gone up to the room after all, but maybe he'd score a few hot moments on the ride up. And now here they were.

The lift had barely dinged past the ground floor when she shot him one of those heated looks of hers, eyes gone all smoky dark. Then she lowered her gaze to his mouth, and Logan didn't need any more invitation than that. The attraction between them had sizzled until it seemed to be a tangible thing, her body sending out a signal that his body was more than ready to answer.

He pulled her to him and kissed her, the whisky on his tongue mingling with the fruity taste of her drink. Sour and sweet. Soft and hard. Christ, she was so soft and he was hard . . . and getting harder by the second.

Logan sucked in a breath as Cassie brushed a hand down the front of his jeans, her fingers outlining the shape of his growing erection. Here he'd been thinking *he* was the one who had been too forward. He couldn't believe he'd asked those questions about her sex life. Bloody alcohol always loosened his tongue. But he'd found her honesty attractive. *How about a bit of honesty of your own, mate? You find everything about her attractive.*

They missed her floor—twice—and when they finally tumbled out of the lift and into the hall, Logan seriously considered pulling her back inside and not getting off until . . . well, they got off. Before he could make good on that plan, the doors slid shut behind them.

She led him down the hall to her room, and Logan valiantly tried to ignore the fact her dress was riding higher up her thighs than it had been before they'd entered the lift. He tried, but failed miserably. Instead, he focused on pulling himself together and smoothed the tails of his shirt down over his jeans. On the lift, she'd undone the first few buttons on his fly, releasing the tip of his swollen cock. Fastening them back up now would risk serious injury.

Cassie swiped her key and opened the door to the silent, unlit room. Logan tugged on her hand. "I guess this is goodnight?" he asked, whispering, in case her roommate was already asleep.

The fact he was supposed to ask the lass something else flashed through his mind, but the thought was gone before he could hold on to it. He leaned down to kiss her, but she stepped inside, opening the door wider. She glanced over her shoulder, peering into the dark quiet of the room behind her for a moment, before turning to face him.

"Bonnie must have decided to wait up for the others over in their room." Cassie shrugged. If she'd meant to appear nonchalant, she ruined the effect with a naughty smile that sent a surge of lust snaking down his back to settle at the base of his spine.

The light from the hall caught the wicked promise curving her cheek as she tipped her face up to his. His balls tightened with anticipation.

"Would you like to come—"

Answering her with his body, he followed her into the room and kicked the door shut behind them.

CHAPTER 4

THE SOUND OF the door banging shut reverberated through Cassie, her pulse leaping exponentially with each step Logan took toward her. She stumbled backward, reaching for the lamp on the desk and flicking it on.

"Aye, that's good." Logan pressed his body close, trapping her against the desk. "I want to see you." He lifted her, setting her on top of the desk. Cool polished wood kissed the backs of her thighs as he hiked her dress up to her ass. "You are so fucking gorgeous. This dress . . . Christ, lass." Logan nudged her knees apart, moving to stand between her legs. It was the most natural thing in the world to wrap her legs around him, ankles locked against his back.

She could feel him now. Barely restrained inside his open jeans, the hard length of him pressed against the thin barrier of her panties. He circled his hips, the teasing friction of each rotation making her warmer, wetter, wilder. A groan of need tore from Cassie's throat, and she flexed the muscles in her thighs, tightening her hold and pulling him closer.

But rather than move nearer, he eased back. She made a sound of protest, and he silenced her with a kiss, pressing his mouth to hers at the same time he pressed his hand between her legs. He rested the heel of his palm against her, exerting a firm pressure that made Cassie's legs twitch uncontrollably.

"You feel amazing," he rasped against her lips as he slid her panties out of the way and dipped a finger inside her. He kissed her again, his tongue thrusting deep into her mouth while his finger thrust deeper into her slick heat.

Cassie moaned and rubbed against him. It felt good, so good. But she wanted more. She unclasped her legs and scooted back, working the rest of the buttons of his fly. "Oh." She sucked in a breath as he sprang free. "Oh, my." Unable to resist touching him, she wrapped her hand around the base of Logan's cock. "You, ah, feel pretty amazing too," she said, sliding her hand up his thick, full length.

As she stroked her thumb over the swollen head, it was his turn to suck in a breath. The sound made her mouth go dry with need. "I want this—I mean you—inside me." She tore her gaze from his cock and met his eyes. "The desk."

"I ken you're on the desk, lass," he murmured. "Do you want to move—"

"No." She shifted her legs. "Open the desk."

He hesitated a moment, and then pulled open the drawer, comprehension dawning on his features when he glanced inside. He picked up the condom box and stared at her, eyebrows arching—in surprise or curiosity, she didn't know and sure as hell didn't care.

Finally, she was getting to the good stuff.

She grabbed the box from him and ripped it open. She'd been carrying this damn thing across Europe for long enough.

"A bit anxious, lass?" He closed the drawer and chuckled, a throaty sexy rumble that made something low in Cassie's belly tremble.

"You have no idea," she said and tore open a foil wrapper.

He took the condom from her, rolling it over his shaft while she watched, so very glad she'd turned the light on. He tugged her panties off and moved between her thighs, pressing close, positioning himself. "Are you ready?"

"God, yes." For years, she'd been so focused on work that trying to find time to date felt like, well, work. The guys she met were usually at events she was covering for the show, so flirting was out of the question. And even when she did find someone she was interested in pursuing something with, her schedule got in the way. The timing never seemed right. So she gave up trying and appeased the occasional twinge of loneliness by promising herself one day, she'd find the time to say yes.

Now was that time, and Cassie was ready. *Very ready.* Legs splayed wide, she braced her palms on the desk. This was what she'd been waiting for for much too long. He was the right man, this was the right moment, and she was done waiting. She arched her body up to meet his. When he entered her, she opened herself to him without hesitation, welcoming his invasion, relishing the way he stretched and filled her. The sharp sweet sting as he slid deeper inside her.

He reached between their bodies and flicked the pad of his thumb over her clit. She gasped. The move caused everything inside her to hum, setting off a chorus of tingling tremors that rolled to the beat of his body rocking in and against hers. Another thrust of his cock, another stroke of his thumb, and the rhythm ricocheted.

"Oh, that's it," Cassie breathed, her body pulsing,

clenching tight around Logan as her orgasm swept over her, flooding her senses. "That's it, that's it, that's it," she chanted as he continued to move within her, coaxing wave after wave of shuddering sensation from her.

"Hold on, lass," he grunted, his hands gripping her hips. "I want you to come for me again."

Was the man serious? Her legs were like water, loose-limbed and heavy. She could barely muster the energy to lift her head and look at him. But then he raised her hips off the desk and pushed forward, thrusting deeper than ever, and she gasped, her body quivering around him as he filled her completely. She grabbed on to his shoulders for balance, tilting her face up to his. He stared down at her, the gold flecks in his green eyes glinting in the glow of the lamp. He kept his eyes locked on hers as he continued to thrust, his movements growing rough and fast, making the desk drawers rattle and shake.

Cassie couldn't look away, couldn't stop staring back at him any more than she could stop the second orgasm that ripped through her, as sudden and unexpected as summer lightning. She screamed, and he covered her mouth with his, absorbing the sound. His body jerked and a growl erupted from his throat while he pumped into her one fierce, final time.

Spent, he collapsed against her, his breath coming in harsh pants that tickled the hair at her temples. Several heartbeats later he eased back, a roguish grin breaking across his handsome face. "Ye did well," he said, the last word curving playfully around his Gaelic tongue.

"I didn't know I was doing this for a grade," Cassie scoffed, though his praise was a burst of sunshine blooming inside her chest. It had been a long time for her, after all.

"Ye're a smart arse." Logan shifted, pinching her back-side as he withdrew.

He turned away from her to deal with the condom, and Cassie realized her "smart arse" was propped on top of a hotel desk, her panties were nowhere in sight, and her dress was hiked up to her belly button. "Oh my God."

"A religious experience, was it then?" He teased, tossing a smug glance over his shoulder.

"With the devil, maybe," she said, feeling utterly debauched and a bit depraved as she scooted off the desk. She spied the box of condoms on the floor at her feet, contents spilling across the hotel carpet. *Yep, definitely depraved.*

Channeling the delicious sense of naughtiness, Cassie kicked the box toward Logan. "How about we try that again?" she suggested, pulling her dress over her head and tossing it aside. "But actually naked this time, and maybe on an actual bed."

Something was poking her. Cassie shifted and rolled on to her side, the crisp hotel sheets sliding across her naked skin.

Wait, I'm naked? Her eyes snapped open. The soft gray-white light of very early morning filtered through the sheer curtains. The outlines of the room's furniture appeared as hazy as her head felt. She lay still and stared straight ahead. After a few moments of squinting, the shape of Bonnie's bed came into focus and Cassie realized it was empty. *No way Bonnie got up before me. Girlfriend might be the last to fall asleep, but she's also the last to wake up at every slumber party we've ever had in the history of forever.*

Then two things happened. Cassie noticed Bonnie's bed was still made, which meant her friend hadn't slept in it, and whatever had been poking her before returned, now a distinct pressure against her bare backside. Her entire body stiffened as she mentally hit replay on the events of last night.

Oh, good God. I slept with him. And by slept, her brain promptly reminded her with a blurry slide show on fast-forward, she meant, had wild, hot, better-than-epic-romance-novel sex. Yesterday morning she'd been starting to think she'd packed the box of condoms for no reason . . . but this morning . . . this morning she was very, very glad she had.

Cautiously, she rolled over. Sure enough, Logan's head was on the pillow next to hers. He was on his side facing her, and the curve of his naked shoulder rose and fell in time with his deep slow breaths. *Not a snorer. I'll put that in the plus column.*

Also a plus? He was freaking gorgeous. His hands were tucked beneath his cheek in a pose that could almost be described as angelic. She watched him, enchanted by how, even in sleep, the devilish slant of his eyebrows and teasing curve of his mouth still held an element of mischief. Asleep, Logan looked like a little boy, innocent but impish, the kind who would steal an extra cookie and then charm his way out of a scolding. The rest of him, though, was all man. He had been right—ridiculously full of himself—but right. Nothing about his body could be considered boyish, and sure as hell not innocent.

Her attention drifted toward the spot where the stark white of the sheet met the warm golden glow of his skin. He wasn't really tan, but he wasn't pasty either. More like . . . Cassie's lips quirked as the image came to her . . . a perfect piece of toast.

"What's got you smiling so early in the day?"

The low timbre of his voice vibrated through her pillow and she looked up to meet his gaze, her smile growing wider to match his. "Toast."

Logan laughed, a deep, rich rumble, husky with the remnants of sleep. "Are ye hungry, then?" He leaned closer, and the thing that had prodded Cassie awake in the first place now pressed against her belly, which had gone all fluttery at the sound of his laugh. Other parts of her started to wake up.

"Maybe." She slipped her hand under the sheet and let her fingers travel down the warm space between their bodies.

"I dinna think you'll be finding your breakfast down there."

"Oh, I bet I'll find something to satisfy me." Her hand bumped up against him. Apparently, his brogue wasn't the only thing that got thicker in the morning. She could barely wrap her fingers around him, and the hot hard feel of him triggered a desperate sense of need to have him inside her, the same as last night.

While many of the details of what they had done together were fuzzy, that part she remembered clearly. The sense of wanting him so badly nothing else mattered. Cassie slid her hand up his length and back down again. He groaned deep in his throat. Again, her body responded to the sound.

But then she heard another sound that froze her in place. Her hand still gripping him, Cassie met Logan's eyes and held her breath, listening. After a moment, the sound came again, a knock rapping sharply on her hotel room door. She considered ignoring it, considered ignoring anything and everything that wasn't Logan. He seemed to be considering the same thing, his gaze drifting down to where she continued to hold him, then back up to her face, one devil's brow quirked in question.

Bonnie's voice answered for Cassie, calling her name through the door. At the buzz of a key card sliding in the lock, Cassie let go of Logan and rolled out of bed. She looked at him, sprawled naked across the sheets, looked down at herself, equally naked, and panicked.

"Um . . ." Not ready to handle the barrage of questions the tableau they presented was sure to prompt, and desperately in need of a few minutes alone to gather her thoughts, Cassie jumped out of bed and raced for the bathroom. "Be right back."

Left to face their morning visitor alone while bare-arsed and sporting a painful hard-on, Logan hastily covered himself with a pillow. At least the room was separated from the door by a short, narrow entryway, saving him from being on display to any passersby in the hall outside. The door clicked shut, and a moment later the redhead who'd had a drink with him and Cassie at the bar last night appeared around the corner.

"Bonnie, right?"

The girl nodded mutely, blue eyes wide as saucers as she stared at him. He quickly glanced down to make sure the pillow hadn't slipped. Gritting his teeth and putting on his best smile, after all Mam did always say you're never fully dressed without one, Logan bid the lass a good morning.

She mumbled something in return and backed up, stumbling over the shoes and clothes scattered on the floor before disappearing around the corner again. At the sound of the door closing, Logan rolled onto his side and pressed his face to the mattress, muffling a growl of frustrated laughter.

A few minutes later, Cassie emerged from the loo. Her chestnut hair was piled high on her head, providing a lovely view of her neck and shoulders, all freshly scrubbed and deliciously pink. She was wrapped in a towel knotted just above her breasts. He'd like to undo that knot and reveal more of that dewy skin, and he'd *really* like to finish what they'd started earlier.

"The shower's all yours," she said, nodding toward the door.

He considered asking her to join him, but she probably wanted a few minutes alone to get dressed. Besides, he was feeling a wee clatty after working up a pretty good sweat last night and could do with a scrub himself.

The Caldy earned its posh reputation. The loo was a study in luxury, the shower sporting a series of high-powered jets that could sandblast the skin off one's arse if turned up too high. Logan wrapped a fluffy towel around his hips and used another to wipe steam from the mirror.

The air was infused with the scent of the lass's soap and shampoo, and he popped the cap and took a sniff. The shampoo smelled nice enough, but it didn't compare to the natural scent of the woman herself.

A scent now burned in his brain, along with the taste and feel of her. He'd slept with girls on the first date a time or two, aye, but he'd never had an experience like last night. Never wanted to get out of his clothes and into a woman so fast or so bad. He'd sure as hell never jumped into bed— or Christ, on top of a desk—with a woman he'd literally just met.

Logan shook his head of wet hair, sending droplets of water spraying everywhere. He wiped the counter down, smiling. When they were younger, Janet used to call him Red Rover and would get mad as a hornet whenever he'd come out of the bath shaking like a puppy after a swim.

Janet. Oh, Christ.

He'd completely forgotten about the contract, forgotten about the telly deal, forgotten *Shenanigans* completely. If he didn't come through with that release form, his sister wasn't going to just be mad as a hornet, she was going to kill him. Janet would say he'd been thinking with his willy—and she'd be right. He was surprised she hadn't called him a few times already . . . and then realized with a sinking feeling in his gut, she probably had.

His phone, always on silent so not to muck up filming, was in the pocket of his jeans, which, along with the rest of his clothes, lay scattered about the hotel room. Logan opened the door and was met with the sound of soft feminine humming. On the other side of the room, Cassie stood in front of the desk, *the desk he'd fucked her on last night*, looking in the mirror as she twisted her hair into a glossy braid.

Logan had liked how she looked in her blue jeans yesterday morning, and had loved the soft clingy dress from last night, but the pretty wee number she had on now was taking the top spot in his affections. Well, maybe second. After naked. She wore a bright, flirty sundress, loose and playful around her legs, but nipping in at her waist and hugging her tits. Abruptly, he began searching for his pants.

"Looking for these?" Cassie asked, toeing his jeans out from behind a chair. She bent down to hook her finger through a belt loop. As she leaned forward, her braid swung over her shoulder. The dress was tied at the nape of her neck, and the ends of the dress ties trailed down her back.

Logan stepped toward her. He wanted to stand behind her and run his fingertips up her smooth, bare skin. Untie the bow at her nape and push her dress down, filling his hands with her breasts as he bent her over that same bloody desk and pushed into her from behind—

"Here." She stood and swung the jeans toward him.

"Aye, thanks." He swallowed hard and grabbed his pants, retreating to the bathroom before the Caldy hotel's generously proportioned towel was unable to hide what was going on beneath the fluffy fabric. Sure, Cassie had seen his own generous proportions last night (and got a handful this morning before her roommate almost got an eyeful), but he doubted she'd appreciate an impromptu full monty.

Logan quickly pulled his jeans on, wincing as he buttoned up over the part of him suffering from a serious case of one-track mind. He pulled his phone out of his pocket and winced again. Three missed calls from Janet. He slumped against the wall and started scrolling through his sister's dozen or so texts.

Cassie watched Logan retreat, enjoying the play of muscle in his back and arms. She had felt those arms around her last night, traced the strong lines of sinew connecting biceps and triceps as he'd hovered above her. Dug her nails into the taut skin of his shoulders when he'd kneed her thighs apart and . . .

A residual quiver rippled through her. Cassie glanced at the mangled box on the bedside table before searching out the crumpled foil wrappers on the floor. Yes, *wrappers*—as in plural, multiple, more than one. She giggled like an idiot. There had been multiples of another kind last night as well.

As she bent to pick up the condom wrappers, she recalled a conversation she'd once overheard between her mother and some of her mother's colleagues at a dinner party. She'd been thirteen at the time, and aside from being scandalized her mom would discuss sex, let alone be having any, Cassie clearly remembered one of the women in the group, a sweet home ec teacher whose classroom was decorated with an elaborate collection of garden gnomes, raise her wine glass and declare with ringing authority, "It's not the quantity, my dear, but the quality."

Last night Logan had scored high on both counts. Cassie had to give credit where credit was due. And to concede, perhaps, that there *was* a difference between men and boys, and it wasn't just the size of their toys. Though there'd been a noticeable difference in that department as well.

Not that she'd had *bad* sex before, she'd had perfectly nice sex . . . and between the three boyfriends she'd had it with, she'd even managed some perfectly agreeable orgasms. But nothing could have prepared her for the raw need she'd experienced last night. The desperate desire to have Logan on her, in her, again, and again, and—Cassie grabbed the third wrapper off the floor—again. She'd wanted a foreign fling, and damn, had she got one. It had taken until almost the end of her vacation, true, but what was that saying about good things coming to those who wait?

"You're not planning to put those in a scrapbook, are you?"

Cassie jumped, sending the wrappers flying. She scowled at Delaney, whose face peered around the corner of the entryway hall. "Ever hear of knocking?"

"I did knock." Delaney stepped into the room. "And before you ask, I also listened at the door first for any hint of sexy times."

"You're disgusting."

"Says the girl who leaves condom wrappers all over the place." Delaney gathered up the wrappers and tossed them in the trash. "Bonnie sent me over to check on you."

"Was that her at the door earlier?"

"Yep. Made a very hasty exit. I think you scarred her for life."

Cassie groaned. Damn those Edinburgh Brambles. And

damn Logan Reid. The man was too sexy for his own good.

Delaney surveyed the tumbled bed sheets, the trail of clothes, and the ripped box on the nightstand. "Speaking of making an exit, where is your Scottish Studmuffin? Did he head for the hills, er, highlands, already?"

Before Cassie could reply, Logan emerged from the bathroom and answered for her. "Not yet. No."

Scottish Studmuffin fit the bill and then some. He'd put his jeans on, but was shirtless, drops of water from his still-damp hair beading on his bare pecs and sliding down over his rippled abs in decadent temptation.

"Who needs a cup of coffee with you to wake up to?" Delaney chirped, eyeing the broad expanse of dripping naked male chest with objective appreciation. "Me, that's who." She turned to Cassie and waggled her eyebrows. "We're having breakfast downstairs. Join us when you're ready." She pulled the men's dress shirt from where it lay strewn across a chair and offered it to Logan. "You too, beefcake. You look like you've worked up quite the appetite."

Before Cassie could go after Delaney for that saucy dig, her friend was out the door, strawberry-blond ponytail swinging jauntily behind her. Cassie turned to face Logan, suddenly shy as she watched him do up the buttons on his shirt. How did one go about handling the morning after a one-night stand?

That's what this had been, right? She'd never had one before. And while she might have liked to spend a few more nights exploring this particular piece of Scotland, she and her friends were scheduled to hop the train to London early this evening.

"So," she said, pausing as he began to undo the buttons

on his fly. She swallowed hard, stealing a glance at the box on the end table before realizing he had only undone his pants so he could tuck his shirt in. *Oh. Okay, then.*

"So," Logan echoed, sitting in the large leather chair and resting one ankle on his knee as he rolled a sock on his foot. He finished putting on his other sock and dropped his foot to the floor, leaning forward, rubbing his hands on his jeans.

Was he feeling as awkward and unsure as she was? Cassie sat on the edge of the bed across from Logan. She hadn't planned out exactly how she'd go about scoring her one-night stand, and she definitely hadn't given any thought to what she'd do with him the morning after. She swung her legs and twisted her braid around her finger, again wondering what to say after a night of lots (and lots) of amazing sex. *Thanks?*

"Would you like to join us for breakfast?" she finally asked.

"I am a wee famished," he confessed, hungry eyes roaming over her legs.

She began to kick her feet faster.

Logan reached out and took hold of one of her ankles, drawing her foot onto his lap. Immediately, heat sparked up her calf. She'd planned to wear a pair of sandals today and had left her feet bare. Logan pressed the pad of his thumb against the arch of her foot and made a slow circle. Cassie melted, leaning back, elbows sinking into the mattress. He pulled her other foot onto his lap and began to massage that one as well.

"I like that." She sighed, closing her eyes, his touch a delicious blend of calming and enticing, relaxing yet arousing.

"Aye?" he asked, and wrapped his fingers around her ankle, kneading the tender skin.

"Aye," she echoed, opening her eyes. She liked the way her body looked in his hands, liked how his long, strong fingers made her feel feminine and delicate.

"I like it too," he said, and trailed one fingertip up the line of her shinbone.

Cassie shivered, glad she'd taken a minute to shave this morning. She wasn't proud of the fact she'd freaked out and abruptly abandoned her overnight guest by jumping out of bed and escaping to the shower. Also part of her (and she was not proud of this either) had hoped, maybe a teensy bit, that he'd sneak out while she was in the bathroom. Then she could avoid the awkward conversation they were having now. Though, with his hands stroking her legs, it was oddly not half as awkward as it had been a few minutes ago when they weren't touching.

"Do you have to go down for breakfast?" he asked, fingers trailing higher up her thighs.

"I should." She pressed her knees together, blocking his progress. "It's our last day in Scotland, and I'm sure Bonnie has our final hours planned almost to the minute."

"Where are you off to next?"

"London." Cassie pulled her legs off his lap, not missing the impressive bulge that hadn't been so obvious moments ago. *Good.* She couldn't help smiling to herself as she slipped her feet into her sandals. Maybe he had enjoyed last night as much as she had. She hoped so.

But last night was over. Tonight she'd be in England, and by the start of next week, back home in Chicago. Meanwhile, Logan Reid, the guy who smiled like a naughty boy but was all man in bed, would still be here in Scotland.

CHAPTER 5

"I HAVE FOUND heaven," Ana declared, standing stock-still in the middle of Edinburgh's bustling farmer's market, tiny wooden spoon hovering at her lips while people streamed past her, browsing the stands and stalls lining the street in the shadow of Edinburgh Castle.

"It can't be that good." Sadie grabbed the spoon and dipped it into the little foil cup Ana held. She licked up a miniscule bit of dessert. Violet eyes going wide, Sadie swallowed the rest of what was on the spoon before shoving the cup back at Ana. "Sweet baby Jesus, take this away from me before I inhale it." She grabbed Ana's wrist. "Wait." She stuck the spoon in the cup again. "Just one more taste." She leaned her head back in ecstasy as she swallowed another bite. "Okay, now I'm done."

"That good, huh?" Cassie asked. An actress, Sadie rarely indulged in sweets. Despite already being naturally petite, Sadie was usually on some fad diet—prepping for an audition or a role or a photoshoot—so if she was willing to spend the calories, whatever was in that cup must be damn good indeed.

Having obviously reached the same conclusion, Bonnie was already making a beeline to order one too. Cassie quickened her steps to catch up and scanned the small chalkboard menu of the Crema Caravan, a food truck (more of a food van, really) whose specialty was crème brûlée. Cassie ordered the same as Bonnie, watching with fascination as the guy behind the makeshift counter torched the tops of their cups of creamy custard, scenting the afternoon air with caramelized sugar.

"Who would have thought we'd end up finding the best crème brûlée in Europe on a van in Scotland, rather than at a café in Paris?" Bonnie asked, tapping her wooden spoon against the hard crust to crack it open. Steam drifted up from her cup, and she inhaled in appreciation.

Cassie stared at the golden crystals dotting the rim of her own foil cup. She chipped away at a piece of the crust and took a bite, letting the burnt sugar melt on her tongue. Crème brûlée wasn't the only thing that turned out to be better in Scotland than what she'd expected to find in France.

As if reading her mind, Bonnie slanted a glance her way. "Better desserts . . . better men . . ."

Cassie choked on a spoonful of custard. She'd managed to avoid the Logan discussion all morning. He'd ended up declining her offer to join them for breakfast. The Scot had been a perfect gentleman about it, had even kissed Cassie's hand in farewell, but still she couldn't help feeling bereft, thinking, *So that's it then?*

It had been a one-night stand. What did she expect? It was right there in the description—*one* night. She didn't want any more than that.

Well, maybe another night or two might not be so bad . . .

No. She'd had her foreign fling. She'd gotten what she'd

wanted. Besides, there was still the issue of who Logan was and what he'd wanted from her, other than sex. She was both surprised and impressed he'd not mentioned the media release to her, not even once. He hadn't tried to get her to sign on the dotted line . . . hadn't really even tried to get into her pants. She'd been the one to get into his.

Her own forwardness had shocked her, and couldn't be blamed entirely on alcohol. Cassie had flirted while tipsy plenty of times in her life, but she'd never had the urge to go for broke in an elevator. There was something about Logan that shoved her inhibitions aside and put her libido in the driver's seat—replaced logic with lust.

Obviously, Bonnie had caught on to this development and wasn't going to let Cassie off the hook so easily. Cassie took another bite of custard and looked back to where Ana, Sadie, and Delaney stood huddled around a cart selling handmade soaps and candles. That should keep them busy for a while.

She turned to Bonnie and gestured toward a park bench a few stalls down. They settled back and after a few more bites of custard, Bonnie gave her the side-eye and Cassie knew she'd better start talking. "Gabe is pretty lucky. A bar full of hot Scottish guys in kilts and you ditch them to come back to the hotel with me."

Bonnie blew out a breath, fluttering the red curls framing her face. "Somebody had to keep an eye on you." She tilted her left hand and gazed down at the gold band on her finger. "Hopefully when we get home, Gabe will be ready to set a date. I'm thinking next summer. June. I'll be done teaching for the year, and he'll finally be finished with his thesis . . ."

"And you've always dreamt of a *Midsummer Night's Dream* theme wedding." Cassie nodded. "See? I remembered."

"You don't think having the bridesmaids dress up like fairies will be too much, do you?"

"Not at all," Cassie assured her, impressively maintaining a straight face. "What about the groomsmen, though?"

"I was thinking . . ." Bonnie halted, rosebud mouth pinching with suspicion. "Hold on, you're *not* getting me sidetracked. We were talking about you. And Logan." Bonnie scraped the bottom of her cup and licked her spoon. "Do you think he'll call you?"

Cassie stirred the remains of her custard. "Why would he call me? He doesn't even have my number."

Bonnie stared fixedly into her now-empty cup.

"Bonnie?" Hope and dread flickered through Cassie, sending the crème brûlée in her belly churning. "You didn't."

Her best friend met her gaze, eyes wide with feigned innocence. After twenty years of friendship, Cassie thought Bonnie would have known better than to try to fool her. From the time Bonnie had drawn a mustache on Cassie's favorite Barbie doll when they were six (she claimed Barbie wanted to be an undercover detective), to the surprise party for Cassie's twenty-first birthday (Cassie was still proud of how well she'd acted surprised, even former soap star Sadie couldn't have performed better), Bonnie had never been able to hide anything from Cassie.

After another moment, Bonnie lost the staring contest. "Okay, fine. I gave him your number."

"When did you do that?"

"At the bar last night." Bonnie shrugged. "I could tell you really liked him, and it was clear he liked you. So I figured . . ." She trailed off, waving her hand in front of her as if rolling a ball forward.

Cassie groaned and set her cup down on the bench next to her. "What have I said about playing matchmaker?"

Bonnie set her own cup down and bristled. "You weren't complaining last night when I left you two alone and stayed out of *our* room." She pouted. "I had to share a bed with Sadie, and you know how she likes to kick."

Cassie grinned. Sadie slept like she was competing in a tae kwon do tournament. Even in her dreams, that girl was exercising. "You're right. I'm sorry." She patted Bonnie's knee. "You're not bruised, are you?"

"Nah, I think she was too tired for her usual horizontal jab-kick-uppercut routine. The three of them didn't get back until almost two in the morning. And then Delaney spent an hour hypothesizing about what you were doing with your 'sexy Scot.'" Bonnie blushed, though given her fair coloring, it might have only been the afternoon sun.

Cassie passed a baleful eye over the trio still clustered around the candle cart. "I can imagine." She shook her head, wondering how someone whose regular vocabulary included the word "tushy" and who had a habit of exchanging curse words with the names of desserts—only yesterday Delaney had smashed her toe in a door and shouted, "Snickerdoodle!"—could be so graphically descriptive when it came to sex. Repression combined with a healthy imagination, Cassie supposed.

"What are you going to do?" Bonnie looped her arms over the back of the wrought-iron bench.

"About what?"

"About your sexy Scot, you bampot."

"What the hell is a bampot?"

"It's Scottish. Means stupid person, an idiot." Bonnie dropped her head back and groaned. "Which is what I should call myself every time I let you distract me." She frowned at Cassie. "Come on now, I'm serious. Would you like to see him again?"

Cassie shrugged. "Sure, I'd like to see him again." At

the thought, the custard in her stomach started auditioning for Cirque du Soleil. Served her right for eating something off a truck—correction, van—though she knew full well her rumbling insides had nothing to do with food. "But it doesn't matter because by tonight, we'll be hundreds of miles away."

Logan turned off the footpath running along the Leith River and headed up the street toward the tricked-out warehouse complex housing *Shenanigans'* workspace. Converted from an old whisky storage facility, most of the units in the complex had been remodeled, equipped with state-of-the-art acoustics and soundproofing. Even so, the muffled thump of a heavy bass line kept time with his footsteps as he made his way across the "square," a central brick courtyard facing the river and lined on three sides with freight doors.

The Mermaids, an all-girl band who favored hard rock covers from the late 80s, also favored rehearsing with their freight door cranked open, guitar riffs pounding through the square. Thick bass notes rumbled in the midmorning air, and Logan recognized the opening to an old glam rock ballad. As he passed their door, Logan gave the girls a thumbs-up. Clara waved her drumsticks in greeting.

Lynne, the guitarist and lead vocalist, eyed his rumpled clothing with a saucy grin. She dipped her head toward the mic. "Someone had a fun night."

"Aye, well." Logan shrugged. "I had a wash this morning." He smoothed back his nearly dry hair and rubbed a hand over the rough stubble on his chin.

"Stash your knickers in your handbag, did you?" Clara teased.

"What knickers?" he deadpanned, catching the drumstick Clara chucked at him.

"Cheeky bastard," the drummer growled.

The bass player, Erica, looked him over as she plucked out the *bow-chicka-wow-wow* of a low-budget skin flick. "Honestly, mate, you look like you've had a hell of a time."

"I have, and my sister is likely going to give me hell for it. If you'll excuse me, ladies . . ." Logan waved the drumstick in farewell and turned away.

"Oy!" Clara sputtered. "Give that back!"

With a chuckle, he tossed the stick to the drummer, who snatched it out of the air and twirled it in her fingers. "Say hi to your sister for me." She lifted the drumstick to her lips and blew a kiss. "And tell her I'm still waiting to hear when we'll be featured on your show."

The pounding beat resumed, growing fainter as Logan passed through the door of his unit. The sound wouldn't penetrate the studio at the far end of the hall. Most of the first floor was taken up by the tech booth, as well as storage space for *Shenanigans'* growing collection of costumes and props and video equipment. Even with all that, there was still room for a cozy sitting area with sofas and footstools and a telly, adjoined by a serviceable kitchenette.

The sharp tang of licorice and mint lingered in the room. Janet must have made a pot of tea recently. Logan added more water to the still-warm kettle and flicked it back on before rummaging in the pantry, pulling out a box of biscuits along with the tea tin. While his sister liked drinking exotic stuff with names he couldn't pronounce, Logan preferred a simple cup of black tea, with a scoop of sugar, poured over a generous splash of milk. Milk first— the proper way. No matter what his best friend, Theo, had to say about it, the British prat.

The kettle shrilled a whistle, and Logan munched a

handful of biscuits while the tea steeped. Best not face Janet on an empty stomach. He'd have much preferred joining Cassie for breakfast rather than rushing home, but knowing his sister, he'd pushed her patience to the limit as it was. Stuffing a few more biscuits in his mouth, Logan grabbed his mug of tea and headed for the studio at the far end of the hall.

"Oh good, you're here. I'll cancel the search-and-rescue party then, shall I?" Janet didn't look up from the computer screen.

"Ha-ha," Logan grumbled and tried to swallow the rest of the biscuit that had turned thick and sticky on his tongue. He took a gulp of tea.

"Did you get it?" Janet glanced up expectantly.

The hot liquid caught in his throat, and Logan grimaced. "Good morning to you too, dear sister." He sat next to her.

"You didn't get it." She frowned, opening a folder and shuffling the contents. "Did you find out *anything* useful about Miss Sugar Lips?"

Logan stared down at his mug, suddenly fascinated with the tiny speckles of color embedded in the clay.

"Oh my God, tell me you didn't."

"Didn't get her to sign the form?" He ventured a glance up. "You're right, I didn't."

She took in his scruffy face and rumpled clothes and rolled her eyes heavenward. "Men. Always thinking with their knob."

"And here I was betting you were going to say willy."

Janet snorted. "If we're making wagers, I should have bet you were going to fanny about. Though I don't blame you, she is a hot piece of ass."

"Nettie."

"Don't worry, you know I prefer blondes." His sister tossed him a grin, the cocky arch of her brow as familiar as his own.

"That reminds me, Clara says hello."

"The drummer?"

"Aye." Logan eyed his sister through the steam rising from his mug. "She wants to know when we're going to feature the Mermaids. Did you promise we'd put them on 'Live in a Lift'?"

Janet ignored his pointed look and shifted the conversation back to the waiver. "I can't believe you got in the girl's pants but couldn't get her signature."

"What's the big deal? We'll make another video. I have loads of ideas."

"We don't have time. If *Shenanigans* doesn't rack up higher numbers in the female demo soon, the producers are going to pass, and the host of that new show is going to be a chit who wears horrid lippy and sings about her cat."

"Not going to happen."

"Wanna bet?"

Logan's jaw tightened. "The telly deal is going to be ours. I didn't get the lass to sign the waiver, so what?" He gestured toward the pile of papers in Janet's folder. "We filmed a bunch of other takes with other girls who were all perfectly happy to sign the waiver. Why is this one so important?"

Janet exhaled and turned her attention back to the screen. "Watch the video and then we'll talk." She rolled the trackball of her mouse, rapidly sliding through a series of screenshots.

Logan recognized clips from the castle and frowned at his sister. "You edited this? I asked you to wait."

"And I asked you to get that release form signed."

He ignored the dig and scooted closer, taking control of the trackball. Janet had set up three files from yesterday's footage. Logan clicked on the first. In moments, Cassie's head appeared around the door of the castle bedroom. The camera they'd rigged on the fireplace mantle was directly opposite the door and set to catch a panoramic sweep of the room.

"The overhead camera works best for this next scene, I think." She swiped the last biscuit off the desk and hit play, tapping the screen with the corner of the biscuit. "You want to talk about close ones, your girl almost blew everything when she stuck her head in the passageway. What happened? You were supposed to maneuver her over to the fireplace."

What happened was, he'd completely forgotten what he was doing. "The important thing is I managed to pull her out of there and distract her." On screen, Logan watched as Cassie lifted her hands and trailed her fingers through his hair. His scalp tingled at the memory. He recalled the feel of her as he brushed his palms down her back and whispered something about devils and angels. Then she had kissed him, and his brain had misfired.

"Remind me again who's distracting whom?" Janet's smug voice knocked Logan out of his thoughts. He stared at the monitor, not even able to blink as he relived the most amazing kiss of his life. That wasn't an exaggeration; it was a simple fact. She had taken him completely off guard. He couldn't blame a bit of what happened next on "getting into character," and his sister well knew it.

As he watched the kiss play out, he saw the moment he'd stepped out of his role. Nobody else might catch the shift, but Logan did. He could pinpoint the exact second he had stopped playing the part, stopped running the gag, stopped doing anything beyond kissing the girl who had boldly taken him by surprise and kissed him first.

Logan had seen himself on-screen countless times, in all kinds of potentially—and often purposefully— embarrassing situations. But watching himself now, seeing his hands grasp Cassie's waist and pull her closer, the whole thing was making him uncomfortable. The moment was intensely private, something between him and Cassie. Something he didn't want to share with his sister or anyone else.

"Damn, brother, when did you learn to kiss like that? That is one sexy snog session." Nettie stroked her chin. "I'm thinking I should have made you lose the shirt."

Especially not his sister. That's probably what was making him feel weird. His sister was watching him make out. Logan clicked on the file to close it, hating the rush of heat burning his cheeks. Downside of being a redhead, he tended to blush like an altar boy who'd found a dirty magazine stashed under a pew. He picked up his mug and took another sip of tea, hoping Janet would chalk his flushed face up to the steam. "Did you edit all the takes or only this one?"

Janet stared at him. "What do you think? Why waste my time on the others when we know this *is* the one?" Her face scrunched up. Logan knew that face—a storm was brewing. "Oh wait, I *did* waste my time. Because instead of getting Miss Kissy Face to sign the waiver, you were busy dipping your quill."

"Cassie."

"What?"

"Her name is Cassie. Not Sugar Lips or Kissy Face or whatever name you've got queued up to say next."

The storm eased for a moment as the frustration in Janet's face shifted, her eyebrows shooting up with incredulity. "I beg your pardon. Does Miss Hot"—he shot her a warning glare—"Miss *Cassie* have a last name?"

Logan relaxed. This at least he knew. "Crow."

"Cassie Crow, huh?" Janet took a fresh release form from the folder and placed it on top of the pile. She tapped the paper with her pen. "Catchy."

His tea had cooled. Logan chugged the rest of the lukewarm liquid, wishing Janet hadn't stolen all his biscuits. Still peckish, he rose from the desk to fetch another snack when his phone vibrated. He slipped it out of his pocket and glanced at the number, then sank back onto his chair, appetite gone.

Logan cleared his throat and let the phone ring one more time before answering the call. "Logan Reid."

At the professional tone of his voice Janet scooted closer, the wheels of her chair rolling silently over the studio's foam floor. "Who is it?" she mouthed.

He held up a finger to her as the man on the line said, "Logan, hey. It's Bob from Second Studios."

"What can I do for you, Bob?" Logan stuck his leg out and blocked his sister from scooting any closer.

"Yeah, hey look, the network is on my case. There's an issue with one of the shows in our fall lineup. We have an opening and need to get rolling on this earlier than expected. How are your stats looking?"

"I'm expecting there'll be a strong uptick soon." Logan thrust out an elbow, scowling at his sister. Nettie was practically breathing down his neck as she listened in on the call.

"Excellent," Bob said. "I gotta tell ya, my money is on you, but my coproducer thinks otherwise. I need to win him and our sponsors over."

Tension gathered in a snarl between Logan's shoulders. "I understand. We're working on an idea right now."

"When do you think you'll have something for me?"

Nettie held up the release form with Cassie's name on it, waving the paper at him. He ignored her. "Soon. I'll be in touch." He wrapped up the call and snatched the waiver from his sister. "Go ahead and finish the edits."

"On it." Janet scooted back to the keyboard. "What's your plan?"

Logan dug in his pocket for the napkin from the Caldy bar. "I'm taking a wee trip."

"Where?" Janet called after him as he headed for the door.

"London."

CHAPTER 6

"STILL DRIVING THIS sorry excuse of a car, I see." Logan tossed his duffel bag into the boot of Theo Wharton's aging Roadster and hopped into the front seat. With its smooth, sexy lines, the old MGB could have starred in a James Bond film . . . three or four 007s ago. An unhealthy gurgle of smoke belched from the exhaust pipe as the car lurched out of the Sandy Station parking lot. Logan glanced over at the driver with a twinge of guilt. It had been too long since he'd seen his best mate. "I thought things were grand."

"*Grand* might be an overstatement," Theo said, as he eased onto the A1 and shifted into a higher gear. The car jerked forward, sputtering a moment before picking up speed.

Logan braced himself against the dash, his palms absorbing the shuddering rattle of the engine. "Meaning?"

"Meaning that while I'm pleased to report the Wharton family is no longer in imminent danger of losing its ancestral estate, we still can't afford to do much more than pay the taxes on the bleeding place." Theo tugged on the cuff of his tailored shirt. He may not have deep pockets, but they were custom-made, on shirts likely cleaned and pressed each morning by a maid who'd been with the Wharton family as long as the Roadster.

Logan remembered asking about that once. He'd been invited to spend the winter holidays with Theo and had been surprised by the number of servants. Confused too, since Logan knew Theo was working toward a degree in estate finance, hoping to save his family from financial ruin. When he'd asked Theo why the family kept such a large staff if they were having money issues, his friend had shot Logan one of those patently British *Good Lord, you're such an idiot* looks and said, "They need us more than we need them."

Logan had laughed at first and accused his friend of classism. But then Theo pointed toward the other end of the dining room, where an elderly woman was arranging a tea tray. "Ms. Cathy has worked for this family since before I was born." Theo lowered his voice. "It's not just about money, Lo. For her, and many others like her—the gardeners, the maids, the laundresses—the Wharton estate is more than just a job; it's their life. And this home is as much theirs as it is mine."

Ms. Cathy set the tray in front of them, and Theo smiled up at her in thanks. He waited until the woman had retreated from the room. "And you want me to tell that sweet old lady we don't need her anymore? Take away her livelihood?" Theo shook his head. "I can't do that. I won't."

It was then Logan had realized how much the Wharton estate was like his da's business. The people of Lochalsh depended on Reid's Fishery for their jobs and for the income those jobs provided. Their homes, the welfare of their families, it was all linked. Like Theo said, it was their livelihood. Theo had stepped up and done the hard thing;

he'd made personal sacrifices in order to provide for his family and those that depended on him.

Unlike Logan, who had run away from his responsibilities.

Shrugging off the memory, Logan leaned over and pushed the button to retract the car's hood. Theo winced at the series of whines and hisses emanating overhead as fabric and metal folded in on itself.

"Maybe I should have asked you to meet me at King's Cross instead. Are you sure this bucket of bolts is going to make it to London?"

"Don't listen to him, sweetheart." Theo patted the car's oversized steering wheel gently, probably afraid anything firmer would knock something loose. "She'll get us to London," he assured Logan. "What are we doing there, anyway? *Shenanigans* prank?"

"Sort of. More like a post-prank follow-up, aye?" Logan leaned back and let the fresh, cool air wash over him. The train ride down from Edinburgh had been hot and stuffy. Since he'd booked his ticket at the last minute, he'd not really had his choice of seats. He stretched his legs, glad Theo had agreed to swing by and pick him up at the station in Bedfordshire. The Wharton family seat was in Sandy, about an hour outside London.

After his conversation with Second Studios, Logan had called his old mate up, still unsure of the game plan. But at the sound of that distinctly British voice, crisp and confident and a shade impatient, Logan felt better. With Theo's help, Logan knew he could pull this—whatever *this* ended up being—off.

Logan had met Theo in an economics class when they were both bejants at St. Andrews. While many of the blue-blooded blokes at the elite university were royal pricks born with a silver spoon stuck between their in-bred teeth,

Theo was the real deal—noble in spirit as well as name. Noble yes, but Logan quickly learned Theo had a mischievous streak, coupled with a wicked sense of justice Logan had no qualms exploiting. Theo enjoyed a good prank and liked it even better if the prank involved serving some aristocratic blighter a hearty comeuppance.

Theo had often been Logan's partner in crime, luring unsuspecting marks into place. Clean-cut, well-mannered, and good-looking, Theo was the proper English gentleman from head to toe. Unlike Logan, who always looked guilty even when he hadn't done anything wrong, Theo had the kind of face people trusted. Logan intended to use that magic face to his advantage.

Theo glanced over his shoulder before crossing lanes. "I need details. Who does this escapade involve?"

"A gorgeous American and her pack of gorgeous friends."

"I knew we were mates for a reason." Theo grinned. "Go on."

Logan chuckled. "The lass doesn't know it yet, but she has a hot date with me this evening." He reached into his pocket and pulled out the cocktail napkin from the Caldy's bar. Two nights ago, Cassie's friend had slipped it into his hand, accompanied by a finger over her lips and a series of odd blinks that Logan realized must have been her version of a conspiratorial wink.

Theo downshifted as they approached the city limits. "I'm not complaining about getting away for a few days, mind you, but what's my role in all this?"

Logan looked over at Theo and winked (he was much better at it than the redheaded lass had been). "How do you feel about playing wingman?"

Tracking Cassie and her hive of friends in London had been cake. At the bar, her friend had mentioned one of their traveling companions had a hookup with the Waldorf hotels, and Logan was glad he'd filed that detail away. As Theo maneuvered the antique heap of metal into town, Logan directed his friend to the West End.

"We're meeting them at the theatre?" Theo asked as he drove past the shops of Covent Garden.

"No." Logan pointed. "Turn here." The hotel's elegant facade came into view moments later. "This is it. Pull over and let the valet park this dustbin—though if they drove it into the Thames, they'd be doing you a favor." Logan got out of the car and glanced back at his friend, who hadn't moved. "For Chrissakes, Theo, don't have kittens. It's where the girls are staying."

Logan shouldered his duffel bag and waved over a valet. "Careful with her, lad, she's an old gal who should have been put out to pasture years ago." He handed over several quid, hoping the generous tip would ensure a tender hand, or at least guarantee the car would be returned in one piece.

Theo yanked a leather valise out of the boot and joined Logan on the sidewalk. He looked up at the bold, classic lettering announcing the Waldorf Hilton, his mouth a hard line. Logan threw a hand over his friend's shoulder. "Don't worry about the price. I'm bankrolling this escapade."

"I'm not a bloody charity case, Lo."

"No, you're not." Logan steered Theo through the hotel's entrance. "But you came here as a favor to me, and I expect you to earn your keep." He nodded toward the front desk, where a pretty brunette stood behind the counter. "Start by chatting up the hotel staff for some intel."

Theo paused at the top of the small flight of steps leading into the lobby. "I thought you already knew this girl of yours and her friends were staying here?"

"I *think* they are, but I want to be sure. Besides, I don't know what room she's in."

"Then call. You have her number, right?" Theo smoothed a hand over his hair, though Logan wondered why his friend even bothered, it always looked impeccable. When they were in school, Logan had nicknamed Theo's meticulously styled head, "Prince Charming Helmet." And while a bit longer now, Theo's dark hair still appeared picture-perfect, despite the windy drive.

Logan, on the other hand, knew his own messy mane hadn't fared the journey quite as well. He hoped he'd have time to clean up a bit before putting his plan into action. "I can't call yet. I don't want to scare her off."

"Fair enough, but if that's the case, you may need to freshen up." Theo gave him a once-over, taking in not only Logan's tousled hair, but his travel-worn jeans and crumpled shirt.

"We can't all look like bloody Prince Charming," Logan grumbled and shoved Theo toward the front desk. "Now go work your magic. I want to find out what floor the girls are staying on."

They approached the counter. Logan may have perfected his own brand of charm, but it didn't compare to the smooth finesse that came as naturally as breathing to Theo. While Logan gave the clerk his information and began the check-in process, Theo simply leaned against the counter and smiled.

Under Theo's gentle gaze, a soft blush rose in the girl's cheeks. She cleared her throat and refocused her attention on Logan. "How long will you be staying with us, Mr. Reid?"

"A few days, I expect." Logan glanced at Theo. "What do you think?"

"Well, here's the thing, Miss . . ." Theo lowered his gaze

and read the name tag pinned to her bosom, letting his eyes linger there a moment longer than necessary, ". . . Swanson."

"Beth," the girl breathed, her chest expanding. "Call me Beth."

"Nice to meet you, Beth." Theo reached across the counter, letting his hand brush hers. "I'm Theo." He raised her hand to his lips.

Logan studied the lobby's ceiling. He often borrowed that move from Theo. You can never go wrong with a classic.

Theo crooked a finger at Beth, and she leaned closer. "I have some friends staying here too. I believe they arrived yesterday, and I was hoping I could get their room number so I could stop by and surprise them."

Beth pulled back. "I'm not sure I can do that."

Theo's face fell, a dejected puppy. "I understand. Maybe you can just let me know if they checked in." He raised his eyes and stared soulfully at her. "Please?"

"Well . . ." The girl melted under Theo's warm gaze. "I suppose there'd be no harm in that. What's your friend's name?"

"Cassie." Theo stole a subtle glance at the napkin Logan had given him. "Cassie Crow."

The girl stiffened at the mention of a female name, and Logan jumped in before the mission crashed and burned. "She's the sister of one of our mates, here on holiday with some of her pals. We promised we'd look in on her while we were in town."

Theo nodded. "Right. He's a protective sort of bloke. You know how big brothers are."

Beth relaxed. "I do. I have two of them myself."

"Sounds like quite a challenge for the lad who'd like to date you," Theo mused with just the right hint of possibility.

Boom. Logan smothered a laugh. Theo was a master.

With a flirtatious toss of her hair, Beth started typing rapidly. "Our records show a Cassandra Crow checked in late last night. She's on a shared reservation." Her eyes widened as she continued reading. "Bonkers. Your friend must be loaded; he booked a block of suites for his sister on the executive floor." She bit her lip and looked up. "Oops. Pretend you didn't hear that last part."

"What last part?" Theo chucked the girl under her chin. Anyone else would have looked like a chauvinistic ass, but Theo pulled off the gesture with charismatic flair. "Thanks, love."

Logan handed over his charge card. "Two rooms on the executive floor, please."

Beth seemed to finally recall there were other people standing there. She pulled her eyes away from Prince Charming and processed the reservation. "I hope you gentlemen enjoy your stay with us. If there's anything I can do to make your visit more pleasant, just ask." She leaned over the counter and said low in Theo's ear, "I get off in time for tea."

Theo winked and blew Beth a kiss before turning to follow Logan.

"Smooth, mate." Logan handed Theo a key card. "But you need to tell your new girlfriend you've got plans tonight."

"Hey, I earned my keep." Theo handed back the cocktail napkin with Cassie's name and number. He narrowed his eyes in challenge. "Until you grow a pair and call this girl, I'm free to do what I want."

"All right." Logan pocketed the napkin and shouldered his duffel bag, chuckling. "I'll call her."

CHAPTER 7

HE DIDN'T CALL.

All through her first day in London, as she and her friends checked off the must-sees on their list, Cassie alternated between hoping her phone would ring and praying it didn't. At the Victoria and Albert Museum, Cassie passed through the rooms with subdued interest, barely perking up when they encountered the larger-than-life plaster copy of David.

The girls had already viewed the impressive original in Florence, but Delaney was fascinated with the detachable fig leaf on display here. As the story goes, Queen Victoria was so shocked when she first saw the statue in all its impressive naked glory that the fig leaf was created to cover David's twig and berries whenever HRH planned a visit. Delaney moved in close and examined the statue, claiming she was trying to find the hooks to see how the leaf was hung.

"Yeah, you're looking to see how it's hung, all right," Ana had quipped.

Cassie smiled at the memory and slid another glance

at her phone. Nothing. What did she expect? What did she want? She knew what she *didn't* want—she didn't want a video of her sucking face with a man she didn't even know plastered all over the internet, that's for sure. Especially not now.

Her boss had finally responded to Cassie's email and agreed to discuss her role in the upcoming season of *Chi-Chat*. After weeks of waiting to hear back from Therese, suddenly Cassie had a meeting scheduled for next Monday morning, barely eighteen hours after she was supposed to get off the plane at O'Hare. If all went well, Cassie would get a crack at doing real stories, like a real broadcast journalist. She could sign-off on being the show's pop culture poster girl and finally be taken seriously. If her boss agreed to the change, Cassie would need to have a plan in place and be ready with the story she'd cover first. She had a couple of ideas, but needed to decide which one she should lead with.

"You're doing it again," Bonnie said, not even bothering to look up from the brochure she was reading about a dinner cruise on the Thames.

"Am I?" Cassie covered her phone with her palm, not knowing why she bothered trying to play dumb. Crammed next to Bonnie as she was, there was no denying the obvious. It was late afternoon and their train car was packed with commuters, rank with the scent of sweat, stale air, and rancid coffee. Just like home. But unlike Chicago's "L," which for the most part traveled above the city streets, the Tube hurtled passengers through the dark corridors of London's underbelly. Over the course of the day, as she and her friends hopped from station to station and rode down escalator after escalator, Cassie was shocked at how deep below the city some of the tunnels traveled.

The train slowed to a stop, the distinctly British reminder to "Mind the gap" chiming as the doors slid
open—a marked change from the garbled voice she was
used to hearing announce the next station on the red line.
Cassie looked over the heads of the mass exodus of hu-
manity and examined the color-coded map plastered near
the ceiling. She counted the stations left until their stop and
figured they had about twenty minutes to go.

She'd barely thumbed the screen awake when Bonnie
grabbed it out of her hand.

"Aw, come on!" Cassie made a grab for her phone, but
Bonnie dodged her and dropped the phone into the hobo
bag slung over her shoulder. "You have *got* to stop doing
that to me."

"Sure, as soon as you stop checking your phone every
ten seconds," Bonnie agreed. "Therese got back to you. No
excuses. You promised you'd stop thinking about work."

"I wasn't thinking about work," Cassie muttered.

"Oh." Understanding lit Bonnie's eyes. "He hasn't
called, then?"

"Who hasn't called? I don't know what you're talking
about." Cassie bit her lip. Why was she was even trying to
lie? Her best friend could read her way too easily. And the
truth was, ever since she'd run into Logan at the castle,
work had taken a back seat to . . . other things.

Bonnie fiddled with the brochure in her hand. "I never
should have told you I gave him your number."

"No," Cassie countered, grabbing on to the dark blue
pole as the train thundered to another stop. "You never
should have given him my number, period."

"Whatever." Bonnie shrugged and went back to her brochure. "What's past hope is past care, right?"

"*Hmph.*" Bonnie may know her well, but that knowledge

went both ways. Cassie had a feeling her friend wasn't done playing matchmaker. Though, what could Bon do? The man in question was hundreds of miles away.

The thought both cheered and depressed her. She shifted to check on the others. Delaney, of course, had nodded off, shoulder pressed to the window, her not-quite-so-perky-anymore ponytail listing to the side. Farther down, Ana and Sadie were also seated, currently arguing over which play they should try to get rush tickets for. When the train stopped again, Cassie took the opportunity to nab a spot next to Delaney.

A small snore escaped Delaney as she sat up. "When's our stop?"

Cassie squinted at the station map. "Two to go, I think."

"Okay." Delaney blinked the sleep out of her eyes and glanced around the train car. "Who's Bonnie talking to?"

"What?" Cassie jerked her head toward Bonnie, who was still standing, one hand gripping the pole, bulging bag swinging from her shoulder, the other holding a phone to her ear—Cassie's phone. Bonnie glanced back, cheeks flushing with guilty heat when she caught Cassie watching her.

Immediately, Cassie knew exactly who Bonnie was talking to.

Mother effer.

CHAPTER 8

"FIRST A POSH hotel room, and now a fancy supper cruise. You sure know how to show a lad a good time." Theo straightened his already straight bow tie.

How the nob managed to wear one of those hoity-toity getups and still look like chickbait, Logan didn't know, but he'd take it. He needed Theo to keep Cassie's flock of friends occupied. For a brief moment, Logan considered if it was selfish on his part to use his friend in such a way, but he suspected Theo didn't mind.

"Remind me to get together with you more often, mate." Theo winked and tossed back a flute of champagne.

Suspicions confirmed, Logan returned the wink and polished off his own champagne. A server crossed the deck, and Logan traded their empty glasses for two fresh ones. He raised the bubbly aloft. "To old friends and new adventures."

"Here, here." Theo accepted his glass and clanked it against Logan's. "What's the plan?"

"Divide and conquer." Logan propped his elbows on the boat rail, the champagne glass resting loosely in his hand, almost empty already. He'd have to slow down if he wanted to keep his wits about him tonight. He couldn't risk getting sloshed and letting his dick do the thinking for him again. Though, when Logan recalled his night with Cassie Crow, it wasn't the time they'd spent in bed occupying his mind.

Oh, he thought about that part too—he was only human—but more often he found himself replaying the time they'd spent alone together in the hotel lounge, the amber light on the low table between them casting a golden glow over her chestnut hair and shining in her dark eyes as she smiled at something he said. Logan liked her smile.

"Look sharp, I believe our quarry is boarding." Theo shouldered Logan, hitching his chin toward the dock where a bevy of females were making their way up the gangplank.

Logan straightened. "That's them."

Theo considered each girl as she stepped onto the boat. "Which one's yours?"

"The one in green. And she's not *mine*," Logan grumbled, wanting to knee his friend in the bollocks for eyeing Cassie, even for a moment. If he had to make a wager, though, he'd say Theo's attention seemed focused on the little redhead.

As if on cue, Bonnie turned toward them and waved, cheeks curving in an ebullient smile. When Theo returned the wave, the girl's smile wobbled uncertainly. She abandoned her friends and hurried across the deck to greet them. "Logan! Nice to see you again." She cast a wary glance up at Theo. "I didn't realize you'd have company."

"Theo Wharton, at your service." Theo took Bonnie's hand and bowed over it.

Instead of swooning, the girl pulled her fingers out of Theo's grasp before he could brush his lips over them. If

Theo was surprised by her apparent immunity to his charm, he didn't show it.

Logan finally managed to recover his wits, which seemed to have abandoned ship the moment he saw Cassie. "I did mention in our wee chat on the phone that I'd come to town to visit a friend, remember?" From the expression on Bonnie's face, Logan figured she'd thought he'd made the friend thing up as a ruse for following Cassie to London—which was more or less true. "Besides, entertaining five beautiful lasses is hard work. Promise me you won't begrudge my need to call in reinforcements."

"Well . . ." Bonnie hesitated.

"I don't bite, I promise." Theo grinned. An answering grin reluctantly teased the corner of Bonnie's lips. Encouraged, Theo dropped his voice to a husky murmur. "That is, not unless you want me to."

The smile fell from Bonnie's mouth, and she flushed, dropping her gaze to the polished beams of the deck.

The raven-haired lass with the set of brilliant knockers sailed forward, stepping between Theo and Bonnie. "Is this guy bothering you?" She turned to Theo and froze, her face losing its confrontational edge as she stared, mouth agape. "Holy shit, it's Prince Eric."

"Sorry?" Theo asked, confusion furrowing his aristocratic brow, whether over Bonnie's continued immunity to his charm or the buxom lass's peculiar comment, Logan couldn't tell.

The wee blonde joined them. "Ignore Ana, she's obsessed with princess movies."

Ana, that was the dark-haired girl's name. And the blonde was Katie . . . no, Logan searched his memory for a moment . . . *Sadie.* That was it. Sadie preempted Theo by holding her hand out to him expectantly. Brave lad that he was, Theo stepped back into the fray, lifting the blonde's fingers to his lips with unruffled formality.

Unlike Bonnie, Sadie had no problem letting her hand linger in Theo's as she met his eyes with a seductive smile. "Ana is right. You *do* look like Prince Eric."

Theo looked to Logan for help, but he had no idea what the lasses were nattering about. Theo wasn't a prince. He was a noble, aye, but not a royal one. Besides, they didn't know that. Logan shrugged. "Must be some American thing."

"It's a Disney thing," Ana huffed, as if that explained it.

"Like the mouse?" Theo asked.

"Like *The Little Mermaid*. You know, Prince Eric and Ariel . . ." Ana trailed off, glancing between Bonnie and Theo. She started to laugh.

Just as Logan was beginning to wonder if Cassie's friends were a bunch of nutters, she joined them. After boarding, Cassie had remained on the other side of the deck, sipping champagne with the leggy strawberry-blonde and ignoring him completely. He'd been keeping tabs on her, trying to ignore the roiling tide of nervousness in his gut that had nothing to do with the gentle sway of the boat.

"What's so funny?" Cassie asked, addressing Ana while still ignoring Logan.

Ana waved a hand between Theo and Bonnie. "Look at those two. Who do they remind you of?" When Cassie didn't answer, her friend began to hum a tune. Though unfamiliar to Logan, the other girls seemed to recognize it.

The strawberry-blonde blinked. "Oh my God."

"Delaney, don't encourage her," Bonnie said. If possible, the little redhead's cheeks flushed a deeper shade of crimson, and Logan felt a pang of empathy. Ginger problems.

A server stopped to collect their glasses and ushered

them through a glass doorway. The dining area was on the main deck, in a structure that looked like a garden conservatory, all windows. There was room to seat about fifty people, with three long tables, each sitting eight, lined up in the center of the room, surrounded by several four-tops and two-tops, elegantly adorned with fine china and silver.

Many of the smaller tables were already occupied with couples, laughing and chatting and absorbing the gorgeous view of twilight on the Thames. Logan maneuvered through the group, trying to negotiate a chair next to Cassie as they settled themselves around one of the long tables. She dodged him and slipped fast as a cat into the seat between two of her friends.

Undeterred, Logan shot around the table and took the seat facing her instead. He stared at Cassie across the snowy linen, daring her to continue to pretend she wasn't aware of his presence. She bent her head and fingered her place setting. With a smirk, she held up her fork. "Remember, Bonnie, this is for eating, not brushing your hair."

"Ugh, not you too." Bonnie grabbed the fork out of Cassie's hand. "Give me that before I stab you with it." She set the silverware down and glanced across the table. "Cassie, you remember Logan, don't you?" Bonnie smiled at him. "I'm so glad you could join us this evening."

Logan knew the syrupy-sweet grin Bonnie poured over him was for Cassie's benefit, a dose of female revenge, but he didn't mind. At least it brought him into to the conversation. "Delighted to be here. Your suggestion couldn't have been more perfect."

It was true, the girl's idea had been a lifesaver. When he first took off for London, he'd had no idea what his plan would be beyond tracking Cassie to her hotel. Once he'd finally grown the bollocks to call Cassie, and Bonnie had answered instead, Logan was worried he'd misunderstood the redhead, and that she'd slipped him *her* number that night at the bar. After Logan oh-so-casually mentioned he was in London (to see a friend, total coincidence of course, he had most certainly not chased after them), Bonnie bubbled over with excitement and within minutes had Logan agreeing to meet them later that evening on the dinner cruise.

Now here he was, and the stubborn Miss Cassie Crow was trapped with him on this boat for the next three hours—unable to escape. Aye, perfect.

Un-freaking-believable. Cassie gave the waitress her drink order—a Dark and Stormy, don't scrimp on the rum, thank you very much—then sat back in her chair and stared across the table at the man she was going to be stuck with for several hours. Logan fucking Reid, with his shit-eating grin and his ginger mane tamed, except for the sexy tousle of hair that fell over one sexy, sinful eyebrow. He was in a crisp jacket and tie, and damn if he didn't wear the fancier threads well. Kilt, jeans, suit, or naked—she liked the way he looked in every variation.

What she didn't like, however, was the way he was looking at her now. Speculative. Considering. Determined. He'd followed her to London for a reason, and she had a pretty damn good idea what that reason was. Just as she'd known Bonnie had been up to something when she'd handed Cassie back her phone with a sheepish grin, Cassie knew Logan was up to something now.

Her drink arrived, and Cassie lifted the glass, letting the scent of ginger and lime fill her senses. She took a healthy sip. The waitress, bless her, had taken Cassie's request to heart. The dark potent rum slid over her tongue, barreled through her belly, and shot straight down to her feet. She wiggled her tingling toes. She was wearing a pair of strappy heels she'd borrowed from Sadie, whom Cassie was convinced traveled with an entire suitcase devoted to shoes. The girl needed one. The number of pairs Sadie had bought in Milan alone were enough to fill a suitcase.

To Cassie's left, Sadie was sporting a new pair of suede pumps with a peek-a-boo toe. Sadie tucked a blond curl behind her ear and poured a glass of water from the pitcher on the table. It was one of her rituals; Sadie always drank two full glasses of water before any meal. Cassie tapped Sadie's arm and motioned for her to pass the bread, which as usual, Sadie hadn't touched. How anyone could ignore the amazing smells wafting from the basket, Cassie couldn't understand. She slipped a roll from beneath the cloth napkin, the still-warm bread heating her palm.

"Send that my way, please," Ana ordered, eyes caressing the basket like a long-lost lover. Seated between Logan fucking Reid and his buddy, Prince Eric, or whatever his name was, Ana held the basket to her bosom and inhaled deeply. To their credit, neither man took the opportunity to sneak a peek down Ana's dress.

Prince Eric was busy answering Sadie's barrage of questions. No, he didn't live in London, but an hour or so west of the city. Yes, he and Logan had been friends for a long time, since university. Where did they go to school? St. Andrews.

At the mention of St. Andrews, Bonnie looked up from where she'd been pouting into her wineglass. "Wait a minute. *The* St. Andrews? As in the same school Prince William attended?"

Prince Eric turned to face Bonnie, at the opposite end of the table from him. "Yes, his highness attended, though he was a few years ahead of us."

"What about Kate? Was she in your year?" Delaney

asked, surprising Cassie. A pint of Newcastle midway to her mouth, Delaney caught Cassie staring at her and lifted a shoulder. "Hey, I spend a lot of time in grocery store checkout lines."

Prince Eric (she really needed to get the man's real name) turned to Delaney with a question in his big, princely blue eyes. Delaney set her beer down and wiped the foam from her upper lip with the back of her hand. "Don't tell me you don't have tabloids in England."

"Oh. Red tops, you mean," he said, holding out a napkin to Delaney. "We've plenty of those. My mum reads them, though she'd disown me if she knew I told anyone."

"Ah, a guilty pleasure, huh?" Delaney took the napkin and grinned conspiratorially. "Well, Theo, your mum's secret is safe with me." *Theo. Right.* Delaney took another sip of her beer and dabbed at her mouth with the napkin. "Sorry, when you spend most of your time with three- and four-year-olds, your table manners take a hit."

"Delaney is a preschool teacher," Sadie said, nudging herself back in to the conversation. She twirled a loose golden curl around one dainty finger.

Uh-oh. Cassie knew that move. Sadie was in flirtation mode. Cassie glanced over at Delaney, but she'd already caught on too.

"That's right. I am," Delaney agreed before calling down the table to Bonnie. "Hey, switch spots with me."

Bonnie tightened her grip on her wineglass. "Why?"

"Because, talk of my profession has put me in the mood for a game of musical chairs, that's why." Delaney stood, rounded the table, and shooed Bonnie out of her chair. "Hurry up, before the waitress comes back to take our order."

"It's a prix fixe menu. We don't need to order anything,"

Bonnie protested as Delaney pulled her out of her seat and took her place.

"Oh, well that's nice." Delaney handed Bonnie her wineglass. "Here, go talk to university boy about books or something."

Bonnie looked over at the empty seat next to Theo. "Fine," she growled, taking a large swallow of wine before circling the table.

"That was generous of you." Cassie took another long pull on her drink as Delaney settled in next to her.

"Generous?" Delaney dug her thumbs into a roll and cracked the crusty bread open, releasing a billow of fragrant yeasty steam.

"You switched seats so the very taken and very not-looking-to-hook-up Bonnie would be Sadie's only competition." Cassie slid the butter urn toward Delaney. "We both know Ana won't make a move on any guy Sadie's staked a claim on."

Delaney slathered butter on both sides of her roll. "Oh. Well, there is *that*." Delaney set the knife down and leaned closer to Cassie. "But there's also the fact I wanted a front-row seat to the Cassie-Logan show." Delaney lifted her roll, wiggling her eyebrows at Cassie before sinking her teeth into the bread.

Beneath the table, Cassie swung her foot, the narrow heel of her borrowed shoe catching Delaney in the shin. Delaney jumped, spewing crumbs.

"Oh my, are you all right?" Cassie asked, patting Delaney on the back harder than necessary.

"Fine," Delaney wheezed. She flipped her strawberry-blond ponytail over her shoulder, the long ribbon of hair smacking Cassie in the face in the process, and reached for her beer. "So, Logan," Delaney said after she'd drained her glass. "I hear you helped Cassie get her special souvenir."

Now it was Cassie's turn to choke. Delaney reached out and patted her back with reciprocal fervor. Cassie finished her cocktail and gestured to the waitress for a refill.

Delaney lifted her empty glass. "Another for me too." She looked at Logan. "How about you? Ready for another round?"

He shook his head. Cassie noted his glass of lager was still more than three-quarters full. Taking it easy tonight, hmm? That did not bode well for his motives—which were what, anyway? "Are you here on business?" she asked, wondering if that business included her. Cassie highly doubted he'd chased her from Edinburgh to London for a booty call, because chase her he had, she wasn't buying his convenient story of visiting a friend.

"Oh, that's right, you make videos," Delaney said, polishing off the other half of her roll. "Tell me, how does one get in to the business of running a sketch comedy show?"

Logan finished his own roll and reached for a second. "Like most things, I suppose. By accident."

"Ha! Tell that to the Queen of Lists." Delaney waved her butter knife at Cassie. "Nothing happens by chance with this girl. She plans *everything*."

"Really?" Logan considered Cassie from across the table. "What about meeting me? She couldn't have planned that."

"Actually," Delaney said, leaning across the table and whispering to Logan, "she kinda did."

Cassie flushed. She much preferred it when they'd been talking about Logan. He was looking at her again, devil brows quirked into a shape she hadn't seen on him before. He looked . . . perplexed. Before Delaney could elaborate on Cassie's grand scheme to score a one-night stand with a foreign stranger, Cassie grabbed the reins of the conversation. "Tell us more about this accident. How did *Shenanigans* get started?"

Another waitress came around and set plates of salad in front of each of them. "Honestly? I was bored. It was market day, the streets packed with shoppers and tourists and the like." Logan stabbed a tomato with his fork. "I decided to go for a stroll. Bare-arsed." He popped the tomato in his mouth

"You went streaking?" A burst of laughter escaped Delaney.

"Oh, this wasna streaking," Logan assured her. "There was no running involved. I took my time. I had shopping to do, you ken. Spent quite a while at a cart of fresh vegetables, asked a few people for their opinion on the cucumbers."

Delaney snorted into her beer. "Good Lord."

Even Cassie had to suppress a smile at the thought of a naked Logan rambling through downtown Edinburgh, perusing phallic produce. "And you filmed all of this?"

"I didna film it, but plenty of other people did, aye? Camera phones going off like popcorn."

"I believe it," Delaney snickered.

Cassie elbowed her, staring open-mouthed at Logan. "I'm surprised you weren't arrested."

"Oh, I was," he assured her. "My wee escapade bought me my first stint in an Edinburgh holding cell, as well as my first taste of fame."

"Fame?"

"Mm-hmm." Logan poked at the bits of lettuce left on his plate. "After springing me from jail, my sister, Janet— you remember Janet? Well, she and her mates took me out for a pint to celebrate my freedom. The nightly news was on the pub's telly, and a segment featuring a clip of my stunt made an appearance."

"That had to be interesting." Delaney pushed her salad plate aside, mostly untouched except for the candied nuts that had been sprinkled on top.

"One of Janet's mates slapped me on the back and said he could watch shenanigans like that all day." Logan shook his head, grinning at the memory.

"And thus, the show was born," Cassie surmised.

"Exactly," Logan confirmed. "But we're not all pranks, you ken."

"That's right," Delaney said as the salad plates were cleared. "You do karaoke in an elevator."

"'Live in a Lift,' aye. And some other bits. Interviews. Sketch comedy, that sort o' thing." Logan paused while the main course was served.

Cassie glanced down to the other end of the table. Ana was grilling the waitress about the salmon, wanting to know what spices had been used. Sadie was holding court with Theo, but Cassie was pleased to note Bonnie finally seemed to be taking part in the conversation as well.

Bonnie wasn't the type to hold a grudge. Cassie wasn't surprised her friend's annoyance about the *Little Mermaid* cracks faded quickly. Though to be honest, Bonnie had reacted to the teasing with more irritation than usual. What had set Bon off?

Catching Cassie's eye, Bonnie smiled. "We're telling Theo about our trip."

Cassie didn't miss the blush staining her best friend's cheeks when she mentioned Prince Eric's name. *Well, well, well.* Good for her. Cassie had always felt Bonnie's devotion to Gabe, her boyfriend-since-forever, bordered on unhealthy. How could you know what meal you liked best if you always ordered the same thing from the menu?

Unlike Bonnie, Cassie had lived on the sampler platter and had never had a serious boyfriend. She dabbled in dating, but her career, and its often hectic schedule, came first. With the changes she hoped to make to her role on *ChiChat* when she got home, Cassie wondered if perhaps it wasn't time she moved on from the appetizers and considered something else on the menu too. Something more substantial.

Cassie took a bite of the salmon. Cooked to perfection, the flaky fish all but melted on her tongue. She could understand why Ana, who owned a catering company on Chicago's North Shore, wanted the recipe. Maybe that was what Cassie needed to find—a hearty meal to sustain her, one with enough spice to keep things interesting. A relationship with a man she could look to build a life with, not a fling with a sexy Scot who had the potential to screw up her plans before she even got the chance to execute them.

Logan wasn't an appetizer—he was dessert—sweet and sinful and totally bad for her. She set her fork down and observed him making short work of the rest of his meal, her gaze tracing the path of his fork from plate to mouth. She remembered the feel of his hands, the taste of his mouth. Yes, Logan Reid was certainly delicious. But tempted as she was to have a second helping, Cassie knew he was an indulgence best not repeated.

CHAPTER 9

THEO HAD DONE an excellent job juggling three of Cassie's friends all through dinner. Over on Logan's side of the table, Delaney was more than willing to let him talk to Cassie uninterrupted while she polished off her own dessert as well as most of Cassie's, and even some of his—the lass must have a hollow leg in addition to her obvious sweet tooth.

Stretching, Delaney stood up. "I feel like an overstuffed Thanksgiving turkey. I could use some air. Anyone want to join me?"

Cassie scooted out of her chair. If she thought she could escape him, she was wrong. Logan got to his feet too, casting a glance at Theo, still deep in conversation with the blonde and the redhead. Good man. The dark-haired lass, Ana, had left soon after dessert was served. At the first bite she'd let out a groan of intense pleasure, pushed back from the table, and announced she absolutely must speak to the chef.

Logan followed Delaney and Cassie out of the dining room. Stepping up onto the observation deck, he offered an arm to each of them. "Shall we go for a stroll?"

"Thanks, babe." Delaney patted his hand. "But I'm more of a speed walker. You two enjoy." Delaney waved goodbye, winking at Cassie over her shoulder. In seconds, her long legs had carried her out of sight around the bow of the ship.

"I guess it's just the two of us, then." He held his arm out to Cassie again, who stood glaring after her friend with the dagger-stare he recognized from their first meeting. After a moment, she sighed and looped her arm through his, resting her hand on his biceps. Logan resisted the urge to flex. Tight as the suit was, he might bust a seam. Instead, he covered her hand with his own, warming it against the slight chill in the air. The August night was warm, but the breeze off the Thames had a bite to it—a promise that fall wasn't far away.

The thought reminded him of his conversation with Second Studios. With the sudden break in their fall lineup, the producers were antsy. They wanted to move on a new show soon, but were still hesitant to make a deal until Logan proved he could improve the ratings in his weakest demographic.

Logan swore he could feel that damn release form searing his skin. Before heading to the boat, he'd slipped the paper into the inside pocket of his jacket. If the opportunity presented itself, he wanted to be ready.

Now was a perfect time. They were alone. The other couples walking on the deck and admiring the glittering skyline paid them no mind. He should talk to Cassie, explain the bind he was in—make her understand why he needed her to sign the bloody release form. But try as he might, the words wouldn't come. He was enjoying his stroll with her too much.

They wound around the aft of the ship and made their way up the port side, the quiet darkness punctuated by the sound of her sexy heels striking the wooden deck, her stride matching his. He'd set a casual pace. Delaney had already lapped them once, the lass hadn't been kidding about the speed walking.

As they passed the entrance to the dining room a second time, Ana exploded up the steps, bursting with excitement. "I got it!" she crowed, grabbing Cassie's arm. "The toffee parfait, I had to find out what was in the filling. I knew the chef had used some kind of tea as a spice. I was right; it was Earl Grey. I thought the fruit might be fig, but do you know what it was?"

Both Cassie and Logan shook their heads.

"Prune!" Ana declared. "Who'd have thought?" She examined a scrap of paper in her hands, reviewing the recipe she'd hastily scrawled on it. "This is going to be a hit at the next octogenarian's birthday I cater."

Delaney joined them, catching the last part of the conversation. "Hold up." She grabbed the piece of paper from Ana. "Did you say prune?" She wrinkled her nose, her light dusting of freckles bunching together. "I ate prunes?"

"Aye. A *lot* of them," Logan murmured.

Delaney gave him the stink eye but then bust out laughing. "Well, they were delicious." She glanced at the paper again and then up at Ana. "Do you think my preschoolers would eat this? Their parents would adore me if I could sneak healthier crap into the snacks."

Ana took the recipe back, considering. "We'd have to modify it, remove the tea, maybe replace it with nutmeg, hmm . . . come to the galley with me. We can ask the chef what he thinks."

"And we can see if any of those tiny cakes are left," Delaney added.

"The petit fours?" Ana grabbed Delaney's arm. "Sure.

Unless you already ate them all," she said, pulling Delaney back toward the dining room.

Logan shook his head. "Where does the lass put all that food?"

"Delaney? We've all wondered the same thing. You should have seen her in college. Half a dozen donuts for breakfast every morning and still skinny as a rail. Drove Sadie batty." Cassie shrugged. "Genetics."

"Then you've all known each other since university?" Logan asked, taking Cassie's arm again for another turn around the deck. He was pleased she didn't protest, but instead snuggled against him.

"Bonnie and I have been friends forever. Since the first day of first grade when the teacher lined us up alphabetically. Bonnie Blythe and Cassie Crow." She smiled, her face alight with the memory. "B.B. and C.C.—Bonnie declared it was destiny."

"Really?"

"Oh, yeah. Even at six years old Bonnie used words like that. I swear she was reading Shakespeare in the cradle. In third grade she discovered *Anne of Green Gables,* and from then on she was Anne, I was her bosom friend Diana Barry, and Gabe was, of course, her Gilbert."

"Who's Gabe?" They'd reached the bow of the ship again, and this time Logan paused. He leaned on the rail and looked out at London Bridge stretched before them, its reflection on the water's surface blurred like an artist's canvas.

"Bonnie's fiancé." She joined him at the rail. "They got engaged last Christmas, but haven't set a date yet."

Logan recalled the look on Theo's face when he'd first met Bonnie and felt a pang of sympathy for his mate. "Someone have cold feet?"

"I'm not sure." Cassie glanced up at the night sky, as if seeking answers from the heavens. "She and Gabe truly are like Gilbert and Anne. He teased her mercilessly in grade school, but then they started dating in junior high and have been together ever since. She's never had another boyfriend."

"What about you?" Logan asked, shifting so his side brushed against hers. "How many boyfriends have you had?"

"Oh, we're not playing this game again." Her voice held a note of warning, but Logan caught how she didn't move away from him, didn't break the contact of their bodies.

Over the smells of city and river, he caught the scent of lavender and vanilla and recalled all those bottles of soaps and lotions he'd seen in her loo at the Caldy. "Fine." He dipped his head and whispered in her ear, "What game *would* you like to play?"

A yip of surprised laughter escaped her, and she turned, leaning her back against the rail to face him. "You are shameless."

"Completely," he agreed, moving to stand in front of her, bracing his hands on the rail on either side of her. "Remember, you're talking to the man who once shopped for produce in the buff."

"How could I forget?" She tilted her chin to meet his eyes. "Cucumbers? Really?"

"Aye, and it put me in quite the pickle."

Her mouth twitched at his lame pun. "I don't know . . . Things seemed to have worked out pretty well for you, popular website and all that."

"I suppose, but it's not what I really want."

"Oh?" She cocked her head. "What do you want?"

Christ, how to answer that question. The paper in his jacket pocket was a hot stone, a weight burning a hole in his chest. *Now.* He should tell her about the telly deal now. He ran his hands up her back, the green silk of her dress sliding across his fingers and palms in an erotic caress.

Yes, he wanted her to sign that bloody waiver. He wanted to move past *Shenanigans* and do something more with his joke of a life. Logan traced the line of silk up over her shoulders and down past her collarbone, his fingers following the dress's neckline until they joined above her heart. She sucked in a breath at his touch, her breasts rising, a mere whisper away from filling his hands. He ached to cup her. To feel her.

Holding his gaze with her own, she stepped closer, brushing all that lush round softness against him. When her lips touched his, he couldn't help but smile at how good it felt—how right. He wrapped his arms around her, ignoring the crackle of paper as he tightened his hold. His future was in his pocket, but his future could wait a little longer.

He wanted her to sign the waiver. But in this moment, he wanted her more.

Cassie cuddled closer to Logan, the warmth of his body eased the chill blowing in off the water, while the scent of clove and mint she'd already come to know as *him* melted her resolve. Walking along the deck, tucked against his side, sharing stories . . . the romance of the evening had chipped away at her willpower. Temptation shadowed her footsteps, and nipping at her heels was temptation's insidious twin—rationalization. They'd already slept together, what could spending time with him now hurt? It was just a little walk, a little talk. Some flirting, some touching . . . some kissing.

Same as that impetuous moment in the castle when she'd chucked caution to the wind, pulled him to her, and kissed him, Cassie once again surrendered to impulse. His hands, which had been featherlight as they'd trailed over her shoulders and across the tops of her breasts, were almost rough as he gripped her waist and urged her closer. His fingers were warm and firm when they slipped around her and traced the line of her back down, down, until his palms rested in the dip at the base of her spine. He kneaded her with his knuckles, loosening the knot of tension trapped there.

Cassie arched her back, wanting more. He bent his head and responded to her demand with an increase of pressure, mouth hot and wicked on her neck as he moved his hands in tight circles that sent waves of pleasure rippling through her body. She threaded her fingers through his thick hair, groaning. Her hips had begun to move, swiveling, matching the pace of his fingers against her back, the stroke of his tongue on her throat.

She had wondered if their night together in Scotland had been a fluke. A magical combination of time and place that could never be replicated. But now, with his hands on her, she knew the magic was still there. She needed his hands on other parts of her, wanted him to work those strong, talented fingers lower. Deeper. She pressed kisses along his rough jaw, licking and sucking the smooth skin above his collar, relishing the contrast, inhaling his scent. Then she returned her mouth to his, nipping his bottom lip and tugging it between her teeth.

He growled when she bit him and cupped her ass, pressing into her. *Yes*, that was what she wanted. Her hips circled faster and she ground against him.

"Whoa, check that out!"

The shout was a direct hit, smacking the bull's-eye and plunging Cassie into the dunk tank of reality. She pulled back and stared up at Logan, trying to collect the scattered thoughts of her rum-and-kiss-addled brain. Logan was no help. His ginger locks were wilder than ever, green-gold eyes hooded—hazed with lust. The man was a walking advertisement for Dude-About-To-Get-Some. Cassie glanced over his shoulder. Delaney was headed their way, Ana in tow. She sighed, reaching up to swipe her thumb across Logan's lower lip.

He leaned toward her as he wiped his own thumb across his mouth. "What was that for?"

"Lipstick," she whispered into his ear, noting a small patch of purple on his throat. *Oops.* Nothing to be done about that. Cassie hoped her own neck didn't sport similar bruises. Good God, she was worried about hickies like some freaking out-of-control horny teenager. Which made sense—she kind of felt like one too.

As if reading her thoughts, Logan smirked. She stuck her tongue out at him before turning to smile at her friends when they joined them at the rail.

"This is amazing!" Delaney breathed. And for the first time tonight, she wasn't talking about food.

Their view beyond the bow of the ship *was* amazing. Somehow Cassie had completely missed how close the boat had come to the Eye—London's Ferris wheel on steroids. *Hmm, fancy that. What on earth could have been distracting me?*

Ana nodded, her attention also focused on the pods of people orbiting the immense structure. "Sort of reminds me of home." She was right, the scene spread out in front of them did bring to mind Navy Pier, but rather than the host of skyscrapers that stood sentinel beyond Chicago's Ferris wheel, here the enormous circle of rotating light shared the skyline with Westminster Bridge and Big Ben. Ana turned toward the iconic clock tower and gasped. "It's really there!"

"What is?" Cassie asked.

Ana leaned over the rail and pointed a finger. "The second star, of course."

"Huh?" Delaney, a smidge near-sighted, squinted in the direction Ana indicated.

"'Second star to the right, and straight on 'til morning.'" Logan squeezed in next to Cassie at the bow, his big, warm body pressing close. "Neverland is our destination tonight, is it?"

Ana clapped her hands in delight. "Very good, Peter Pan."

Cassie glanced up at Logan, whose gaze was still trained on the enormous glowing face of Big Ben. Her lips twitched as she watched him, the night wind ruffling his hair. Logan was like Peter Pan, the eternal mischievous boy, with a ready smile and unquenchable thirst for adventure. Being with him was a bit like being in Neverland.

Suddenly a burst of light shot across the sky, an arc of shimmering stardust that danced along the horizon before winking out of sight.

"Did you freaking see that?" Delaney whispered.

"Come on, let's make a wish!" Ana pulled Delaney to the other side of the bow, chasing the path of the shooting star.

Alone again with Logan, a reverent hush settled over Cassie as she absorbed the magic of the moment. *Make a wish . . .* Her night with Logan back in Scotland had been magic, a dream, her wish come true. Cassie knew soon enough she'd be heading back home and her fantasy would end. But that was still a few days away. Meanwhile, she was here, and Logan was right here next to her.

She shifted, putting more of her body in contact with his. He responded instantly, adjusting his stance, the angles of his body rearranging to accommodate her curves. The fact they fit together perfectly was another bit of magic that did not escape her notice. Above them, the sky twinkled, a velvet blanket embroidered with diamonds. Cassie leaned back and rested her head against Logan's chest. A sense of peace mingled with anticipation settled over her.

This was her fairy tale. She could go back to working on being taken seriously—to being a grown-up—when her vacation was over. For now, she was going to enjoy her stay in Neverland.

The boat rocked gently against the dock as the dinner guests departed, the murmur of quiet conversation coupled with the shuffle and click of shoes on the gangplank. Bonnie, Sadie, and Prince Eric (she really needed to stop calling him that) had joined them on the observation deck a few minutes ago.

The view was spectacular, the summer breeze sweet, and Cassie was in no hurry to catch up with the throng exiting the ship. Neither was anybody else in her party. They'd seemed to come to a silent agreement, loitering along the railing at the bow while the other passengers finished disembarking. Soon enough, though, the footsteps slowed, the conversations drifted off, and Cassie knew it was time they leave the ship as well.

"Shall we?" Logan offered her his arm.

She accepted, and again they fell into the same easy rhythm they'd found on their stroll around the deck. The muscles of his arm were thick and firm beneath her hand, his body warm against hers. Behind them, she heard Prince Er—Theo—volunteer as escort to Bonnie.

A moment later Delaney said, "If you don't want him, I'll take him."

At the top of the stairs leading to the gangplank, Cassie glanced over her shoulder. Bonnie was standing, arms crossed, mouth pinched, while Delaney stepped around her and grabbed hold of Theo. Sadie and Ana brought up the rear, looping their arms behind Bonnie, carrying her forward with them.

When Delaney and Theo reached the stairs, Cassie leaned forward. "What's going on with Bonnie?"

Delaney shrugged. "Don't know. Must be something this one did." She poked her escort in the chest.

"Ow! I object." Theo rubbed the spot and turned to Cassie. "I've been perfectly polite all evening. I haven't the faintest idea what your friend's problem is."

Cassie had a few guesses. Tall, dark-haired, with cobalt-blue eyes and a pleasant smile that didn't quite hide the brooding undertones hinting at something *more* swirling beneath his civilized surface—and of course, there was that cultured aristocratic accent—Theo was an Austen hero incarnate. Throughout their entire vacation, while the rest of her friends had ogled and flirted and fantasized, Bonnie had remained immune to the charms of the men in each country they'd traveled through . . . until now. Cassie had known Bonnie most of her life, and she knew without a doubt what her friend's problem was—Prince Eric was her kryptonite.

Once off the boat Bonnie shook out her curls, a sure tell she was nervous, and tapped her phone awake. "We better hurry," she said.

"For what?" Cassie asked. Bonnie had made all the arrangements for the evening, and Cassie had no idea what else her friend had planned for them.

"For that." Bonnie pointed toward the Eye.

Ana hooted in excitement. "Excellent!"

Next to her, Sadie frowned. "Are you sure it's safe?"

Ana looked at her best friend. "You're kidding, right?"

Theo grinned, a smile that would put a long-tailed cat in a room full of rocking chairs at ease. "It looks intimidating, I know, but I assure you, it's perfectly safe."

Sadie relented, melting beneath his charm like butter on a stove. She sidled up next to him, clearly ready to launch round two of her "Bag Theo" campaign. "Will you ride with me?"

"We'll all ride together." Bonnie swept past them, her words tight and clipped, matching the sharp staccato click of her shoes as she headed for the Eye. "Each of those capsules are built to fit twenty-five people."

Once they were nestled inside one of the egg-shaped pods, Cassie clutched Logan's hand, a little nervous herself. Logically, she knew hundreds upon hundreds—probably thousands upon thousands—of people rode this thing every day, but it was hard to think logically when your tummy was doing somersaults while a steel bubble hefted you skyward.

Rather than tease her, Logan squeezed her hand back. The small gesture put Cassie instantly at ease. She relaxed and gazed through the window, absorbing the view of London spread out below her.

"It really is like Neverland," Ana said, her voice full of childlike wonder. "My favorite ride at Disney World is Peter Pan's Flight. The part where you fly over a miniature version of London at night. There's a tiny Big Ben and the Westminster Bridge and little twinkling lights all along the Thames." She released a sigh of pure joy. "God, I love it."

Next to her, Sadie rolled her eyes, specks of violet flashing with annoyance. "Yes, I know. You made me ride that thing with you at least a dozen times." Sadie turned to Theo. "We took a trip down there together for spring break our senior year of high school. Here I was thinking we were headed to Florida for some fun in the sun, and the closest I seemed to get to a beach was Mermaid Lagoon."

"Don't let her fool you. She had a great time," Ana assured him. "I have plenty of pictures of Sadie posing with princesses to prove it."

"Do you always travel on holiday together?" Theo asked.

"The two of us have gone on a bunch of trips," Ana said, gesturing between herself and Sadie, "but this is the first time all five of us have traveled as a group."

"Yep." Sadie nodded. "We made a pact. Five years after graduation the five of us would visit five European countries, taking the vacation of our dreams."

Cassie smiled, recalling the day they'd first hatched the plan for this trip. It had been freshman year, the bargain struck late one night during a brain-draining study cram session.

At first it was just for fun, a game she and her friends would play to help get them through the college grind. Bonnie's mom was a travel agent, and Bon would constantly bring glossy vacation brochures back to their dorm. Over bowls of crappy cafeteria pasta, they would debate whether France or Italy would have the best food. As they slogged through another harsh Midwestern winter, they warmed each other by emailing pictures of sunny verandas in Spain. If one of them was suffering from a post-breakup heartache, they would take her out for drinks and console her with detailed descriptions of hot European guys with sexy accents.

Eventually all those hours of debating and planning had bred a determination to make the dream come true. Come hell or high water, they had promised that no matter what they were doing or where they were living, five years after graduation they would take their trip. And damn if they hadn't succeeded.

"How did the five of you decide where to go?" Theo asked, bringing her back to the conversation.

"We each selected the country we wanted to visit most." Cassie glanced at the bracelet on her wrist. Each charm marked a moment on this journey. She'd collected so many charms, and yet even now, here in London, on their last stop before the trip came to a close, it still seemed incredible.

Logan quirked an eyebrow at her. "No doubt Scotland was *your* choice."

"It was mine," Bonnie piped up from the other side of the pod where she stood next to Delaney.

"Bonnie is our resident Anglophile," Sadie explained. "She insisted Ireland, Scotland, and England all counted as one."

"It does," Bonnie sniffed. "I said I wanted to visit the United Kingdom."

Theo chuckled, a low throaty laugh, masculine and pleasant. Cassie didn't miss the way Bonnie flushed at the sound. "Did you hear that, Lo? It's official, Scotland counts as part of England."

"I dinna think so." Logan scowled.

"Promise me you won't wax patriotic," Theo begged. "I'm trapped in here with you, and if you decide to launch into a diatribe on the oppression of the British monarchy, I might launch myself into the Thames."

Logan shoved his friend in the shoulder. "Don't tempt me." He turned back to Cassie and lifted her hand, studying the charms on her bracelet. "What country *did* you choose?"

"France." Cassie shrugged. "I thought it would be romantic."

He touched the miniature Eiffel Tower dangling from her wrist before glancing up to look into her eyes. "And was it?"

Cassie had the sense he was asking more than whether or not she'd liked Paris. "Oui." She blinked, pretending she had missed his meaning. "Trés romantic."

A slight frown tugged at the corner of his mouth. "Oh."

Cassie took pity on him. She leaned over and whispered in his ear, "But not nearly as romantic as finding a kilted Scotsman hidden inside the wall of a castle."

His face split in a grin, and Cassie swore she could see his chest swell with male swagger. Still holding her hand, he shifted his grip and stroked her wrist, the rough pad of his thumb rubbing back and forth across the delicate skin there. Cassie shivered as a thrilling tingle shot up her arm and across her breasts.

"Could you guys knock it off? The sexual tension in here is suffocating me." Delaney shook her head. "Sheesh, you two are almost as bad as Ana and her Italian stallion . . . what was his name?"

"Lorenzo," Bonnie supplied, "like from *The Merchant of Venice.*"

"Oh, please don't mention his name," Ana groaned.

"Has he called you again?" Sadie asked.

Ana shook her head. "No idea. I blocked his number after the Spanish incident."

"What's the Spanish incident?" Theo asked.

Sadie filled him in. "Ana has a stalker."

At Theo's quizzical expression, Ana elaborated. "This guy I had a fling with in Italy wouldn't stop calling. Said he was in love with me, that he had to see me again. The lunatic tracked us down in Spain and showed up at the hotel we were staying at in Barcelona, can you believe that?"

"No," Theo said, with an odd quirk to his voice. He turned and eyed Logan. "I can't. Who would do such a dodgy thing?"

Logan cleared his throat. "Who chose Italy?" He flicked the tiny replica of the Leaning Tower of Pisa, sending it swinging back and forth on Cassie's wrist.

"That would be me. People always think Paris is where the fashion is, but in my opinion the best shopping happens in Milan." Sadie kicked out a leg, displaying her gorgeous, outrageously expensive footwear. The men dutifully admired her shoes.

"And I chose Spain," Ana said. "I've always wanted to learn how to make paella. And the wine there is to die for. Nothing beats a crisp, Spanish white." Ana clasped her bosom. The men dutifully avoided admiring her cleavage.

"Let's see . . ." Theo lifted a hand, "Italy, Spain, France, the UK . . ." He ticked off his fingers, pausing at the last. "What was number five?"

Delaney took Theo's pinky and wiggled it. "The Netherlands."

"Let me guess." Logan grinned. "You went for the danish."

"No." Delaney raised a haughty chin. "I wanted to visit the Van Gogh museum in Amsterdam."

"But she did devour an Alps-sized portion of stroopwafels," Sadie added.

"They were *so* good." Delaney wrapped her arms around her middle, clutching her stomach. "Oh, man, I want some right now."

"Good thing you packed half a suitcase with boxes of them." Bonnie patted Delaney on the arm.

"I can't eat those," Delaney moaned in misery.

"Why not?" Bonnie wrinkled her nose.

Cassie laughed. "Because they're not for her. She bought them for her students."

"Those pip-squeaks better be grateful," Delaney growled.

"She's joking," Cassie assured him. "Delaney loves her kids. She's an awesome teacher."

"I'm sure she is." Logan released the bracelet and began to stroke Cassie's wrist while Ana helped Delaney do the math on how many boxes she had packed, how many cookies were in each box, and how many she could get away with eating before she risked seriously cutting in to her supply of student souvenirs.

"What about you? What do you do for a living?" Logan asked, as his fingers traveled up the inside of Cassie's arm, tracing a nerve-tingling path to the cleft at her elbow. The movement was ticklish and sensuous at the same time. Kind of like him—silly but sexy.

Before she could answer, a pleasant voice replaced the piped-in notes of the London Symphony Orchestra and crisply announced their capsule was approaching the disembarking zone. The voice continued, explaining the exit process in various languages.

"Hold up. This thing doesn't stop to let us off?" Sadie stood and gripped the handrail lining the capsule as she stared at the other pods rotating below theirs.

"Weren't you paying attention when we got on?" Delaney shook her head. "You're worse than one of my kids. We walked on while it was moving, right? Which means we'll walk off *while it's still moving*."

Ana joined Sadie by the rail. "There's nothing to be scared of. This thing moves slower than your nana on her electric scooter."

"I can ask the operator to pause the ride." Logan gestured toward a call box built into a panel of the capsule.

"I ken they do that for elderly folks and those with disabilities."

Sadie shook her head. "Thanks, but I think I'll be okay."

He nodded, but as their pod swung into position, Logan moved to Sadie's side and wrapped his arm around her. Theo took up a similar position on her other side. When it was time, the two men lifted Sadie and carried her petite frame between them, exiting the capsule together.

Cassie was touched by the thoughtful gesture. Sadie was too, and more than eager to show her gratitude. She hugged both of them. Cassie noticed Sadie embraced Theo with significantly more enthusiasm.

Bonnie noticed too. "What a drama queen."

"That's not very charitable of you," Cassie admonished. "You're not usually so petty, Bon. You've been cranky most of the night. What's up?"

"Nothing. I don't know. I miss Gabe, I guess."

Cassie eyed her best friend and debated pointing out what was painfully obvious. She decided to take the passive-aggressive approach. "Theo certainly is good-looking."

Bonnie frowned and looked over to where he stood on the curb, helping Logan hail a cab. "I suppose." She shivered. "I hadn't noticed."

"Liar," Cassie teased, shivering too. The night air had turned from crisp to frosty and gooseflesh pebbled Cassie's skin. She lifted her hands to rub some warmth back into her arms and was surprised when a man's coat, heavy and warm, settled around her shoulders.

"Thank you," she told Logan, pulling the lapels of his dress jacket closer, inhaling mint and clove. She wanted to snuggle into the silk lining of his coat, cocoon herself in his heat and scent.

"My pleasure." Logan placed a soft kiss on her cheek, his lips a welcome heat on her chilled skin. "I've got us a cab to see you back to your hotel, aye?"

"Aye," she echoed, and this time she wasn't mocking him.

When she'd stepped aboard the boat this evening, Cassie had been completely unprepared for the sight of Logan—Bonnie's ability to keep a secret was definitely improving. Despite her initial hesitation when she'd realized what her best friend had done, Cassie was glad she'd allowed herself to open up to him. She'd had a lovely time. The evening had been wonderful.

Cassie thought what she'd wanted was a one-night stand, had believed the experience of a hot night of foreign action would fill that place in her that, *for years*, had sat waiting, wanting more . . . needing more. But tonight, this perfect shining jewel of a night with Logan, *this* was what she'd been waiting for. This was the souvenir she'd craved, and the memory she would keep with her always.

CHAPTER 10

LOGAN RODE UP to the executive floor with Cassie and her friends. He watched her, wondering if she too was remembering what they'd done the last time they were in a lift together. Only this time they were not alone. When they'd arrived at the hotel, Theo had bid the ladies good night and headed for the bar while Logan offered to see them to their rooms.

When the bell to their floor dinged and the doors opened, Logan pondered his next move. Should he invite Cassie to his room? After that story about the Italian prick who tracked the lasses to another country, he was reluctant to admit he'd booked a room on the same floor of their hotel.

Her friends waved and murmured good night as they split up and slipped into their rooms. Looked like Cassie was sharing with the little redhead again—so much for option B.

"So . . ." Cassie paused outside the hotel room door Bonnie had just entered.

Logan wondered if the lass was feeling the same awkward combination of eagerness and uncertainty as he was. Only two nights ago, they'd slept together. Christ, had it only been two days? And here they were, standing outside her door again. He'd like nothing better than to pick up where they'd left off the last time they were in a hotel room together—*exactly* where they'd left off, if possible.

"So . . . ," he echoed. *Way to charm her with your excellent conversational skills, numpty.*

She fiddled with her purse string, her gaze focused on the ground. Logan wanted to slip a finger under her chin and lift her face, so he could see those pretty, dark eyes. He wanted to look into their depths and know what she was thinking—what she was feeling. She had very expressive eyes. He'd seen the sable brown of her irises turn almost black as they snapped with anger, or glow amber with fiery passion when she'd shoved him against the wall of the lift and kissed him. He loved watching her eyes, loved watching how they shifted and changed and told him what he needed to know.

From inside the room he heard the telly click on. Her roommate was obviously settling in for the night. Again, Logan considered inviting Cassie to his room, only a few doors away. Before he could muster up the courage, she stopped fiddling with her purse and looked up at him.

Her eyes were dark and warm, but a color he'd not seen yet, a shade of brown that made him think of sweet sticky things like honey and toffee.

"It was nice seeing you again."

He nodded, unable to respond, his mind too focused on trying to come up with the right way to accurately describe the swirls of amber around her pupils.

"Will you be staying with your friend long?" she asked.

"What?" *Topaz . . . was topaz what he was thinking of?*

"Your friend, Prince, er, I mean, Theo."

"He's not a prince, he's a duke." *Shit, how had he let that slip out?* It wasn't like his mate's rank was a secret, but Logan knew when Theo met someone who didn't know he was a member of the peerage, he preferred not to enlighten them. People sometimes got weird when they found out they were in the presence of honest to bleedin' God nobility.

"Oh. Well, good for him." Luckily, the lass didn't seem to give a fig about Theo. Maybe it was because she was tipsy, or maybe it was because she had her mind on other things. She leaned back against the door of her room and continued to stare up at him. "Are you guys staying at his castle or something like that?"

He grinned. "Something like that."

"Is it far?" She reached out and straightened his shirt collar, her fingers brushing the skin of his neck

"Not too far," he replied, swallowing hard. *It wasn't a lie.*

"Maybe the two of you could join us for breakfast in the morning—share some pointers on what sights we should go see." She trailed her knuckles up the column of his throat, her eyes following the movement. If she thought he hadn't noticed the wee nookie badge she'd given him on the side of his neck, she was wrong. "You owe me a breakfast, after all."

"I do?" Logan took her hand in his and pressed her palm to his lips.

"Mm-hmm. You skipped out on breakfast in Edinburgh."

He kissed the tip of each finger. "I recall *you* skipped out on something else in Edinburgh."

"Not fair. We were interrupted, remember?" Her pupils dilated, amber swirls filling with shadows, as she watched him nip gently at the pad of her thumb. She gasped when he sank his teeth into her skin. Her response made his cock, still primed from their snogging session on the boat earlier this evening, throb with need.

Abruptly, the door behind her swung open, and Cassie stumbled backward. She would have landed on her lush little arse if her friend hadn't been there to break the fall.

"Oh!" Bonnie dropped the ice bucket she'd been holding and locked her arms behind Cassie's elbows, helping steady her. "You're still here."

Balance and composure back in place, Cassie tucked a chestnut wave behind her ear and smiled at Bonnie. "Uh, yes. Logan and I were just discussing plans for the rest of our stay. I asked him if there were any must-see sites we should visit."

Bonnie bent and retrieved the ice bucket. She was wrapped in a fuzzy bathrobe with tiny teacups printed all over it, toes tucked into equally fuzzy slippers with what looked like miniature teapots sewn on top of each. "Yes, there are." The redhead scooted between them. "Hampton Court and Windsor Palace. We're touring both tomorrow." She headed down the hall, stuffed teapots bobbing authoritatively on her toes.

"Well." Cassie waited until the sound of her friend's slippers shuffling on the carpet had faded. "What she said."

"I haven't been to Hampton Court in years." Logan recalled a school trip, he and his mates in their ties and sweater vests, running like hooligans through the garden maze, their professor threatening to leave them behind. "There's a hedge maze; it's a lovely place."

"Would you like to join us? I mean, I've already invited you to breakfast, you might as well make a day of it." A smile lifted the curve of one cheek, and Logan tried not to think about a similar smile she'd given him, standing outside another hotel room door, as she'd asked if he wanted to come in.

When he hesitated, the smile faded, and she hurried to add, "Your friend is welcome too. Unless, of course, you have other plans already."

"Nothing important." He processed logistics. The girls had probably planned to hop a tour bus, but that was hardly an ideal setting for a cozy conversation, and Theo's bucket of bolts wouldn't hold them all. Logan decided to book a rental, something big enough for all seven of them to ride in. Or maybe two cars. Then Theo could drive some of the girls, and Logan could have some alone time, or almost-alone time, with Cassie.

"Is it a date?"

Logan realized he hadn't answered her. He grinned, liking very much the idea of spending more time in her company. He couldn't have her tonight, but he would have her all day tomorrow. "It's a date," he agreed, bending down to kiss her. He'd meant it to be a chaste kiss, a good-night kiss, short and sweet. But the moment his mouth touched hers, lightning surged in his veins and he wanted more. He tracked the lush curve of her lower lip with his tongue before plunging deeper, devouring the hoarse moan rising in her throat.

Over that delicious sound came the curt noise of someone pointedly clearing her throat. Before he could break the kiss, Bonnie tapped him on the shoulder. "Can I get by please or do I need to dump this bucket of ice on your head?"

Down his pants would probably be more helpful at the moment, but Logan decided not to share that with her lest she take him up on the suggestion. "Sorry. I was just leaving."

Cassie moved aside to let Bonnie through the door. "Logan is going to join us tomorrow."

"Oh, happy day." Bonnie shuffled past them. Her normally perky voice had taken on a very droll tone. Logan wondered what her problem was. The lass had seemed keen enough to help him get together with Cassie before. He'd never have been able to arrange the meeting on the dinner cruise this evening without Bonnie—it had been her idea, in fact. What had changed?

"Don't mind Bonnie." Cassie slipped his jacket off her shoulders and crossed the threshold of her room. She turned to face him around the edge of the door and passed his jacket back to him. "Meet you in the dining room tomorrow morning. Around eight?"

He folded his jacket over his arm and nodded, already counting the hours between now and then.

"Good night." She blew him a kiss and shut the door.

CHAPTER 11

AFTER LEAVING HAMPTON Court, Ana suggested they head for a trendy Indian place she'd been eyeing right in Covent Garden not far from the Waldorf. Ana had a knack for finding amazing restaurants, and this place was no exception. Everyone stuffed themselves on naan, soft and fluffy as a cloud, and samosas so irresistible, even Sadie indulged. Cassie and Logan sampled each other's curry, cooling their tongues with tall glasses of lassi mixed with rum, a house specialty.

On the walk back to the hotel after dinner, Cassie strolled between Logan and Bonnie, ensconced in the mellow, happy glow that only comes after a good meal shared with good company. "What a perfect day." She took in a deep breath of the warm summer night. "I think that was my favorite palace yet."

"It's not that grand," Logan grumbled. "Nothing as fine as some Scottish castles I could show you."

"Aw." Ana stepped closer and squeezed Logan's shoulder. "Are you feeling a bit of palace envy?"

Logan gave Ana the side-eye, throat working in a Gaelic sound of amused disgust.

Sadie snorted with laughter and gave Ana a fist bump.

Cassie laughed too, enjoying the banter. It was fun to see Logan joking around with her friends, engaging in playful teasing. *Careful*. This was starting to sound like more than just a one-night stand. Well, it *was* more—wasn't it?

To be perfectly honest, Cassie would like nothing better than to spend what was left of her trip in Logan's company. Her voice of reason had been on vacation ever since meeting the sexy Scot. Why pay attention to it now? She gave Logan's hand a playful squeeze. "Bonnie told me she's planning to stay in Delaney's room tonight."

Hint taken, Logan glanced past Cassie to beam at Bonnie. "You have the best roommate ever."

"It's true, she does." Bonnie winked at them and moved ahead to join Delaney, who was grilling Theo with questions about whether the nursery rhyme about blackbirds in a pie was based on something King Henry really ate.

"Does that mean you'd like to come up?" Cassie asked, not sure why she felt nervous. Maybe because he'd been acting different today. More likely because she always seemed to be the one making the first move.

"Aye, lass. Lead the way."

"That's what I've been doing," she muttered under her breath. Three times now she'd been the one to get things started—not that she was counting—okay, fine, she was, but she wasn't trying to. So far she'd been the antithesis of hard-to-get and decided this time he needed to work for it a little. Tonight, she wanted Logan to initiate things. Though technically, she'd already done that by inviting him up to her room.

When the elevator dinged, Cassie slipped out ahead of

Logan and fumbled for her keycard. She swiped her key and opened the door, leaving it up to him to follow her inside. Cassie dropped her purse on the small occasion table in the suite's living room and clicked on a lamp. Pulling out the clip holding her french twist in place, she shook out her hair, rubbing the spot where the accessory had pressed against the back of her head.

When she turned around, she caught Logan watching her. Holding his gaze, Cassie ran her fingers slowly through her hair, letting the long, brown waves fan out over her shoulders. She wrapped a fat lock around her finger and considered him. He still hadn't moved, but stood frozen, his back pressed against the closed door of her hotel room, eyes hooded and hot.

She glanced at the impossible-to-miss bulge in his pants. Unless that was a stray cucumber for some new prank, he wanted her. What was he waiting for? He wanted to stand there and watch her? *Fine*, she'd give him something to watch. This was her vacation—her fantasy fling—and if she had to take the lead, *again*, she would.

Cassie let her hand drift lower, to where the ends of her hair curled slightly, grazing the top of one breast. From there she traced the lace trim of her dress, her fingers following the curve of the sweetheart neckline. When she reached the dip between her breasts, she paused.

Logan leaned forward, his anticipation tangible. Cassie bit down on a triumphant grin and let one finger slip beneath the fabric, then two. He swallowed hard and continued to watch.

The glow from the lamp cast her body in highlight and shadow, and she wondered if he could see the pebbling of her nipples. She glanced down at her chest. *Yep, the headlights are definitely on.* But just to be sure he didn't miss the show, Cassie raised her hands to her shoulders and tugged gently. The straps of her dress slipped down her arms, baring her to the waist. She stared down at herself, at the dark pink circles of her areolas and the jutting tips of her nipples, which had tightened further in the air-conditioned hotel room.

She flattened her palms and pressed them against her breasts. When she began to move her hands in slow circles, the gentle brush of her own skin against her was both wicked and delicious. Cassie closed her eyes and let her head drop back, giving herself over to the pleasure as she continued to lightly stroke her breasts.

A hoarse sound broke the silence of the room, and Cassie lifted her chin, not sure who had been the one to moan. Meeting Logan's gaze, she straightened her spine and thrust her body forward. Taunting him. Daring him. His eyes dropped to her chest once again, and she cupped her breasts, the weight of his stare making them feel heavy in her hands, hot and full and aching.

Watching him watching her was turning her on. Wanting to reveal more of herself to him, Cassie slid the dress down. The fabric clung to her hips, and she shimmied until it fell in a heap at her feet, pooling around her strappy sandals. At any other time, she'd have thought she looked ridiculous standing there in her undies and shoes, but right now, with his gaze intent on her, she felt sexy as hell.

She stepped forward, kicking free of her clothes, and pressed her fingers to the hollow at the base of her throat. Her pulse a throbbing rhythm against her fingertips, Cassie stood perfectly still, waiting until she had his attention right where she wanted it. Once she was sure Logan was watching her hand, she trailed her fingers slowly down the valley between her breasts, over the softly rounded curve of her stomach, pausing when she reached the satin edge of her panties.

Logan licked his lips. His chest rose and fell rapidly. Cassie thought she saw a muscle clench in his jaw. She closed the distance between them, stopping when her bare breasts were a breath away from his chest. The crisp linen of his dress shirt grazed her nipples every time he sucked in air. The fleeting, teasing contact made her ache for more.

She looked up at him and allowed herself to be naked, truly naked—letting him see all her desire, all the passion and hunger she felt for him. Their first night together had fulfilled her long-standing fantasy of a foreign fling. Tonight, she was going to make a few more of her fantasies come true.

They hadn't said a word to each other since they'd gotten in the elevator. Hadn't spoken since entering her hotel room. Now, Cassie discovered she had something she very much wanted to say to Logan. She pressed the tip of one finger against the top button on his shirt. There was one benefit of making the first move. Since she started the game, she got to make the rules. "Your turn."

Logan didn't want to presume anything, but he thought he knew what the lass intended by inviting him upstairs—after all, it wasn't like this was unchartered territory between them.

However, once the lift doors slid shut, an awkward silence descended, and he hesitated. Throughout the day, he hadn't been able to stop thinking about his hotel room or the unsigned waiver waiting in his jacket. They'd been a constant pressure, an albatross around his neck, choking him with guilt.

He'd planned to tell Cassie about his room at the hotel, he really had. But after their conversation last night, he'd been paralyzed by the possibility she'd think his following her to London was Lorenzo-level creepy. And she'd be right. He *had* followed her. But not because he was obsessed with her, though that may no longer be strictly accurate. He couldn't stop thinking about her.

So now he was nervous *and* guilty—to the point he couldn't bring himself to make a pass at her. No matter how badly he wanted her, and Christ did he ever, he'd rather suffer the biggest case of blue balls on God's green earth before he'd take something from her that she wasn't willing to give.

Except her signature on that damn waiver.

He needed to tell her about the waiver, about his room at the hotel, a few doors down from her own. It was best he come completely clean, and hope she understood. *Get it over with, mate. Now.*

"Your turn," she'd said. Did that mean she was going to undress him or did she want him to undress for her? He decided things would go better if she kept her hands off him for the time being. There was no telling what would happen if she touched him in the state he was in right now. Logan lifted her finger from where it pressed against the top button of his shirt. He bent his head and brushed a kiss over her knuckles. "As you wish."

He released her hand and peeled off his jacket, tossing it on the couch. Finally managing to tap his inner reserves of control, he took his time with the buttons on his shirt. As each one came undone, he took another step forward, forcing Cassie to retreat deeper into the room.

Christ, she was a picture, tits high, completely nude save for a scrap of red satin . . . and those shoes. Logan had never been one to notice footwear, but suddenly he was very aware of how the shiny strappy heels looked paired with the rest of her clothes, or rather, the lack thereof. He'd thought the time he took unbuttoning his shirt gained him some control over himself, but looking at her was making the whole endeavor harder—in every way imaginable.

Once he finished unbuttoning his shirt, Logan spread the fabric wide. Cassie's gaze roamed over his naked chest and abs. A surge of pleasure washed over him in the wake of her appreciative stare. Shirt off, his jeans were another matter. Logan undid his belt buckle, sliding the leather strip through the loops in one swift motion. He thumbed the button on his jeans, the tip of his cock just below, aching to be released.

Cassie watched him intently. He paused, fingers hovering over his fly. *What's good for the goose is good for the gander, aye?* Instead of undoing the rest of the buttons, Logan palmed himself and began to stroke his cock through his jeans. He was so fucking sensitive that the contact, even from his own hand, was enough to make his hips thrust forward of their own volition.

Cassie gasped, and he grinned. Feeling more like his cocky old self, pun totally intended, he undid the next two buttons on his fly and stroked himself again. She stared at his hand, tracking his movements with feverish intensity.

Logan reached out and grabbed her wrist. She looked up at him, cheeks flushed, eyes dark and hungry. He shifted her hand so her palm pressed against the hot, hard flesh of his erection, straining beneath the remaining buttons. He raised an eyebrow and tossed her challenge back at her. "Your turn."

For a moment Logan wasn't sure she would accept his dare, but then she laughed, a bold rich sound that made his balls ache and his heart skitter in his chest. Her fingers traced the shape of him, her touch tentative at first, gentler than his own. Logan groaned, and she stopped immediately.

"Don't stop," he rasped. "Please."

"Am I hurting you?"

"Only when you stop." He bucked his hips, pushing himself into her hand.

She tightened her hold on him and increased the pressure, slow at first, her strokes growing bolder with each grunt of pleasure her touch ripped from him. The muscles in Logan's legs started to tremble.

"Wait," he breathed, looking around the room. They were in the parlor of the suite, and he didn't think he could make it all the way to the bedroom. He guided her to the couch, hands at her waist. Then he dropped to his knees in front of her, slid two fingers beneath her knickers and tugged. The slippery fabric slid down her legs. Logan gripped her now naked hips and pressed her backward. She fell onto the sofa. He yanked her knickers past her calves, over her shoes, and off—a flash of bright red sailing across the room.

"Oh!" The startled sound escaped her, quickly followed by a deeper, throatier, "Ooooh" when he opened her thighs and moved to kneel between her legs, pressing his mouth to her hot wet center. He licked and nipped and sucked, circling her clit with his tongue. She tasted so good. Logan slid his hands beneath her, lifting her to his mouth so he could taste more of her salty sweetness.

Her fingers fisted in his hair, knees locking on either side of him as she rocked against him. Tiny gasps of excitement told him she was close, the sound a siren's song calling him to her. He wanted to crash against her, slam his body into hers. But he held on, determined to give her this first. He pulled a hand out from under her and slipped two fingers inside, matching the rhythm of his tongue, pressing into her, opening her, moving harder and faster until Cassie was moaning his name over and over and over.

Her hips jerked, and she screamed as she came. Logan pressed his free hand to her mouth, muffling her cries, while his other hand kept working her, his fingers not relenting, his tongue not slowing, not until he'd wrested every last quiver from her. At last she lay still, and he relaxed, resting his cheek against the soft curve of her inner thigh. He breathed in the scent of her, her dark curls tickling his nose.

"What are you doing down there?" She was still a little breathless, her voice both curious and amused.

Without lifting his head, he responded, his mouth brushing against her delicate skin with every word he spoke. "Och, *now* you ask me? You weren't too concerned a bit ago."

She giggled. He levered himself into an upward position, still on his knees between her legs. Logan tilted his chin and looked up, his attention caught for a moment on the pale swell of her breasts. She was so beautiful, so fucking lovely. He could stay like this all night, just gazing at her. Her nipples puckered under his stare and his balls tightened.

He licked his lips. Well, maybe not *all* night.

She ran a hand through the messy tangle of her hair. "Oh good Lord," she mumbled, staring down at her feet.

"What?" Logan's pulse sped up. Had he done something wrong? Had she not liked it as much as he thought she had?

"I still have my shoes on." Her cheeks, already flushed, turned a deeper shade of pink.

He grinned and grasped a feminine ankle in each hand. "Aye, you do."

"I don't think I've ever done . . . this." She waved an arm, indicating her naked torso.

"Ever?"

"I mean, um, not while wearing shoes."

"There's a first time for everything." He winked and rubbed his thumbs along the leather straps crisscrossing her calves.

She smiled, the wicked smile he was learning promised good things for him. Cassie leaned forward, the curtain of her dark hair tumbling over her shoulders and covering her breasts.

"I was thinking," she said, licking her lips.

"Aye?"

"There's something else I don't think I've ever done . . ." her gaze drifted down the length of him, the speculative look crossing her face again, ". . . while wearing shoes." She reached for him, curling her fingers into his belt loops and pulling him toward her.

CHAPTER 12

CASSIE DOZED, HALF-AWAKE, listening to the rain spatter against the skylight. She rolled over, snuggling against the warm lump of Scot taking up most of the bed. After their first round on the couch, Logan had carried her to the suite's bedroom where they promptly got started on round two.

Though the night had begun with Cassie annoyed at how she seemed to be the one always making the first move, things had changed quickly once Logan finally peeled himself away from the door. He may have been slow to get in the driver's seat but damn, once the Scot decided to take charge—the man meant business.

She cracked an eye open and smiled at the tousle of red hair popping up from the nest of blankets. Logan had major bed head. Cassie was tempted to run her fingers through the wild mess, but she didn't want to risk waking him.

Not yet. Not with the rain pitter-pattering on the glass above, making shadows dance over their warm, cozy cocoon below. The moment was too perfect. Cassie contemplated the pros and cons of spending her last full day in London right here in bed with Logan.

The only negative she could think of was food, but that's what room service was for, right? They could order piles of scones with clotted cream and fresh berry jam. Her eyes drifted closed as she pictured a lazy breakfast in bed with Logan, licking crumbs off each other's fingers before turning the pages of the *London Times*, which the hotel delivered to each suite on the executive floor every morning.

She had begun to nod off again, her mind full of the things she and Logan could do to each other with the cream and jam after they'd finished eating, when a sharp knock on the door startled her awake. Next to her, Logan mumbled something in his sleep, the top of his head disappearing completely as he burrowed deeper under the covers.

The knock came again, and Cassie struggled to unwrap herself from their bed burrito. She stumbled into the front room, yanking on a hotel robe. Quickly tying the sash, she peered through the peephole.

"Bonnie?" Cassie unlatched the security bar and opened the door.

"I'm sorry, were you still asleep?" Bonnie asked, standing in the hall in her fuzzy teacup robe and slippers.

"Not anymore." Cassie opened the door wider.

"I need to talk to you." Bonnie scurried past Cassie into the room and began to pace in a frantic circle, the stuffed teapot on the top of each slipper swaying like they were riding a tidal wave.

Cassie picked up the waiting newspaper on the floor outside her room and shut the door. She was about to take a seat on the couch when she recalled what had happened on that particular piece of furniture last night. She shifted course, choosing instead to sit in one of the low-backed leather chairs by the window. She placed the paper on the coffee table and waited for her friend to calm down, or at least tell her why she was agitated.

On her fourth circuit of the room, Bonnie paused. She leaned forward and reached for something hooked on the corner of a large framed picture—something shiny and red. "What is . . . ?" she began, stopping when Cassie leaped up and pushed her aside.

"Nothing. That's nothing." Cassie yanked her panties down, cramming the satin fabric into a tight ball inside her fist.

Bonnie blushed as scarlet as Cassie's underwear. "Oh." Her eyes snapped wide, and she glanced around. "Is he still here?"

"In bed, yeah. Where else would he be?" Along with her panties, Cassie gathered up her dress and Logan's jeans and tossed everything into the bedroom. The mountain of satisfied male hidden under the covers didn't move. She gently slid the pocket door separating the sleeping area from the front room of the suite shut. "Come on, sit down. I don't think he'll be waking up anytime soon."

Bonnie eyed the closed door. "It's not really a big deal. I, uh, I can talk to you later."

"Are you kidding? I got out of a very nice, warm bed where I was all snug and cozy with a very nice, very warm, *very naked* Scot. Now talk, don't make my sacrifice be in vain."

After a moment of hesitation, Bonnie joined Cassie. "Well, it's about Logan's friend."

"Theo?" Cassie started, surprise making the question come out louder than she'd intended. Her insides raced. Did something happen between Theo and Bonnie last night? *Oh my God, what if it did?* She lowered her voice and struggled to remain calm, aiming for polite, but casual, interest. "What about Theo?"

"Never mind. I told you, it's no big deal. I don't know why I came rushing over here." Bonnie tried to stand, but Cassie yanked the belt of her friend's robe and pushed her back down.

"Unacceptable," Cassie declared. "You do not get to drop a bomb like that and then run away."

"It's not a bomb!" Bonnie tugged on an auburn curl that had escaped from the loose bun on top of her head. "It's just, I saw him this morning."

Cassie cocked her head, not sure where her friend was going with this. "Where? Here? At the hotel?"

Bonnie nodded and fiddled with the dish of hard candy on the table.

Cassie wondered why Logan hadn't mentioned it. Maybe his friend had booked a room last night after it was obvious Logan was staying. A twinge of guilt stabbed her. That had been rather thoughtless of her. Not once had she considered what Theo would do if his friend abandoned him for the evening. In her defense, Logan hadn't seemed worried about it either.

"I stepped out of Delaney's room to grab the paper, and a door across the hall opened, and there he was." Bonnie's cheeks were turning crimson again. "He was getting the paper too, and he was, uh . . ." Bonnie swallowed hard.

"Don't tell me he was naked."

"No!" Bonnie dropped the mint she had just finished unwrapping. It clattered across the table and bounced onto the hotel carpet. She hunched over and made a grab for it. "No, he was not naked." She sat back up and stared at the candy, now covered in specks of lint. She picked at the fuzz, concentrating hard. "He was in a towel. And, um . . . he must have just had a shower because his hair was wet and there were drops of water on his, uh . . ." Bonnie stopped and swallowed again. She reached for a new piece of candy.

"Bonnie Blythe, I do believe you have a crush on him."

"I *do not* have a crush on anyone," Bonnie whispered fiercely.

"Methinks the lady doth protest too much." Cassie grinned.

"First *Romeo and Juliet*, and now *Hamlet*?" Bonnie stared across the table at Cassie. "When did you get so well versed in Shakespeare?"

"Since I've been friends with you." Cassie shrugged. "But if it helps, I thought that line was from *Macbeth*," she admitted.

"Nope. *Hamlet*. And it's 'The lady doth protest too much, methinks,' actually."

"Actually, methinks the lady is trying to change the subject." Cassie watched as Bonnie organized the candy, separating the butterscotch and mints into individual piles. "When's the last time you were attracted to a man? Other than Gabe, I mean."

Bonnie didn't meet her eyes.

"Bon?" Cassie placed a hand over her friend's. "It's okay to think someone besides your fiancé is cute. Hot, even."

The mumbled response was too low and garbled for Cassie to understand. She leaned closer, squeezing Bonnie's fingers. "Can you try that again please? In English this time?"

Bonnie squeezed back and sighed. She looked up. "I had a dream about him. Last night."

"Who, Gabe?"

Bonnie shook her head, blushing furiously.

"Theo?" Cassie asked. She knew it had to be, but she was enjoying making her friend squirm, just a little.

"I'm guessing it was a good dream?"

"No, it wasn't a good dream. It was . . ." Bonnie paused, blushing more furiously than ever. "It was wrong."

"Dreaming about doing something isn't the same thing as doing it."

"But if I dreamt those things, it must mean I want to do all *that* . . . with *him*." Bonnie pulled her hand from beneath Cassie's and twisted the engagement ring on her left ring finger.

Cassie leaned back in her chair, considering her friend. She really wanted to hear more about this dream, and what "all that" entailed, but didn't want to press for details if it was going to upset Bonnie. "Remember sophomore year of high school, when we had Mr. Getzl for chemistry?"

Bonnie nodded, staring down at the small diamond on her finger as it flashed in the gray light from the window.

"Remember the dream I told you I had about him?"

Bonnie stopped twisting her ring and stared up at Cassie, blue eyes narrowed as she dug through her memory. "You brewed a love potion in class, and when you drank some of it, he was the first person you saw so you pulled him into the supply closet and . . ." She dropped her gaze again.

"And I kissed him. Between shelves of beakers and Bunsen burners, I rubbed my hands over his bald, shiny gnome head and pulled him to me by that vinyl pocket protector he always had on and kissed him." Cassie laughed, shaking her head at the bizarre workings of her fifteen-year-old brain. "So I kissed Mr. G in my dream. Do you think that meant I wanted to kiss him in real life too?"

"I hope not."

"No. It was just a dream. People dream crazy shit all the time."

"But this dream seemed so *real*. And then, I got out of bed to get the paper, and Theo was there, wearing only a towel, and he has this line of dark hair that starts just under his belly button and goes down . . ." Bonnie paused, her eyes going unfocused.

"Mm-hmm," Cassie murmured, her mind immediately conjuring an image of Logan's bare torso, buttons on his jeans popping open one by one, revealing the masculine trail of hair marking a path from belly button to parts farther south. The carpet definitely matched the drapes. Cassie cleared her throat. *God, she would kill for a cup of coffee right now.*

She rubbed her eyes and focused on Bonnie. Her friend needed her help. Cassie tried to think of the right thing to say, not what Cassie thought was right, but what she knew would be right for Bonnie. She decided to go with an interview tactic she'd learned on *ChiChat*. Restate the facts.

"So, you had a hot, sexy dream about Theo."

"I didn't say it was hot and sexy," Bonnie protested. Cassie pursed her lips and narrowed her eyes at her friend. Almost immediately, Bonnie relented. "Fine. Yes. It was hot and sexy."

"And then you saw him this morning, looking hot and sexy," Cassie continued, and this time Bonnie didn't argue. "After which, you pounded on your best friend's door, even though you knew she was probably still sleeping, and probably still in bed with her own piece of hot and sexy."

"That's not fair, Cass. I didn't know Logan was still here."

"Look, I'm not mad you woke me up. I'm your friend— you need me, I'm here. But come on, where else would he have been? Last night you all but invited him up here for me. Thank you, by the way."

"You're welcome." Bonnie sniffed. "One of us should be having fun, right?"

"You're not having fun?" Cassie hoped that wasn't true. Not on their big dream vacation.

"I am. That's not what I meant." Bonnie started putting the piles of sweets back into the bowl. "It's just . . . I think it's because I miss Gabe. I've been gone almost six weeks. We've never been apart this long before."

"Absence makes the heart grow fonder, right?"

Bonnie sighed. "I hope so."

Cassie caught the note of worry in her friend's voice. "You don't think Gabe would . . ."

"What? No!" Bonnie shook her head. "Of course not. Gabe would never cheat on me. It's just that, if I can have these . . . *thoughts* about someone else . . ."

"Who's to say he's not having them too?" Cassie finished.

"Right." Bonnie smiled, a little wan around the edges. "But we're going home tomorrow. It's only one more day."

"Remind me what's on the agenda for today?" Cassie asked. She glanced at the closed door to the bedroom.

"A bunch of Shakespeare stuff in Stratford-upon-Avon and a show at the Globe tonight."

Cassie yawned. "Sounds like a packed schedule."

"You know that's how I roll." Bonnie snorted. "I don't mind if you want to ditch. Sadie and Ana already bailed and are going shopping at Harrods, but Delaney will still come with me."

"Sorry. I just need coffee, really." Cassie stifled another yawn and thought of the warm bed waiting for her in the other room, and the man who was keeping it warm—much more tempting than a day spent tromping around in the fog and rain.

"Look, if you prefer to spend the day with your sexy Scot rather than the Bard, I understand."

Cassie smiled. "Thanks, Bonnie. You really are the best roommate ever."

Bonnie stood and tightened the knot on her robe. "I know. And also the best friend ever."

"My bosom friend," Cassie agreed, repeating a favorite childhood phrase of Bonnie's, borrowed from *Anne of Green Gables*.

"A kindred spirit." Bonnie beamed. "I'll go steal a few snacks from Delaney and come back in an hour," she said, giving Cassie a quick hug before heading for the door. "But *only* one hour, I still have to get my clothes and we'll need an early start to fit everything in."

"Thanks for the heads-up." As Bonnie pulled the door open, Cassie called after her. "Why don't you see if Theo is free today? I get the feeling he likes Shakespeare."

Cassie caught the mint Bonnie threw at her head, laughing as the door slammed shut.

CHAPTER 13

LOGAN STRETCHED, RELISHING the luxurious pull on the muscles in his arms and legs and back. He'd dropped like a stone after their third go late last night—or maybe that had been early this morning. He couldn't remember when he'd slept so deeply. He reached a hand out and felt for Cassie, but the lass wasn't there. Her side of the mattress was cool. He grimaced and hoped he hadn't chased her from the bed. As dead to the world as he'd been, he wouldn't be surprised if he'd been snoring like an old badger.

He pulled the covers down to his shoulders and popped his head out, looking around the room. No Cassie. Rain tapped against the windows and skylight, a steady beat, heavier than the morning shower typical in London. This storm had legs and would likely last awhile.

Logan swiped the tangle of hair off his forehead and lay back on the pillow, contemplating how he might go about convincing Cassie to stay in bed with him all day. Where could the lass be? He sat up, the door to the bedroom was closed. Logan thought he heard the soft murmur of feminine voices beyond, but the sound was almost drowned out by the thrum of rain.

Rolling out of bed, he made for the pile of clothes lying on the floor by the door. After he picked up Cassie's dress and draped it across her roommate's still-made bed, he grabbed his jeans and pulled them on. A flash of red caught his eye, and he glanced back down and grinned. Logan retrieved Cassie's knickers from the floor, letting the silky fabric slide between his fingers. For a brief moment, he considered pocketing them, but decided against it. He was already worried enough about being accused of stalker behavior, he didn't need to add pervert to the mix. He tossed them on the bed next to the dress.

He was glad he did, because a second later he'd have been caught red-handed, quite literally, as the door to the bedroom slid open.

"Morning." He looked Cassie up and down. The lass was wrapped in a hotel robe, her dark hair was an unholy tangle, and there was a smudge of makeup under one eye. She looked good enough to eat, a delicious, well-boffed mess.

"Morning, yourself." She returned the appraisal, hungry gaze snagging on his groin, where he hadn't finished doing up the buttons of his jeans, having been distracted by a pair of red knickers at his feet.

Lust coiled at the base of his spine as his cock responded to her attention. Christ, after last night, he'd have thought the randy bastard would be in need of a break. But no, here the lad was, up and ready for action.

"Who was at the door?" he asked, seeking distraction.

Cassie tore her gaze away. Reluctantly, he was pleased to note. "Bonnie." She moved to the coffee maker tucked into a nook next to the closet and popped one of those pod things into the top. "She saw your friend Theo this morning. I guess he has a room down the hall?"

Tell her, mate. Get it over with already. Before he could say anything, she pressed a button on the machine and then headed for the loo. The sound of running water was soon overpowered by a series of hisses and gurgles erupting from the coffee maker. Logan eyed the machine warily, wondering if an explosion was imminent. After another minute of menacing noises, the smell of something one could loosely define as coffee wafted through the room. Logan peered into the mug Cassie had placed at the base of the machine.

Cassie poked her head into the room. "Hey, that's mine. Make your own." She pointed her toothbrush at him, and he supposed she meant it to be a threat.

He laughed and made a grab for her toothbrush. She yelped and escaped back into the loo. Logan followed.

"Here." She ripped the plastic wrapper off a new hotel toothbrush and handed it to him.

"Thanks." Logan joined her at the sink. It was oddly pleasant to stand next to her like this. He didn't think he'd ever brushed his teeth with a lass before, not even Nettie.

As she rinsed her toothbrush under the tap, she met his gaze in the mirror, her thoughts echoing his. "I've never brushed my teeth with anyone before . . . other than Bonnie, maybe."

He wiped his mouth with a towel and grinned. "We'll add that to the list of firsts you've experienced with me then, aye?" He could see his own eyebrow arch in the reflection. Mam was right, it really did make him look like a satyr. Devilish, even. He was feeling devilish. He moved behind Cassie, wrapping his arms around her waist and nuzzling her neck.

She raised her hand and rubbed it along his jaw. He

heard the soft rasp of his stubble against her fingers. He tilted his head and pressed a kiss to her palm, wishing time could stop so they could stay in this room together for as long as they liked. To hell with everyone and everything else.

Again, as if reading his mind, Cassie stepped out of his embrace. "I better get dressed. Bonnie is coming back soon."

"Aye." Logan trailed after her. "I suppose you have plans for the day?"

"Shakespeare." She picked up her coffee.

"The Globe?"

She shrugged and sat on the edge of her bed. "I think so, and some other stuff Bonnie has planned." She hesitated. "I don't have to go with, though."

"No?"

Cassie shook her head and stared at her coffee. "I told her I might stick around here today."

"Oh, aye?" He moved to join her on the bed. "And do what?"

"Well . . ." She peered up at him over the rim of the mug, eyes full of mischievous speculation. "That depends on you."

Suddenly the room seemed bright, filled with sunshine despite the rain outside. This incredible, beautiful, sexy woman had only one more day of her holiday left, and she wanted to spend it with him. He could not believe his good fortune. "I'm all yours."

Cassie made a gagging noise, and Logan hesitated. "Lass?"

"Sorry, this *coffee* is disgusting." Cassie stood and set the mug on the dresser. "It's my fault. Paris has ruined me forever. I'm hopelessly spoiled. Maybe I could get the hotel to send up a French press."

"Or maybe," he said, standing up and pulling on his shirt, "we could order some real coffee from room service and have it sent to my room."

She turned to face him. "Come again?"

That's exactly what he hoped would happen. Logan shoved the thought back to the part of his brain that had never matured past age fifteen and forged ahead. "You mentioned your friend had seen Theo a few doors down from here, aye?"

"Aye," she repeated, her voice hedged with suspicion.

Logan swallowed, too late to back down now. "We booked a room."

"Oh, that's perfect!"

He could leave it at that. She seemed fine with the revelation he'd gotten a room in the same hotel as her, why provide any additional unnecessary and potentially damaging details?

"Wait." She frowned.

Damn. This was it. Logan braced himself, but instead of the tirade of accusations, demanding to know why he had followed her from Scotland to England, she bit her lip and looked up at him, a question in her eyes.

"Just one room for both of you?"

Relief flooded his cowardly veins. He grinned broadly. "Not a chance. Theo is over in 757." He fished his hotel key out of the back pocket of his jeans and held up the card. "I'm Room 762."

"In that case," she said, matching his grin, "why don't you head over to your room now? I'll meet you there soon. I need to tell Bonnie there's been a change of plans."

Logan yanked on the belt of her robe and pulled her to him. He kissed her hard on her minty-fresh mouth.

Cassie kissed him back just as hard before pushing him toward the door. "Go on. And order up some real breakfast to go with that real coffee, please. I don't think we'll be leaving your room for a long time." She smiled at him, the wicked curve of her cheek launching a thousand fantasies.

A day in bed with Cassie? *Hell yes.* On his way to his room Logan stopped outside 757 and knocked.

Theo opened the door. "Go away."

Logan stuck his foot out to stop Theo from shutting the door in his face. He pushed it open again and stepped inside. "Can I come in?"

"You are in, you rude bastard." Theo left Logan at the door and retreated into the suite. His mate was already dressed for the day in freshly pressed slacks and a crisp blue-and-gray striped button-down. BBC News droned in the background.

"My, don't we look smart. Looking to impress someone, are we?"

"I was thinking I'd take care of some business this morning since I'm in town."

A tray of tea and breakfast pastries perched on a small table by the window. Logan grabbed a scone. "Can it wait? I have something I'd like you to do."

"Help yourself," Theo said drily as he poured a measure of tea.

"Thanks." Logan grinned and bit off a hunk of scone.

"Don't mention it," Theo said. "This is all on your tab, after all." He took a swallow of tea and set his cup down. "Speaking of, did you get your precious contract signed?"

Logan choked. "Not yet."

"I thought you planned to walk your American lady friend to her room and then talk—"

"I know what the plan was. It was *my* plan, after all," Logan growled. "I just . . . It didna feel right, ya ken?"

Theo chuckled. "You've got it bad."

"Shut yer face," Logan snapped, but his jibe lacked heat. Theo was right, and they both knew it.

"I suppose I should warn you . . ."

"About what?" Logan asked before popping the rest of the scone in his mouth.

"The cat is out of the bag." Theo swatted Logan's hand away from a thick slice of frosted lemon loaf and grabbed it for himself. "Bonnie saw me in the hall this morning. She knows I have a room here."

"Aye, I heard."

"You did?" Theo glanced up in surprise.

"I did, indeed." Logan brushed crumbs from his fingers.

"How? It only happened an hour or so ago. She spotted me outside my door when I was grabbing the *Times*." Theo paused, a rare smile tugging at the corner of his mouth. "Did you know she has a robe with teacups printed all over it? And fuzzy slippers—"

"—with matching stuffed teapots on the toes. Aye, I know that too." Logan swiped a square of shortbread.

Theo's face darkened. "And how, pray tell, did you happen upon that knowledge?"

Oho, am I getting a whiff of jealousy? "Easy, lad. I saw her in that getup our first night here, when I walked Cassie to her room. Come on, it's not like she was wearing something naughty." Logan wondered what kind of pajamas Cassie favored. Was she into fuzzy, quirky stuff too or did she prefer silky, satiny, sexy sleepwear? He hoped it was the latter. So far, they'd spent all their time in bed together naked—not that he was complaining.

Thoughts of being in bed with Cassie reminded Logan he had to hurry. "Bonnie stopped by this morning, told Cassie she saw you."

"Ah." Theo pressed his fingertip to the plate of pastries

and picked up spare crumbs of lemon cake. "Did you tell Cassie you had a room here too?"

"I did." Logan left out the fact he hadn't come clean on the timeline. "Which leads me to what I need from you."

"Oh?" Theo crossed his arms over his chest.

"I'm supposed to meet Cassie in my room in a few minutes." Logan raised a hand to ward off whatever comment he saw brewing on Theo's face. "She's skipping out on her plans with Bonnie. I thought it might be nice if you stood in. They're touring Stratford-Upon-Avon and some other Shakespeare touristy stuff."

"That's a lot of time in the car." Theo sighed. "Fine. I'll do it."

"You're a prince," Logan said, smothering a knowing smile. Theo had capitulated much too quickly. It had been a long time since Theo had fancied a lass; he was usually too busy fighting off the wealthy title hunters his mother kept thrusting on him. Too bad the lass in question was spoken for. Not wanting his friend to get hurt, Logan thought it best to inform him of that fact. He paused at the door and turned. "She's engaged."

"Who?"

"You know who. Bonnie. Cassie told me the lass got engaged last Christmas."

A muscle twitched in Theo's jaw, but beyond that, his expression didn't change. British stiff upper lip firmly in place, Theo held the door open for Logan. "I appreciate the warning."

"Right, then." Logan clapped Theo on the shoulder and stepped into the hall. "You're a good man, Theo."

"Don't remind me," Theo grumbled and shut the door.

CHAPTER 14

ANTICIPATION PUMPING MORE adrenaline than a caffeine rush, Cassie zigzagged around her hotel suite like a drunken bumblebee as she dove for her suitcase. In preparation for her foreign fling, along with the box of condoms, she'd also packed some fancy new lingerie. It'd be a shame if those silky pretty things traveled all this way and never had a chance to strut their stuff. Sweaters and T-shirts went flying as she dug down to the bottom of her suitcase.

She was starting to wonder if she'd forgotten to bring the matched set Sadie had helped her pick out in a boutique on the North Shore. As someone who usually purchased bras and pajamas a few aisles over from the milk and toothpaste, Cassie had almost suffered heart failure when she saw the price for what amounted to less than a fistful of fabric. She wouldn't have been surprised if her inherently frugal nature had subconsciously left the ludicrously expensive underwear behind. To be returned later, the money spent on something more prudent—like a month of groceries, possibly two—when she got back home.

Cassie was about to give up when a pair of sweatpants she hated and had no idea why she'd bothered packing unrolled, revealing a small vellum-wrapped packet tucked inside. *Aha!* She gingerly removed the featherlight bundle and set it on the bed. Untying the satin bow, she peeled away the delicate sheets of cream and gold paper, and then gasped in surprise, having forgotten how exquisite her splurge had been.

She fingered the price tags, still attached to the garments by a satin ribbon, elegantly secured with gold pins. Hell, the fancy pins probably cost more than what her usual bra and panty set did. She unfastened the pins and made a point to tuck them and their satin strung price tags inside a pocket in her suitcase. Then, before the frugal, prudent side of her brain found its voice, she shrugged the hotel robe off and slipped the more-expensive-than-a-Brazilian-blowout panties on.

Oh. They felt nice. Very nice. The fabric managed to be snug without pinching, and the touch of silk brushing against her lady bits was downright sensual. Cassie lifted the other half of the set from the layers of vellum. She couldn't remember what Sadie had said this thing was called. A chignon? No—that was a hairstyle. Whatever it was, it was gorgeous, and surprisingly easy to get on. Delicate straps held up the fitted cups, with three tiny satin buttons that fastened between her breasts, almost like the clasp on a bra that opened in the front.

As she did up the buttons, Cassie focused on the movement of her hands in the large mirror over the dresser. The silk was pale lavender, wisps of fabric flowing from bodice to hips in a dreamy cloud, sheer enough to be nearly see-through. Okay, not nearly, it was *totally* see-through. The satin trim on the bra and panties was darker—a rich, royal purple. Watching her reflection, Cassie felt like royalty.

Damn—Logan was waiting for her. Cassie pulled the hotel robe back on over the lingerie and hurried to the front parlor, mentally scrambling to recall the room number Logan had told her. She'd almost left the suite when she remembered she was barefoot. She ran back to the bedroom and dove through the piles of stuff she had tossed on the floor during her mad lingerie hunt. A pair of flip-flops appeared, and Cassie tugged them on. Good enough, she wasn't planning to wear them very long anyway.

She dashed out of the bedroom again before realizing she needed her key. Sure, she planned to spend most of the day in Logan's bed, but at some point she might want to come back here for actual clothes. Flip-flopping her way over to the side of the couch where she'd dropped her purse last night, Cassie grabbed her keycard and her phone, shoving them both into the deep pockets of the robe.

At last, she was ready to head out the door when she caught a glimpse of Logan's jacket hanging over the back of the couch, flung there and forgotten. She'd missed it when she'd hurriedly cleaned up the rest of their clothes after Bonnie's discovery of the errant panties.

They had been a little wild last night, that's for sure. The thought reminded Cassie of something else she was forgetting, and she headed back to the bedroom one more time to grab the condom box. She crammed the whole crumpled mess into her other robe pocket and was making her way to the door for real this time when it opened.

Bonnie entered the room, jumping as she almost ran smack into Cassie. "Oh! I didn't think you would still be in here."

"I was just leaving," Cassie said.

Bonnie looked Cassie up and down. "You going for a swim or something?"

"Huh?" Cassie wasn't even sure the hotel had a pool.

It probably did, but what did that have to do with any-thing?

Bonnie pointed to Cassie's flip-flops.

"Ah." Cassie shook her head. "No, these were just the first things I found to put on."

"In a hurry, are we?" Bonnie smirked. "I need to hurry too. I told Delaney I'd meet her downstairs, and I better not be late. She's already mad at me."

"Why?"

"I ate her entire stash of shortbread." A knock sounded at the door, and Bonnie yelped, rushing for the bedroom. "That's probably Delaney."

The knocking increased, and Cassie tightened the belt on her robe. "She'll be ready in a minute," she called as she opened the door. "Oh! It's you."

"A pleasant morning to you as well," Theo shot back.

"Sorry. Good morning." Cassie fiddled with the door handle. "Are you looking for Logan?"

"No. I'm here for Bonnie."

"You are?" She opened the door wider and stepped back.

"Logan sent me over." Theo entered the suite. "Some-thing about the two of you having made other plans? He suggested I take your place and escort your friend on her Shakespeare expedition today." Theo blithely ignored the fact Cassie was standing there in a robe and flip-flops, crumpled box of condoms spilling out of one terry cloth pocket.

"Um, okay." Cassie gestured to a chair. "Have a seat. I'll let Bon know you're here."

Cassie crossed the room as quickly as her flip-flops would carry her. "So . . . ," Cassie said as she slipped into the bedroom and slid the door closed. "Do you want to guess who's out there?"

Bonnie was standing in front of the wardrobe, where her own clothes had been neatly hung. Unlike Cassie, who preferred to live directly out of her suitcase, Bonnie enjoyed the ritual of unpacking and organizing her clothes at each stop on their trip. She turned and glanced over her shoulder at Cassie. "Delaney?"

"Ah, no. Not Delaney." Cassie cleared her throat. "It's Theo. He said he's planning to accompany you today."

Bonnie paused, dropping the ends of the plaid scarf she'd been draping across her sleeveless turtleneck. "What?"

Unable to meet her friend's stare, Cassie began to gather the multiple hills of her clothing into one giant mountain. "Apparently, he heard I would be staying at the hotel today . . . and apparently he is under the impression you could use some company."

At her friend's silence, Cassie looked up and met Bonnie's eyes. "Apparently, you are not happy about this," she finished lamely.

Bonnie's cheeks flushed, and she turned away, fussing with her scarf. "I don't know what you're talking about. I don't care if Theo comes with. Why should I care if Theo comes with?" Flustered, she gave up trying to tie the scarf and flounced onto her bed. "Did you know Theo was planning to come with?"

"No, I didn't." Cassie maneuvered around the remaining piles of clothes and sat next to her friend. "Look, I know I teased you about Theo earlier, but honestly, Bon, I didn't know. If it's going to bother you, I can ask him not to come."

Bonnie waved toward the front room of the suite. "He's already here. What would you say?"

"I'll tell him the truth. I'll tell him I decided to go with you and he's off the hook." Cassie stood and slid her suitcase closer to Mount Clothing.

"But weren't you planning to spend the day . . . you know?" Bonnie wiggled her eyebrows.

Cassie tossed a flip-flop at Bonnie's head. "Not anymore." She kicked off the other flip-flop, making up her mind in an instant. Logan must have talked to Theo after he left here. He knew Cassie was ditching her friend to spend the day with him, and he'd taken the time to make sure Bonnie wouldn't be all alone. The action had been kind. And certainly more thoughtful than she'd been. She grabbed Bonnie's hands and squeezed. "This is our last full day in England, the last full day of our once-in-a-lifetime-vacation. We should be spending it together."

"Are you sure, Cass?"

"Absolutely." Cassie nodded, working at the knot on her robe. She smiled, knowing she had made the right decision. Besides, this may be their last full day of vacation, but a full night still lay ahead as well. The thought made her giddy with possibility.

"Okay," Bonnie agreed, her tone dry, "but I just have one question."

"What's that?" Cassie tugged the robe off.

"What, exactly, are you wearing?"

Cassie glanced down at the skimpy array of frothy lavender silk. "Two months of groceries," she grumbled.

"I see." Bonnie stood, biting the inside of her cheek as she gave Cassie a once-over. "Well. Hurry up and get ready then."

Cassie put on a pair of jeans and riffled through the mess of clothes left in her suitcase, looking for a shirt that would work over the flowy-chignon-bra-thing she was wearing. She pulled a peasant top over her head and smoothed the brocade fabric down her sides, surprised at how good it looked. The fancy lingerie top worked really well under the Boho cut of the blouse, which was tight at the bosom but flowed loose around the torso. She checked her reflection for any stray bits of lavender poking out. Nope. The long top covered everything, and the smooth layer of satin beneath made the shirt swish jauntily around her hips.

Satisfied, Cassie stopped primping and turned around. "You wanna go tell Theo he's free to go?"

Bonnie heaved a sigh, sending the curls at her temples fluttering. "No, it's fine. If he wants to come, he can come." She grabbed her purse and slid the door open, stopping to deliver a parting shot. "But your sexy Scot better be coming too."

If Theo was surprised at the change in plans, he hid it well. With Austen-worthy manners, he escorted Cassie and Bonnie to the lobby and left them to wait with Delaney while he "fetched Logan and had the car pulled 'round."

"Prince Eric is coming with us today?" Delaney smacked her lips suggestively. "Sweet."

"Stop calling him that." Bonnie scowled.

"What's got your fin in a knot, Ariel?"

Bonnie ignored the jab.

Delaney cast a knowing look at Cassie. "I bet she's crabby as old Sebastian because she has indigestion. She ate all my shortbread."

"I heard." Cassie suppressed a grin. It felt good to be in the thick of her friends' typical good-natured teasing. And though it might not be as exciting as spending the day in bed exploring a sexy Scot, she was looking forward to spending the day exploring Shakespeare's England.

As if conjured by her thoughts, her sexy Scot appeared. She wondered if he was upset about the change in plans, but like his friend, Logan was the perfect gentleman, all manners and grace as he took her arm and kissed her cheek. He gestured toward the front of the lobby where Theo stood waiting by the rental car. Big enough to seat five, they'd only be taking the one car today. It would be snug, but comfortable. "Ladies, shall we?"

"We shall." Delaney pretended to pick up the skirts of an imaginary ballgown and sashayed forward. She patted Theo on the cheek as he held the door of the sedan open. Cassie climbed in and was about to scoot over so Logan could sit next to her, but Bonnie popped open the back door on the other side and hopped in.

"Guess you're taking the front seat," Cassie told Logan with a note of apology, as Delaney squeezed closer, making room for Bonnie.

"So it seems." The twinkle in his green-gold eyes let her know he understood. He closed her door with a wink and got in front next to Theo.

Cassie glanced across the back seat at Bonnie, but her friend refused to make eye contact. After a moment, Cassie shrugged and put on her seatbelt. Message received. Bonnie had agreed to let Theo come along, but that didn't mean she was happy about it.

It seemed that Theo, too, had gotten the message. He was studying Bonnie in the rearview mirror, brow furrowed.

"What's the matter?" Bonnie leaned forward. "Is something wrong? Do you want me to drive?"

"Bloody hell, woman." Theo straightened in the driver's seat. "Absolutely not."

"What's that supposed to mean? You think I can't?"

Bonnie poked the back of Theo's headrest. "I am completely capable of driving this car. I have family in Ireland, you know. I've driven on the wrong side of the road plenty of times."

"The wrong side, she says," Theo muttered, shaking his head. "American *and* Irish—heaven help us."

"So." Logan stepped into the fray, his voice braced with cheerful politeness. "Where to first?"

Bonnie thrust a list between the seats. Logan glanced over it and punched the coordinates into the car's GPS.

Once the route loaded, Theo put the sedan into drive. "Anne Hathaway's house it is. Next stop, Warwickshire, followed by Stratford-Upon-Avon."

Delaney leaned forward and patted Theo on the shoulder. "Where were you on the rest of our vacation?"

Theo chuckled and eased into London traffic. "Doing something far less interesting, I assure you."

"Oh?" Delaney settled back into her seat. "What do you do for a living?"

Cassie studied Theo's profile. Logan had told her that Theo was a duke, an actual member of the British aristocracy. Had he been telling the truth? If so, would Theo admit it now?

"I suppose you could say I'm in finance." Theo glanced at the GPS and switched lanes.

"Do you work in a bank?" Delaney asked.

"Not exactly."

"Secretive, aren't we?" Delany nudged Bonnie's knee. "What do you think, Bon? Does he look more like a banker or an accountant?"

Bonnie swatted Delaney's hand away. "I couldn't say." She slumped down in her seat and stared out her window, where the city buildings had begun to give way to townhomes. It was still raining steadily, but the fog had all but abated.

"Hmm," Delaney mused, "I say he's dressed like a banker, or maybe one of those stockbroker guys. Hey, what's the equivalent of Wall Street in London?"

"I believe that would be Lombard Street," Theo replied.

"Do you work on Lombard Street?" Delaney asked.

"Not directly."

"My goodness, such shady answers, Mister . . . what was your last name again?"

"Wharton." Theo's response was clipped.

Was it her imagination, or did Theo sound guarded? Cassie made a note to remember Theo's last name and look it up later.

The sound of crinkling paper interrupted her thoughts, and she glanced over to see Delaney unwrapping a giant Kit Kat. Unlike the Kit Kats she was used to back home, the UK version was a single monster size bar that had to be at least two inches thick. And America was supposed to be the one guilty of supersizing everything.

Delaney caught Cassie's eye and smiled. "Want some?"

"Sure." She held out her hand, and Delaney broke off a healthy chunk and passed it to her. Cassie bit into the candy, letting the buttery-rich cocoa melt on her tongue. If she wasn't going to spend the day indulging in hedonistic sex, the least she deserved was some chocolate.

As if reading her mind, Logan glanced over his shoulder, one brow raised in question. Rather than answer him, she leaned forward and offered him the rest of her piece. "Chocolate?"

He took it and popped it in his mouth.

"Not how you were expecting to spend the day, I bet," she said quietly near his ear.

He shook his head and swallowed. "I've learned to expect the unexpected." He laughed, but Cassie thought she
caught a note of bitterness tainting the sound.

Theo must have heard it too, for he looked over at Logan, eyes thoughtful. "Life is rarely what we expect, right,
mate?"

"Aye, isn't that the bloody truth," Logan agreed, turning on the radio.

From her spot behind Logan, Cassie couldn't see his
face or read his expression. While he flipped through
the stations, Cassie contemplated the exchange between
the two men. Something had piqued her journalistic instincts . . . There was more to the story here, she'd bet on it.

The notes of a familiar song pumped through the car's
speakers, a British boy band that was popular in the States.
When Delaney started to sing along, Logan turned the vol-
ume up another notch, and Delaney sang louder. Cassie
shrugged off the urge to dig deeper into the vibe she'd
picked up between the men and joined her friend in the
chorus. When the song ended, Delaney put on the accent
of a snooty British matriarch and tapped Theo on the
shoulder. "I say, how much longer, Jeeves?"

Theo checked the GPS. "We're halfway there, madame."

"That did not answer my question, Jeeves."

"It's a two-hour drive from London to Stratford. Do the
math," Bonnie snapped.

"My goodness, aren't we testy?" Delaney dropped the
accent and shoved the remainder of her chocolate bar into
Bonnie's lap. "Here, you need it." Then she tapped Theo
on the shoulder again, back to playing the British matriarch. "Jeeves, is the cranky redhead correct?"

"Yes, madame," Theo confirmed, playing along. "One
hour 'til we arrive at our destination."

"Thank you, Jeeves, I believe I shall retire for a nap. Carry on." She scooted back and let her head lull, her long strawberry-blond ponytail trailing over the headrest.

"Naps and candy." Cassie shook her head and leaned forward to whisper to the front seat, sotto voce, "Have I mentioned Delaney is a preschool teacher?"

"I say she gives Mary Poppins a run for her money." Theo glanced over his shoulder for a second, smiling wide, and those killer dimples of his made an appearance. Engaged or not, Cassie could see how her best friend had found herself dreaming about this gorgeous piece of blue-eyed Brit.

Poor Bonnie. Cassie looked across the already snoring Delaney and offered her friend a grin. Bonnie rolled her eyes but after a moment returned the smile. The chocolate must have helped. And the sunshine. The clouds were breaking up, and the sun had decided to make an appearance. Bonnie opened her window and a summer breeze rushed in.

Cassie opened her window too. The air was still tinged with the scent of rain, overlaid by the smell of fresh-cut grass from the meadows beyond the road, where fat rolls of hay sat drying in the late morning sun. Her last day of vacation was showing promise to turn out perfect after all.

CHAPTER 15

THAT EVENING, LOGAN paced around the lobby of the Globe Theatre, waiting for Cassie and her friends to return from their post-show expedition to the loo. "Why must lasses piss in packs?" he asked Theo.

Theo glanced up from the program bill he was reading and smirked. "Bloody hell if I know."

"You have three sisters, aye?"

"Yes, but I don't believe I've ever broached this particular topic of conversation."

Logan snorted. Theo had a point. He could imagine Nettie's reaction if he tried to ask her about the mysteries of peculiar female behavior. Whatever the reason, he hoped the girls would hurry up. He was starving. After spending the day touring all the famous Shakespeare landmarks, they had met up with Cassie's other two friends at the Globe to catch a performance of *Othello*. In Logan's opinion, the play was not one of the bard's more cheerful endeavors. Personally, he'd thought the final scene a bit overdone, too much weeping, but the lasses seemed to enjoy it well enough.

When the girls finally appeared, Logan crossed the lobby and guided them toward the exit. Cassie fell into step with him and smiled. "What's next?"

"A late night dinner on the Thames." He held the door open.

She stood waiting next to him while the others filed out. "Again?"

"Well, not *on* the Thames, *off* the Thames would be more accurate." He planned to take them to one of his favorite spots in London—an old hole-in-the-wall that looked like something out of another century, with thick-paned windows that opened onto an incredible view of the river and thick-cut steaks that tasted like heaven. Logan offered his hand to her. "Do you trust me?"

Ana brushed past them and headed down the steps. "Aw, he sounds like Aladdin."

He shot Cassie a quizzical look, but she only giggled and took his hand.

Sadie glanced over her shoulder with a sly smile. "I wonder if she'll get to ride his magic carpet."

Catching the obvious innuendo of *that* comment, Logan grinned. "No magic carpet, just the Tube," he said, directing them to a station at the corner. As they took their seats on the next train, Logan felt Cassie's gaze on him. "What?"

She shook her head. "I was just thinking, you *are* a bit like Aladdin." She leaned toward him, her mouth curving in a sweet grin. "My very own diamond in the rough."

He'd no idea what Cassie was nattering on about, but the way she was looking at him made his chest swell with a bubble of happiness. Logan leaned back in his seat and draped an arm around Cassie's shoulders. The move came naturally, as though they were a couple—a real couple out on a regular Friday night date—not two people who had met less than a week ago and would probably never see each other again after tonight. Before that thought could burst his bubble, he pushed it away and cuddled Cassie closer, taking her hands in his.

"Oh God, if the two of you are going to break into song, warn me so I can prepare my gag reflex," Delaney said, flipping her ponytail.

"You didn't have to come along, you know," Cassie muttered, and he wondered if she was wishing they could be alone too.

"Oh, yes I did." Delaney nodded her head sagely. "Otherwise I'd end up spending the night back in my hotel room, alone, watching bad British TV and snorting stroop-wafles." She paused and poked Bonnie in the side. "I'd be snorfing shortbread but *someone* ate my entire supply."

"Now hold on," Theo objected.

"Don't bother defending her." Delaney waved a finger at Theo and then pointed it back at Bonnie. "I watched her commit the crime."

"My objection is with the other half of your state-ment," Theo said, stalwartly ignoring Bonnie's burning blue gaze. "I happen to think the BBC offers some qual-ity programming."

"Of course you do," Delaney quipped. "You're British."

Cassie laughed, a low chuckle that made Logan go warm all over. She lifted her chin and met his gaze, amuse-ment lighting the dark depths of her eyes, sparking like bright shards of amber.

When Theo had come to Logan's room and told him, "Change of plans, old chap, you're joining the caravan," Logan had been all kinds of frustrated. But the day had proven more enjoyable than he ever could have predicted.

Cassie was so happy, so at ease, laughing and teasing with her friends. This was her last day of holiday, it was only right she spend it with her friends. He didn't begrudge the hours shared today, as long as he had her all to himself tonight.

The lass was fortunate to have such a close-knit group of friends. In this, Logan realized, he was fortunate as well. He looked across the aisle of the train car to where his best mate sat, arguing with Bonnie about the merits of a couple of long-dead poets. Logan could tell Theo was growing fonder of the redhead despite himself.

A twinge of guilt passed through him. Maybe it hadn't been such a good idea to invite Theo along for the day. Though Theo and Bonnie had bickered endlessly, as Sadie had said yesterday, their arguing seemed more like some kind of perverse foreplay, the sexual tension between them tangible.

Or—Logan shifted on his seat—maybe that was just him. After all, he had spent most of the day fantasizing about what he would do with Cassie once they were finally alone again. The train rumbled to a stop, interrupting his dangerous line of thought. As they stepped off the Tube and onto the platform, Logan clasped Cassie's hand. She twined her fingers in his, and he savored the skin-on-skin contact.

After ordering their meal and a round of drinks, Logan chugged his pint, hoping the alcohol would take the edge off and dull the sharp ache of need pulsing through him. Christ, he couldn't wait for supper to be over so they could be on their way back to the hotel. Hungry as he was, he was hungrier still for Cassie.

"Logan, you mentioned this restaurant was one of your favorite spots in London," Cassie said. Over the rim of her wineglass, she sent him a naughty side-eyed glance that made every part of him rise to attention.

"Aye?"

"Well, I was wondering if you wanted to give me a tour of the place. You know, while we waited for the food to arrive." She set her glass down but kept those hot eyes on him.

"Uh, aye. I could do that." He cleared his throat and rose from the table, trying to think of what he could show her. The restaurant was fairly small, and aside from the view of the Thames, which was clear from their table, there wasn't much to see. He took her hand as she rose, and when she squeezed his fingers, understanding finally clicked in his lust-addled brain.

Trying not to appear too eager, Logan pushed Cassie's chair in and shrugged an apology to Theo, who rolled his eyes as only a blue-blooded aristocrat could do, before turning his attention back to Bonnie, who was still fervently defending the poetry of Shelley . . . or maybe she had moved on to Byron now, Logan wasn't sure.

"Don't be gone too long," Sadie warned.

"Yeah," Ana chimed in, "it would be a shame if your meat got cold."

The girls snickered. Cassie's mouth twitched, but she only shook her head. Logan wrapped an arm around her waist and walked with her to the wide spread of windows. Late as it was, the summer moon was high in the night sky, painting the city in a palette of shadow and light, transforming the river into a swath of glittering dark magic.

Cassie let out a sigh of pleasure, and Logan was instantly glad he'd thought to bring her here. Morgan's wasn't located in one of the posher areas of London, but it was open 'til the wee hours and had a quiet vibrancy to it, a familiar atmosphere that reminded him of the pubs back home. She laid her head on his shoulder, her chestnut hair soft against his cheek. He bent his head toward her. "This is pretty much all there is to see . . . unless . . . you want to have a look belowstairs."

She lifted her chin and considered him. "What's down there?"

"Och, not much really. The kitchens, and a wee bar."

"Sure, let's go check it out."

He steered her toward the stairs. While the dining room on the second floor of the restaurant was full of light from the wall of windows and the bright candles dotting the cluster of tables, downstairs was dark, the air hazy. The small pub area was crammed with second shift blokes sharing a pint and a smoke after work. Logan maneuvered Cassie past the crowd of men, who barely cast a glance their way, too focused on their beer and the grimy telly in the corner where a Manchester United match was playing.

The breezeway to the kitchen was redolent with the smell of grilled meat and fried potatoes. Logan's stomach rumbled loudly.

Cassie laughed. "Somebody's hungry." She tugged his arm. "Come on, let's go back up. I don't know what I was thinking, dragging you away from the table."

"Och, I know what you were thinking, lass." Logan held fast to her hand, pulling her past the kitchen. "And you didn't drag me, I came willingly, aye?" He glanced around, looking for a quiet corner to give her a quick kiss. Spotting a curtained alcove at the end of the hallway, he tugged her toward it.

They slipped into the makeshift storage closet. A waist-high pile of wooden pallets lined one wall, and propped against the other wall was a rickety shelf holding stacks of menus. He maneuvered amongst the clutter and turned to face Cassie. In the faint light seeping in from beyond the burlap curtain, he could just make out her features. She took a step forward, bumping against him in the narrow space.

Not the most romantic of locations, but it was dark and quiet, and they were finally, blessedly, alone. Unwilling to wait another second, Logan wrapped his arms around her and brought his mouth down on hers. She responded instantly, leaning into him, tongue thrusting against his.

His hands skimmed beneath her shirt, seeking her soft, heated skin. Slick, smooth silk brushed his fingers, and he shivered at the delicious contact. "Christ, lass, what have you got on?"

Cassie giggled against his lips, tickling and teasing him at the same time. She shifted, breaking the kiss to yank her shirt over her head. She tossed it onto the shelf and stepped into his arms again. "Do you like it?"

"I canna really see it, but if looks even half as good as it feels," he murmured, sliding his hands up her back, "then I love it." Logan traced the dainty straps over her shoulders and down, encountering a row of tiny satiny buttons fastened between her breasts. He splayed his fingers wide and felt her nipples pucker into tight buds beneath his touch. Then he dipped his head and licked her through the fabric, letting his tongue swirl around the taut peak.

She sucked in a deep breath, the movement causing her chest to rise, filling his mouth with more of her sweet, soft flesh. He scraped his teeth across the tips of both silk-covered tits, savoring the shudder that ran through her.

Returning his mouth to hers, he kissed her, tongue plunging deep as his hands reached around to palm her ass, loving the feel of her lush bottom encased in tight denim. Logan cupped a cheek in each hand and lifted her until she straddled him, the vee of her thighs pressed snug against the swollen ridge of his cock. She groaned and swiveled her hips, rubbing against him, nails digging into his shoulders.

Close, but not close enough. Logan shifted his grip and set her back on the floor, needing to get the layers of clothing separating them out of the way.

Cassie must have agreed, because while he worked at her fly, she undid the buttons of his shirt. He shrugged out of his shirt and peeled her jeans open. His fingers slipped beneath the fragile wisp of satin she wore underneath, and he willed himself to be gentle.

She wiggled restlessly, urging him on. The limited space in the alcove hampered his movements. With a grunt of frustration, he stepped back and grasped her waist, twisting her around so she faced away from him. Logan looped his fingers through her panties and jeans and shoved them both over her hips and down to her knees in one swift motion. She gasped as he pressed into her from behind while making short work of his own fly.

His body tensed and teased against hers, and she bent forward over the stack of pallets, spreading her legs to give him better access. He pressed closer, the head of his cock nudging, skimming. She was so hot and so fucking wet, and he was so very, very close to being inside her.

He wanted to be inside her. Right now.

Logan held himself in check and leaned over her, his bare chest against her back. The silky texture of the lingerie she wore rubbed across his pecs and torso, making his skin tingle. He threaded his fingers through hers and stretched their arms out overhead, pressing both their palms flat against the wood.

She brought her legs together, clamping down, trapping him between her thighs. A rush of air hissed through his teeth. He arched his back and pulled away slowly, pressing his face into Cassie's hair and biting his lip at the delicious friction. Unable to resist, he shifted forward again, coming just to the brink of entering her before sliding back.

He did it again, and again, the pressure building. With each slide of his cock between the tight grip of her thighs, she grew hotter, slicker. Their breath quickened, matching the pounding of his heart. The sound was a rush in his ears, so loud he barely heard her cry his name as she suddenly tilted her hips, pushing up and back. Her move met him midthrust. Caught off guard, his body acted before his brain could think. He surged forward, and they both gasped as he slid inside her.

Logan could feel her pulse around him. Hot. Wet. Exquisite. Need, raw and brutal, laced every muscle in his body with tension. The tendons of his hips flexed as he fought the urge to move. His body's desire to push deeper was so intense he thought he was going to die if he didn't.

Beneath him, Cassie moaned and twitched her ass.

"Don't," he growled. Christ, he barely recognized his own voice. "Be still, lass," he begged, pressing his chest down hard against her back. If she moved again, Logan wasn't sure he could stop himself, and that scared the shit out of him. They held motionless for an extended moment, inhaling and exhaling together, the sound of their breathing filling the small, dark space.

A muffled chorus of cheers from the bar down the hall broke the spell. What the hell was wrong with him? Here he was, jeans around his ankles, only a thin burlap curtain and a short hallway separating his bare arse from a restaurant full of people.

And Cassie. Bloody hell, he'd been on the verge of fucking her in a supply closet without an ounce of protection. And she'd been about to let him.

Stupid. Stupid, stupid, stupid.

Janet was right—he had to stop thinking with his knob.

The thought of his sister brought everything tumbling back into place. Logan's brain kicked on, taking control of things again, reality a very effective boner-killer. He pulled back, ignoring the protests of his body as it withdrew from hers.

Cassie shifted, looking over her shoulder at him. "Logan?"

Beneath brows raised in confusion, her eyes glinted, dark pools of desire. Logan swallowed hard. Even in the dim light he could see the rosy flush of her skin, and . . . mother of God, her fine backside, gloriously naked. Before he changed his mind and did something they would both regret, Logan bent and hauled her jeans and panties up. Then he grabbed his shirt from the floor and turned away to adjust his own clothing.

As he did up his buttons, he could hear her shuffling around behind him. At the sound of her jeans zipping, he took her blouse off the shelf and handed it back to her. She tugged the shirt over her head. The loose fabric floated down, swishing around her hips, completely hiding the sexy thing she had on underneath. But he knew it was there. Despite himself, that little secret made Logan smile.

Cassie returned the smile tentatively, almost shyly.

He pulled her close and smoothed her mussed hair back from her face. "I'm sorry, lass. I let things get out of control."

She snorted and pushed his hand away, any momentary sense of shyness gone. "It's not like you did it alone. I was there too, bud. We both got carried away." With deft fingers, she put her hair to rights. "After being out all day, I just wanted a few minutes alone with you . . ." She paused and looked around the tiny room. "Good thing they didn't run out of menus."

Logan laughed. "Aye. Good thing." Not able to stop himself from touching her, he brushed a finger down her cheek. "I wanted the same. It's been torture, being near you all day and yet . . . not. I only meant to kiss you."

"Is that all?" she pressed, the teasing lilt to her voice making him smile.

"Well, until you started to strip for me," he admitted. "And now that I ken what kind of knickers you're hiding under there"—he quirked an eyebrow at her, pointedly staring her up and down—"supper is going to be torture for sure."

"Well, come on, then," Cassie said as she peeked around the curtain. "Let's hurry. The sooner we eat the sooner you can eat me."

She stepped into the hall and Logan followed, not quite sure he had heard her correctly, but praying to all that was holy he had.

CHAPTER 16

"YOU SURE YOU don't want to hang out downstairs with the others for a few drinks?" Cassie asked Bonnie as she followed her into their hotel room.

"Not a chance." Bonnie unzipped her boots and kicked them off.

"But it's the last night of our trip!"

"Exactly," Bonnie said, shrugging out of her jacket, "and for the first time in more than a month, I'm going to have a room all to myself."

Cassie watched as Bonnie unwound the plaid scarf around her neck. The movement reminded her of the conversation they'd had this morning, when Bonnie had been putting that same scarf on. Cassie knew exactly why her best friend wanted to spend her last evening alone . . . It was easier than spending any more time in the company of a very dashing Brit.

"The best way to resist temptation is to avoid it, hmm?" Cassie asked, and ducked when Bonnie whipped the scarf at her.

"Don't you have somewhere to be?" Bonnie groused.

Cassie laughed. "In a minute." She headed for the bedroom to gather up a few things for her "sleepover."

After she and Logan had rejoined their friends at the table, dinner had been a fun, if slightly awkward, affair. Sadie and Ana kept the conversation flowing with detailed descriptions of the spoils of war from their shopping spree. Cassie was sure everybody knew exactly what she and Logan had been off doing together, but was surprised to discover how little the knowledge embarrassed her.

No, what made her squirm in her seat, aside from the residual pulsing ache of a repressed orgasm, was the fact she had been about to have an orgasm in the first place—in the storage closet of a pub.

Ever since Cassie first met Logan, he had fulfilled one fantasy after another. But this . . . this unbridled passion, this need to have him went beyond reason, beyond logic. Despite whatever secret desires she'd held inside her, Cassie had never, ever expected to experience such feelings outside the pages of a book. It was thrilling . . . and also terrifying.

Thank God Logan had kept his wits about him long enough for her to relocate hers hiding beneath the layers of lust clouding her brain.

Which reminded Cassie. She grabbed the remains of the condom box and tucked it in to the backpack she used as her carry-on bag, along with a change of clothes and her toothbrush. The bedroom was still in shambles from this morning's frantic lingerie hunt, but she didn't care. She'd come back here tomorrow and cram all her stuff into her suitcase. There'd be plenty of time to sort through it when she got home.

There were only a few precious hours left for her to be with Logan. She glanced at the clock on the nightstand, it was almost midnight. All too soon she'd be boarding a plane away from her Scot. She picked up her bag and hurried to the parlor, a warm glow spreading through her as she recalled what he'd said to her in the elevator on the way up.

"I'll wait for you in my room, lass, but don't take too long, aye?" He'd leaned closer, whispering low and quiet in her ear so Bonnie wouldn't hear, "We don't have much time left, and I intend to be inside you for as much of it as possible. You ken?"

Oh, she kenned all right. She absolutely kenned. Cassie waved goodbye to Bonnie, who had taken up residence on the couch, a BBC miniseries on the hotel's wide flat-screen television.

"Austen?" Cassie asked.

Bonnie nodded. "*Pride and Prejudice*." She plucked a Cadbury chocolate bar from the pile on her lap.

"Did you get those from the minibar?"

"I got *this* from the minibar." Bonnie held up a tiny bottle of peppermint schnapps and downed a shot. Then she started to unwrap the candy. "I got this out of Delaney's purse."

Cassie shook her head and grinned. Austen, booze, and chocolate—her friend would be fine tonight. She blew Bonnie a kiss and headed for the door.

"Hold on," Bonnie called around a mouth full of chocolate. She pulled something off the back of the couch, and Cassie realized it was Logan's jacket, still here from last night.

She snatched the coat from Bonnie, heat infusing her cheeks. It's not like Bon knew what had taken place right where she was currently sitting. Cassie cleared her throat. "Thanks!" she said brightly to cover her embarrassment. "See you in the morning."

She hoisted her backpack on her shoulder. As she tossed

Logan's jacket over her arm, a small jewelry box tumbled out and fell to the ground. She bent forward and scooped it up.

"Everything okay?" Bonnie called from the couch.

"I don't know." Cassie set her backpack down and turned to show her friend the box.

Bonnie jackknifed into a sitting position. "That's not . . ."

"I don't know," Cassie repeated as she stared at the little box. "It can't be . . . right? That would be crazy."

"You think? You've known each other what, all of three days?"

"Four—almost five, thank you very much." Cassie moved to sit next to Bonnie. "Not everyone starts dating their future husband while still wearing braces."

"I never wore braces."

"You know what I mean." Cassie held the box out to Bonnie. "Here, open it."

"I'm not opening it! You open it." Bonnie pushed the box back toward Cassie.

"I don't think I can," Cassie said, swallowing hard.

"Oh, just give it here," Bonnie grumbled, "it's probably not even for you." She grabbed the box out of Cassie's hands and pulled the top off. "Aaaaw!"

"What? What is it?" Cassie asked, her eyes squeezed shut.

"I was wrong." Bonnie shoved the box back in Cassie's hands. "It is for you."

Cassie peeled one eye open, relaxing when she didn't see the flash of a diamond ring. Nestled in the box were two charms, silver miniature versions of London Bridge and the Eye. "They're for my bracelet!"

"Yes, yes, very sweet of him," Bonnie said, nudging Cassie off the couch. "Now get out of here and go thank the man properly before you make me miss the part where Darcy comes out of the lake."

Cassie closed the lid, a flock of joyful butterflies taking flight inside her as she pictured him picking the charms out. She wondered when he'd had the time to find these. As she tried to shove the box back inside Logan's coat, a piece of paper slipped out of the pocket. Thinking it was probably the receipt, she grabbed it and was about to tuck it away with the box when something on the paper caught her eye . . . something familiar.

Her back stiffened. She'd seen this document before. Almost five days ago, in fact. The same day she'd met Logan for the first time. Cassie unfolded the paper and scanned the document. *Mother-effer.*

The butterfly wings turned razor sharp, shredding her happiness. She wanted to do the same to the waiver, tear it to shreds and stamp on the pieces, maybe light them on fire. She tore off a corner, but as she began to rip the paper, the echoing rip across her own heart made her stop. Cassie took a shallow breath, then crumpled the paper in a ball and threw it across the room. It bounced off the wall and landed on the desk. "Sorry, Bon," Cassie said, struggling to keep her voice level as she picked up her backpack and retreated to the bedroom. "Looks like you don't get a room to yourself after all."

Before Bonnie could reply, Cassie slid the pocket door dividing the suite closed. She stood still and took several slow, deep breaths. What she wanted to do was throw herself across the bed and cry, but instead, she began to pack. With sharp, precise movements, she gathered up her mess of clothes and began to fold each item, taking more care than she usually ever did.

She was halfway through the pile when she heard the bedroom door slide open behind her. She dropped the sweater she was folding and glanced over her shoulder, equal parts relieved and disappointed to see Bonnie. For a brief second, she'd thought Logan had come to see what was taking her so long. Without a word, Cassie returned to her pile, not wanting to talk, not wanting to think.

After a moment, Bonnie entered the bedroom and began to place the folded piles of Cassie's clothes in the suitcase. They continued to work together, the silence of the room broken only by the soft murmur of Darcy and Elizabeth from the television in the suite's parlor. In no time, all of Cassie's things were neatly packed. Bonnie zipped the suitcase and rolled it across the room to stand next to hers. "Want to talk about it?" she asked, fiddling with the luggage tags on one of the handles.

Cassie sat on the edge of her bed and shook her head, her eyes filling with tears.

Bonnie joined her on the bed, wrapping her arms around Cassie in a tight hug, auburn curls tickling Cassie's wet cheeks. Cassie leaned into her friend, pressing her face into Bonnie's shoulder, absorbing the quiet strength and love Bonnie silently offered with the simple gift of her presence. After a time, Cassie looked up to see Bonnie watching her. Her friend's face was full of curiosity and concern, bright blue eyes brimming with questions.

But when Bonnie finally spoke, she asked only one thing. "What do you want first: booze or chocolate?"

Cassie groaned and rolled on to her side. Something crinkled beneath her cheek and she shifted, plucking out a candy wrapper. As she pulled herself into a mostly upright position, a few tiny bottles of alcohol tinkled to the floor. She cracked one eye, still gritty with sleep, to see Bonnie slouched across from her, face buried in the couch cushions. Cassie nudged Bonnie with her knee.

"What time is it?" Bonnie croaked.

"Time to get moving." Cassie stood and shuffled to the window. A rosy glow was barely creeping above the rooftops of tightly packed buildings lining the London horizon. Her last sunrise in Europe.

"It's barely dawn, our flight isn't until this afternoon, and I have a sugar-and-alcohol-fueled hangover." Bonnie yawned and burrowed deeper into the couch cushions. "Now, if you'll excuse me, I'm going to sleep for another few hours."

Cassie shoved the curtains open wider, letting the meager light spill across the room. "Come on, Bon. Don't you want to get home to Gabe?"

Rolling back over, Bonnie pushed the tumble of red curls out of her face and stared bleary-eyed at Cassie. "This isn't about Gabe, is it? It's about him."

At the mention of *him*, Cassie felt nauseous, the montage of minibar staples she'd downed last night deciding to launch a parade in her gut. "Never mind. Go back to sleep, Bon. I'm going to take a shower." Evading her friend's questioning gaze, Cassie escaped to the bathroom.

The room started to fill with steam as the shower heated up. Cassie swiped a hand across the mirror, clearing the mist away. *Ugh, you look like hell.* The left side of her hair was sticking straight up, as if she'd spent the night with her face pressed against the arm of a couch . . . which of course she had. She was still in her clothes from yesterday, the peasant blouse now hopelessly wrinkled, her jeans sagging at the knees.

And underneath that, she still wore the damn lingerie set.

She stripped off all her clothes and debated flushing the uber-expensive underwear down the toilet—it's not like she was going to wear it ever again—but decided against it. The last thing she needed was to get in trouble, and knowing her luck, fined for plugging the hotel's plumbing. The damn outfit had cost her enough as it was. She rolled everything together and crammed it into a ball before stepping into the shower.

The water was prickly hot. As heat eroded her hangover and the remains of her fatigue evaporated, the facts of last night settled in. Cassie grabbed the hotel shampoo and lathered her hair with quick, angry strokes. He'd lied to her. She remembered when she saw him on the dinner cruise and first realized he was in London. She'd been cautious then, wary. But he'd crept past her defenses . . . not that she'd made it very difficult for him.

Logan fucking Reid had followed her here from Scotland, carrying that damn waiver with him. All this time, every minute he'd been with her, had been part of his plan. He was worse than Ana's loony Lorenzo. At least Lorenzo had chased after them because he wanted to marry Ana. The only reason Logan had chased her down was because he wanted her fucking signature.

Cassie leaned her forehead against the tile. No. If she was honest with herself, that wasn't all he wanted. He'd wanted her too, as badly as she wanted him. If all he'd wanted was to get her to say yes to airing his stupid prank video, he could have asked her that night on the boat. But he didn't. Instead, he'd talked to her, laughed with her, spent time with her . . . made love to her.

How could he do that? She lifted her face to the spray, letting the pounding stream work out the knots of tension. How could he be with her the way he had these last few days, all the while hiding an ulterior motive? Cassie finished rinsing her hair and shut off the water. She dried off briskly, searching her memories of her time with Logan for any signs she may have missed.

The problem was, she told herself as she brushed her teeth hard enough to scrape enamel, she'd been so happy to see Logan again, so eager to continue her foreign fling, that she'd been oblivious to everything else. Or at least ignored the warning bells.

And they had been ringing. Loud and clear, like her head was now, pain pounding between her ears. A tiny but persistent troll banging away inside her skull. *I need coffee*. Not wanting to wake Bonnie again, and in need of something better than the sad excuse for caffeine that was the in-room coffee, Cassie decided to head downstairs. As she slipped on her shoes, her gaze landed on the jacket again and an idea struck her.

The dark-haired girl at the front desk smiled pleasantly when Cassie strode up. "Morning, miss. May I help you?"

"Yes"—she glanced at the girl's nametag—"Miss Beth Swanson, you may." Cassie slapped Logan's jacket on the counter. "This belongs to a guest at the hotel, can I leave it here for him?"

"Um," Beth hesitated.

"Logan Reid," Cassie added.

"Oh, yes!" The girl's face brightened. "You're his friend's sister, then?"

"Pardon?" The troll started hammering inside her head again. Maybe she should have got the coffee first.

"Aren't you Miss Crow?"

"Yes," Cassie said slowly.

"Your brother's friends . . ." Beth beamed at her. "Theo, er . . . Mr. Wharton and Mr. Reid. When they checked in Wednesday afternoon, they mentioned wanting to make sure they looked in on you."

Cassie smiled weakly. She had no clue whose brother Beth was referring to, but that wasn't the part her caffeine-starved brain was struggling to make sense of. Logan and Theo had met up with them on the river cruise Wednesday evening. "You mean Wednesday *night*, right?"

"Oh, no." Beth shook her head. "My shift ends by afternoon tea. I checked them in myself."

"Right." *That lying asshole.* She clenched her fists, digging her nails into Logan's jacket.

Beth leaned across the counter and offered Cassie a commiserating sigh. "I have two big brothers, and they're both overprotective pains in the bum."

"You know . . ." Cassie pasted a smile on her face. "I think I'll drop this off myself."

"As you like." Beth's rosy complexion grew even pinker. "Could you . . . would you mind saying hello to Theo for me?"

"No problem." In fact, Cassie decided as she took the elevator back up to her floor, she'd go see Mr. Might-Be-A-Duke right now. Heart pounding, Cassie gathered Logan's jacket in her arms. She didn't want to talk or see the effing Scot . . . but maybe she could get some answers from his British buddy. *"Theo is over in 757, I'm 762."*

A minute later, she was knocking on the door of Theo's suite. Cassie glanced down the hall to Logan's room and fought the urge to go bang on his door instead. If things had gone as planned, right now she'd be in his room, still in his bed.

Instead, it was almost nine o'clock in the morning, and Logan hadn't even tried to reach her. She'd checked her phone. No missed calls, no new texts. What did he think when she didn't show last night? That the jig was up? The fact he hadn't come to find her was further admission of his guilt. She stifled a frustrated yawn. She still hadn't managed to get a cup of coffee yet.

"Cassie?" Theo asked when he opened the door, looking

confused but very handsome and extra Prince Eric-ish in a white fisherman's sweater and dark jeans.

"Good. You're awake. Can I come in?" She pushed past him before he could reply.

With his typical impeccable manners, he didn't protest the intrusion. Closing the door behind her, he asked, "Can I help you with something?"

"What do you know about this?" Cassie pulled the wadded up contract out of one of the pockets. She'd stuffed that and the jewelry box back inside the jacket before she'd gone downstairs.

"It's rubbish?" Theo suggested, then narrowed his eyes at the crumpled paper. "Oh." Running a hand through his thick, dark hair, he gestured toward the couch. "Why don't you have a seat?"

Cassie sat, fidgeting with a torn edge of paper.

"He's not a bad chap, you know." Theo joined her on the couch, his voice gentle.

Cassie glanced over at him. "I know he's a liar."

"What makes you say that?" Theo's voice was still gentle, but she sensed a note of challenge.

"Well, for starters, he lied about when you checked in to this hotel." She watched Theo's face, looking for a reaction. "Beth says hello, by the way."

"Ah." He had the decency to look embarrassed.

Cassie pressed on. "He also told me you were a duke."

Theo's hands tightened at his sides, but he didn't respond. He also didn't look embarrassed anymore . . . if anything, he looked ticked off.

Cold certainty rolled through Cassie. She stared at his profile . . . his very aristocratic profile. "He wasn't lying about that, was he?"

A muscle leapt in Theo's jaw. "You can stop staring now." His voice was clipped, all trace of gentleness gone.

Cassie jerked back. "Sorry, I didn't mean—"

"Bloody bastard. He shouldn't have told you."

"It's not his fault," Cassie said, surprising herself by rising to Logan's defense. "He was sauced. And I kept calling you Prince Eric. And he said you're not a prince, you're a duke, but I shouldn't say anything . . ."

"Did you?"

"Did I what?"

"Say anything." Theo nodded in the direction of the suite she shared with Bonnie. "To your friends, perhaps?"

Cassie shook her head. "No. To be honest, I'd pretty much forgotten all about it until now. It was the night of the river cruise. I was tipsy too, and had, er, other things on my mind." Her cheeks heated as she recalled the kisses she and Logan had shared on the boat, in the hotel hallway, against the door to her room . . .

"I wager you did." Theo chuckled, amusement lightening his tone. His flash of anger was gone as quickly as it had come.

Cassie stared down at the contract. Unlike Theo, she was still angry. Only now she realized she was angry at herself too, possibly more than she was at Logan. It was her own damn fault.

When he'd shown up that night on the boat, she'd let her attraction to him and the magic of that perfect night convince her to ignore reality, pretend, play make believe. She'd wanted to visit Neverland . . . and so she had.

Her phone vibrated. On reflex, Cassie almost pressed the answer button before she remembered to check to see who it was.

Theo glanced over. "Is it him?" he asked, voicing her thoughts.

She shook her head. "It's Bonnie." Relief and regret roiled in her gut. "Hey, Bon."

"Cassie? Thank God. I woke up and you were gone. Where are you?"

"I'm um . . ." She cleared her throat. "I'm in Theo's room."

"Oh." There was a moment of silence as Bonnie processed this information. "Okay. I thought maybe you'd run away or something."

"Why would I do that?" Cassie paused, thinking. "You know . . . that's a great idea. Hold on, Bon, I'll be right there."

Fifteen minutes later, Bonnie joined Cassie outside the hotel and shoved a banana into Cassie's hand.

"What's this for?" Cassie protested.

"Breakfast."

"Thanks, Mom. A coffee would have been better."

"Where's your boarding pass?" Bonnie asked, unperturbed.

"On my phone."

"You sure you don't want to print it?"

"I'm sure." Cassie stuffed the banana in her pack and shouldered it. "I'll get through security and wait for you guys in the lounge."

Bonnie nodded. "I'll let the other girls know and make sure they're ready to go. You know how long Sadie takes."

"Right. And remember, if you see *him*—" Cassie hesitated.

"I'll handle it," Bonnie said, eyes flashing.

If Cassie didn't know better, she'd say Bonnie was kind of enjoying this. But Cassie did know better—and Bonnie *was totally* enjoying this. Her friend wasn't happy about the fact Cassie was hurt and upset and looking to escape. It was more that Bonnie was excited about the act of escape itself. Like her fictional doppelgänger, Anne Shirley, Bonnie had always had a flair for the dramatic. And as Bonnie's best friend, Cassie—like her own fictional doppelgänger, Diana Barry—had ridden sidecar on more than one madcap adventure, the passenger to whatever escapade Bonnie dreamt up next.

Only today it looked like she would be riding passenger next to Theo. She had intended to call a cab to take her to the airport, but Theo insisted on driving her himself. Cassie wondered if it was British manners or a guilty conscience that prompted Theo's offer, but decided she didn't care. A free ride was a free ride.

A vintage roadster rolled to a stop in front of them. Theo stepped out and Bonnie gasped. "Is this yours?"

"No, I lifted it from James Bond," he shot back, straight-faced.

The car did look like something straight out of a 007 film. Cassie snickered and rolled her suitcase over to Theo. "Thanks again for doing this."

He heaved her suitcase into the trunk. "Anything for a damsel in distress."

Was that what she was? Cassie didn't think so. Pissed, yes—distressed, no. She also didn't think she was the damsel Theo was interested in helping.

Cassie hugged her friend close. "Thanks, Bon. You're the best."

"Tell me about it." Bonnie squeezed Cassie back, giving her a quick kiss on the cheek before pushing her toward the car.

Theo, who stood holding the door for Cassie, quirked a dimpled grin at Bonnie. "Got one of those for me?"

To everyone's surprise, probably none more than Bonnie's, Bonnie rushed forward and went up on tiptoe, brushing her lips, soft and swift, against Theo's jaw. Short as she was, that was all she could reach. "Thank you," she said, stepping back as quickly as she had stepped forward.

"Anytime, love," Theo said, blue eyes bright with sincerity and a bit of something more.

Hmm. Cassie eyed Theo as he shut her door and went around to the driver's side. She rolled down her window—literally *rolled*, the car had those old-fashioned crank handles—and gave her friend a knowing look as she waved goodbye.

Bonnie ignored the look and waved back, blowing kisses and generally acting ridiculous. After all, they were going to see each other again at the airport in a few hours. Still, Cassie wouldn't have it any other way. With a surge of love for her friend, she blew a few kisses back as the car pulled away from the curb.

Cassie took a deep breath. The trip, her glorious once-in a lifetime vacation, was coming to an end . . . and not at all like she had expected.

They were barely outside London's city limits when the first call from Logan fucking Reid came through. Cassie ignored it. She also ignored LFR's second, third, and fourth calls. Eventually, she turned her phone off, not wanting to risk the temptation to answer it, to explain why she left . . . to say goodbye.

As they approached Heathrow, a wild guitar riff blasted through the silence of the car and Cassie jumped. "Jesus!"

"Sorry," Theo said, keeping one hand on the wheel as he pulled his phone out of his jeans. "It's Logan."

"Don't answer it!" She grabbed Theo's phone, wincing as the ear-piercing sounds continued for a few more seconds. "What the hell kind of ringtone is that?" A second later, another call came through—Logan again—his name popping up on the screen. "Think he knows you're helping me?" She raised her voice over the screech of a guitar.

Theo switched lanes, waiting to answer until the phone

stopped wailing. "If not now, I wager he'll find out soon enough."

"Will he be mad that you did?"

"Probably." Theo shrugged. "But he'll get over it."

Cassie dropped the now blessedly silent phone in her lap and rubbed her pounding temples. "Guns N' Roses fan, huh?"

"I'm impressed," Theo said.

"I'm surprised." Cassie nudged him. "And please, everybody knows 'Welcome to the Jungle.'"

"Then why are you surprised?" They passed a sign announcing the Heathrow exit, and Theo switched to the far lane.

"I mean, come on," she said, "'Paradise City' would have been a better choice."

Theo laughed. As he entered Heathrow's circle of traffic, he began to sing.

The airline terminals ticked by, and Cassie mused on the strangeness of life. When she'd set out on this trip almost two months ago, she'd never predicted it would end with her running away from a sexy Scot, riding shotgun to a duke, listening to him mimic Axl Rose's powerful whine in a crisp English accent.

Take me home, indeed.

Her terminal approached, and with a start, Cassie realized this was it. Panic set in as she wrestled with a sudden flurry of emotions.

Theo slipped the car into an open spot. "I'll get your luggage." A moment later, he opened her door and offered her his hand. "You ready?"

Cassie took a shuddering breath. No. No, she was not ready.

The sharp, annoyed bleat of horns started to sound around them. Theo cleared his throat. Cassie thought she heard him tell someone to "piss off" but couldn't believe the rude remark had come from polite, princely Theo. No, not prince, *duke*, she corrected herself, grabbing her backpack and placing it on top of her suitcase.

"Do you want me to park and walk you in?" Theo asked.

Cassie shook her head. "You've already done so much. I can't ask you to do more." She jumped out of the car.

"Is there anything you *can* ask me to do?" Another horn. He jerked a hand out and yelled, "Move on, you bloody tosser!"

"You know? There is," Cassie said, struck by a sudden impulse. She pulled the crumpled contract from the back pocket of her jeans and smoothed the paper out. She'd left the jacket and jewelry box with Bonnie, but perhaps she should leave this behind too.

Yes. It would be best to leave it all behind. Leave *him* behind.

"Do you have a pen?"

CHAPTER 17

LOGAN LIFTED HIS head from the couch and raised an arm to block the laser beam of sunlight threatening to burn his retinas. *What the hell time was it?* Well past dawn if the bright ball of fire outside his hotel window was any indication. He rolled his head to the side and squinted at the clock on the desk.

That couldn't be right.

He sat up and dug his phone out of the back pocket of his jeans. Tapping it awake, he swore at the number that blinked back at him. How was it five fecking minutes past nine in the morning?

Christ, what had happened to Cassie?

Last night, after he'd dropped the lass off at her room to pick up a few things, Logan had hurried down the hall and tidied up both himself and his suite a bit. Then he put on some music, purloined a wee bottle of whisky from the minibar, and settled down on the couch, figuring she'd be along any minute. He'd sipped the whisky and relaxed, fantasizing about all the things he'd do to her once she arrived. At some point, he must have nodded off. Christ knew it had been a long day and he hadn't had much sleep recently.

He grinned, recalling what he'd been doing instead of sleeping these last few nights, but the grin quickly faded . . . He should have been up doing more of the same last night. Again, he wondered what had happened to Cassie. Had she been waiting for him? Standing in the hall outside his door, knocking, while he'd slept through it like an idiot?

Logan dropped his head into his hands and rubbed his temples. Then grabbed his phone again and checked his messages. Three texts from Janet, a few from some mates, but nothing from Cassie. No missed calls either. If he'd been passed out and hadn't answered his door last night, she would have tried calling him . . . right?

A tremor of uncertainty shook him, and he jumped to his feet. Not bothering with shoes, he grabbed his key card and rushed out of the room. A moment later he was pounding on Cassie's door. Nothing. He dialed her number and let it ring until voicemail picked up. He clicked off and called again, getting voicemail once more. Pinpricks of foreboding tripped up his spine.

When Cassie's voicemail clicked on for the third time, Logan left her a message. "Cassie? It's Logan. Where did you go last night? I'm afraid I fell asleep waiting for you." He tried to laugh, to keep his tone light, but his throat was too tight. He swallowed. "I'm at your door now, but no one's answering. Your flight's today, aye? I'd hate to miss a chance to see you before you go." Logan turned and slid down the wall, clutching the phone to his ear. "Please, lass," he begged, not caring how desperate he sounded, "let me know you're all right."

He ended the call and shoved a hand through his hair.

"She's fine," he whispered to himself. Deep down, he wasn't truly worried anything had happened to her. No, he was fairly certain he knew exactly what had kept Cassie from coming to his room last night.

Somehow, someway, she had found out, either about the fact he'd lied to her as to when he'd checked into the hotel (though he still maintained he hadn't lied exactly, he just hadn't corrected her assumptions) or worse, she knew about the contract.

Logan jumped to his feet. *The contract.* The bloody fucking contract.

He raced back to his room and tore through his things. But in his gut, he knew. He could see his jacket in his mind's eye, still feel that damn piece of paper burning him through the pocket. With painful clarity, he recalled standing in her hotel room, watching her undress. He remembered the slow, sexy smile she'd given him as she'd said, "Your turn."

He'd tossed the jacket on the sofa and hadn't spared another thought for either his coat or the contract as he'd proceeded to do all kinds of wonderfully wicked things to her on that same damn piece of furniture. *Shit.*

Stupid, stupid, stupid. For the second time in less than twenty-four hours, Logan found himself cursing his brain for letting his dick take over.

He should have told Cassie the truth that first night on the boat. And then what? She'd throw the contract overboard and tell him to never see her again? No. Logan wouldn't trade these last few days he'd spent with her for anything. Not even for a guaranteed shot at that telly deal.

The realization shook him. When had this thing between them become something more?

Had Cassie felt what they had was more too? If she had, he'd fucked it up royally now.

Logan glanced at the clock again. It was almost ten. He racked his brain, trying to remember what she'd told him about her plan for today. He knew her flight was in the afternoon and that a hired car had been arranged to take them to Heathrow. *Bingo.*

Logan tugged on his trainers and raced out into the hall again. As he waited for the lift, he dialed Theo. He would have stopped and knocked on his mate's door, but he wanted to get to the lobby as fast as possible. Theo's line cut to voicemail, and Logan ground his teeth. Why wasn't anyone answering any of his fecking calls this morning? He jammed his phone in his pocket and punched the button for the lobby.

The doors slid open, and Logan cut through the foyer. The swish of a long, strawberry-blond ponytail caught his attention, and he turned, catching sight of Delaney exiting the breakfast room with a plate stacked high with scones.

"Hey!" he called, hurrying toward her as she made her way to the hotel's entrance.

She glanced behind her, almost dropping the plate when she saw him. Logan reached her side in time to catch a scone that teetered and fell off the top of the pile.

"If I let you keep that, will you go away and leave me alone?" Delaney asked.

"Not a chance," Logan said, making short work of the pilfered pastry as he kept in step with her, following her through the revolving door and out of the hotel. Near-side the curb stood Cassie's other friends, all of them talking over each other, attempting to direct a livery driver while he packed their many suitcases into the boot of a limousine.

But no Cassie.

Bonnie glanced up. As soon as she saw him, her Cupid's

bow mouth tightened into a hard, stubborn line. She shifted her gaze to Delaney. "Nice work. You just had to go back for seconds, didn't you?"

Delaney flushed with guilt. "When will I have another chance to have an English scone in England?" she asked, holding the plate out as a peace offering. "Want one?"

Logan was surprised the pile of dough didn't burn to a crisp, singed by the icy fire in Bonnie's blue eyes. He came to the rescue, taking the plate and smiling wide. "Aye, thank you."

The lass didn't seem to appreciate his heroic gesture. "I wasn't talking to you." Delaney tugged the plate back and moved to a bench near the valet stand, where she sat and proceeded to power through the stack of scones.

He shook his head, once again impressed at the sheer amount of food the tall, thin girl could devour. He turned back to Bonnie, who was arguing with Sadie about the number of suitcases still lined up behind the boot.

"There is no way all of these are going to fit!" The red-head's curls bobbed back and forth. "I swear, Sadie, you've doubled your luggage since we started this trip."

"If I may make a suggestion," Logan said as he approached the curb.

Bonnie stopped him with another icy glare. "I'm not talking to you."

He was sensing a theme here. "Where's Cassie?"

"She's not talking to you either."

Aye, definitely a theme. The scone he'd hastily scarfed started to crawl back up his throat. So far, he'd held out hope Cassie had not answered her phone because she'd been busy packing and getting ready to fly home. Or, if the lass was angry with him, it was due to the fact he'd fallen asleep and missed their tryst. "Is she fashed with me then?"

"If by 'fashed' you mean mad enough to never want to

see your face again, then yes," Bonnie said, stepping off
the curb to join Ana, who was busy rearranging the bags
that had already been packed.

Sadie sighed. "Sorry, guys, I thought there'd be plenty
of room since Cassie already went on ahead—"

"What's that?" Logan's head snapped in the wee
blonde's direction.

Sadie shrugged her pixie-like shoulders. "Ah, nothing,"
she chirped, eyes darting to Bonnie.

Logan met Bonnie's gaze, and in that moment he understood.

Cassie was gone.

He felt numb, unable to sense the ground beneath him
or hear the rush of morning traffic in the street beyond the
hotel square. The harsh slam of a car door brought him
back to the moment, and he jerked, looking up to see Bonnie walking toward him.

"Delaney!" she called. "We're leaving."

Delaney rose, brushing the crumbs from her lap, and
handed the lads at the valet stand her plate, generously offering them the last two crumpled scones. As she passed
him on the way to the car, she patted Logan on the back.
"Well, Scottie the Hottie, it was nice knowing ya."

Despite himself, Logan laughed. "Same to you." He
turned to give the tall, sassy lass a hug, whispering a bit
of Gaelic in her ear.

"Do I want to know what you just said?" she asked,
pulling back and giving him a peck on the cheek.

"Probably not." Logan waved her off, the cold weight
of Bonnie's blue gaze pressing down on him as he waved
farewell to Ana and Sadie as well. Once the other women
were settled in the limousine, he turned to Bonnie. Before
he could ask her about Cassie, she stepped closer and
poked him in the chest.

"Ow!" Logan rubbed his smarting skin; the little vixen was fierce. "What was that for?"

Bonnie waved her finger in his face. "I don't know what you did to hurt Cassie, but I know you did something." She moved to poke him again, and he jumped back, holding her wrist. Bonnie shook herself free and walked away from him. She reached into the car, pulled something out, and marched back toward him.

Logan stood frozen at the curb. She was carrying his jacket.

"I was going to leave this at the front desk, but since you're here—" Bonnie whipped the coat at him, venom in her voice and her aim.

Ducking to avoid getting smacked in the face, Logan caught the jacket. Immediately, he checked the inside pocket, guts churning, feeling for the contract. Nothing. He checked the other pockets, hoping to find a note from her tucked into one of them, but she'd left without a word.

After everything they'd shared the past few days, he was more than a little hurt.

He recalled the jewelry box with the charms that he'd been planning to give her as a going away present. Something to remember him by. The box was gone too. "She didn't happen to leave anything else for me?" he asked, hoping she'd kept the charms. He wanted her to have them.

Bonnie reached into her purse and pulled out a familiar-looking jewelry box. "Something like this?" She slapped the box into his open palm.

Logan shook his head, wordless. That Cassie hadn't wanted to keep the charms stung more than he was willing to think about right now.

Bonnie turned away and returned to the car. "Oh, and there is one more thing." She paused and faced him again.

His breath caught as hope and fear warred in his gut. "Aye?"

"Please be sure to thank Theo for me."

"Thank Theo?" Logan repeated dumbly. "For what?"

"For driving Cassie to the airport. She was going to take a cab, but he insisted on taking her. Unlike some guys . . ." she paused, glaring at Logan as she entered the limo, ". . . your friend Mr. Wharton is a gentleman."

The driver closed the passenger door after Bonnie and, with an apologetic tip of his hat toward Logan, took his place behind the wheel. "Yes," Logan silently agreed, mouth tight as he watched the limousine pull away and maneuver into the flow of traffic, "such a gentleman."

A gentleman who was going to get his arse kicked.

Logan stormed down the hall back to his hotel room. As he passed Theo's door, he punched it. He knew the blighter wasn't there, but still, it felt good to hit something. By noon he was at the train station. His temper hadn't cooled, had instead remained at a steady simmer, fury burning just under his skin, ready to boil over at a moment's notice.

During the past few hours he'd considered and dismissed a slew of scenarios. He could hire a cab and race to Heathrow, run through the throngs of travelers, and try to track Cassie down like some lovesick dobber from the cinema. And likely end up tossed in the clink for his efforts. Or he could buy a ticket on the next flight to Cassie's town.

Except, Logan realized with a start, he didn't know where she lived.

How could that be? How could he have shared so much with Cassie these past few days and not even know where she was from? He racked his brain, searching for clues, replaying conversations, analyzing them for anything that might help. Most of his memories from that night centered on Cassie's mouth, specifically those moments when it was on his.

He decided to head home. He sent his sister a quick text letting her know he'd be back in Edinburgh tonight, but didn't elaborate, in no hurry to admit defeat and face Janet's wrath. When his phone buzzed, he ignored it, assuming it was Nettie calling to demand more details. When it buzzed again, he yanked it out his pocket, ready to turn the blasted thing off.

It was Theo.

The pot boiled over, blood sizzling in his veins. "Hello, traitor," Logan snarled into the phone.

An elderly gent on the bench opposite lowered his newspaper and eyed Logan with concern. Logan smiled at him, a wolf's smile, all teeth. The man abruptly folded his paper over his arm and stood. Wise choice. As Logan watched the man relocate to a seat several benches away, he considered all the things he wanted to say to his *best* mate. In the end what came out was one question. A single word. "Why?"

"She was going to leave regardless." Theo's voice was guarded. "I thought it best she didn't go alone."

Had she been so upset then? So mad that she'd wanted to get away from him as fast as possible? Couldn't even wait the few blasted hours until her ride to the airport arrived? Couldn't say goodbye? "And you had to be the one to go with her, aye?"

"Bonnie thought it was a good idea."

Despite himself, Logan laughed. "Oh, Theo," he groaned, shaking his head, his anger waning. "You poor sot—couldn't resist the chance to play hero, could you?"

"It was the right thing to do," Theo countered.

Logan detected the note of defensiveness in his mate's voice and pressed his advantage. "No, the right thing to do would have been to stand by your friend. Tell him that the girl of his dreams and key to his future was planning to run away, not bloody help her escape."

Theo ignored the accusation. "I came back to the hotel looking for you. Where did you take off to?"

"King's Cross."

Theo sighed. "What time's your train?"

"Soon."

"Wait for me," Theo ordered.

"Why the fuck should I do that?"

"Get stuffed. I'll be there in ten."

"That eager for a pounding, are you?" Logan glanced at the departure board. His train would be boarding in fifteen minutes, departing in twenty. What the feck did it matter if he heard the blighter out? "Fine. I'll be here. Platform six."

A dozen minutes later Logan spotted Theo's perfectly coiffed dark head amid the crowd swarming toward the platform. Logan dropped his duffle bag to the ground and straightened, wrapping a hand around the post he'd been leaning on.

Theo approached, eyes wary. "Hey."

"Hey, yourself." Logan tightened his grip on the post, fingers digging into the wood as he imagined plowing his fist into the turncoat's face.

Theo must have read the violence in Logan's stance for he held back a few paces. "I didn't come here to start a fight."

"Oh, the fight's already on, mate." Logan shifted, trying to release the sharp knot of tension trapped between his shoulder blades. A speaker crackled overhead, announcing that passengers may begin boarding. "If you've got something to say, you better say it quick."

"You shouldn't be mad at her."

"Don't tell me what I should and shouldn't be," Logan snapped. There was no question over who the "her" was.

"Fair enough." Theo reached into his pocket and pulled out a wad of paper. "Here."

"What's that?"

"You know what this is." Theo held the crumpled mess out to him.

Logan stiffened, his heart pounding. He dropped his hand from the post but didn't reach out to take the paper. "Did she give this to you?"

Theo nodded. "She asked me to make sure you got this, said you'd earned it. Said she got what she wanted, so it was only fair you got the same."

Logan grabbed the paper from Theo's hand. What the hell did the lass mean by that? What had Cassie wanted? His mind cartwheeled backward and forward. "Did she say anything else?"

When Theo hesitated, Logan surged forward. "You have to tell me."

"Only . . ." Theo tensed, and Logan knew whatever his mate was about to say next, he wouldn't like it, ". . . that you were a liar. She knew you'd lied about when we checked in to the hotel. And thought you'd lied about a few other things as well."

"Like what?"

Theo glanced around the nearly empty platform. "The fact your best friend is a duke, for one."

"That was my fault." Logan winced. "It slipped out."

"You don't say," Theo grumbled. "Well, I cleared her

up on that point, at least. If your ship's going down, only fair to have it sink under the weight of your own sins."

"Don't think that saves you from an ass-kicking."

"I'm not sorry, Lo. I did what I thought was best."

The speaker blared, announcing final boarding time. "Aye, I know. You're a git," he said, and punched Theo in the arm, "but you're a good friend too, Theo. And a better man than me."

"Get on with you. You're a better man than you give yourself credit for." Theo waved Logan off. "Send Janet my love."

Logan cringed at the mention of his sister, whom he still hadn't called back. "Och, speaking of ass-kickings." He shouldered his bag and saluted Theo, who was chuckling now, before joining the few remaining stragglers scurrying toward the train.

It wasn't until the train had pulled out of the station and was chugging north at a steady clip that Logan finally worked up the courage to smooth the mangled paper and look at the form.

She'd signed it

The lass had fecking signed it after all.

CHAPTER 18

IT WAS CLOSING in on ten o' clock at night when Logan finally made his way across the square and let himself into the Leith studio flat. Janet was curled on the sofa, face lit by the glow of her laptop, a bowl of crisps at her side.

Logan dropped his duffle bag at the door and collapsed next to her.

She leaned over and rumpled his hair. "Welcome back." She pressed a quick peck to his forehead before returning to her computer.

Logan grabbed the bowl of crisps and dug in. "Theo sends his love," he mumbled around a mouthful.

"That's sweet," Janet said, not looking up from her screen. She slapped Logan's hand. "Stop eating all my crisps."

"Too late." He handed his sister the empty bowl, licking salt from his fingers.

She gave him a look of disgust and set her laptop aside. "Glutton," she said, crossing to the kitchenette and depositing the bowl in the sink.

"Can you get me a beer while you're up?" Logan asked,

leaning back against the cushions and shooting his sister a coy smile.

"Careful I don't throw it at your head," she warned, but the threat lacked heat.

He heard the pop of two caps and a moment later Janet returned, handing him a short-necked bottle of Newcastle. Logan took a deep pull on his beer as she settled back down next to him.

"How was your trip?"

"Fine." Logan brushed crumbs off his lap.

"Fine? You take off for London with barely a warning, don't answer a single one of my phone calls or texts—save to tell me you arrived in one piece, thank you very much— and all you can say is *fine*?"

He took another drink, hiding a grin as his sister's face puckered in frustration. The interrogation had begun. It was old hat between them. The summer after Da died, Logan would often come home late, well past curfew, and Nettie would demand to know where he'd been, what he'd been doing. Logan always kept his answers brief, avoiding detail whenever possible. It was a prat move, since she was only looking out for him, but he'd been barely seventeen at the time, angry at the world and in no mood to be nice to his nosey parker of a sister.

"Did you find our girl?"

"I did." Logan tipped the bottle back and chugged the rest. He stood and headed for the kitchen. "You want another?" he asked as he popped the top on his second beer.

"What I want," Janet said, eyeing him over the rim of her still full bottle, "is to know what the hell happened in London. Second Studios has called twice since you left."

Logan paused, the fresh beer halfway to his mouth. "What did you tell them?"

Janet shook her head. "Not a chance. You first. You found the girl. Did she sign the waiver?"

The paper Theo had handed him at the station was in Logan's back pocket. He resisted the urge to pull it out and instead planted himself on the arm of the sofa. Countless times over the long train ride home, Logan had retrieved the mangled form and stared at Cassie's signature, wondering what the hell the lass had meant. Wondering what he was going to do next.

A few days ago, the answer would have been obvious. But now, he wasn't sure. Cassie had given her permission, but did that give him the right? At the castle, she had been dead set against the idea of having her video posted on *Shenanigans*. And yet, in the end, she'd signed the waiver. Why? He frowned. He was missing something, and he didn't like it. He needed to talk to her, damn it.

"Well?" Janet set her bottle down and crossed her arms.

"Aye, she signed it," Logan finally said.

Janet dropped her arms and relaxed against the sofa cushions. "Perfect." She pulled her laptop close and began typing.

"I'm not sure we should post the video . . . not yet, I mean." Logan rubbed the back of his neck. Everything felt stiff, his body tight and tired from long hours on the train, adding to the tension that hadn't left him since he awoke this morning and found Cassie gone. Christ, had that only been this morning? It felt like a lifetime ago.

"Are you daft?" Janet continued typing. "Second Studios is chomping at the bit. They want to set up a meeting with you. In person. That's why they've been calling." She looked up from the screen. "We *need* that video. Scots, kilts, time travel, it's all super-hot right now with the female eighteen-to-forty-nine demographic." His sister waggled her eyebrows. "I told you, the ladies are going to eat that shit up. If you weren't my brother, I'd even think it was hot."

Logan ran a hand over his face. Janet was right, he knew she was, but it still felt wrong. He needed to think. "I said she signed the waiver, but I'm not entirely sure it's legal."

"What the hell does that mean?" Janet stared at him.

Logan stood and pulled the ripped and crumpled waiver from his pocket. "I'm not sure this would stand up, should she decide to challenge it."

Janet squinted at the line of ink scribbled on the bottom of one scrap. "That's her signature?"

"Aye."

"Then what's the problem? Did she change her mind after she signed it and try to rip it up?"

"No. As I understand it, she crumpled it up *before* she signed it."

"Well, what happened? Did you force her to sign it? Threaten her life?"

Logan stared at his sister, not sure if she was serious. "A fine opinion you have of your brother."

"Piss off." Janet inspected the mess. "If she signed it, we're good. A pound note spends the same no matter how grotty it looks."

"True." Logan hesitated.

"What is it?" Janet set the papers aside and studied him. "There's something you're not telling me."

His sister knew him too well—aside from suggesting he was capable of coercing a girl into signing something against her will. Logan moved to the kitchen and set his second empty beer bottle next to the first. He debated getting a third. How to tell his sister what he couldn't fully explain to himself?

"*Logan Cameron Reid*," she prodded, using his full name and sounding exactly like Mam.

Logan bit the inside of his cheek. He decided to forgo the beer and instead rummaged in the freezer, pulling out a tub of ice cream. He nicked two spoons from the drawer and joined his sister on the sofa.

She took a spoon, parrying his out of the way and scoring the first scoop for herself. "Talk," she ordered.

Icy crystals clung to the container, stinging his palm. He rubbed his thumb across the side, melting the frost. "Remember how mad the lass had been about the video? How she was dead set against letting us post it?"

Janet took another spoonful of ice cream. "Mm-hmm. Glad to see your charm hasn't lost any of its persuasive power."

"I'm not so sure about that." Logan scraped his spoon across the surface of the ice cream, working at a piece of chocolate. "It's a long story, but before we move forward with the video, I'd like to talk to Cassie first."

"Then call her." Janet waved her spoon in the air.

The bit of frozen chocolate came loose and Logan scooped it up, letting it melt on his tongue. The taste brought him back to the morning before, in the car on the way to Stratford, eating a piece of the giant chocolate bar Cassie's friend had shared. Did everything have to remind him of her? Something deep in his chest shifted—a heaviness that wasn't heavy at all.

"I'm not sure what time her flight gets in," he said and dug his spoon into the carton again, seeking more chocolate. "I'm not even sure what time zone she is in."

Janet paused, spoon hovering at her lips. "Wait. You don't know where she lives?"

He shook his head and poked harder at the ice cream.

"Her name is Cassie, right? Cassie Cardinal?" Janet dropped her spoon and turned her attention to her laptop.

"Cassie Crow." Logan dug out another chunk of chocolate.

"Cassie Crow, right," Janet muttered, her fingers flying over the keys. Seconds later, she whooped in triumph.

"What?" Logan tightened his grip on the ice cream. Janet rarely smiled, and when she did, it usually meant trouble, and usually for him. Right now her face was wreathed in a Cheshire Cat grin of epic proportions.

"Have I told you how fond I am of image search?" Janet tilted her laptop toward Logan. A picture of Cassie's face smiled back at him.

He squinted at the screen, trying to identify the city skyline behind her. After a moment, he recognized the bright round circle of light on the horizon, and everything snapped into place. The London Eye had reminded her friend of home—like the Ferris wheel at Chicago's Navy Pier.

Chicago. Where Second Studios was located. A shiver passed through Logan, a prickling of anticipation or apprehension—or both. Either way, the coincidence was unnerving.

Oblivious to his discomfort, Janet turned the laptop back her way and started typing again. "That's her, isn't it?"

"Aye, that's definitely her," Logan said.

"Oh, this is too perfect." Nettie tugged the tub out his hands.

Appetite gone, Logan gave up the ice cream without a fight. "What's perfect?"

"You want to talk to Cassie. Second Studios wants to talk to you. Both are in Chicago."

Well, hell. "Wanna come with me?" Logan asked, regaining his composure.

"Nah, this is your party. They want to see the face of *Shenanigans*, not the brains." Janet smirked. "Besides, one of us needs to hold down the fort. Check on Mam and such."

A surge of guilt cut Logan off at the knees. In his typical selfish fashion, in all his plotting and scheming to land the telly deal stateside, he hadn't spared a moment's thought for what they'd do about Mam if the plan was successful.

"Wipe that look off yer face."

"What look?"

"The look that says, 'I'm a horrible son and deserve to be drawn and quartered.'" Janet shook her head. "Mam's going to be so proud of you."

"Aye, sure," Logan agreed reluctantly. "But what about Da?"

Nettie's face softened. "He'd be proud too, Lo. You must know that."

Logan didn't know any such thing. He desperately wanted to believe his sister, but the self-doubt was too strong. The familiar fear and vulnerability eating away at him, leaving a hole he couldn't seem to fill. He hated it.

As if sensing his discomfort, Nettie's rare moment of sweetness passed. "Stop stewing and go pack, ye fouter." She pushed him off the couch, back to her usual tart self. "I've got an important meeting to arrange."

CHAPTER 19

"HEY, MOM." CASSIE shifted the phone to her other ear and opened her closet.

"Cassie! You're home!"

"Yep. My flight got in last night." She filed through the row of hangers, determined to look as professional as possible for her meeting tomorrow.

"Oh my goodness, tell me everything. What was your favorite part?"

Getting it on with a sexy Scot? Cassie cleared her throat. "It was all great, really. So much fun. Lots of memories."

"I'm glad, dear. I know how long you've been planning that trip. Did Bonnie enjoy herself too?"

"Oh yeah. Loved it." Cassie pulled out a couple of outfits and tossed them on her bed. "But she's glad to be home with Gabe."

"Has she finally set a date for her wedding?"

"Um . . . I'm not sure." Cassie quickly changed the subject. "How's Dad?"

"Oh, *that man*." Cassie grinned at her mom's familiar refrain, colored with fond irritation. "He's off checking on all his gardens. The migration season is starting, you know."

"Right, I forgot." An entomologist, Cassie's father had always been more at home with bugs than people. "I guess that means school is starting soon for you too." Cassie dug around the floor of her closet for her favorite pair of work heels.

"Oh goodness, are you kidding? We've been back in session for two weeks already." Her mother was the principal of a small charter school near their home in the northern suburbs. Cassie had always felt equal parts sad and relieved she'd graduated from middle school before the charter opened. Her mom's school was amazing and did some really cool things, but gah—to have your mom be your principal. Like junior high wasn't awkward enough.

"Oh, yeah." Cassie kept forgetting that while the city schools didn't go back until after Labor Day, most suburban schools started in late August, and the charter schools often began even earlier.

"Have you been taking vitamin B" her mother asked.

"What? Why?"

"I'm worried about your memory."

"Nothing's wrong with my memory, Mom. I just have a lot on my mind."

"I'd think you'd be nice and relaxed, coming home from a long vacation and all."

"Well, that's the problem. I just got back from vacation yesterday and have a big meeting at work tomorrow morning."

"You'll be fine, you've been planning this for months. Which project do you think you'll start with?"

"The literacy initiative." Cassie had spent some time on the plane ride home debating her options and had decided, since *ChiChat* would start filming their new season in

September, she could take advantage of the increased focus on education during back-to-school time and boost her project's interest and visibility in the media.

"That's such a fabulous concept. I'm so proud of you for thinking of it." Her mother paused and added, "You know, I have some ideas that might help, if you're interested."

"That's great, Mom. And I totally want to hear about them later, okay? But first I need to land the new position."

"I'd wish you luck, but you don't need it," her mother insisted. "You got this."

"You got this," Cassie whispered to herself the next day as she straightened the lapels of her most polished and professional suit jacket. On her morning commute, her mom's parting words became Cassie's mantra. "You got this," she repeated at each stop on the "L," channeling all the love and confidence that had been in her mother's voice as she rode up the elevator and strode through the halls of the television station's offices.

"You got this," she said again, under her breath, as she approached the receptionist for *ChiChat*'s executive producer.

"Morning, Cassie."

"You got this!" Cassie said, wincing when she realized what had come out of her mouth. "Ah, hi, Maria."

The receptionist grinned. "Suffering from vacation brain?"

"I've been told I need more vitamin B." Cassie pasted a smile on her face. "I have a meeting with Ms. Rey?"

Maria clicked away on her computer for a moment. "Yes, you do." She put a call through to confirm, then nodded at Cassie. "Go on, she's expecting you."

"Great." Cassie started to turn away, but Maria called her back.

"Oh, Cassie?"

"Yeah?"

"You got this."

"Thanks," Cassie said, the receptionist's chortles of laughter following her down the hallway. The wall outside Therese's office was lined with plaques and awards. Cassie took a moment to smooth her palms down her neatly pressed linen skirt. She hadn't managed to unpack her suitcase or do a single load of laundry yet. Instead, she spent most of Sunday agonizing over what to wear for this meeting. She'd probably regret the decision in a few days when she had nothing clean left to wear, but at least she looked good today. "You got this," she promised herself one final time.

"Cassie, how was your trip?" Therese Rey stood when Cassie entered and shook her hand. Cassie's boss was a striking woman, tall, with elegant cheek bones and great lipstick. Under her guidance, *ChiChat* had gone from being a poorly rated afterthought, something people only watched if they forgot to turn off the TV after the morning news ended, to an award-winning talk show that everyone, from politicians to celebrities, artists to scientists, jumped at the chance to appear on.

If Cassie could convince Therese to give her idea a try, she'd be golden. Nobody said no to Therese.

The problem was, she first had to get Therese to say yes.

"Amazing," Cassie said, taking the seat Therese gestured toward.

"I'm sure it was." Therese leaned back in her chair. "The summer replays wrap up in a few weeks. Are you ready for the new season?"

"Actually, that's what I'd like to talk to you about." Cassie resisted the urge to twirl the charm bracelet on her wrist.

"Oh?"

"Yes." Cassie cleared her throat, refusing to buckle under Therese's sudden intense stare. "I've been covering Chicago's social scene and the pop culture beat for a few years now, and while I enjoy it and am grateful for the opportunities the position has afforded me—"

"You're ready for something new," Therese concluded.

"Well . . . yes."

"I had a feeling that's what this was about." The barest hint of a smile crossed her boss's face. Therese steepled her long dark fingers and considered Cassie. "Did you have something in mind?"

This was it. Cassie straightened her shoulders and sat taller in her seat. *You got this.*

Several hours later, Cassie shuffled toward her cubicle, exhausted, elated, and starving. Therese had said yes—a provisional yes—but a yes. With her boss's greenlight, Cassie could move forward with making the transition from pop culture princess to respected reporter. An agent of change, covering stories involving social activism and cultural improvement projects. First up, drawing attention to the city's abysmal youth literacy rates.

After leaving Therese's office, she'd spent the rest of the morning ironing out a production schedule, then skipped lunch to research urban reading programs and set up interviews with local school officials. Now, it was after two. She slumped into her chair.

Her cubicle looked pretty much the same as it had before she'd left for vacation. Sticky notes on every surface, and stacks of paper and books everywhere. Cassie yanked the July page off her desk calendar. In a few days it would be time to pull August too. There was much to do during the few weeks until the new season launched mid-September.

"Guess what, Charlie, I got it!"

Cassie pulled her potted plant, Charlie, to the center of her desk, running her fingers over his velvety leaves and healthy green tendrils. "You're looking good. Someone must have taken care of you while I was gone."

"You're welcome."

Cassie glanced up. Tiffany Hunt, her office nemesis, was hovering in the entry to her cube. "You? You watered Charlie?" Whenever she saw Tiffany, Cassie half expected to hear a clap of thunder or the opening notes of an ominous dirge.

Tiffany tossed her curtain of smooth, dark hair over one shoulder. "I didn't want it to die and start rotting and getting all smelly."

"Oh. Well, thank you?" She gave Charlie a final pat, then pushed him back into his patch of sunlight on the corner of her desk. Tiffany was the last person she'd expected help from, which meant there was something Tiffany wanted. Sure enough, when Cassie turned around, Tiffany was still standing there.

"Did you need something?" Cassie asked, doing her best to be pleasant, for Charlie's sake. The fact of the matter was, Tiffany hated her. It hadn't always been that way, though. She and Tiffany had started their internship at the station around the same time. And for the first year or so, they'd gotten along relatively well, climbing the ladder together as they passed through the early stages of gofer grunt work, often collaborating on assignments.

Then Cassie had happened to be in the right place at the right time, tasked with covering the wedding of a Bears player to a famous actress. The interview earned her an on-camera segment. Before long, she had a regular spot on the morning talk show, covering all the local celebrity gossip, weaving in food and fashion trends as well. If it was hip and happening in Chi-town, Cassie was on it.

Meanwhile, Tiffany was still behind the scenes, hardly ever appearing on-air, instead prepping material for the show's two lead talking heads. Cassie figured Tiffany felt betrayed—like Cassie had stolen an opportunity from her or something.

"I heard you're starting a new segment." Tiffany sidled closer. "A project with books or reading or something?" She dropped her gaze and rummaged through the romance novels stacked on the side of Cassie's desk. "Hmm. I didn't realize it was going to be pornographic."

"Those aren't pornographic." Cassie pulled open a drawer and slid the books in. Geez, word traveled around the office fast.

"Oh really?" Tiffany smirked, holding up a book with naked man-chest splashed across the cover.

"Really." Cassie grabbed the book out of Tiffany's manicured hand and crammed it in with the others. She slammed the drawer closed. "Cut to the chase, Tiffany. What do you want?"

"I want your spot."

"Huh?" Cassie's brain felt fuzzy. Maybe her mom was right, she needed more vitamins.

"If you're going to be busy doing this new book segment or whatever, someone needs to cover the pop culture scene." Tiffany leaned toward Cassie, aggressively plucked eyebrows narrowing. "That someone should be me."

"Ah, okay, sure." Cassie nodded, too tired and busy to care. "You want the job, it's yours."

"Perfect." Tiffany popped up, white teeth flashing. "I already talked to Therese, she said it was up to you."

Could have told me that in the first place you little . . . Cassie gritted her teeth. "Great. So we're done here?"

"Sure, I'll let you get back to your plant . . ." The acid in Tiffany's smile could peel paint. "And your porn."

* * *

Cassie spotted Bonnie's red curls at their usual booth and hurried forward. "I got it!"

Bonnie jumped up and screamed, loud enough to be heard over the mariachi band. "Yes!" She grabbed Cassie's hands, hopping around in a quick, happy jig.

"Margaritas on me tonight," Ana said, beaming as she held up four fingers to the waitress.

Cassie laughed and dug into the basket of house-made tortilla chips.

"Delaney would be here too, but she's running a new parent open house tonight," Sadie said, dipping a celery stick in the salsa. "Now, tell us everything."

"Therese loved it, said my idea had a lot of potential."

"Potential?" Ana frowned. "I thought you said you got it."

Cassie swallowed, her appetite curbing slightly. Ana was never one to pull punches. "I did . . . but on a trial basis."

"Which means?" Sadie asked.

"It means that she's willing to let me try my idea. In my new role as *ChiChat*'s reporter for social change, I get to launch one project, and she'll see how it goes." Cassie swirled a chip through the salsa bowl. "Therese said if the response from viewers is positive, I could run the segment permanently."

"What happens if the response isn't positive?" Bonnie asked after the waitress set their drinks on the table.

Cassie popped a straw in her glass and took a deep pull on her margarita before answering. "Then I might be out of a job."

"Wait—what?" Bonnie dropped the chip she'd been about to eat. "Like fired?"

"I'm not sure." Cassie ran her finger along the rim of her glass. "Maybe." She shrugged and licked the salt from her finger.

"But why? Couldn't you just go back to doing what you did before?" Sadie asked.

Cassie shook her head and took another sip of her drink.

"Why not?" Sadie asked.

"One, I don't want to be the pop culture princess anymore. And two, even if I did, I couldn't. They're giving the job to someone else."

"Who?" Bonnie twirled her straw, making the ice in her glass tinkle. 'Ritas on the rocks with salt. Never frozen. Their standard order.

Cassie drained the rest of her own 'rita. "Tiffany."

"*No,*" Bonnie gasped.

Cassie nodded.

"Why would they give it to her?"

"Because I sort of suggested it." Cassie opened her menu, even though she already knew what she was going to order. She was surprised the waitresses still bothered to ask.

Bonnie didn't bother with her menu. Instead, she kept her eyes trained on Cassie. "Why would you do that? She *hates you.*"

"It's a long story."

"Was the b-witch grateful, at least?" Bonnie asked after they'd placed their order. "I never liked her, you know."

"Yeah, we know," Sadie said.

"You're jealous of her," Ana agreed.

"Am not," Bonnie protested.

Ana chuckled. "Of course you are, Bon. You guard your status as Cassie's best friend doggedly and Tiffany was like, Cassie's work wife."

"Whatever," Bonnie grumbled.

Cassie hid a smile and started in on her second drink. Ana was right, Bonnie had never been a fan of all the time Cassie and Tiffany used to spend together, even if it was for work. Sometimes her bosom friend could be more jealous than a boyfriend. Thinking of boyfriends, Cassie glanced up at Bonnie. "Gabe must be glad to have you home, huh?"

"I guess." Bonnie stared down at the melting ice cubes in the bottom of her glass.

Cassie leaned closer to Bonnie as the waitress set their plates in front of them. "Are things okay between you and Gabe?" she asked quietly.

"Of course, why wouldn't they be?" Bonnie stabbed her fork into her food.

Ouch. She'd have to tread lightly here. "I don't know Bon, I just get the sense that's something's up with you, that's all." She bit into her fajita, not wanting to say more.

Bonnie continued to poke at her meal, but with less violence. "It's just, we were apart for most of the summer, you know? Gabe and I have never been away from each other so long."

"Okay . . ." Cassie said, taking another bite and hoping Bonnie would continue.

"And now, things feel kind of weird between us."

"What kind of weird?" Sadie asked, picking olives off her salad.

Bonnie dropped her gaze to her plate. "Just . . . different, I guess." She set the fork down. "I'm sure it's nothing. We just need to spend some time together, and everything will be back to normal."

"Exactly. You and Gabe will be able rekindle the flame," Cassie teased.

"There you go, sounding like one of your romance novels." Bonnie rolled her eyes, but Cassie was glad to see her friend pick up her fork and dig into her meal.

"Hey, there's nothing wrong with enjoying a happy ending." Cassie smiled, unoffended.

"Are there any stories where the heroine is stuck waiting in limbo for her happily ever after to finally begin?" Bonnie asked. Her voice was light, but Cassie could sense the weight behind her friend's remark.

"Still no date for the wedding?" Ana guessed.

Bonnie shook her head and pulled Cassie's drink toward her.

Cassie patted Bonnie's hand, the one with the engagement ring. "Like you said, you just got home. Give it some time, I'm sure he'll come around."

"You're right." Bonnie sighed. "I know he's focused on his doctorate right now. But he graduates in May. I wanted the wedding to be in June. He knows that. He knows how much I want a wedding on Midsummer Day. I don't think it's a big deal to go ahead and set the date now."

"It's *not* a big deal," Ana agreed. "These things take time to plan. What's he waiting for?"

"Maybe he's waiting until Christmas," Sadie suggested. "You know, since he proposed on Christmas too?"

"If this were one of Cassie's romance novels, maybe." Bonnie shrugged.

"Oh, come on Anne of Green Gables, your story is textbook romance," Cassie argued. "You have your whole life with Gabe planned out."

"There's nothing wrong with being prepared." Bonnie straightened in her seat, chin set.

"Agreed," Cassie said. "But sometimes it's hard to prepare yourself when you don't know what life is going to throw at you."

"Like a Sexy Scot popping up unexpectedly?" Bonnie asked coyly.

Cassie eyed her friend across the booth, lips pursed at the low blow. "Indeed."

CHAPTER 20

ON MONDAY AFTERNOON, Logan entered the offices of Second Studios prepared for battle. Unsure what would happen when he got to Chicago, he'd told Janet to upload "The Hidden Highlander" (as she'd so snarkily informed him she'd named the clip) to the *Shenanigans* webpage, but asked her to keep the file marked private. Logan wasn't ready to release Cassie's video to the world, but he wasn't ready to forfeit the opportunity either. Depending on what the producers had to say, he needed to keep that ace in the hole.

Turns out he didn't have to play a hand at all. The interview had gone well, better than he could have hoped for. Minutes after he'd walked into the conference room, shook hands with the producers—both of whom, it turned out, were named Bob—and exchanged the briefest of pleasantries, Logan found himself brainstorming a twelve-episode mini-season. He'd been ready to fight, but rather than rake him over the coals for not providing new content targeted at his weakest demographic, the production team conducted the meeting as if they'd already hired him.

"I don't get it," he told the Bobs, "not that I'm complaining, but what changed?"

Over a celebratory meal of thick gooey slabs one of the Bobs proudly declared was "Chicago-style pizza," Logan learned why things had gone so smoothly. Turns out Second Studios had decided to hire both Logan *and* the twit with the cat. That's what they'd been calling about while he'd been in London, chasing after Cassie.

By the time he'd finished his second pint of 312, another Chicago staple the Bobs insisted on, Logan had outlined sketches for all twelve episodes. He'd meet again with Bob and Bob tomorrow to nail down logistics, deciding on interview guests. Filming would start by the end of the week. The timeline was tight. They'd have less than a month to film most of the pre-taped sketches before the fall season launched. After much backslapping made heartier by a third round of beers, Logan bid his new bosses a good night, waving off offers of a ride back to the hotel.

His first mission accomplished, Logan was itching to get started on the second. He'd considered staking out the floor *ChiChat* studios was on and arranging an "accidental" run-in with Cassie, but too many of their meetings had been based on subterfuge already. The fact she lived in the same city as his new job, worked for the same channel as his new show, was a real, mind-blowing coincidence.

Could it be fate? Was there such a thing? Logan didn't know, and he didn't care.

Right now, all he cared about was seeing Cassie again. All he knew for sure was he and the lass were in the same city, breathing the same air. He sucked in a breath of that air and focused on the sidewalk in front of him. One step at a time, that was his motto. Don't make too many plans, and don't think too far ahead. Live in the moment because you never know when the whole bloody thing will come crashing down around your fecking ears.

Barely a week had passed since she'd discovered him behind a castle bookshelf, and now here he was, across the ocean, strolling through downtown Chicago at sunset, the mile-high skyscrapers of the Windy City casting long shadows across his path. As Logan walked, he soaked up the vibe of this new city, her city, trying to get a sense of the world Cassie lived in . . . the world that would, for the foreseeable future, be his as well.

Who could have predicted the wild turn his life had taken?

"People plan and God laughs." That's what Da would say.

Logan had been thinking about Da a great deal the past few days. *The joke had sure been on you, huh, Da?* He doubted his father would have predicted any of this. A wave of anguish rose in his chest and Logan pushed it down. He wasn't going there. He crammed his hand in his pocket and pulled out a faded cocktail napkin. Swallowing hard, he took out his phone and started to dial.

As Cassie headed home after dinner, her mind swirled with to-do's and tequila. She still needed to unpack, and she really needed to do laundry. Part of her acknowledged putting off these chores was her way of extending her vacation—like, maybe the vacation wasn't really over if her bags were still packed.

Also, she really didn't want to wash the clothes that smelled like Logan, and had in fact spent the last few nights sleeping in one shirt in particular. She had just finished brushing her teeth and was about to change into the same shirt again when her phone buzzed. She absently swiped her thumb over the answer button. "Hello?"

The familiar delicious burr caught her off guard, and she almost dropped her phone. "Logan, is that you?"

"Aye, it's me. Look, I uh, happen to be in Chicago and I thought . . ."

"Wait, hold on," Cassie demanded. "You're in Chicago?"

"Aye."

"Right now?"

"Aye," Logan said again.

"I don't believe it." Cassie laughed, collapsing onto the pile of laundry on her bed. "Prove it."

Less than twenty minutes later, Cassie watched from her window as a tall figure bounded up the front steps to her building. The nape of her neck prickled with awareness. There was no mistaking those broad shoulders or the tousle of bright hair.

Logan fucking Reid was indeed in Chicago. Right now.

"Holy shit."

Cassie let him inside her apartment and closed the door. Leaning against it, she drew support from the feel of solid wood beneath her back, a welcome sensation since the rug had been pulled out from under her feet.

"Thanks for having me up," he said, that same mischievous grin she remembered all too well tugging at the corner of his mouth.

"Don't thank me yet," she warned, watching as he shrugged out of his jacket. It was *that* jacket. The man sure had nerve. That, or he didn't own a lot of coats. Cassie reached to take his jacket and folded it over her arm, the warmth the fabric still held from his body seeping into her skin.

"On or off?"

"Hmm?" Uncertainty rooted Cassie to the spot.

"Shoes. Do you prefer them on or off?" He quirked an

eyebrow in question, one of his wicked devil brows she also remembered very well.

"Oh. Off, please." As he bent to remove his boots, the muscles in his back and arms bunched and, despite herself, Cassie briefly considered suggesting he remove a few other things. Shoes, socks, shirt . . . pants. *Settle down, girl.*

She'd always considered her apartment's tiny entry nook cozy, but with Logan's broad shoulders filling the space, it was downright intimate. She swallowed hard and squeezed past him to open the closet. "You can toss those in here," she said, as she placed his jacket on a hanger. His boots landed with a thump on the hardwood floor, and she glanced up, startled.

Behind her, Logan caught her gaze in the hall mirror. He bit his lip in a sheepish gesture. "Sorry. My mam calls them anchors."

"For your boat-sized feet?" Cassie guessed.

"Aye." His eyes crinkled as he grinned, and Cassie's insides turned to porridge.

She slid the closet door shut and focused on his stocking feet. "They are rather big." Cassie slid her foot across the floor and nudged his toes with hers, unable to resist making contact.

"Well, I'm kind of big too. What, you think I should be walking around with dainty fairy feet? I'd fall on my face for want of balance."

"Ah, it's a matter of proportion then." Cassie lifted her gaze to his face, her eyes taking the long way to get there. And at Logan's height of six foot four, it was a long way indeed.

"Proportion, is it?" he purred, one auburn eyebrow quirking.

"That's *not* what I was talking about," she protested, keeping her gaze astutely away from the area in question.

"Really?" he asked, his burr rolling, playing with the word, teasing her.

Cassie turned away from him and headed into the living room. Less than five minutes in his presence and already she was talking about his cock. Well, not talking about it, exactly, but thinking about it. She honestly had been referring to the size of his feet at first—and Lord knew it was true—the man was built to scale. It was just kind of hard not to think about his other, ah, proportions, which she recalled in vivid detail.

"Have a seat." Cassie gestured toward the one chair in the room while she took a spot on the couch. If the temperature of her cheeks was any indication, she was blushing furiously. She considered shoving her face into one of the pillows, but figured that would likely draw more attention to the problem. She leaned back and waited for him to get settled in the chair.

Rather than sit, he strolled about. Cassie glanced around and tried to see her apartment through his eyes, wondering what would catch his attention. What story would her things tell him?

What was *his* story anyway? What was he doing in Chicago?

Logan finished his circuit of the room, ignored the chair she'd indicated, and sat on the couch. Right next to her.

Of course he did.

Cassie tried not to think about how his leg was pressed against hers, tried to ignore how her professional business skirt didn't look quite so professional when hiked up her thighs as his added weight caused her to sink deeper into the thick cushions of the couch. She tugged at the hem of her skirt, hoping he wouldn't notice.

His gaze followed her movement, lingering on her legs. *Real smooth, Cass.* If he hadn't noticed before, he did now. Not in the mood to play games, Cassie cut to the chase. "Why'd you call me?"

"I missed you, lass." His voice was whisper soft, and Cassie felt a tickle low in her belly. She'd missed him too, but that wasn't the point. The problem, however, was being so close to Logan made it hard for her to remember exactly what the point was supposed to be.

She leaned away from him and gathered her thoughts. In London, he'd played her, carried that contract around with him the *entire* time he'd been with her. She had to remember that. "Why didn't you post the video?" she asked. "I signed your stupid contract. Didn't Theo give it to you?"

"Aye." His face darkened. "Why didn't you give it to me yourself? And by the bye, what did you mean when you said I'd earned it?"

"Never mind. I was angry when I said that."

"No kidding." He snorted. "I suppose you had a right to be."

"You *suppose*?" She jumped to her feet, fuming. She'd been feeling bad about what she'd said, but Logan's attitude stirred the ashes of her anger. "You followed me to London. Tracked me down so you could get me to sign that contract. Do you deny it?"

A bright red flush crept across his features. "No. I dinna deny it." A muscle leapt in his jaw, and he stood as well, towering over her.

If he thought he could intimidate her with his height, he was wrong.

"Look, you damn Scot, the one thing I wanted from my vacation was a night of hot sex with a stranger. A foreign fling." Cassie went toe to toe with the man and glared up at him. "Thanks to you, I got the souvenir I wanted."

"Are you saying that's all there was between us?" His voice was low, pained. "That you used me?"

Cassie wasn't buying his hurt feelings routine. The only thing hurting this man was his bruised ego. "Oh, please, like you weren't using me."

"It wasna like that. I mean, aye, at first. And I meant to tell you, I did. But then . . ." He stopped, closing his eyes as he sucked in a breath. "Then I . . ."

"Then you what?" Cassie asked, her own breath caught in her chest.

He shook his head. He opened his eyes and stared down at her. They were standing so close she could see each individual fleck of gold in his green eyes, the bright shards orbiting his pupils. He bent toward her, mouth hovering inches from hers, and for a moment Cassie thought he was going to kiss her.

And she realized, despite everything, she *wanted* him to kiss her.

"I'm sorry, lass," he said, briefly touching his lips to her cheek before he stepped back.

His words drained the last of her anger, and in its place crept remorse. "I'm sorry too." What they'd shared had been more than a one-night stand. At least, that's what she'd begun to believe—until she'd found that contract. Maybe, instead of running away, she should have given him a chance to explain.

A rueful chuckle broke the silence between them. "And to think," Logan said, shrugging his broad shoulders, "in the end I didn't need your signature on that bloody contract after all."

"What are you talking about? I thought you had to have it. For your show." Cassie thought back to that day in the castle, trying to remember what his sister had said. "Something about a big important deal?"

Logan nodded and pulled her back on to the couch. "Aye, I thought I needed it too." He rubbed his thumb across the inside of her wrist. "But the producers at Second Studios came up with a compromise, so I get my shot after all."

"So I don't have to be humiliated? Thank God." Cassie sighed.

"I hardly see how getting caught winching me is humiliating," Logan mused.

"Winching?" Cassie frowned. "What's that?"

"Kissing." He grinned. "With, ah, tongue."

Cassie stared at his mouth. He licked his lips.

She tried very hard not to lick her own lips.

She failed.

He moved closer, green-gold gaze meeting hers. Intense. Focused. Knowing. "I don't think it's the winching that has you worried."

"You don't?"

"Nae. I've had time to consider. And I think you're upset because I got you."

"You . . . got me?" Cassie asked, suddenly finding it hard to breathe.

"When you first saw me in the castle"—he lifted his chin and gazed down at her, devil's brow arched in challenge—"part of you thought maybe . . . just maybe . . ."

"What? You were actually a time-traveling Highlander?" Cassie sat still, holding her ground. "No way."

"Admit it, lass." He pressed closer, speaking soft and low in her ear. "For a moment, you believed. For a moment," he continued, his words caressing the curve of her neck, "I got you."

Cassie shivered, his ability to read her affecting her

even more than his touch, his nearness. Because the truth was, he was right.

For a split second, she *had* believed. Not really, not logically. Not in her head.

But in her heart . . . yeah.

"Fine, I admit it," Cassie acquiesced. "You got me, okay? But only for a second."

He chuckled, a throaty triumphant sound that ticked her off while still making her nipples tighten.

"I can't believe you're working for Second Studios now." Cassie shifted on the couch, scooting her traitorous boobs away from him.

"You're looking at the host of their new late-night talk show." Logan grinned. "We start filming the end of the week."

"Does this mean you'll be staying in Chicago for a while?"

"The next few months, for certain." Logan reached into his pocket and pulled out a familiar box. He opened the lid. "These were meant for you, lass," he said, taking her hand and spilling the charms into her palm.

Cassie bit her lip, staring down at the miniature silver replicas of Big Ben and the London Eye. "You know, when I first found this box, I thought it might be an engagement ring."

A strangled noise gurgled in Logan's throat, and his eyes bulged as if he had indeed just been strung with a hangman's noose.

"I didn't say I *wanted* it to be one," she rushed to reassure him. "That's outrageous."

"Bloody bonkers," he agreed. "Especially seeing as I don't intend to ever get married. I just meant it as a farewell gift, aye? Something to remember me by." His voice tightened. "But you ran away before I had a chance to give them to you."

"I didn't run away," she protested, but they both knew she was lying.

"You didn't give me the chance to say goodbye." He held her gaze with his, and the hurt she saw there was real. He wrapped his hand around hers, closing her fist on the charms. "These are yours. No strings attached."

No strings, huh? Cassie wondered. When she'd first signed Logan's damn waiver, that had been her intention—to cut any strings tying her to the Scot. It had been an impulsive act, one she'd regretted almost immediately. But now she was glad she'd signed it. If she hadn't, and he'd called her, told her he was here in town, she'd have been sure it was for one reason and one reason only. She narrowed her eyes at him. "You don't want anything else from me?"

"Well, since you ask . . ." He paused.

Cassie tensed, her spine going rigid as he stared down at their clasped hands. *Here it comes.*

Logan squeezed her hand. "I'd like to see you again. Take you out for another drink, perhaps?"

Oh. The steel went out of her spine, and Cassie exhaled. When she'd run away from him in London, part of her had hoped he would chase after her. And in the end, he had. Regardless of motive, he'd followed her across the ocean.

In any of her romance novels, that would have been enough. The heroine would have taken one look at her hero and thrown herself into his arms. God knew Cassie wanted to do just that . . . but this was real life. Happy endings weren't lurking around every corner. "Logan, I think there's something you should know."

"You're not seeing someone, are you? Engaged, like your friend Bonnie?"

"Um, no. Definitely not." She pulled her hand from his and opened her palm, studying the charms again. "The exact opposite, actually. I haven't dated anyone in a long time. I haven't *been* with anyone—present company excluded—in a really long time." She swallowed. "The Cassie you met in Scotland was a completely different person."

"Ah. You have an evil twin," Logan deadpanned.

Cassie laughed. "No. But real-life Chicago Cassie is not the same person as fantasy vacation Cassie. When I was in Europe, I gave myself permission to indulge, to be spontaneous, to—"

"Fuck a Scotsman on a desk?"

"Exactly," she said, cheeks burning.

"I dinna mean to sound crass." He touched her cheek gently, lifting her face to his. The tender gesture turned Cassie's knees to water. Good thing she was sitting down. "I'm not going to lie. I liked holiday Cassie . . ." He paused, brow quirking. "Verra much."

The roll of his Gaelic tongue made other parts start to liquefy. She squeezed her thighs together.

"But I'd also like to spend time getting to know Chicago Cassie," he said, smoothing back a lock of her hair. "What do you think?"

What did she think? Logan was here, in her city, and didn't want anything more from her than the chance to go out on some dates. Get to know her better.

For so long, she'd been focused on getting ahead at *Chi-Chat*. Meanwhile, her love life had taken a back seat . . . more like been stuffed in the trunk. Now, everything seemed within reach, the job she wanted, the man she craved. And she was in the driver's seat.

Cassie laughed, giddy with possibility.

"What's so funny?" Logan asked.

"It's just . . . it all seems too good to be true."

"Life is short, lass." Logan winked at her, and there he was, her Peter Pan holding out his hand, offering another taste of Neverland. "When good things happen, try not to question it."

"I do have one question." Cassie took a breath, lifting her gaze to his. "Did you happen to pack your kilt?"

CHAPTER 21

A MONTH LATER, Logan glanced at the clock in Cassie's kitchen and cursed. She'd be home in under an hour and everything was going wrong.

So he did what he always did when things went wrong. He called his best mate.

"Logan?"

"Hello, Theo," Logan drawled pleasantly. "How's things?"

"What's wrong?" Theo demanded.

"Everything's great," he lied, pinching the phone between his ear and shoulder and stirring a pot of melting butter. "I'm making clootie dumplings." He poured flour into a bowl. *Trying to, anyway.*

Theo snorted. "Never say you're cooking?"

"I wanted to surprise Cassie." *Oh, she'll be surprised, all right.* He glanced around the kitchen, which looked like a battlefield, the counters and floor littered with the sad remains of his failed attempts. The hiss of water bubbling over reminded Logan he'd left the range on. He hurried to the stove and yanked the pot off the flame, cursing as hot liquid splattered his arm. "Shit!"

"Sounds like things aren't going well," Theo said, doing nothing to hide his amusement.

"Things are going verra well," Logan growled.

"Really?" The suspicion in his friend's voice traveled clearly all the way across the pond. "Then why are you calling me?" Theo knew him too well.

Logan surveyed the disaster surrounding him and sighed. "You got me. I need your help."

"I'm not flying to Chicago."

"I'm not asking you to."

"Then what's up?"

"Did you know clootie dumplings have to be boiled for four hours?" Logan glanced at the recipe for the hundredth time, still not believing the treat he'd enjoyed every holiday of his life took so much effort to make.

"I had no idea," Theo said in his I-could-care-less-snooty-English voice. "Thanks for enlightening me."

"Don't be a wanker."

"Hey, *you* called *me*," Theo countered. "You do know it's almost midnight here, right?"

"Och, sorry." Logan rubbed a hand over his face, then cursed again, realizing he'd just covered himself in flour.

"It's fine," Theo grumbled. "Not like I'm doing anything important right now, anyway."

"No hot date?" Logan teased.

"Hardly. But sounds like you and Cassie are carrying on well enough. Still seeing each other then?"

"Aye, it's been a month now."

"A month? My, things *are* getting serious," Theo cooed. The git was teasing him.

"Did I mention her friend Bonnie is looking well?"

Logan shot back. "Adorable redhead. You remember her, right?"

"I remember she's engaged," Theo replied stiffly. "Remind me, was there a reason for this call?"

"Right. I wanted to do a wee something special for Cassie, to celebrate, you ken? But I left my kilt back in the hotel room."

"Ugh. I don't need to hear about your kilt kink."

Ignoring that, Logan continued, poking at the lump of dough in the pot. "And now this dumpling belongs in a dumpster."

"Here's my suggestion. Give up on the cooking, clean up the mess I'll wager my left nut you've made, and take the girl out for a proper meal."

"Now, that's a fine suggestion."

"Of course it is," Theo agreed. "How's everything else? How's the new show?"

"Coming along."

"Have you talked to your sister?"

"A bit."

"Lo," Theo chastised.

As the oldest child and only brother to three sisters, his best mate had expectations in the sibling department. Like everything else, Theo was better at managing his responsibilities, carrying out his family duties. Meanwhile Lo was a selfish fuckwad.

Sharp stabs of guilt lashed him. Logan gripped the phone tighter. "You're right. I'll call her again soon."

"I won't give you any more shit, then," Theo said. "Give Nettie my love, and don't bloody call me in the middle of the night again."

"Hey, Theo?"

"What?"

"Thanks, mate."

* * *

Cassie settled in the chair Logan held out for her and smiled as he took his seat across from her. "This is a nice surprise."

"For me too." He ran his hand through his hair and paused, looking up. "I mean, yes, this is nice."

"You've got something there." Cassie touched her own cheek, indicating a spot where Logan had a smudge.

"Christ, I thought I got it all. It's probably flour." Logan rubbed furiously at his face. "Is it gone?"

She shook her head, trying not to laugh. Instead of wiping the stuff off, he had smeared it more. "Here." Cassie reached out and brushed her thumb across his cheek. His skin was warm beneath her hand, the faint bristle of new beard tickling.

As always, touching him made her tingle all over. Cassie had thought the sensation would begin to dull over time, but it hadn't. If anything, the feelings had grown stronger these past weeks they were together. Like a junkie, she never seemed to get enough of Logan and was always looking for her next fix.

Luckily, Logan seemed to feel the same and was constantly touching her. He gripped her fingers in his, pulling her hand toward his mouth and pressing a soft kiss in the center of her palm. Liquid heat flowed from his lips up the length of her arm, thick and sweet as honey.

Cassie tugged her hand away. If he didn't stop, they'd end up under the table . . . or on top of it. "Flour? Was this for your show?" She knew he'd been busy filming pre-taped sketches that were used during the live broadcast.

Logan shook his head and glanced at the wine list. "Ah, no."

"Then what were you up to today?"

"Och, nothing much." His face turned crimson.

Like Bonnie's, Logan's fair ginger skin was always a dead giveaway. He'd definitely been up to something. "Logan?" Cassie pressed.

"I was trying to cook for you," he mumbled into his menu.

Of all the answers she could have predicted, that was not one of them. Cassie's heart did silly little flip-flops in her chest.

When she didn't reply, he looked up. "I was going to make you a clootie dumpling, but I muddled the time, and then I boiled myself like a damn lobster." He pushed the sleeve of his shirt up, revealing a smattering of angry pink marks puckering the skin on his forearm.

"My poor, wounded Scot." Cassie patted his arm.

"Ow!" He jerked his hand away. "That smarts."

"Sorry," Cassie said, swallowing a giggle. Men were such babies. But still, it had been very sweet of him. She pictured Logan standing at the stove, cursing as he cooked, his brogue growing thicker as it always did when he got angry . . . "Wait a minute," she said, putting the whole picture together. "Was this in *my* apartment?"

"It was." His face was all little-boy innocence.

"Maybe I shouldn't have given you that key after all."

"I cleaned up everything, I swear."

"I hope you did a better job on my counters than you did on your face," she teased.

"Your kitchen is as clean as the pope's arse, I assure you."

"I'll take your word for it on that one." Cassie wrinkled her nose.

"Come now, it's not as though you do much cooking in there yerself."

"That's a low blow, Scottie." Cassie play-pouted, not really offended. He did have a point. "It's not my fault my mother never taught me how to cook."

"What about yer da?"

"My dad's more interested in what bugs eat."

"Bugs?"

This time she couldn't resist the giggle that escaped at his blank look. "Yes, bugs. My father is an entomologist. He studies insects."

Logan's brow furrowed. "What does he do with the wee beasties?"

"Well, right now his big project is helping save the monarch butterfly population. A few months ago he launched a countywide waystation program."

"Oh?" Logan asked, but Cassie could tell he had no idea what she was talking about.

"Every fall monarch butterflies migrate hundreds of miles, but areas where they can stop along the way have been vanishing. Dad has been working to build havens—waystations—for them."

"Your da is helping butterflies get home, and you're helping kids get books. Crusading for causes must be an inherited trait." Logan leaned back, and the smile he gave her across the table made the sweet honey feeling expand, spreading through her, leaving her warm all over. She fiddled with her silverware, ridiculously pleased at the note of admiration in his voice. She'd never thought of it quite like that.

"Tell me about your family." She'd met his sister, but didn't know much beyond the fact Janet looked a lot like her brother and was equally stubborn. Logan explained Janet had been an art major, and aside from running *Shenanigans* with him, designed website marketing, mostly for up-and-coming bands.

"I know you two got off on the wrong foot," Logan said, referring to Cassie's encounter with Janet in the castle, "but she's great, really."

The way he said "gr-eat," his tongue tickling the *r*, made her insides melt. Cassie bit back a smile, wondering when she'd stop finding his accent so darn sexy. Plus, he was adorable when he spoke sweetly about his sister. "Do you have any other siblings?"

"No. Nettie's enough, aye?" He chuckled. "And you, lass? Any brothers or sisters?"

"Nope." Cassie shook her head. It was one of the reasons she was so grateful for Bonnie. Her bosom buddy was the sister she'd never had. "But back to you. What's your mom like?"

"Mam's grand."

"I bet she's a fantastic cook, right?"

"The best."

"Your father is a lucky man."

Logan shifted in his seat, his humor evaporating. Cassie didn't need the instincts of a journalist to know she'd stumbled on a sensitive subject. Were his parents divorced? He had mentioned he never wanted to get married, and she'd filed that bit of information away for further speculation. She'd have to tread carefully. "What's your dad like?"

"My da . . ." Logan stopped, a muscle rippling along his jaw as he inhaled. "Da is dead."

"Oh." Cassie's heart squeezed at the weight of grief packed in those three small words. *So much for treading carefully.* "Oh, Logan."

He sat ramrod straight, broad shoulders stiff against the dining chair. She wanted to go to him, put her arms around him and hold him, but something in the cut of his gaze and tense line of his back told her now was not the time. She remained in her seat, whispering, "I'm so sorry."

"I doona wish to speak of it," he said, brogue thick, voice clipped.

Yeah, I kind of got that. She wouldn't press the issue. He'd tell her more when—and if—he wanted to.

Luckily, a moment later their server appeared. After they'd placed their order, Cassie changed the subject. "Not that I'm complaining about the special treatment, but what's the occasion anyway?"

"You wound me, lass." Logan arched an eyebrow, but she was glad to see he seemed to be recovered and was teasing her. "You don't know what today is?"

Cassie gasped, "Your show doesn't preview tonight, does it?"

Logan stared at her. "No, that's next week, remember?"

"Right, sorry." Cassie racked her brain, trying to recall what could be special about today. Ever since returning from vacation, she'd been completely absorbed in two things: Logan and her new role at work. To the point that unless an event was entered in all caps on her calendar and accompanied by a notification alert, she was likely to forget it existed. Her mother still hadn't forgiven her for missing Aunt Eleanor's birthday.

The wine arrived and Logan raised his glass. "I'd like to propose a toast."

"A toast," Cassie echoed, lifting her glass too, still not sure what they were celebrating.

"To the day I arrived in Chicago," Logan said, grinning expectantly, "and you agreed to start seeing me, exactly one month ago."

"Oh," Cassie breathed, "is that all?"

His grin slipped and Logan coughed.

"That's not what I meant," Cassie backpedaled, relieved and thrilled at the same time. Relieved she hadn't forgotten some major event—not that dating Logan for a month wasn't major—and thrilled he'd obviously thought it important enough to celebrate. Who could have known her sexy Scot was the kind of man who remembered one-month anniversaries and cooked for his woman . . . or tried to, at least.

And he says he never wants to get married, hmm? Were they going too fast? Honestly, she had no idea. Technically, Logan hadn't moved in. He still kept the hotel room provided by Second Studios, but he did spend most of his nights at her place. She'd given Logan the spare key to her place a week or so ago. It had been Bonnie's, and her friend had handed it over to him with a knowing wink.

Now that Logan was filming the live broadcasts, he usually finished up well past midnight. Cassie had decided it would be easier if he could let himself into her apartment rather than use the buzzer and wake her up. Or worse, possibly her neighbors, especially Delores Crabtree, who *of course* had been in line behind Cassie at the corner drugstore this summer when Cassie had purchased her Europe-bound industrial-sized box of condoms. The old lady had been giving Cassie the side-eye ever since. Whatever. Her nosy neighbor could think what she wanted.

She smiled up at him. "I'm sorry. I've had so much on my mind with work. I guess I didn't realize—"

"Dinna fash yourself, lass," he said, turning the brogue up a zillion notches. "You can make it up to me later, aye?" He winked at her.

"Aye," Cassie croaked, mouth suddenly dry. She swallowed a gulp of wine and leaned across the table. "Can later be now?"

CHAPTER 22

THE FOLLOWING MORNING, Cassie paused in the hall outside the studio's dressing room to drink her coffee. Inhaling deeply, she took a sip of the dark, fragrant brew. It was rich and strong, exactly how she liked it. She smiled into her cup and made her way to the makeup department on legs that still felt wobbly. Maybe heels weren't a good idea today. After what went down in her apartment last night, Mrs. Crabtree was really going to give her the side-eye now. If that was how the man celebrated being together for a month, she couldn't wait to see what happened after a year.

Let's not get ahead of ourselves. She set her coffee on the counter, cutting off that line of thinking. She had to stop doing that. She sighed and settled into one of the swivel chairs lining the room, sliding a romance novel out of her purse and popping it open while she waited her turn.

"That looks like a good one," Anita, the makeup artist, said as she pulled her cart up next to Cassie.

"It's a re-read," Cassie admitted, holding the book up

so Anita could admire the cover. "One of my favorites. You want to borrow it?"

"You know it," Anita said, tucking a tissue into the neckline of Cassie's on-camera dress to protect it. "I love the last one you gave me."

"You finished it already?"

"Like two days ago." Anita wiggled her gorgeous, perfectly plucked eyebrows. It was always a good sign when the person doing your makeup did such a fabulous job on their own face. Cassie liked the girl a lot. She'd been the one to get Anita hooked on romance novels in the first place, and now they often swapped books.

While Anita got to work, Cassie tried to read, but her mind kept drifting back to Logan. She'd criticized Bonnie for planning too far ahead, and here she was contemplating her one-year anniversary to a man she'd been dating for scarcely a month. She groaned in frustration. "Anita, I think I might be crazy."

"Why do you think that?" Anita asked, pursing lips lined in a gorgeous shade of ruby.

"I've seen her talk to her plant," an unpleasantly familiar voice scoffed. "Isn't that, by definition, crazy?"

Cassie stiffened, but managed to hold still while Anita applied primer. "Morning, Tiffany," she said when her co-worker came into view.

Tiffany stopped directly in front of Cassie. Bitch face firmly in place, she leaned against the counter and parked her pert Donna Karan–covered derriere inches from Cassie's coffee.

"How can I help you?" Cassie asked, making only the tiniest of wishes Tiffany would lean back a *teeny* bit farther and bump into the cup.

"I'm supposed to check in with you and get an updated

list of venue contacts." Tiffany shifted and crossed her arms.

"I thought I sent those over to you already." As Anita applied mascara, Cassie peeked between her lashes, watching her cup wobble. Logan had got up early to brew the coffee for her, and she'd come out of the shower to discover her disheveled Scot wearing nothing but bed head and a pair of snug boxer briefs, his broad bare shoulders taking up most of the available space in her kitchen as he fussed with the French press. She'd padded over to him, her feet leaving mini-puddles on the hardwood, and rained kisses over his delicious cinnamon-toast back. She'd never realized how sexy freckles could be.

An exaggerated huff interrupted her mental replay.

Cassie started, her book almost slipping from her lap. "You wanted the contacts, right?" She wiggled in the chair and pulled out her phone, opening her email app. She pointed at a line in her outbox dated over a week ago. "See? I told you I sent them."

"Hmm." Tiffany leaned in, her hair draping over her shoulder in a cascade of smooth perfection.

Cassie had always been jealous of Tiffany's hair, had even debated doing a *ChiChat* fashion segment on getting hers straightened. But in the end, she decided it would be too much work and way too much money to try and make her wavy mane behave on a regular basis.

"Send it again." Tiffany tossed her hair back over her shoulder.

Typical Tiff. No "please." No "Sorry, I must have missed it." Cassie had worked hard to create that list of contacts, cultivating relationships with club managers and bartenders to stay in the know. She swallowed a retort, fantasizing about the pair of scissors on Anita's cart and wondering how Tiffany's silky-smooth locks would look styled in a mullet like the hero on her romance novel's cover.

"Sure," she said instead, and clicked resend. She opened her book again. When Tiffany didn't move, Cassie glanced up once more. "Look, if that's all you needed . . ." She pointedly trailed off.

As *ChiChat's* new Queen of Fluff sauntered away, Cassie reminded herself that she had made the choice to give up that role. She didn't regret her decision, but her new job was harder than she'd anticipated. Getting her project off the ground was requiring serious effort, and she was the one doing all the heavy lifting. But she wasn't complaining. This was what she'd wanted.

So far Cassie had conducted interviews with the mayor's office, and today she was interviewing some members from the teachers' union. She'd had a difficult time making headway scheduling meetings with anyone from the Chicago Public School board, but last week Cassie had done a docuseries featuring several of the controversial charter schools sprinkled across the city—a passive-aggressive move on her part that paid off.

She had her mom to thank for that idea. As her mom had predicted, once the segments covering Cassie's visits to city charter schools started airing on *ChiChat*, the Chicago Public School board, which up to that point had glacially slow to respond to her requests, contacted her immediately. Things were lining up. There was only one more duck missing to complete her row.

The pièce de résistance of her media campaign would be an interview with a board member of the Chicago Public Library, and the higher up the food chain, the better. Her goal was to unite the city's schools and libraries in a joint endeavor on the literacy campaign, but first she needed to get the library board to make a commitment on record. So far, Cassie hadn't gained much traction with the library officials, but she wasn't giving up. She'd found a weakness in the school board's armor, and if she poked around enough, she'd find what drew a reaction from the library board members too.

"What is it going to take?" Cassie groaned to her friends over margaritas. Almost a month had passed since Cassie's run-in with Tiffany, and she was still struggling to get that last duck in line. Over the past few weeks she'd interviewed several Chicago Public School board members and filmed site visits at city schools where a pilot program of the after-school literacy project had already been launched. And yet the powers that be at the Chicago Public Library continued to dodge her calls.

"I saw the piece you did on the pilot program, it looked great. Really promising." Bonnie, ever the loyal cheerleader, smiled encouragingly.

"Yeah, at this point, I don't see why you even need the library's help." Ana spooned some guacamole on her plate.

"Schools are only half the battle. Getting the library on board will double the outreach efforts and give kids more opportunities to engage with books. Most of the trouble kids get into happens during the hours between when school ends and parents come home from work." Cassie plucked a chip from the basket on the table. "Library programs targeted during this time would be a win-win."

"Makes perfect sense." Bonnie nodded. "And you'd think the library would be all over an opportunity like this. What's the problem?"

"Funding." Cassie pointed her chip at Ana's plate. "Think of that pile of guac as state funding for education." She scooped up a healthy bite. "All these programs are fighting for their share." She scooped up another bite and then another.

"Hey!" Ana frowned at the rapidly diminishing amount of guacamole on her plate.

"Sorry." Cassie pushed the bowl of guac toward Ana. "That's why I want to get the library involved, a joint venture would not only mean a joint effort but joint funding."

"And that's *exactly* why they won't meet with you." Sadie squeezed another lime into her water glass. "Cassie, this is Chicago. You gotta play the game, baby."

Cassie stirred the ice in her margarita. "Do you have any suggestions?"

"Do what my daddy taught me." Sadie schooled her features and lowered her voice, mimicking her father. "Follow the money."

"That sounds just like your dad." Ana snorted. "It's true, though, Cass. You gotta get 'em where it hurts. Go after the donors."

"How is she supposed to do that?" Bonnie wondered.

"You mean the library's benefactors," Cassie mused out loud, spidey senses tingling. Her friends might be on to something.

"Your dad knows his shit," Cassie told Sadie when they met up for margaritas the following Monday.

Sadie's violet eyes twinkled. "So you followed the money?"

"I did. And hit pay dirt, literally." Cassie licked a bit of salt from the rim of her drink. "It took some digging, but I found an annual donor who was very interested in my literacy campaign."

"And?" Ana prodded.

"And I got a call the next day, from the secretary of the

Chicago Public Library's board herself." Cassie grinned. "Get this, not only did she apologize for the delay in responding, but she told me the CPL would be delighted to team up with *ChiChat* on this reading initiative."

"Does that mean you got your interview?" Bonnie gasped.

"I got my interview." Cassie nodded. "With the vice president of the library's board of directors!"

"Woo-hoo, all the way to the top, baby. Well played." Ana raised her glass and they all joined in.

"Well, almost all the way to the top. I'd have loved to get the board president, she's amazing, but I'm not complaining."

"When does the big gig go down?" Sadie asked.

"Not for another month yet." Cassie smiled. "It's scheduled for December sixth."

Next to her, Bonnie beamed. "Aw, that's St. Nicholas Day."

"I know, I'm taking it as a sign of good luck." She'd circled the date on her coffee-stained desk calendar with a red sharpie, grinning when she'd realized it was going to happen on St. Nicholas Day. Everything was falling into place. Her ducks lining up in a beautiful, perfect row. She may have even picked up Charlie and danced with her plant around her cubicle.

"Do you know what they're talking about?" Ana asked Sadie.

"Nope, not a clue." Sadie cocked a golden eyebrow across the booth at Bonnie and Cassie. "I grew up in a house with both a Christmas tree and a menorah, and I have never heard of this holiday."

"I learned about it from Cassie's family when we were kids." Bonnie snagged a chip from the bowl. "Involves shoes."

"Oh?" Sadie perked up.

"And chocolate."

"Oh, really?" Ana asked, echoing Sadie's note of interest.

"The chocolate isn't a requirement." Cassie laughed, tossing back the rest of her margarita. "But seriously, guys, I can't remember when things have gone so well for me. Professionally and personally."

"Don't jinx it," Sadie warned, picking olives off her salad.

"Those are like ten calories each," Ana said, poking Sadie. "Just eat the damn things."

"I've got an audition coming up." Sadie aimed an olive at Ana's head before turning back to Cassie. "Everything is great with your Scot, then?" Sadie leaned across the table. "How's his cute British friend . . . what was his name?"

"Theo," Bonnie cut in. Her cupid's bow mouth pinched for a moment before curving in the coy smile of a gossip with juicy details. "And things must be really great with Logan . . ." She paused for effect before continuing, "Cassie gave him my key to her apartment."

"Oh really?" Ana gasped dramatically. "So the two of you are living in sin?"

"Not all the time." Cassie couldn't stop the wicked grin from creeping across her face.

"Just most of the time," Sadie teased. "How long has it been now, two months?"

"Actually . . ." Cassie paused, doing some quick math in her head. "It's been *exactly* two months." She jumped up, slurping the rest of her 'rita and tossing some cash on the table. "Hey, I gotta go."

"Ditching us for a hot date, huh?" Sadie laughed.

"If I'm lucky." Cassie waved and headed for the door. On the way to her apartment, she dialed Logan. She knew he was probably in the middle of hosting his show, and sure enough, after a few rings, his voicemail picked up.

"Hey," she said, a little breathless and tipsy as she hurried to catch a train, "you know what tonight is, right? Get ready to celebrate." She glanced around, lowering her voice to a husky whisper. "Oh, and this time, remember to bring your kilt."

Logan clicked play on the message again. At the sound of her sexy purr, he couldn't stop the goofy grin from spreading across his face. Christ, he was a sap. Two months— had he really been in this city so long already? Time had flown. Fall in Chicago was bonny, the changing leaves a canvas of bright colors, almost as brilliant as the shades of scarlet and gold that hedged the burns and blanketed the hills back home. Of late, the wind off the lake had a bite to it, making Logan think of Scotland more and more. A month had passed since he'd promised Theo he'd call Nettie. He'd do it soon. Tomorrow.

But tonight was for Cassie.

A few hours later, as Logan bounded up the steps of her building, he wished the lass had asked for something else. Chicago wasn't called the Windy City for nothing. It was only a few block's walk from the train to Cassie's flat, but most of that was toward the lake, with nothing to stop the wind from flying up his kilt and biting his arse. To add insult to injury, his cock and balls were now bloody Baltic.

Thank God he had a warm lass waiting to heat him up.

Once in her apartment, Logan shucked off his boots, tossing them in the closet, his legs raw and chapped with cold.

"Did you wear that all the way here?" Cassie asked, surprise coloring her voice.

He turned and gave her a look. "Of course, I did. You bloody asked me to."

"I said to *bring* the kilt, not wear it." She smirked and shook her head, looking him up and down. "You must be freezing."

"Aye, I am," he growled. "Now get over here and make yourself useful, woman." He lunged, reaching for her. She was wearing the dusky blue sweater dress, the one she'd been wearing that night at the Caldy.

She wiggled out of his grasp. "Your hands are like ice!"

"That's nothing." He stalked toward her as she backed away from him. "You should feel my cock." He launched himself at her and she squealed, turning to run. "Lord help me," he groaned, watching the lass's curves shift and sway beneath the magic of her dress.

She'd headed toward the bedroom, which suited him fine. He followed on her heels, and when she dove for the bed, he caught her, collapsing on top of her. She was warm and soft and smelled delicious. He nuzzled her neck, teeth nipping at the delicate skin behind her ear.

She shivered.

"Cold?" he asked.

"Not as cold as you are." Her hand drifted beneath his kilt and she gasped, "Holy shit, you weren't kidding!"

"Pipe down, lass, you'll scare the poor frozen bugger," he warned. "Then he'll never want to come out and play."

Cassie giggled, and he felt the vibration of it all through his body. He loved hearing her laugh, the sound warming him as much as her touch. He rolled, pulling her on top of him.

She straddled his hips, palms braced against his chest, the tight vec of her thighs cradling him with exquisite heat. He lay back on the pillows and closed his eyes, relishing the feel of her, the weight of her body pressing down on his. The tickle of her hair on his face as she bent down to kiss him, the brush of her lips against his.

Eyes still closed, he let her take her time, her tongue exploring his mouth while her hands explored his body. Slowly, her fingers worked the buttons of his shirt loose, spreading the fabric wide. She flicked her fingers over his nipples and then trailed them slowly down the line of hair low on his belly. Everywhere she touched him his body burned, and as his temperature rose, so did his cock.

Cassie broke the kiss and shimmied lower, her breath hot against his skin. She shoved the swath of kilt up and took him into her mouth. Pure pleasure bolted through him and Logan moaned, tangling his hands in her hair while she sucked him, her lips and tongue snug and sure. Unable to stop, he arched his back, lifting off the bed as he pressed deeper into her mouth, so deep he was afraid he would hurt her. Still she took him, took more of him than he believed was possible, warm and wet and so fucking perfect.

He let her bring him to the brink before he stopped her, tugging her hair gently, urging her mouth back up to his. He kissed her, hard and deep, tasting himself on her tongue. He reached for the hem of her dress, bunching the soft fabric in his hands.

The feeling triggered a host of sensory memories, and he smiled in the shadowy cocoon of her bedroom. "You're wearing that dress," he said, not needing light to see what his touch remembered. In his mind's eye he could see Cassie walking ahead of him, leading the way down the hall to her hotel room, this very dress riding up her thighs after he'd ravaged her in the lift—after they'd ravaged each other.

"You remembered," she said, sitting up. "I was wondering if you'd notice."

"Och, I noticed." Logan brushed his hands up her bare legs, rucking her dress higher. "I may have been frozen as a corpse, but I'm not dead."

She was still straddling him, rubbing against him with every shift of her body. He curled his fingers around her panties, and she helped peel the silky fabric off before settling back down on top of him. A groan of appreciation escaped him as he palmed the ripe round curves of her ass.

Cassie leaned back, pulling a condom from her nightstand. Logan watched, mesmerized, while she slipped the rubber around the swollen head of his cock, her fingers swift and sure as she rolled it down his thick hard length. When she began to tug her dress over her head, he stopped her.

"Leave it," he growled, pulling her to him again so he could nip at her lips, at the delicate line of her jaw, tasting her in little nibbles. "I fucking love this dress," he breathed, his hands roaming over her back, down to her waist, where he held her in place and thrust up into her.

She gasped as he entered her. "I know you do."

He tilted his hips and rocked, groaning as the move pushed him deeper inside her. "I fucking love you."

She stilled atop him, and he pulled back, reeling, his words hanging in the air between them, suspended in the sudden silence as neither of them moved, or even breathed. He stared up at her, searching her face, unable to read her expression in the dim light of her bedroom.

Finally, she exhaled and leaned forward. "I love you too," she whispered in his ear, her voice low and sexy as hell. "Happy two-month anniversary."

* * *

Later, after they'd raided the kitchen for a midnight snack, Logan drowsed on the couch, Cassie nestled against his side.

"This is nice," she said, snuggling closer.

"It is." He pressed a kiss to the top of her head, her chestnut curls tickling his cheek as he inhaled her scent, a mix of coffee beans and something softly floral. Was it strange how comfortable he'd become with a lass he'd only known two months, in a country he'd been in for less than that? Once more he was reminded of home and of his promise to call his sister.

An idea struck him, and for the second time tonight his mouth was in motion before his brain could catch up. "Would you like to come home with me, lass?"

Cassie glanced at him from beneath the shadowed crescents of her eyelashes. "What, back to your hotel room downtown?"

"No." He chuckled. She was giving him an out, but he didn't want to take it. He'd already jumped in the lake, might as well go for a swim. "To my family's home, in Lochalsh."

"Scotland?" She sat up, meeting his eyes.

"Aye. I've been meaning to pay Mam a visit for a while now."

Cassie bit her lip. "I want to, but I've got so much going on at *ChiChat* . . . how long?"

"A few days, perhaps?" He figured he could swing a stay of three days, four at the most. Enough to appease his conscience.

"When?"

Logan shrugged. "Soon. Before the end of the month. I've got a wee break before we tape the final episodes of the season."

"Hmm . . ." Cassie tapped a finger against her chin.

"You know, that could work. I get some time off for Thanksgiving. But," she hesitated, her brow furrowed, "I don't want to crash a family holiday."

"It's an American holiday, aye?" Logan reminder her, smiling. "Though I'm sure my mam will be happy to prepare a feast for you." He paused, suddenly shy . . . an alien sensation. "I've never brought a lass home before." He'd never told a lass he loved her either, but she hadn't said anything more about that moment in bed, and he sure as hell wasn't going to bring it up now.

"Never?" Cassie beamed, and it was like morning sun cresting over the brochs atop the hills back home, golden and sweet and full of promise. Suddenly, Logan couldn't wait to be back in Scotland with Cassie by his side.

CHAPTER 23

A YEAR AGO, if someone had told Cassie she'd be spending the following Thanksgiving in the Highlands with a sexy Scot by her side, she'd have laughed and wondered if there was more than tryptophan in the turkey because they had to be tripping.

Cassie was so excited, she felt a bit high herself. She couldn't wait to start exploring Logan's hometown and planned to see and do as much in the three days—five, if she counted travel days—as possible. She'd done some research, okay, a lot of research, and Lochalsh looked like something straight out of a fairy tale. A harbor city bisected by the sea and skirted by the soaring hills of the Highlands, Logan's hometown was in throwing distance of such historic landmarks as Eilean Donan Castle and Glen Shiel.

Logan handled the travel arrangements, refusing to hear a word about her paying her own way. Their flight was scheduled for Wednesday, the day before Thanksgiving, the flipping busiest travel day of the year. When Cassie told Logan they should head to the airport over three hours before their flight, he'd laughed. But she insisted, and she'd been right.

As expected, even at the crack of dawn, O'Hare was a circle of hell straight out of Dante's *Inferno*. They trudged through international check-in, making sloths look speedy. By the time their flight got underway, she was tired and cranky and more than ready for the glass of complimentary champagne the attendant offered her.

Cassie had never flown first class before, even the perks courtesy of Sadie's dad hadn't stretched that far. She had to admit, she liked being pampered. She settled back in her seat and sipped her bubbly. "All right, I have to ask. How can you afford all this? I mean, I know *Shenanigans* was popular but . . ."

"Aye, well," he huffed, his tone gruff, "I've got other funds." He fiddled with the stem of his glass, not quite meeting her eyes.

"Sorry, that was rude. It's none of my business." Cassie searched his face, holding back from saying more. Something had triggered his melancholy mood, but rather than pry it out of him like she was dying to do, instinct told her to leave him be, and let whatever was troubling him come to the surface on its own.

An awkward silence crept between them. She swallowed the last of her champagne, studying him over the rim. After the attendant came around and took their glasses, Logan shifted toward her. Even in the roomier first-class seats, his broad shoulders and long legs looked cramped. Maybe her instincts were wrong. Maybe he was crabby from the O'Hare ordeal too, or maybe he just didn't like flying.

"Everything okay?" she asked. That was a safe enough question. General. Open-ended.

His response was a noncommittal shrug. Or, at least she

thought it was a shrug. With the way he was bottled up in the seat, it was hard to tell.

"Logan?" Was he regretting this trip? Wishing he'd never asked her to go? They still hadn't talked about that moment in bed the other night, when they'd said . . .

"The show does pay well," he mumbled, interrupting Cassie's thoughts.

"What? Oh, we don't have to talk about that, I never should have asked—" Cassie began, embarrassed she'd ever mentioned the subject.

"But there was a settlement too, you ken," he cut her off, his voice muted, almost strained as he added, "from Da's death." He shifted again, turning away from her to stare out the small window.

"Oh." Cassie's breath caught in her chest. She reached out her hand, and his muscles tensed beneath her touch. She recalled that night in the restaurant on their one-month anniversary when she'd asked about his family. Just like now, he'd closed up, his body stiff, voice clipped. She ached to say something, do something to ease the pain etched in every taut line of his body. "I'm so sorry."

"It was a long time ago, aye?"

"How old were you?"

"Seventeen."

Cassie thought about herself at that age, tried to remember what's she'd been like at seventeen, tried to imagine what it would have been like to lose her father then—God, what it would be like to lose her father now. Her dad had never been the coddling type, devoted to his own passions and interests and often lost in his own little world, but she'd never doubted that he loved her, never doubted that he would be there for her whenever she needed him.

"I'm sorry," she repeated, at a loss for anything else.

"It was an accident," he said, his voice low as he continued to gaze out at the endless expanse of sky.

She stroked his back, not saying anything, hoping he would open up to her.

After a few moments he let out a breath and faced her. "Da had gone out for his usual gloaming bike ride. He always took a turn on his bike after work." A twisted half smile cracked the frozen façade of Logan's face. "For his health, he'd say. Da always joked, he didn't . . . he didn't . . ."

Logan stopped, his breathing shallow. Cassie sat absolutely still, eyes and throat burning as she watched him struggle to get the words out.

"He didn't want Mam to outlive him." A broken, bitter laugh escaped him, the sound unlike anything Cassie had heard before. "The doctors said Da had been lucky, that he'd died instantly. 'Luck,' what an interesting word." Another bitter laugh. "I wonder, did Da feel lucky when he saw death coming around the bend at three hundred plus kilometers per hour?" He rubbed a hand over his face, body shuddering.

Cassie pulled her big Scot toward her, pushed his head down to lay against her, wrapping her arms around his shoulders. He leaned into her, burying his face in her breasts as she kissed the tip of one ear, the top of his head, offering the comfort of human touch, the giving and receiving of solace. She glanced around the quiet cabin. While there was nothing inappropriate in their movements, still, there was an intimacy to the moment she didn't feel like sharing.

On the attendant's next pass down the aisle, Cassie made a request, and a few minutes later, a soft travel blanket was draped over them both. She rested her chin on

Logan's tousled mane, inhaling the woodsy scent of his
aftershave. He snuggled against her under the blanket,
nuzzling a wordless thank you in the hollow of her throat.

Emotionally wrung out, lulled by the steady hum of
the plane and the subtle thrum of alcohol in her veins,
with the quiet weight of Logan's cheek pressed against
her heart, Cassie was asleep before they even reached
the Atlantic.

After landing in Inverness, they rented a car for the two-
hour drive to Lochalsh. Cassie stared out the window, en-
tranced by the view. She'd only had a chance to visit
Edinburgh on her trip this summer, and while they'd explored a bit of the Irish countryside, this was different. Unlike the rolling green hills outside Dublin, the Highlands
rose in craggy brown and gray peaks, tall Scotch pines
peppering the landscape.

For most of the ride, Logan was a silent lump slumped
behind the wheel, eyes on the narrow road ahead. Occa-
sionally he would respond to Cassie's oohs and ahs, sup-
plying names of the many lochs they passed. They rolled
off his tongue like magic spells, conjuring mist and re-
fracted moonlight: Loch Garve, Loch Luichart, Loch
a'Chuilinn, Loch Dùghaill, Loch Carron, and at last, Loch
Alsh.

It was approaching ten o'clock at night when he finally
turned off the main road and headed up a gravel path.
From out of the darkness a house appeared, whitewashed
walls shining in the glow of an almost full moon, the many
windows framed by shutters painted a blue so deep to be
almost purple.

"It's lovely," Cassie breathed.

"It's home," was all Logan said as he unloaded their
bags.

But Cassie heard the note of pride in his voice, and something else too. She swept a glance over the warm and welcoming house and wondered if coming home was hard for him. Of course, it probably was. He hadn't spoken about his father again, but as they drove, she could sense the tension building in Logan the closer they'd got to his home.

Come to think if it, Cassie was feeling a bit tense herself. She'd never done the whole "meet the parents" routine before. She'd never been serious enough with a guy for things to get this far.

The front of the house lit up in a blaze of light as a woman stepped outside, waving while they approached. Cassie waved back. *What am I supposed to say?* She wondered, nervous energy flooding her veins. *Hi, I'm Cassie, the girl who's been banging your son silly for the past three months. Oh, and I think I'm in love with him?*

As it turned out, Cassie didn't have to say much of anything. Logan's mother did plenty of talking for everyone, chattering nonstop, starting with the moment she introduced herself at the door. "Fiona Reid, my dear, and you must be Cassie. Welcome, welcome."

Before Cassie could reply, she was wrapped in a fierce hug.

"I can see where your red hair comes from," Cassie said to Logan, glancing up at him over his mother's head. Fiona's wild mane of bright red hair was sprinkled liberally with white, but the top of her head barely brushed Cassie's chin. Considering Logan was six feet and then some, Cassie was taken by surprise. The height must be from his father. She kept that observation to herself.

A grunt was Logan's only response as he heaved their luggage through the door.

"Let me help you with that." She hurried to follow Logan inside.

"Don't fash yerself, sweeting." Fiona patted Cassie's hand before opening her arms to her son. "It's good to see you, laddie. Now, come here and hug your dear old mam."

Logan grabbed his mother around the waist and lifted her. "Good to see you, Mam," he said, wrapping her in a hug while the woman's feet swung several inches above the floor.

"Mind you don't drop me," she said. "My bones are getting as brittle as Hilda Heyworth's shortbread."

Logan set his mother down and bent to kiss her cheek.

"That's better," she said. "Are you peckish at all?"

"Starving," he growled, his *r*'s rolling thicker than ever. "I think I'd even eat some of old maid Hildy's shortbread right about now."

"Not in my house," his mother scolded. "Off to the kitchen with you. I'll put the kettle on the hob, and there's a batch of dumplings, made fresh this morning." Fiona strode down the hall, motioning for them to follow.

Logan grabbed Cassie's hand and pulled her down the hall after his mother. "You're in for a treat."

She squeezed his hand back, relieved to see the familiar twinkle in his eye.

As Fiona set out bowls and spoons on a table made from wide planks of a glossy, honey-colored wood, she pelted them with questions. Not waiting for an answer before asking more questions, she bustled about the kitchen, making tea and asking how the drive down from Inverness was.

Finally, after she'd served each of them a heaping portion of dumpling and set out a fresh pot of sweet-smelling cream, Logan's mother settled herself on the bench across the table. "Well, don't be shy, hen. Eat up, eat up."

Cassie examined the contents of her bowl, staring down at what resembled a spongy fruitcake. She copied what

Logan was doing and poured a generous helping of custard cream over the top of her dumpling before digging in.

Biting into the dumpling while Fiona stared intently at her should have been unnerving, but Cassie was used to people watching her eat. She'd often featured hot new dining spots on her *ChiChat* segment, covering everything from Michelin-starred restaurants on the Magnificent Mile to trendy food trucks on the South Side. Being filmed taking giant bites out of a candied bacon burger or slurping noodles at a new ramen joint had been a regular part of her job.

The dumpling's texture was surprisingly soft, the taste spicy—a cross between bread pudding and gingerbread. "This is delicious," Cassie said, spooning up another bite, glad she meant it.

"Thank you, dear. It's my gran's recipe, you ken. I've messed with it a bit, to be sure. I prefer to make lots of wee dumplings rather than one portly ol' pudding. But the ingredients haven't changed much in more than fifty years." As Fiona set another dumpling in Cassie's bowl, she continued to chatter, and by the time Cassie finally set her spoon down, tummy full to bursting, she had gotten a comprehensive education on the history of the clootie dumpling. She almost wished she'd taken notes to share with Ana, who probably would have loved to try her hand at the Scottish treat.

Cassie glanced over at Logan, who was seated next to her on a bench cut from the same honey-colored wood as the table. He gave her a lazy smile and scooped up the last bite from Cassie's bowl, popping it in his mouth. When Fiona stood and began to gather up the dishes, Cassie rose to help her, but Logan's mother waved a hand, insisting Cassie sit and rest after the long journey. Logan eyed the remaining dumplings piled on a tray in the center of the table. He reached for one, and his mother slapped his wrist.

"Don't make yourself sick, loon." Fiona grabbed the plate and brought it to a sideboard. Over her shoulder she said, "You can have the rest of these in the morning, I'll fry 'em for brekkie, aye?"

"Fine," Logan grumbled.

He was such a picture of thwarted petulant boy Cassie laughed.

Fiona grinned, her lips curving with the same promise of mischief that so often crossed her son's face. "Clooties are his favorite, you ken."

"Is that what you were cooking in my kitchen that day?" Cassie asked.

"You tried to cook?" Fiona chortled in disbelief.

Logan shrugged. "*Try* is the key word," he said, cheeks growing pink.

Fiona turned to Cassie. "Well," she said, and her Gaelic lilt drew the word out, giving it weight. "You must be something special indeed, if my son was willing to risk the danger of such a domestic endeavor."

This time, when Fiona stared at her, Cassie was unnerved by the weight of the woman's shrewd gaze taking her measure. It was her turn to blush.

Logan came to her rescue, rising from the bench. "Speaking of domestic endeavors"—he took the now clean dishes from his mother and stacked them in the cupboard—"I told Cassie you'd insist on preparing a grand feast when you heard she was missing out on Thanksgiving back home to be here with me."

"Of course I would." Fiona laid the dish cloth over the sink and crossed her arms. Her brows wrinkled as she glanced at Cassie. "About that. I know the holiday is on

Thursday, but I was hoping we could wait to celebrate on Friday, as Nettie won't be here 'til then."

"That's fine, really. You don't have to do anything special—"

Logan's mother cut Cassie off with a click of her tongue. "No more of that, now. It's my pleasure."

"Aye, and now that I know how much trouble it all is, it will be my pleasure to help you with the cooking," Logan said, bending down to kiss his mother's cheek.

"Is this one of your jests?" she asked, staring up at him. Fiona turned to Cassie. "Stay on your guard with this one, you never know when he has something funny planned."

"Oh, I'm aware," Cassie said, smiling as she met Logan's eyes over his mother's head.

Fiona shook her head. "Like his da, that man always had some shavie up his sleeve."

This was Fiona's first mention of her husband, and Cassie hesitated, unsure how to proceed. "Shavie?" she asked.

"A joke, you ken—a prank. Full of mischief, my Cameron was." Fiona tilted her chin, looking heavenward, eyes shining. "He's probably running a shavie on some poor angel even as we speak, the good Lord bless him." Fiona crossed herself and offered Cassie a watery smile. "But there was never any malice in his pranks." Logan's mother retrieved the dish towel and wiped her eyes. "The man had a tender heart."

"Well, he sounds like a wonderful man," Cassie said, careful to keep her voice gentle. *And a lot like his son.* She risked a glance at Logan. He was staring at the floor, and in the gleam of firelight from the hearth she caught the twitch of a muscle in his jaw.

"He was. He was indeed." Fiona set the towel aside

again and took a deep breath. "Now then, it's late and I'm sure you're both tired. Let's find you some beds then, shall we?"

When Logan's mother had said "beds," she'd indeed meant beds, as in plural, separate bedrooms. Fiona had escorted Cassie to a guest room on the first floor, a lovely suite with an attached private bath and a breathtaking view of the loch. Not long after, Logan dropped off her bags and kissed her good night, but he'd been different. Not cold exactly, but stiff . . . distant. Before Cassie could talk to him and try to chip away at the wall rising between them right before her eyes, he'd excused himself, taking his things upstairs to what Cassie presumed was his boyhood room.

She wished he would talk to her some more, share what he was feeling, let her comfort him as she had on the plane. Even though the long day of travel had worn her out, with the way things had been left between them, she thought she'd be up tossing and turning all night. But the fluffy feather pillows and thick down coverlet made her feel like she was going to bed on a cloud. The next thing she knew, it was morning and the decadent smell of fried dough was nudging her awake.

Stretching, Cassie inhaled deeply and realized she was starving. Considering the amount of clooties she'd downed last night, she couldn't believe the way her stomach growled as she dressed and brushed her teeth. When she entered the kitchen, she said as much to Fiona, who was standing at the stove flipping dumplings, her hair tucked in a braid that made her look years younger.

Logan's mother laughed. "Och, that's the Highland air for you. Works up a serious appetite." She pointed her spatula at the sideboard. "There's juice and tea, if you like."

"Cassie prefers to kickstart her day with a jolt of

something stronger," Logan said, his deep, raspy morning voice making both women jump.

"Whisky is in the cupboard to your left, aye?" Fiona winked.

"No." Cassie laughed. "Just coffee, please . . . that is, if it's not too much trouble? I don't want to impose."

"Did that parcel I sent you arrive?" Logan asked his mother. She nodded and waved a hand toward the pantry. He ducked under the low doorway and disappeared.

Cassie couldn't help feeling a flash of disappointment. No good-morning kiss? Heck, she'd not even got a "good morning" from the man, period. A moment later he reappeared, and Cassie watched curiously as Logan began to tear packing tape off a large box. "What's that?"

"You'll see." He raised a brow at her and went back to unpacking the box.

"Is that . . ." She trailed off, not wanting to sound too hopeful.

"It is," he said as he set the French press on the counter. "I know how you like your coffee dark and strong, lass."

Cassie clapped her hands in delight when Logan reached back into the box and pulled out a bag of her favorite brand of coffee beans.

Fiona abandoned her post at the stove and watched with a bemused expression as her son went about setting up the coffee maker. She opened the bag and peeked inside, then turned and eyed the press curiously. "Do you brew the beans whole, then?"

"Christ," Logan swore.

His mother sniffed. "While I agree this smells strong enough to bring the good Lord back from the dead in one day instead of three, curb yer tongue in my kitchen, if you please, laddie."

"Sorry." Logan frowned and took the bag of beans from

his mother. He looked up at Cassie. "Sorry," he said again. "I forgot to order a grinder."

"Oh well," Cassie said, "it's the thought that counts, right?" And it was true. He'd thought about what she liked. Taken the time to do something to make her happy. She smiled at him. An answering grin lit his face, green-gold eyes twinkling, making her heart do funny little cartwheels inside her chest. "I love it," she whispered, going up on tiptoe to kiss his cheek. *I love you*, she wanted to add. But didn't.

"I've an idea." Fiona clicked her tongue thoughtfully, breaking the spell. "You said you wanted to help cook?" She slapped the spatula into Logan's palm. "Here."

Logan stood paralyzed, holding the spatula awkwardly as he watched his mother bustle off to the pantry. The sound of dough sizzling shook him into action, and he hurried to the stove. Cassie watched as he attempted to flip the dumplings. One slipped off the spatula and landed with a splat in the pan, sending hot oil spraying. "Christ!" Logan swore again, rubbing his arm, before glancing up quickly in the direction of the pantry.

"I don't think she heard," Cassie whispered, crossing the kitchen to stand next to him. "I'd offer to take over, but I don't think I'd be any better at this than you."

He winked, the naughty-boy smirk making an appearance. "I ken your feminine talents lay in other places, aye?"

"Watch it, Scottie." Cassie smacked him on the butt. He was wearing an old T-shirt and a faded pair of jeans, and she liked the feel of Logan's firm body beneath the tight, threadbare fabric. Liked it so much she was gearing up to smack him again when his mother returned from the pantry.

"Here it is!" Fiona chirped, setting a large old-fashioned mill on the counter.

Cassie dropped her hand and cleared her throat, moving to join Fiona at the counter.

Fiona poured a measure of coffee beans into the top of the mill and gestured for Cassie to take the handle on the crank. "Give it a go, lass." Cassie twisted the handle and began to grind the beans. After a moment Fiona nodded her approval and shifted her focus to Logan. "Give me that." She took the spatula and shooed him away from the stove, deftly flipping the dumplings out of the pan and into a cloth-lined basket.

While Cassie continued grinding, Logan set water to boil and prepped the press. Just when Cassie thought her hands were going to curl in a permanent cramp, Fiona took over. Logan's mother gave the crank one final turn before pulling out a small drawer at the bottom of the mill. "Will this do?" she asked, tilting the drawer so Cassie could see inside.

Cassie nodded, inhaling the thick, rich scent of fresh ground beans. *Really fresh*, she thought, flexing her fingers.

"I'll handle the rest, Mam." Logan took the coffee grounds from his mother and set about making the coffee.

Fiona watched her son, her expression clearly saying she didn't quite believe her eyes. She cocked her head toward the table. "Come join me," she said to Cassie. "We'll get first crack at the clooties before this guffy can eat them all, aye?"

While Logan finished brewing the coffee, Cassie and Fiona dug into the hot, delicious lumps of fried heaven. Between bites, Fiona peppered Cassie with suggestions of what she and Logan could do today.

"Easy, Mam," Logan said, setting a steaming mug of coffee in front of Cassie. "We're only down for a few days, remember?"

"Och, fine." Fiona made a face and sipped her tea.

"You'll have to be sure to bring her back again for a longer visit soon, then."

Logan rolled his eyes at his mother's blatant hint and joined them at the table. "Let's just get through today, aye?" He pulled the basket of clooties toward him. "I was thinking of taking her up to Eilean Donan."

"That'll be lovely." Fiona nodded. "Perhaps you can stop by the docks? Say hi to Mr. Kinney?"

Logan set a half-eaten dumpling down. "We'll see."

Cassie wondered if that phrase meant the same here as is it did back home. To Cassie, "we'll see" meant "not a chance in hell." The tone of Logan's voice certainly indicated the same, but his mother chattered on as if she expected he'd follow through.

"Wonderful. I know he'd be delighted to see you. He misses you, you know. Says it's not the same without a Reid at the helm."

"Is aught amiss at the fishery?" Logan asked, his voice gruff.

Seated next to him on the bench, Cassie could feel the waves of tension rolling off him.

"No, no." His mother was quick to respond. "Everything's grand."

"Good." Logan let out a breath and pushed back his plate. Cassie noticed he'd barely made a dent in the pile of food he'd loaded on it. But she didn't argue when he rose from the bench and offered her his hand. "Care for a walk?"

Cassie glanced at Logan's mother, not wanting to abandon the poor woman to clean up after breakfast alone. Fiona waggled her fingers toward the door. "Off you go. It's a rare fine morning out there, no need to be stuck inside wi' me."

CHAPTER 24

MAM HAD BEEN right about the weather. It *was* unusually fair for this time of year in the Highlands. Once away from the house, Logan relaxed a bit, the ever-present tightness in the back of his throat easing. He wanted to take full advantage of the bonny day and show Cassie some of the best sites Lochalsh had to offer. She'd mentioned wanting to see Eilean Donan when they'd still been in Chicago, so he decided to start there.

When they arrived at the castle, the sun was creeping over the craggy edges of the stone towers, lighting the long, winding path linking the island fortress to the mainland and sparkling like a blanket of diamonds on the surrounding moat. He gave up counting how many times she sighed and gasped with pleasure as they spent the morning inspecting every nook and cranny of the old place.

After they'd toured the castle, he took her down past Shiel Bridge to Glenelg, where they could view the ruins of the Bernera Barracks and wander around the old brochs.

"I've read about these," Cassie said, poking her head into one of the ancient round structures. She ran a hand along the mossy brick. "Can you believe this has stood here for centuries?"

"Knowing how brutal the weather is in these parts?" Logan shook his head. "Ah, no, I cannot."

She tilted her chin and looked at the top of the tower, awe sparking in her dark eyes. "I wonder what they were like."

"Who?"

"The people who built this."

Logan had to admit he'd never thought much about it. But he liked knowing that she did. There was something sweet and wonderful in the way she wanted to absorb everything. To look and touch and smell.

They were still exploring in the late afternoon when gloaming took over the highland landscape, painting the hills and crags with amber and indigo. "Where did the sun go?" Cassie asked, only half joking as she shivered in the fading light.

"Dusk falls early in the Highlands this time of year." He wrapped an arm around her, pulling her close, sharing his warmth. Day shifted to night, a chill rising with the moon as it crested the horizon, fat and full.

Cassie gasped. "It's so beautiful."

"Aye," he agreed, though it was not the moon capturing his attention. The lass was so very lovely, her cheeks pink with cold, her sable eyes shining. "That's the Dark Moon, you ken."

"The dark moon?"

"Mm-hmm," Logan hummed, brushing his lips across the tender skin of her forehead. "'Tis the Celtic name for the full moon in November," he explained, and let his mouth drift lower to nip a kiss. "Best we be careful, or the Fair Folk will come to steal you away from me."

"You mean fairies?"

"Oh, aye." He pressed another kiss to the smile hiding in the corner of her mouth. "Once a month they abandon their homes deep under the hills to dance and play in the glow of the full moon."

Cassie laughed and twirled out of his embrace, her chestnut hair fanning out around her as she spun. She cast a glance over her shoulder at him, the heat of her gaze cutting through the frosty night and warming him from the inside out. With one pale finger she beckoned to him, and Logan stepped forward, unable to resist. But before he could reach her she turned, wicked as any fey, and ran from him, teasing laughter ringing in her wake.

Logan chased her around the abandoned brochs. With his long legs, he easily outpaced her, but he let her think she was winning, enjoying the sport of it, waiting for the right moment to strike. At the edge of the hill she paused and looked back, and that's when he saw his chance. He leapt forward, wrapping his arms around her waist and tackling her. As they fell he shifted his body so he'd hit the ground first.

She landed on top of him with a yelp. Before she could squirm away from him, he tightened his hold and pitched his weight sideways, sending them tumbling down the gentle slope of the hill. They rolled to a stop in a patch of sweet-smelling clover. She lay trapped beneath him, hair spread in a dark cloud around them. He twined his fingers in the silken mass and bent forward to touch his lips to hers.

A stiff wind roared across the hillside, making the hair on the back of his neck stand on end. He ignored it, pressing into her as he kissed her, wanting to bury himself in her taste. In her heat. He plunged deeper, tongue exploring her mouth, and she moaned in response. The air around them became charged. When Logan heard the rumble of thunder in the distance, he realized it wasn't just the sparks flying between them causing the electrifying shift. With a reluctant groan, he broke the kiss and got to his feet.

"Come on, lass, I'll take you home." He offered her a hand up.

She stood. "What's wrong, are the fairies coming to get us?" she asked, quirking lips that were wet and full, swollen from his kisses.

He chuckled and pulled a purple thistle from the tangle of her hair. "No, but a storm is. Best we go before it catches up." He tugged her hand toward the car, picking up the pace as another round of thunder rolled across the hill.

On the drive back, over the steady thrum of a brisk November rain, Cassie chattered about what she'd liked best from the day's adventuring. She seemed to find all the old places fascinating, recalling the tiniest details with relish. He enjoyed listening to her, warmth blooming in his chest as her animated voice made him see places he'd grown up knowing in a fresh light, through her eyes.

By the time they got to the house, it was late and Mam had already retired upstairs. She'd left a plate of sandwiches on the table for them, along with a note threatening injury if Logan dared touch the pies cooling on the counter. Unable to resist, Logan peeked under the cloth covering the pies. As he'd known she would, Mam had gone all out for Cassie, making three different kinds. Logan didn't have to glance in the fridge to know it would be crammed full with platters of food prepped and ready to pop in the oven come morning.

He took the bench across from Cassie and propped his feet up next to her. "I hope you packed your appetite."

Cassie looked up from the sandwich she'd already

started on. "Don't worry. Ever since we got here I've been starving."

"It's the Highland air."

She laughed. "That's what your mother said."

He smiled. "Well, Mam's right." He looked at her then, watching her face carefully. "You sure you don't mind spending your holiday here? Without your family?"

Cassie shook her head and set her sandwich down. "Are you kidding me? It's fine, really. We usually go up to my mom's sister's place in Minnesota. You've rescued me from a weekend of speed walking at the Mall of America and having to eat Aunt Eleanor's Jell-O."

His confusion must have shown on his face because Cassie laughed again and explained. "Every Thanksgiving Aunt Eleanor makes these awful concoctions of fruit and Jell-O and God only knows what else. And they are always in these molds of animals. Last year it was chicken-shaped. I mean, a turkey would kind of make sense but, a chicken?" She shuddered. "And the thing about Jell-O is it wiggles . . . jiggles, really." She stared at him, her eyes wide with horror. "It was like eating a giant, jiggling, orange creamsicle–flavored chicken nugget. Can you imagine?"

Logan chuckled as he tried to picture what the lass described. "I'm glad I was able to rescue you from such a cruel fate, then." He fussed with his sandwich. "But what about your family? I'm sure they must miss you."

"I doubt it. Does that sound horrible?"

"I dinna ken. Is it?" Logan realized how little he knew about Cassie's family. During the last few months when they'd been together, in an effort to avoid talking about his own parents, Logan had avoided asking too much about hers.

She shrugged. "My mom and dad are usually busy off doing their own thing. I kind of like it, because it allows me to do my own thing too." Cassie finished her sandwich and wiped her mouth with a napkin. "And I have Bonnie, of course. She's like a sister."

An image of Cassie's friend, the redhead Theo fancied, flashed through his mind. "Right. How is Bonnie?"

A small pucker appeared between Cassie's delicately arched chestnut brows. "We haven't talked much lately. I've been so busy with the show and spending so much time with you . . ."

"What does she think of that? Of you spending so much time with me?"

"Well, it was her copy of the key to my place I gave you." Cassie's forehead smoothed and she smiled at him. "She's happy for me. I've never . . ." She stopped, staring at the crumbs on her plate.

"Never what?" he pressed.

She kept her gaze lowered. "I've never been serious about a guy before."

Logan's breathing hitched. He shifted, setting his feet on the ground and leaning forward. "And now?" He reached across the table and nudged her, his fingers gentle.

"I think maybe . . ." Cassie lifted her chin and met his eyes. "I could be."

Later that night, Logan lay awake in his old bed, staring up at the ceiling of his childhood room, a place both familiar and strange all at once. He was no longer the lad he'd once been, the boy who had slept in this bed and stared up at this ceiling.

For one thing, that boy still had a father.

How did Mam do it? How did she stay here, in this house, surrounded by the memories of what was, and face the reality of her loss each and every day? A decade later, his gut still went tight and cold at the memory of how Mam had clung to Da's limp arm as she'd begged her husband not to leave her . . . not to die.

He rolled over and punched his pillow. It was fucked up how he still hadn't gotten past Da's death. It had been ten fecking years. He should be able to come to this town and be in this house without his heart turning to bloody stone, cold and heavy and dragging him under. He should be able to talk about his father without feeling like all the air had been sucked out of the room.

The shadows on the ceiling shrank to nothing as the darkness gave way, dawn filling the room with soft, gray light. With morning, the topic he'd been struggling to keep submerged bobbed to the surface. Like a slick silver fish, it darted through his mind, nibbling at his thoughts.

He'd said he loved her, and she'd said it back. But that had been in a moment of passion when they'd been caught up in each other, in the undeniable attraction they had for each other. But was that all it was?

Was Cassie serious about him?

Christ, was he serious about her? Did he dare risk it?

The questions continued to swim around in Logan's skull long after the sun was full up, pale though it was, and ate at him most of the morning. He pushed the musings down, packing them up with all his other bloody emotional baggage, determined to enjoy the day with Cassie.

Unlike yesterday's touch of warmth, today's weather was cold and wet. Gray, soggy clouds sat heavy and low in the sky, looking as if they had no intention of going anywhere. It was a day for staying inside, for sitting by the fire with a glass of something warm.

As promised, Logan tried to help Mam in the kitchen, but before long she shooed him out, griping about how his "big braw body" kept getting in her way. After risking Mam's wrath to brew Cassie some coffee, he suggested they pass the time playing cards.

"You sure I can't help in there?" Cassie asked for at least the fifth time.

Logan glanced up from the hand she'd dealt him and shook his head. "Mam's in her element. Trust me. She doesn't get many opportunities to prepare a big meal anymore."

Cassie tossed out a card and drew another. "My mom's not much for cooking."

"Like mother, like daughter, hmm?" Logan asked, picking up the six Cassie had discarded. He placed the pair on the table.

"Hey!" Cassie protested.

"What?" he asked, the picture of innocence. "It was a fair move."

"That's not what I'm talking about and you know it." She looked at her cards, mouth pursed. "I can cook. I just don't enjoy it."

"Don't fash yourself, lass. I don't care if you can cook." He flashed a grin. "Remember, I told you I ken your talents lie elsewhere." He waggled his eyebrows, reaching under the table to touch Cassie's knee, his fingers brushing up her inner thigh. He might have explored further if the front door hadn't blown open, his sister flying in on a blast of chill November air.

Cassie jumped, clapping her knees together, almost smashing Logan's fingers in the process. He retreated and set his cards down. "Hello, Nettie," he said drily, standing and crossing the parlor to greet his sister.

"Give me a hug, you pervert." Janet dropped her bag and squeezed Logan tight. "It's good to see you."

"You too," he said, and meant it. He'd missed his sister.

Working in Chicago, he hadn't realized how much. They'd been a team for so long. Seeing her now, he felt the pang of her absence over the last few months.

Janet patted him on the back and turned to Cassie. "Hello, again," she said, moving to shake Cassie's hand when the lass rose from her spot at the card table. "You'll have to excuse my brother, he never could keep his paws out of the biscuit tin."

Cassie blushed, but before Logan could tear into his sister, Mam came bustling out of the kitchen. "Is that my Nettie-girl? It is, it is!"

Soon they were all seated in the kitchen, enjoying the fruits of Mam's labors. There were fat bridies stuffed full of steak and onions, as well as cock-a-leekie soup and fish toasties. Mam had even attempted a few American dishes, including some godawful creamy concoction made of green beans with crunchy fried things on top. Logan smiled at his mother, touched at how much effort she'd put into making this meal special for Cassie.

Mam winked at him and went back to grilling Janet. "What else is new? How have you been keeping yourself busy without this loon here to pester you?"

Janet helped herself to a second serving of the disgusting green bean crunchy thing and shrugged. "I've taken on several new bands as clients, but I'm still doing work on *Shenanigans*." She looked at Logan. "Since there hasn't been any new content to post, I'm focusing on the archives. I created a mobile app, where fans can search for old videos."

"Oh?" Logan asked. "I didn't know you knew how to do that stuff."

"I don't. Clara is helping me."

"The drummer?" Logan cocked an eyebrow at his sister.

Janet didn't miss his look. "Yep, that's the one. When she's not banging sticks with The Mermaids, she's a programmer. Cool, huh?"

"Oh yes, very cool." Logan had ideas about what else Clara was banging. Well, bully for Nettie. Maybe with him out of their flat, his sister had finally decided to come out of her shell and date a bit.

Janet smiled at him, and he knew she'd picked up on his approval. Sometimes sibling telepathy could be a good thing. She glanced around the table. "Hey, where are the clooties? I thought Mam was going to make some."

"I did, a whole mountain of them." Mam tilted her head in Logan's direction meaningfully.

Janet stared at Logan across the table. "You ate *all* of them?"

"I helped," Cassie said. She was seated next to Logan and had been quiet through most of the meal. Though, to be fair, Mam didn't leave much room for anyone else to get a word in.

"Oh, well, that's fine then." Janet grinned. "What did you think?"

"They were good," Cassie said. "Very filling."

"That's nothing. You should try black bun." Janet poured herself a glass of wine.

"Is that like black pudding?" Cassie scrunched her nose in obvious distaste.

Janet laughed. "No." She reached across the table and filled Cassie's wine glass, describing the merits of Scotland's most treasured delicacy.

"This fruitcake wrapped in a piecrust is a Christmas thing?" Cassie asked.

Mam nodded. "Aye, and Hogmanay—that's the New Year—too. Och, do you remember the year yer da stuffed a black bun full of bangers?"

Logan fought the familiar tension that rose at the mention of his father, struggling against the demons of anger, regret, and grief ready to swallow him whole. He would not give in. He would not let the demons win. He inhaled, filling his lungs in a slow, steady breath. He would stay relaxed, stay calm.

Sibling ESP in full effect, Janet cast a concerned eye his way while she continued to smile at Mam. "How could I ever forget?"

Cassie glanced around the table. "Wait, bangers . . . isn't that a sausage or something?"

"Not this time, hen." Mam shook her head. "Fire crackers. Big ones. I told you my Cameron was quite the jokester, aye? Well, at the end of one Hogmanay he had a few left over and decided to stuff them inside a loaf of black bun."

Cassie's eyes widened. "Don't tell me someone tried to eat it?"

"Och, no." Mam quivered with laughter. "The trouble was at the other end, I guess one could say."

"What happened?" Cassie looked from Mam to Janet, who were both laughing too hard to answer. She turned to Logan.

He cleared his throat. "Well, Da had thought it would be funny to put the bangers in the bun, aye? But I don't think he considered what he would do with the thing once it was lit. Not having much time to decide, he dropped the whole mess down the sewer drain."

As the memory of that night filled his mind, Logan felt a rush of love for his da. The bands of iron constricting his chest eased, and he smiled at Cassie. "I suppose he thought the water would put out the fuse."

"I'm guessing it didn't," Cassie said, eyes still wide.

Logan shook his head and chuckled. "No. The bangers went off, and the explosion caused the pipes to back up."

"Poor Auntie Madeline." Janet giggled.

Cassie looked to him again for clarification.

"The water . . . went up . . . and out . . ." Logan
wheezed, laughter making speech difficult, ". . . the loo."
He made a gesture with his hands, laughing harder as he
tried to mimic how the water had gushed, a geyser bursting out of the toilet Aunt Madeline had the misfortune to
be sitting on.

Janet picked up the narrative. "We heard a scream and
then Auntie came running out of the loo, knickers around
her knees, soaking wet with bits of black bun in her hair."

"At least, we all *hoped* it was black bun," Logan
quipped.

That set off another round of giggles.

"I don't think she ever forgave Da," Janet chortled.

"Och, of course she did." Mam wiped at her eyes, but
it was tears of laughter she shed now. "You always forgive
Logan whenever he plucks yer feathers, aye? Well, yer
Auntie Madeline put up with her brother's shavies too. Life
with your da was unexpected, messy at times, to be sure—I
wasna happy about cleaning up after that escapade, let me
tell you—but fun. Always full of craic."

"He sounds wonderful," Cassie said.

"He was, dear, he was." Mam sighed and smiled wist-
fully at Cassie. "He would have liked to meet you."

Abruptly, Mam turned to Logan. "You should bring
Cassie back for Hogmanay," she said, reaching across the
table to pat his hand.

"Ugh, slow down there, Mam." Janet refilled her wine
glass and raised it in a salute to Cassie. "You better watch
out or she'll be planning your wedding by breakfast."

Logan pulled the bottle toward him and filled his own
glass, mouth gone dry at the direction the conversation had
turned. "Or yours," he shot back at his sister.

"Yes," Mam agreed as she cut into the first of the three pies. "I want to hear more about this Clara girl. You know, Nettie, I still have your gran's engagement ring set aside."

Janet rolled her eyes. "Christ, Mam, no thank you!"

"Language," Mam scolded.

Logan hid a grin behind a forkful of blackberry-rhubarb pie. He was off the hook for now. It was his sister's turn for some maternal matrimonial machinations.

His plate full again, this time with a slice of ginger-peach pie, Logan considered his own life. Could he see himself settling down with Cassie? The thought made his entire body go equal parts hot and cold. Life was too unexpected to bother trying to plan so far ahead. Why spend years building a life with someone if it could be snatched away in a flash?

He wasn't willing to face such a loss. Wasn't brave enough to risk that kind of pain. No. Better to enjoy life one day at a time. Celebrate the moments as they come. The familiar mantra soothed him, silenced the questions. He helped himself to a slice of cherry pie. He was already full to bursting, but cherry was his favorite, and he was determined to savor the sweetness of every last bite.

CHAPTER 25

ON SATURDAY LOGAN took Cassie on a tour of the more banal, local sites of his hometown. They wandered through the business district, poking around his favorite shops. Finally, they went for a walk along the harbor, down to the pride and joy of Lochalsh's tourism industry, the aptly named Lochalsh Hotel. The hotel had a very nice lounge attached, of a higher class than the many pubs peppering the docks.

"This is lovely," Cassie said, as they settled into a booth with an impressive view of the loch and Skye Bridge stretching across the horizon.

Logan nodded. "A bit fancier than average, more for out-of-towners than locals, you ken."

The barmaid approached with two glasses of ale.

"I didna order those," he began.

"They're from the gent over there," the barmaid said, tilting her chin toward a booth across the room.

Oh, Christ. Heat rose up Logan's collar.

"What's wrong?" Cassie asked.

"Nothing," he bit off, turning away from the booth where Mr. Kinney sat, waving at them.

"Do you know that man?"

"No, I doona think so," he lied.

"Are you sure?" Cassie prodded.

Jesus, lass, leave it alone, will you? "Quite sure." He kept his gaze averted, feigning interest in the daily specials. Salmon it looked like, courtesy of Reid's Fishery, no doubt.

"Well, I think he knows you," she said, taking a sip from her pint.

"What's that?" Logan glanced up.

She nodded behind him. "He's coming this way."

Logan closed his eyes and held back a groan. A moment later, an aged meaty hand clapped him on the shoulder.

"Mr. Reid, I heard you were in town."

"A few days only." He stood and shook the hand of his father's former foreman.

"Nice to see you, Logan. Aren't you going to introduce me to your lovely companion?"

No. Offering the man a grim smile, Logan turned and held out a hand to Cassie. "Cassie Crow, please meet Mr. Nathaniel Kinney, head of Reid Fishery."

"Oh, so this is Mr. Kinney!" Cassie said, smiling up at the old curler.

Logan winced.

"Och, ye've heard of me?"

Cassie hesitated, gaze shifting between Logan and the older man. "Well, yes . . . Logan's mother, that is, Fiona, I mean, Mrs. Reid . . . she asked us to look in on you."

"Did she now?" Mr. Kinney's ruddy face beamed. "And how is yer mother?"

"Fine," Logan replied, the weight of the man's stare pressing down upon him, suffocating him.

"I'd be happy to accompany you both on a tour of the fishery," Mr. Kinney offered. "Whaddya say, Logan, come on down and see what I've done with the place? Yer father would be happy, I think."

"That would be very—" Cassie began.

"That won't be necessary, thank you," Logan said sharply.

After an awkward pause, Cassie smiled at the foreman. "We're only here a few days," she offered lamely.

"I see," Mr. Kinney said slowly. "I'll leave you to it then." He tipped his hat. "Give my regards to your mother and sister."

The pressure increased. Logan was starved for air, his lungs collapsing. "Aye," he choked out, gripping the edges of the table as the man made his farewell to Cassie.

"Logan?" she asked, reaching for his hand. He pulled away, grinding his fists into his thighs as he sucked in several slow deep breaths. "He's gone now."

He downed his ale, then raised his hand for another. "And add these to my tab," he told the barmaid, gesturing to the pints Mr. Kinney had sent over. He didn't want to owe that blasted man anything. The worst part was, Kinney wasn't the problem. He'd done a grand job taking over the business and ran it in good faith. Da would be happy. And there's the rub.

She sipped her drink quietly for a moment. "Do you want to talk about it?"

"There's nothing to talk about."

"Okay . . ." Cassie said, voice teetering with doubt. A commotion at the front of the lounge pulled her attention. "I think there's a wedding happening."

He glanced over his shoulder. Sure enough, a bridal party was making its way through the hotel restaurant to the banquet room. "That'll be the reception. The hotel hosts them often. It's likely the couple got themselves hitched over at the castle."

"Eilean Donan?" Cassie gaped at him. "The one we toured the other day?"

"That's the one."

"I'd love to get married in a castle," she sighed dreamily. He snorted. "Why?"

"Why get married in a castle?" She tilted her head, considering him. "Because it would be unique and special and ridiculously romantic."

"No. Why get married at all?" The sounds of laughter from the wedding party carried across the bar. Logan shook his head. "Those poor sots have no idea what they're in for."

"But what if you're in love?" Cassie pressed, voice taking on a wary edge.

"Even worse." He thought of his mother, broken-hearted in that hospital room. "Much worse."

She stared at him. "You don't actually believe that."

"I do." He smiled with cold finality.

That seemed to knock the wind out of her sails. "Oh." She stared at the dregs in her glass.

A fiddle began to play, a cheery tune in dreadful contrast to the mood at their table.

"Well, I believe that when two people are in love, they *should* get married," she said, her chin jutting out as she met his gaze. "And someday, I know I want to get married."

"Well, I know I don't," Logan countered, unable to stop himself. Something mean and spiteful curled in his chest, clawing to get out.

"I see," Cassie murmured, brown eyes going soft as a doe's. She blinked and shook her head, and Logan thought he caught the shimmer of tears on her lashes. Her reaction tore through him, but didn't change his mind. Better to feel a little pain now, than be in a world of hurt later.

The moment Logan put the car in park Cassie let herself out. She didn't wait for him, but instead rushed up the walkway and hurried inside, not caring if it was rude to enter his house on her own. She managed a polite greeting to his mother and sister, who were settled on the sofa in the parlor, before scurrying down the hall to her room.

Through the closed door she could hear Logan enter, his deep voice a heavy rumble in counterbalance to Janet and Fiona. Cassie resisted the urge to lean against the door and listen. Instead, she pulled her suitcase out of the closet and began to pack. They had an early morning flight back to Chicago. She might as well get ready.

It didn't take her long. After all, she'd only packed for a few days, and she was almost finished when a knock sounded at the door. She ignored it at first, zipping up her suitcase and pulling off the old travel tags. But when the knock came again, she stormed to the door and threw it open. "What?" she demanded, blanching when she saw not Logan standing outside her room, but his sister.

"It's like that, is it?" Janet raised an eyebrow, the spitting image of her brother.

Cassie gritted her teeth and turned back to her suitcase, yanking aggressively at the remaining airline tags.

Not waiting for an invitation, perhaps because one obviously wasn't forthcoming, Janet stepped inside and closed the door behind her. "You and my brother had a row, then." It was a statement, not a question.

Cassie crumpled the tags in her fist. "Not really."

That wasn't a lie. There had been no fight.

Janet sat and patted the spot next to her on the bed. When Cassie ignored her invitation and remained standing, Janet sighed. "Coming back home is always hard for Logan. I thought it would get easier with time, but . . ." Janet paused, her mouth working, ". . . to be honest, I'm not sure it's gotten all that much easier for any of us."

Despite herself, Cassie moved closer, her heart twisting at the look on Janet's face.

Staring down at the bed, her fingers tracing the pattern on the duvet, Janet continued, "In some ways I think Da's passing was a blessing." She paused and glanced up at Cassie. "I know that's a terrible thing to say—and I don't mean it like that, I'd give anything to have my father back. Anything. But Da's death forced Logan to make choices he never would have had to consider otherwise. Suddenly he had the opportunity to forge his own path."

"You're talking about the family business, right?" Cassie asked. "He was an ass to that man Mr. Kinney today."

Janet winced. "Aye, well. Everything about that place reminds him of Da . . . and Mr. Kinney worst of all." She picked at a loose thread. "Taking over the fishery never would have been a good fit for Lo. He'd have been miserable. But if Da were still alive, my brother would have done it and never once questioned it. Lo didna want anything so much as he wanted to make Da proud." She smiled then, her face soft and wistful.

"It's how he ended up going to St. Andrews. Da was always bragging about me, about how I'd gone on to university. Logan decided if getting a college education would make Da proud, then he'd go for it big time. He used some of the settlement money from Da's accident to enroll in that hoity-toity school."

"That's where Logan and Theo became friends, right?"

"Aye, I forgot. Lo told me you met Theo in London." Janet grinned. "Theo's a gem."

"He is." Cassie nodded. "He helped me out when I, uh, really needed it."

"I'm sure he did." Janet winked. "If I liked dick, I'd be all over his Prince Albert."

Cassie laughed. The sound cleansed the lingering taste of anger sitting bitter on her tongue.

"Did Lo ever tell you how *Shenanigans* got started?" Janet asked, lounging back on the bed, crossing her arms behind her head.

"He said it was your idea." Cassie frowned, wondering where Logan's sister was going with this.

"I suppose." Janet crossed her ankles and stared up at the ceiling. "But my brother thinks the idea for *Shenanigans* first came to me after his streaking incident. The truth is, I thought of it much earlier."

"What do you mean?" Cassie sat on the edge of the bed.

"It was the first Hogmanay after Da passed. We were a sorry lot, Mam, Lo, and I. The three of us mooning about and staring at the walls. Talking about everything but saying nothing." Janet shook her head. "Painful, awkward, awful."

Cassie sank back, settling on the pillows next to Janet. "I'm so sorry."

"Aye, well, it sucked. But then, out of nowhere, my brother comes prancing downstairs in some outrageous costume he'd cobbled together. When Mam demanded to know what he was about, Lo grabbed her hand and told her to get her wrap because we were going out first-footing."

"I don't know what that is," Cassie admitted.

"An old Scots custom. Especially around these parts. Winter can be long and lonely in the Highlands." Janet shifted on the bed, turning to face Cassie. "On New Year's Eve, family and friends bundle up and go visiting, hopping from house to house to share food and drink and wish their neighbors a happy new year."

"That sounds nice." Cassie rolled to her side, tucking a palm beneath her cheek and smiling at Janet.

"It's cold as hell, is what it is. But that's what the whisky is for. They don't say 'drink yer jacket' for nothing. Da had always been a grand one for the tradition. Tall and dark, he was considered lucky." Janet lifted an eyebrow, again with a devilish quirk so like Logan's it was unnerving. "Super-stition holds redheads make unlucky first-footers."

"What?"

"It's true. And redheaded females are the unluckiest of all." Janet made a sound of good-natured disgust. "So there's my brother in his ridiculous outfit, with Mam and me hovering behind." She broke off, chuckling. "The look on our neighbors' faces when they opened the door to see us standing on their porch. Old Hilda Heyworth threw a tin of shortbread at Lo's head, and maybe we redheads aren't so unlucky after all, as it was a wee bit of New Year's luck he didn't end up in hospital."

Cassie nodded, eyes wide. "I've heard about Miss Hildy's shortbread."

"I'm not surprised," Janet made a face. "The stuff is in-famous. Anyway, Mam laughed so hard, I thought we'd end up needing to take her to hospital instead for a busted gut."

Heart squeezing, Cassie wished she could see the mem-ory that brought such a brilliant twinkle to Janet's eyes.

"It was the first time we'd heard Mam laugh—*really* laugh—since Da died. And all from one of Lo's silly pranks. I wished there were some way he could do that all the time. It wasna a conscious thing then, but looking back I know that's when the idea first came to me. If he could help people find the laughter in their life, find a way to laugh at themselves . . ." Janet shrugged.

"You're a good sister, you know," Cassie said.

Janet made a very Gaelic tsking noise in the back of her throat and turned back to stare at the ceiling.

"Really, Logan is lucky to have you. And your instincts were right, *Shenanigans* is a big success. But as far as I can tell, *Shenanigans* was doing really well. Why did Logan want the television show so badly? Why was it so important?"

"Somehow he got it into his head that a show on the telly, especially one in the States, would legitimize his choice. Make it okay that he didn't carry on the family legacy."

Cassie digested that. In a twisted, male-logic kind of way, she could see how it made sense. A few pieces of the puzzle slid into place, but there were things about the man she was pretty sure she was in love with that she still didn't understand. "One more question. What does Logan have against marriage?"

Janet looked at her, face thoughtful. "I think this is where I'm going to play the sister card," she finally said, patting Cassie on the knee and sitting up. "If you really care to know, you're going to have to ask my brother about that yerself."

But Cassie didn't ask him. Not on the drive back to Inverness, nor on the plane ride home. Part of her was afraid of the answer and wished she'd never had that awful, stupid conversation with Logan. But another part of her was glad she did—glad he'd made his feelings clear. Whatever this was between them, whatever they had, it wasn't serious. Maybe she did love him, and he might even love her. But it wasn't going to last—not forever, anyway.

That question, at least, had been answered.

CHAPTER 26

BACK IN CHICAGO, an unspoken truce settled between Cassie and Logan as they eased into the same routine they'd established before leaving for Scotland. And if sometimes Cassie felt like she was tiptoeing around a baby elephant they'd brought back with them, she chose not to mention it. Just as she chose not to ask why a man who enjoyed celebrating monthly anniversaries was so averse to the idea of marriage.

He wanted to live in the moment? Fine. She could do that. They had a good thing going, she should enjoy it. Stop worrying about a happily ever after and embrace her happy for now. Determined to do just that, Cassie pushed the trip with Logan, both the good and the bad, to the back of her mind. Right now, she needed to focus on other things—like her upcoming live interview with the vice president of the Chicago Public Library's board of directors.

A few nights before St. Nicholas Day, on a rare evening when she and Logan were both free at the same time, they sat huddled on the couch in front of the TV, eating plates of Korean beef tacos (takeout, of course) when a commercial for Logan's show came on. "Tomorrow night's the last episode of your mini-season, right?" Cassie asked, dipping the end of one tortilla in plum sauce.

"Aye," Logan said around a mouthful. He swallowed and leaned forward to set his plate on the table. "That reminds me, I probably won't be home 'til late."

Cassie tried to ignore the giddy bubbles fizzing inside her at his use of the word "home." "Big party, huh?"

Logan swigged the rest of his wine and nodded. "The crew wants to go out and celebrate."

"Are you getting a second season then?" she asked, setting her own plate aside.

He shrugged and stood. "We need to see how the ratings compare." Logan gathered up the remains of their dinner and headed for the kitchen. He returned with the bottle of wine, refilling both their glasses before settling back down next to her.

"Thanks." She forced a smiled and took a sip. They hadn't talked about what would happen if his contract didn't get renewed. Like the marriage discussion, she had filed it away in the *I'll worry about this later* section of her brain. She took another sip of wine. The way things were going, that section would need more shelf space soon.

"Always happy to help get you a wee tipsy." He winked at her. "I think I'll pick up a bottle of Glengoyne whisky."

"Ugh, no. I'll stick to wine, thanks." Cassie grimaced, she'd had her fill of the stuff at Edinburgh Castle.

"Not for you, hen." Logan pulled her feet into his lap, tickling her for a second before beginning to rub them. "The lads on set have been boasting how nothing beats their Kentucky bourbon." He made the same tsking noise his sister had. "I'm thinking I have to prove them wrong. Besides . . ." he raised one of his devil brows, ". . . a wee dram may help convince them to grant me the renewal contract."

Cassie laughed, her smile genuine this time. "You are shameless." Her laugh ended on a sigh, and she groaned with appreciation as he continued to massage her feet, his thumbs circling her arches with firm, confident strokes.

"Completely," he agreed, taking an ankle in each hand and spreading her legs, his touch firm and confident as his fingers moved up her calves and thighs.

"Don't forget to leave your shoes out," she murmured.

"Pardon?" He paused, hands hovering at the hem of her pajamas.

"When you get here tomorrow night, make sure to set your shoes out for St. Nicholas."

"Who?"

Cassie rolled her eyes at the comical look of confusion stamped on his face. She wiggled out his grasp. "I told you about this. Friday is St. Nicholas Day. You're supposed to leave your shoes out and he fills them with presents." Cassie loved this holiday. Passed down from her Belgian grandparents, it was a tradition she looked forward to every year.

"Och, right. Now I remember." Logan leaned back against the couch.

"Do you?" Cassie asked in a voice laced with skepticism.

"Certainly." His tongue danced over the word, and Cassie knew he'd done it on purpose, thickening his brogue to distract her. "But remind me again. What sorts of gifts does this Nicholas fellow leave in people's shoes?"

"Mostly sweets and trinkets—little things, really. You can't fit big packages in someone's shoes, after all." She glanced down at Logan's sizable feet. "Unless that someone happens to wear anchors."

"Big shoes mean a big package?" he asked, a wicked gleam in his green-gold eyes.

"Very big." She nodded, feigning seriousness.

"Verra big, you say?" He lowered his voice to the husky, rolling burr that never failed to make her toes curl. "Well then, lass," he said, reaching for her with a naughty chuckle that made her shiver with anticipation, "I'll be needing you to help me unwrap it."

The post-production party was held in a banquet room at the same hotel where Second Studios had put Logan up to stay. Things got under way in a civilized manner, with a catered dinner served around six. Logan and his crew started the celebration with champagne, but quickly moved to the bottle of single malt Highland whisky he'd procured. Not to be outdone, one of the lads ordered a bottle of Kentucky bourbon. A bit of friendly competition ensued as he and the boys talked smack and traded stories while trying to see who could drink whom under the table.

Which meant by eight o'clock Logan and his crew were fairly blootered when Bob and Bob arrived on the scene, one producer holding a bottle of Black Label and the other carrying a bottle of Single Barrel. Before long, Johnnie Walker and Jim Beam were duking it out, and everyone had moved past tipsy to become completely trollied.

Logan closed one eye and steadied himself as he focused on clinking his shot glass against the others raised in the air. It might have been their twentieth toast or their fiftieth. The Bobs had told him not only had they renewed him for another season, but his show was taking over the entire time slot. Seems Kitty Lippy Girl was bowing out. She'd signed a multimillion-dollar deal with a home shopping network for a line of cat spa products.

If he were sober, Logan might have found the fact he'd

beaten the mental missy and her fancy feline by default a little disturbing, but at the moment, he didn't give a fig. The show was his. That was all that mattered. He had another season ahead of him, which meant a reason to stay in Chicago. An excuse to stay with Cassie.

As Logan attempted to pour another round, he contemplated the next step in what he now felt comfortable calling his career. He steadied himself against the table and stared down at the amber liquid filling his glass. How was he going to fill a full hour of television every week? Maybe he could change the show's format, mix things up . . .

One of the Bobs leaned heavily against Logan. "We need to talk about the shhhhow," he slurred, smiling, his face cherubic in its sozzled state.

"I was just thinking about that," Logan agreed.

"Oh, good." Bob straightened and beamed. After a beat, he leaned on Logan again. "We need to talk about your shooooow."

Sober Bob shook his head and turned to Logan. "Now that it's just you in that time slot, we need to focus on the original problem—raising your appeal with the female market."

"Nottaproblem," cherubic Bob proclaimed. "My wife finds him veryveryvery appealing." He tectered against Logan, staring up at him with his baby owl eyes. "Tol' me, 'Scots are hot.' Says she loooooooves your accent."

"My girlfriend does too," Logan confided, and then lowered his voice conspiratorially, "she especially loves the kilt."

"Kilt?" Bob blinked again. "What kilt?" His question came out in an odd chirping noise, reinforcing the baby owl image.

Logan snickered, his own inebriated sense of humor finding the whole thing massively entertaining. He pulled his phone out of his pocket and opened the *Shenanigans* app. Nettie had shown him how to access the archives, including a hidden file that contained any videos they'd uploaded but never posted. It took his soused brain a few tries to remember the password for the private page, but he finally managed to get it open. "Here," he said, holding out the phone in front of him so both Bobs could see the screen. "Watch this."

While the crew secured her wireless mic, Cassie mentally reviewed her interview notes one more time. She'd practiced with Anita during hair and makeup, but was still feeling nervous. Ever since she woke up this morning, a sense of foreboding had hung over her. It was probably because Logan hadn't come back to the apartment last night. He'd warned her he'd be out late, and she figured he was sleeping off his hangover in the room Second Studios provided for him.

Still, she missed waking up next to him. And selfishly missed his coffee. Cassie hoped he remembered to put out his shoes, she was looking forward to celebrating with him tonight. Hopefully, there would be a lot to celebrate. She skimmed the crew surrounding the sound stage and spotted a handler prepping her guest.

"Ready, Mr. Valentine?" She shook the man's hand again. She'd only had a brief moment to introduce herself in the green room, and now it was showtime. The floor manager gave her the signal the booth had cut to commercial, and Cassie led her guest over to their spot on-set. She settled in across from him on the plush chairs, giving her eyes a moment to adjust to the studio lights.

Here we go. On Dave's mark, she slid into action, addressing the camera. "Today on *ChiChat* I'm delighted to be sitting down with Chad Valentine, vice president of the

Chicago Public Library's board of directors." Soon, she was in the flow, and as the interview progressed, the shadowy fear that had been plaguing her all morning began to fade.

While the vice president described how the literacy initiative aligned with the board's own community outreach goals, Cassie did a subtle check-in with Dave. He raised a finger, then bent it at the knuckle. She had thirty seconds 'til transition. Her guest paused, and Cassie deftly shifted the conversation to wrap-up. "And now let's hear what our viewers think. Tiffany, what are people saying on social media?"

From her perch on an adjacent set, Tiffany took over, teeth gleaming in her on-camera smile. "On Facebook, Donna from Rosemont wants to know if suburban schools and libraries will be launching the same program. Sarah from Edgewater says her son is in one of the pilot programs and seems to be enjoying it . . . and what's this?" Tiffany paused, her smile stretching even wider.

Cassie's stomach lurched, her spidey senses were going haywire. There was something devious about Tiffany's smile . . .

"Several viewers on both Facebook and Twitter want to know if that's our very own Cassie Crow in a video surfacing early this morning." Tiffany addressed her via the camera. "Cassie, can you enlighten us?"

Cassie's pulse twitched in her neck. She shifted on her seat, trying to shrug off the unpleasant tickling of sweat beading between her shoulder blades. "I'm not sure I know what this is about . . ."

"Well, let's find out, shall we?" Tiffany nodded at the camera. "John in Calumet was helpful enough to provide a link; let's take a look."

Several of the studio's screens shifted to display the

video currently streaming for *ChiChat* viewers. Cassie sat glued to her chair, face frozen in horror as she watched herself appear in the doorway of a room in Edinburgh Castle.

Oh, no. Not this. Not now.

Across from her, ironically in the seat once occupied by a rapper who became hysterical after watching his video replay in this same studio, her esteemed guest also watched the screen. His eyes widened as vacation Cassie pulled Logan fucking Reid toward her and kissed him. The kiss was bad enough, as it progressed, Cassie realized the video had been edited so it appeared as if Cassie thought Logan was *actually* a time-traveling Highlander. She looked like a horny lunatic.

Snickers from the crew filled her earpiece, and Cassie stifled a groan, a wave of nausea rolling through her as she watched Logan, in all his kilted glory, slide his hands down her hips and grab her butt in high-definition detail.

"Oh my," Tiffany interjected, eyebrows raised in mock surprise. "Maybe this isn't safe for our younger viewers." The screens shifted focus, the video disappearing. For once, Cassie was grateful to see Tiffany's face.

She dredged up the courage to meet her guest's eyes. His face, however, did not make her feel grateful. Cassie swallowed hard. She didn't need her spidey senses to tell her she was screwed.

That night, Cassie trudged up the steps to her apartment building, dodging the swirling eddies of snow. The winter twilight was as dark and depressing as the gray-black sludge lining the sidewalks. She should have heeded the warning she'd felt this morning heading down these same steps.

She'd hoped today's interview would get some attention, and boy, had it ever. But rather than raise the city's awareness of the campaign to get Chicago's youth interested in reading, Cassie had earned insta-fame as the "Kilt Girl." Which was totally unfair since she wasn't even the one who'd been wearing the kilt.

Even more unfair were the months of work that had been undone in a matter of minutes. The credibility she'd slowly built with each interview, the relationships developed with each school visit, each meeting . . . gone in a flash. On the "L" ride home, Cassie had received an email from Therese. Her boss had scheduled a meeting for Monday morning. Nothing specific had been mentioned in the email, but Cassie bet Therese was having second thoughts about continuing the segment.

Already the internet vultures were circling, creating memes and GIFs with startling alacrity. Since the debacle aired on *ChiChat*, the video had been viewed close to a million times. Cassie knew this tidbit because Tiffany was generous enough to stop by her desk and tell her. A million views. A million people thinking Cassie was some fluff-brained female who'd read one too many romance novels. Which was something else to thank Tiffany for. The new princess of pop culture's extended coverage of the escapade had included pics of Cassie's desk, man-titty covers piled high, accompanied by the question "While youth literacy is a serious concern, is *this* how we plan to raise our city's reading rates?"

Personally, Cassie didn't think it mattered what kids read as long as they were reading, but she knew that wasn't a popular mindset. It certainly wasn't a view shared by the Chicago Public Library's vice president, who had stared at her with disgust, telling her that despite what she might believe based on the content of the video, time travel wasn't real. Which was too bad, or else he'd be able to go back in time and cancel this interview.

If time travel were possible, *she'd* go back and slap the snarky smile off his face, board member or not. Better yet, she'd go back to that day in the castle when she'd first met Logan. Cassie remembered the moment she'd realized it was a prank. At the time, she'd wanted to slap the smile off Logan's face. Now, she wanted to pummel it.

He'd lied to her. Again. And this time it wasn't for a few days. The asshole had lied straight to her face for months without once letting that charming bad-boy grin slip. Her lungs felt tight. There was a knot in her chest, twisting and tightening, making it hard to breathe. A constant pressure. A steady, heavy ache carving out her insides, leaving her as empty as the unfilled shoes she'd set out by her door before she left.

Shit. Her shoes. Had he filled them with gifts? Were his shoes sitting out, waiting for her to fill them in return? Oh, hell, was he sitting on her couch right now, waiting for her? Cassie paused outside her apartment. If she opened the door and saw his boat-sized shoes lying in wait, she would have to confront him, something she wasn't ready to do. But she wasn't willing to run away either. Not this time. She'd escaped in London when she'd found the contract in his pocket. And avoided confrontation again in Scotland, when she'd hid in her room after he'd stomped on her marriage discussion, snuffing out any vague dreams she may have had about their future together.

Gritting her teeth, she opened the door. Sure enough, Logan's shoes were there. Cassie bit back a laugh-sob. The urge to flee was strong, but an anchor forged from fury, bigger and heavier than the effing Scot's shoes, held her in place.

"Lass!" Logan emerged from her kitchen, champagne bottle in one hand, two glasses in the other. "I've been waiting for you to come home."

Once again, the way he said "home" made her heart tremble. Cassie fought the tender feelings rising up. She reached down inside herself, drawing on the anger weighing her down. She sucked in air and welcomed the weight. Tied to the dock, her heart was safe. She would not venture from the shelter of that harbor.

Logan set the glasses on the table by her sofa and poured a measure of champagne in each. "I probably shouldna be drinkin' again, considering all I had last night, but I couldna resist a toast." His excitement thickened his burr.

"A toast?" she asked, the words barely able to slip past her tight lips. "Are we celebrating something?" *Was the man serious?*

"I did it!"

"Oh, you did it, all right." Cassie stared at the Scot.

"You heard already, then? Isn't it grand? They've renewed my contract, and for the full hour now." He handed her a champagne glass and raised his own. "Sláinte!"

She threw the champagne in his face. While he coughed and sputtered, champagne dripping off his adorable, arrogant freckled nose, she took the other glass from his hand and tossed that in his face too.

"Christ, what was that for?" He grabbed the end of his shirt and wiped his eyes.

Cassie ignored the flash of washboard abs. Right now, he could do a striptease on her couch wearing only his kilt, and she wouldn't care. "How could you do this to me?"

"Do what?" He blinked, drops of champagne still clinging to his auburn lashes. "Lass? What's amiss?" he asked, confusion reflected in his eyes and the tilt of his head.

"Isn't there something else you want to tell me?" She carefully set the glasses down, her hands shaking with rage. "About a certain video, perhaps?"

Beneath the sprinkling of ginger freckles, his face paled. He swallowed, throat working.

Busted, asshole. "How could you?"

"I didna do it on purpose."

"Right. Like I'm supposed to believe this wasn't some publicity stunt." Cassie laughed. A brittle, mocking sound.

"I'm serious," he protested, the syllables tripping over themselves.

Cassie couldn't give him an opportunity to explain, to charm his way past the fact he had lied to her—used her—again.

No. She had to go on the offensive. "Even if the video got out there by accident, and boy, I'd like to hear *that* story . . . so what? How was it even possible? And the edits . . ." She crossed her arms over her chest, holding back the fear and frustration and fury all clawing for space inside her.

"I told you it was a mistake. I didna mean it for it to go public. I'm not even sure *how* it went public." Logan ran a hand through his hair, further mussing the already rumpled mess.

"If you had told me the video had been released, given me some kind of warning, I could have mentally prepared myself. At least been aware that it was out there." Cassie paused for breath, voice shaking. "Instead, I was taken completely by surprise. I looked like an imbecile."

"You want to be a broadcast journalist, aye? You need to be able to think fast on your feet." He reached a hand out and traced the curve of her cheek with one finger. "Be ready to roll with the punches. Expect the unexpected."

His chauvinistic attitude was tinder, his presumptuous comment the spark lighting her temper on fire. "My God, you are so self-involved," Cassie exploded, shoving his hand away.

"I'm self-involved?" Beneath the mocking curve of his eyebrows, Logan's eyes widened. "Take a look in the mirror, lass. Since the beginning, this has always been about you. About what you wanted. What you needed."

"That's not true," she argued. "You followed me all the way to another freaking country to get that waiver signed."

"But I wasna going to go through with it. Did I ever bring it up in London? Did I ask you to sign it? No. *You* found it. *You* signed it."

Cassie glared at him as he stood, cocky and sure. Peter Pan, the eternal mischievous boy—shrugging off guilt, avoiding both commitment and responsibility. "What would have happened if you came to Chicago and the producers hadn't offered a compromise? If you needed the video? Would you have used it?"

At her question, his face hardened, his mouth growing tight. And when he didn't reply, she had her answer.

"You know, Logan, I think maybe it's time you do some growing up," Cassie continued, so angry, her tongue felt sharp against her teeth. A weapon. A knife to cut him and make him hurt like he had hurt her. "Don't you realize how your actions affect others? Have you ever taken responsibility for yourself?"

He reeled back as if she'd slapped him. "Aye, I'm aware of all the ways I've come up short against my responsibilities. I ken well enough what my flaws are. But I also know life can be the biggest joke of all. Personally, I prefer not to set myself up as the punch line." He paused, jaw working as he stared at her. "Though perhaps, I already am."

"What's that supposed to mean?" Her entire body tensed, ready to strike back, to defend against whatever he might say.

"Do you recall the message you asked Theo to give me, before you left London?" Logan didn't wait for her to reply, but continued, "You told him that since you'd got what you wanted, it was only fair I got the same." He stared down at her, green-gold eyes mocking.

"What was it you'd wanted from me, lass? What did I give you?" He reached out and touched her wrist, fingers brushing over the charms on her bracelet as he closed the distance between them, towering over her, nostrils flaring, his chest rising and falling with shallow, furious breaths. "You came to Scotland looking for someone to fuck, and fuck me you did, right proper." The end of his sentence rasped in his throat.

Logan's cheeks were a mottled red, and he looked so wounded Cassie almost apologized. But she didn't, she refused to back down now. She clamped her lips together and moved away from him, toward the window. She kept her eyes averted and focused on the swirling patterns of snowflakes dancing in the light from the streetlamp. "I think it would be best if you left."

The room was silent for several long moments. *What if he refused to go?*

Before she could work out what she would do if he didn't leave, she heard the entry closet swing open. The rustle of clothing told her he was getting his coat. At the sound of his footsteps approaching the door, Cassie finally turned around. "Leave your key here, please."

He paused, his broad back to her. After a beat he dug into the pocket of his jeans and fished out the key she'd given him—what felt like a lifetime ago. Logan pivoted, holding out his hand.

Cassie stared at the key in his open palm. He wasn't going to make this easy for her. She sucked in a breath and gathered herself, stepping forward to take the key. As her fingers brushed his, she half expected him to grasp her hand—to tighten his grip and beg her to let him stay.

But he didn't. He didn't do anything. Didn't say anything.

Once she had hold of the key, he dropped his arm and walked out the door, closing it softly behind him.

In his wake, her tiny apartment felt big and empty. Cassie stumbled to the door and pressed her face against it, the beveled edge of a wood panel cutting into her cheek. Her gaze dropped to the ground. At her feet lay the pair of shoes she'd set out this morning. Cassie bit back a sob as she crumpled to the floor.

Peeking out from the toe of each shoe was a small, carefully wrapped package.

CHAPTER 27

SOMETIME LATER CASSIE dragged her pathetic ass off her apartment floor and called Bonnie.

"Hey, Cass."

"Hey, yourself." It was good to hear Bonnie's voice. Cassie fingered her spare key, grateful beyond words for her best friend. For more than twenty years, since she was six years old, Bonnie had been her rock, her steady constant. "Do you have a ringtone for me?" she asked, suddenly recalling Theo's screeching guitars.

"What?"

"You knew it was me calling. I mean, I suppose that could have been caller ID," Cassie rambled, not caring she probably sounded like a headcase, "but I was wondering if you have a special ringtone for me. Like a song or something."

"Oh, um. No." Bonnie paused. "Should I?"

"Maybe. I should probably do one for you on my phone too. Why don't we do it together? How about I come over?"

"Ah, sure."

But Bonnie didn't sound sure. "I'm sorry; I'm interrupting something. Do you have plans with Gabe?"

"Don't be sorry. I don't know where Gabe is. Out with some study group, I think. Which is fine, he was driving me bonkers and I've got a ton of papers to get through."

"That's right." This was when Bonnie had her semiannual end-of-semester grading frenzy. "I don't want to keep you." Cassie tried to hide her disappointment. "We can get together another time."

"Actually, now's perfect," Bonnie said, and Cassie could hear the smile in her friend's voice, "as long as you promise to bring ice cream."

"You bet." Cassie laughed, relief oozing through her. "Cookie dough or salted caramel?"

"Both. And I could use some chocolate too. Get a bag of Hershey Kisses."

"Papers that bad, huh?"

"You have no idea," Bonnie groaned. "Better make it the big bag."

Cassie pocketed her spare key. Junk food and girl time were exactly what she needed right now. "Consider it done."

"That hit the spot." Bonnie sighed, shoving the nearly empty pint of ice cream back toward Cassie. "Grateful as I am for the tasty distraction, it's time to spill." She nudged Cassie with her elbow. "What's wrong?"

The concern in her best friend's voice almost undid her. Cassie stared down at the melting dregs remaining in the container. "My big interview was today."

"Oh God, that's right." Bonnie sat up straight. "How did it go? Did something happen?"

"It was an epic cluster fuck." Cassie looked up in disbelief. "You haven't heard?"

"I'm in crunch time, remember?" Bonnie waved her arm at the piles of papers scattered across pretty much every flat surface in the room.

Okay, Bon had a good excuse for being clueless. Cassie shook her head at the mess. She'd long ago given up trying to figure out Bonnie's grading method. When it came to student papers, the normally fastidiously neat Bonnie had a chaotic system that boggled the mind. Bonnie assured her there was a method to the madness, and as far as Cassie knew, she'd never lost a term paper yet, so . . .

Bonnie tossed a Hershey Kiss at Cassie's head.

Cassie blinked, dropping the ice cream carton in surprise. "What was that for?"

"Tell me what happened!" Bonnie prodded.

"Right." Cassie grabbed the empty container and started to pack it with the tiny foil wrappers sprinkled on the floor around them. "Remember what I told you on the flight home from London?"

"You told me a *lot* of things." Bonnie got up and grabbed the other pint of ice cream from her freezer.

Cassie felt her cheeks heat as she followed Bon into the kitchen. "This is about that waiver he wanted me to sign." She dumped the garbage she'd collected from their junk food binge and retrieved her phone from her purse.

"For the video of the prank he pulled on you in Edinburgh Castle?" Bonnie pried the lid off the second container.

"Yep." Cassie pulled up *the video*, and plopped back down next to Bonnie, trading her phone for the ice cream. While Bonnie pressed play, Cassie freed a chunk of cookie dough from its creamy bed, watching over Bonnie's shoulder as the nightmare unfolded. It was all there, from entering that room in Edinburgh Castle, to finding Logan behind the bookshelf, to kissing him.

"It gets worse." Cassie clicked over to the disastrous *ChiChat* interview clip.

Bonnie gasped, eyes on the screen. "But this . . . but you . . . I mean. . . ." she sputtered. The clip drew to a close, and Bonnie looked up at Cassie, mouth hanging open. "I told you Tiffany was evil. How could she do that?"

"Pretty bad, isn't it?" she asked, scooping up more cookie dough.

"Not as bad as some of these comments," Bonnie said, shaking her head while she scrolled. "And I hate to say it, but maybe you *have* been reading too many romance novels."

Cassie choked. "What in the hell are you talking about?"

"I mean, come on, Cass." Bonnie nodded toward the screen. "You tell the guy you know he's some time-traveling Highlander and proceed to cram your tongue down his throat like it's your destiny."

Cassie swallowed past the lump in her throat and set the pint down. "The clip's been edited. Butchered is more like it. What I really said was, 'I know you're *not* some time-traveling Highlander.'"

"Oh." Bonnie had the decency to look chagrined. "Why don't you tell these people that, then?"

"Rule number one of social media: Do not engage." Cassie had covered enough celebrity meltdowns on *Chi-Chat*, including one crying rapper with a snake phobia, to know how true that was. "Besides, if you, my best friend, believed this video is real, what hope is there?"

Bonnie shrugged. "Well, you know what they say, 'What's past hope is past care.'"

"Only you say that, Bon. Only you." Cassie rubbed her palm against her forehead, wishing she could wipe away her memories of today. "How could I be so stupid?"

"Not stupid," Bonnie said, leaning toward Cassie and grabbing her hand. "Foolish, maybe . . . romantic."

Coming from the girl who was convinced her life was a real-life version of a classic novel, this was really saying something. "Holy crap." Cassie squeezed her best friend's hand and groaned, "What am I going to do?"

Bonnie wiggled her fingers out of Cassie's grasp and handed over the ice cream pint. "First, you're going to finish this."

"My boss wants to see me Monday morning." Cassie poked halfheartedly at the container. "Probably so she can fire me."

"For what? Kissing a hot guy in a kilt?"

"For not being strong under fire. For being an empty-headed female who reads romance novels." Cassie gave up on the ice cream and flounced against the embroidered cushions of Bonnie's overstuffed sofa. "Smart women with promising careers in journalism don't read fluff like that, right?"

Bonnie made a scoffing noise in the back of her throat and pulled another stack of papers onto her lap. "I may tease you about your man-chest obsession, but I know plenty of smart women who read romance."

Cassie snorted. "Name one."

"Lisa Martinek."

"The alderman?"

Bonnie glanced up, red pen of doom poised over a student's paper. "The alder*woman*."

"How do you know that?"

"That she's a woman?"

"Bon . . . ," Cassie warned.

"We have lunch at the same deli. She eats her corned beef on rye, extra mustard, while devouring Nora Roberts. I see her there all the time." Bonnie tapped her pen in thought. "I don't know how she avoids getting mustard all over the pages."

"Nora Roberts doesn't count." Cassie slumped deeper into the cushions. "She's got street cred. Everybody reads her."

"Fine. How about my doctor? She loves all those vampire books."

"What vampire books?"

"You know, the ones with the glitter or sparkles or something." Bonnie moved to the next paper in her pile. She attacked the first page with a growl. "Ugh. How does someone reach the ripe old age of nineteen, have lived on this Earth for nearly two decades, and not know the difference between 'their' and 'there'?"

While Bonnie continued her rant on homonyms, an idea began to unfurl in Cassie's brain. Those vampire books had been wildly popular too. But still, to know a doctor was reading them—someone people trusted with their health, their lives . . .

"Who else?"

"Huh?"

Cassie sat up, leaning toward Bonnie. "Who else do you know likes to read romance?"

"Uh . . ." Bonnie's brow creased in thought. "Oh! Francine. She's a professor in the physics department. She's into the ones with motorcycles and half-naked men wearing leather chaps on the covers."

"Nothing wrong with that." Cassie laughed. As her mind continued to whir with possibility, the weight of worry began to ease. She laughed again. "Nothing wrong with that at all."

On Monday morning, Cassie experienced a tickle of déjà vu as she made her way to Therese's office, once again expecting a lecture . . . or worse. But unlike before, when Cassie hadn't been sure why she'd been summoned to her boss's office, this time she knew precisely the reason.

"Before you decide anything, I'm hoping you'll hear me out," Cassie said, hovering in her boss's doorway.

"Good morning to you too." Therese nodded toward a chair.

A pang of unease rumbled through Cassie, but she quashed it and moved to sit across from her boss, diving in before she lost her nerve. "I want to reschedule my interview with the library board, but this time with the president."

Therese considered Cassie, her perfectly lipsticked mouth pursed. After a moment, she asked, "Do you think that's wise?"

"Look," Cassie said, trying to do what any good impartial journalist was supposed to do—put aside her own feelings and focus on what's important, "Chicago's youth reading level is abysmal. Study after study shows how reading is directly linked to success in school and beyond. This interview could help launch a sustainable literacy program and raise student interest."

"I'm aware of the potential benefits of this project, Cassie. I was the one who approved it, after all."

Cassie nodded, swallowing hard. Point made.

"However," Therese continued, "due to recent *developments*, I admit to having some concerns."

"My friend's doctor reads romance novels," Cassie blurted, panicking. "Vampire ones."

Therese blinked. "Pardon?"

Not how she'd planned to broach the subject, but it was too late to start over, so she forged ahead. "And you know Lisa Martinek?"

"The aldcrwoman?" For a fraction of a second, Cassie's boss looked bewildered.

Cassie nodded. "That's the one. She loves Nora Roberts books."

"Well, who doesn't?"

"Right?" Cassie smiled, then stopped. "Wait, you read Nora Roberts?" Cassie had been serious when she'd told Bonnie that everyone reads Nora, but *Therese*?

"I've been known to indulge," Therese admitted, her tone warning Cassie she better tread carefully. "So?"

Pulse racing, Cassie leaned forward in her seat. Before, when she'd presented her original concept, she'd had months of planning backing her up. Now, all she had was a wild idea born out of desperation and too much cookie dough ice cream. But if her plan worked and the project was successful, her own discomfort and embarrassment would be well worth it. "So . . . smart women read romance."

"I hardly see how that has any bearing on the situation at hand."

"Oh, come on," Cassie said, choosing not to dwell on the consequences of contradicting one's boss. "It has everything to do with the situation."

"I'm listening." Therese folded her hands together and rested them on her desk.

A tightrope stretched across the room. On the other side, Cassie could see what she wanted. But to get there meant taking a risk. The prospect was horrifying . . . and thrilling.

"I want to dispel the idea that smart people, smart women in particular, don't read romance." Cassie folded her own hands to stop them from trembling. "Nobody should ever be ashamed of what they read," she told

Therese. "If you love romance novels, fine. If you love comic books, great. Crime stories? Thrillers? Sci-Fi . . . anything goes."

"What's your point?"

"My point is that reading is imperative to an individual's success in life. My point is that it doesn't matter what you read, as long as you pick up a book. My point is people need to come out of the book closet, find stories they enjoy, and *read*."

"Well . . ." Therese paused, pressing her palms flat against the wood as she considered Cassie, eyes narrowed. Judge, jury, executioner.

Cassie stared at her boss's reflection in the highly polished surface of the desk and awaited her sentence.

"You make a good point."

Cassie glanced up, holding her breath.

"Let's see if the CPL board president agrees with you. I'll get that interview rescheduled so you can ask her."

Shoulders collapsing in relief, Cassie exhaled.

"Don't think you're off the hook, though," Therese cautioned her. "Saving this project is only the start. If you want to keep this segment going long-term, I'm going to need to hear what you plan to do next."

"No problem." Cassie had dozens of ideas, but as she sat there, trying not to panic while mentally filing through her list, she knew none of them was the right idea. She needed something to make her journalistic instincts hum, make her spidey senses tingle.

"Think about it and put something together for me," Therese suggested. "Let's plan on a pitch session right after Christmas, before I head to Key West for New Year's. Does that work for you?" She smiled again, still benevolent, but with a gleam in her eye that told Cassie "yes" was the only available option here.

"Sure." Part of Cassie wished she could head to Key West. It would be warm, it would be sunny, and it would be hundreds of miles away from a certain sexy Scot.

Therese stood, her signal the meeting was over. "Oh, and one more thing," Therese called as Cassie reached the door.

"Yes?" Cassie asked, turning to face her boss and struggling to maintain an air of calm control while inside, her mind was a tornado.

"If this bombs, you're done." Therese tapped a slim dark finger against her desk. "I like you, Cassie. But morning television is a cutthroat profession. You have to keep your head in the game."

Cassie nodded. *Gee thanks, boss, no pressure.*

CHAPTER 28

"HEY, MAM." LOGAN shifted the phone closer to his ear to hear better over the slight buzz coming over the line from an international call. Lochalsh didn't have the best cell reception.

"Logan! How are you?"

"I'm well." It wasn't a complete fib. Hearing Mam's voice lightened the heaviness in his chest that had been weighing him down for over a week, ever since Cassie had told him to get out. The December days passed in a gray blur, marked by a hideous blend of slow and slush that the locals referred to as a "wintery mix."

"I was just thinking about ye. I've about finished wrapping up the black bun, and it will be ready when you come home fer sure."

His gut twisted. "About that . . . ," he began, sitting on the edge of his hotel bed, not knowing how he was going to explain to his mother that not only would he not be coming home for Christmas next week, but he'd be absent—for the first time ever—on Hogmanay as well.

"Stop chewing on it and spit it out, laddie," Mam ordered.

"I am so sorry, Mam, but I need to be in the States for the rest of the year."

"Whatever for?" He could hear the frown in her voice, picture the crease forming between her brows right now.

"I've been asked to host a New Year's special."

"Will it be on the box?" Mam asked.

"Aye, I expect it will." He pulled his legs up and lay sideways across the bed.

Mam gasped. "Like Andy Stewart?"

"Ah, not exactly. It's more like a big party with music and dancing and such." He tried to recall the details of the event the Bobs had asked him to host. "I'll be onstage introducing the bands, and keeping the crowd entertained between sets. It's at a place here in the city."

"Not home for Hogmanay?" Mam tsked. "I suppose it was going to happen eventually." She breathed a heavy sigh. "Tell you what, I'll tuck the black bun in the post tomorrow so it's sure to arrive in time for you to enjoy."

"That's grand. Thanks." He should have tried to find a way to get home and at least spend Christmas with her. But the New Year's Eve gig gave him an excuse to stay in Chicago, on the off chance Cassie finally answered one of his calls or replied to one of his texts.

"What else is troubling you?"

"Nothing," he said, struggling to keep his tone light.

Mam, however, knew him too well. "Och, now there's a lie."

The rustling sounds on the phone told Logan his mam was settling in for a long chat. He could picture her in the kitchen, a fire in the hearth and a mug of tea on the table in front of her. The thought of her sitting there, all alone in that house, filled him with a familiar, bitter ache.

"Talk to me, son."

"How do you do it, Mam?" Logan rolled to his side and shoved the boring, standard-issue hotel pillows out of his way. He missed Cassie's soft squeaky mattress and haphazard hill of mismatched pillows. "How do you get through each day? Alone. Without Da?"

The silence following his question made Logan wince. He shouldn't have asked her that. What was wrong with him? Cassie was right, he was an inconsiderate sod who didn't stop to think about how his actions affected others. "Never mind, Mam. I'm sorry I asked."

"No," Mam said slowly, her voice soft and lilting. "I've been wondering when you would finally come around. I ken you don't like it when I talk about yer da."

"Mam—"

"Hush, now. No use denying it. It's all right, I ken it hurts." Mam paused, and Logan wondered if she felt the same tightness in her lungs, if she struggled with the same inability to breathe through the pain.

Christ, of course she did. He could still remember the sound of her broken cries echoing in the dim halls of the emergency wing of the hospital. The sound like shards of shattered glass, shredding Logan's heart and embedding in his soul.

"Aye, talking about yer da hurts," Mam said quietly. "But not talking about him hurts worse."

The simple truth of her bald admission cut Logan to the quick. "I'm so sorry, Mam," Logan breathed, his voice heavy with shame. His eyes burned and he squeezed them shut.

"Shh now, shh," Mam crooned into the phone, into his ear.

With his eyes closed, it was almost as if she were here with him, a tangible, soothing presence in the room.

"I know you're worried about me, here in this house, all alone, with nothing but my memories to comfort me," Mam said. "But I want you to know they *are* a comfort. I loved your da, I loved our life together. And I'll tell you, it's true I regret he was taken from me so soon. I regret the days we should have had. What I don't regret is the time we *did* have." Her voice was strong, resolute. "The pain of missing your da is well worth the joy of having loved him. Of loving him still."

And suddenly Logan realized Mam was right. It was true enough no one could predict what would happen next, but the fact things could change at any moment shouldn't be a reason to avoid life—to avoid love. If anything, it was the very reason to jump in with both feet and cram in as much life as you could.

When you find the person you want to spend your life with, you shouldn't waste a single day waiting. With gut-wrenching certainty, Logan knew exactly what he wanted. He wanted every day Cassie could give him—every day he could give her. Every morning and every night, every kiss, every fight, every laugh, and every tear—he wanted it all

He'd been a selfish ass, lost in his own feelings. No wonder Cassie kicked him out. He was such a blind, bloody fool. Losing Da had made him afraid to take anything seriously. To commit to something was to risk losing it. But now the thought of losing Cassie, of losing what they had, made him grind his teeth in frustration.

"Do you still have Gran's engagement ring?" he asked, surprised how easily the question slipped out.

"Aye, of course I do." Mam's chuckle was warm as a

wool afghan. "I'll jes slip it in wi' the black bun then, shall I?"

"Yes," Logan said, hope lighting all the dark spaces inside him. "Yes, that's perfect."

On Christmas Eve, Cassie wrapped presents for her family and worked up the courage to call her mom and tell her she wouldn't be heading home. Even as low-key as the Crow family holidays were, she didn't have the energy to deal with it right now. Tying a fat bow around the giant bug book she'd bought for her dad, Cassie picked up her phone, deleted all the new texts and missed phone calls from Logan—same as she'd been doing for the past two weeks—and dialed home.

"Now I understand why you ditched us at Thanksgiving." Mom chortled appreciatively. "I'd choose him over Aunt Eleanor's Jell-O molds any day."

"Mother!" Cassie shouldn't be surprised her mother was completely sucked in by the kilted Scot. Like mother, like daughter, right? Cassie had first developed her addiction to Highlander romance novels by stealing them from her mom's stash. "You've seen the video then, I take it?"

"A few times. But I've been watching your *ChiChat* interviews too. 'Coming Out of the Book Closet' was very clever. I love how you turned the whole nasty mess around. Speaking of nasty, who peed in that Tiffany girl's orange juice?"

"She has issues," Cassie said.

"I'll say," her mother agreed. "Maybe she needs to read a good romance novel or two."

For the first time in weeks, Cassie laughed. "Maybe we should get you on the show, Mom. A school principal who reads about sexy Scots."

"Speaking of," her mother continued, "why don't you bring him along?"

"Who, Logan?" Cassie paused, stomach and heart breaking into a messy tango at the thought of Logan spending the holidays with her family. "I don't think so."

"Worth a try," her mother teased. "It would have been nice to see him up close. How about you?" she continued, unperturbed. "When are you coming home?"

"I'm not sure." Cassie looped her finger through the curling ribbons on one of the presents. "I'm sorry, Mom, but once this current segment runs its course, I need to be ready with a new project."

"How soon?" Mom asked.

"I have a pitch meeting with my boss later this week."

"That's *very* soon. What's your plan?"

"I'm still working on it." Which was not exactly a lie, she *had* been thinking of new ideas . . . in the few moments she wasn't sulking about her breakup. She'd ignored Logan's calls, deleted his texts, but she couldn't pretend she liked coming home to her empty apartment and her empty bed each day, knowing he wasn't going to show up sometime in the night, warming her despite the kiss of winter chill he carried with him on his skin. Couldn't convince herself it didn't hurt to know he wasn't going to greet her in the morning with a kiss and a freshly brewed cup of coffee. "What about you, what's keeping you busy?"

"Raising money to buy uniforms for the girls' basketball team," Mom groaned.

"Why?" Cassie asked. Anything to keep her mind occupied and away from Logan and his coffee and kisses.

"For years the girls' team has had to wear the boys' jerseys."

"Gross." Cassie shuddered. "Those poor girls, having to wear a basketball jersey some junior high boy had been sweating in all season?"

"Well, they'd been washed, of course, but yes, that was one of the complaints. Another was the style. Boys' jerseys don't fit the same." Cassie's mother heaved a sigh. "I don't recall all the details, except it was a big enough deal for the parents to storm a few board meetings about it. And then it got worse from there."

"Oh?" Cassie asked, the back of her neck prickling. She leaned forward, recognizing the sensation. Spidey senses activated. There was a story here. A good one. "What happened?"

"The board finally approved a new budget. Great, right? Except, you know what my athletic director does? He makes the genius decision to use the money raised to buy new boys' uniforms."

"What?" *Yep, definitely a story.*

"It was a fiasco." Mom was getting riled up and began talking faster. "Since the budget only provided enough to purchase uniforms for one team, he figured why not buy new boys' uniforms? They were getting old anyway. What's the big deal if girls wore boys' jerseys? They'd been doing it for years. This way both teams could enjoy fresh new jerseys. He thought he was killing two birds with one stone."

"How about this," Cassie suggested peevishly, "how about the school order new girls' uniforms and let the boys wear those? What's the big deal, right?"

"Actually . . ." Mom chuckled. "A parent offered that exact solution. I'm just glad we worked it out before the situation turned ugly. Don't you remember what happened the year you did that candy fundraiser in high school?"

Cassie sucked in a breath. "Oh my God, that's right.

My team sold all those freaking chocolate bars, and the school told us we had to split the money we raised with the boys' team."

Mom laughed. "Well, the boys did buy a *lot* of chocolate from you girls."

"It's not funny, Mom," she fumed. Recalling that memory stirred a sense of injustice that still stung. Cassie's ire dialed back a notch as a hunch formed in the back of her journalistic brain. The idea gathered speed, hurtling down the track in her mind, becoming clearer. A moment later it crystalized, pure and perfect. "That's it!"

"What? What's it?"

"Mom, you're a genius!" She had her next idea, it was a Christmas miracle.

Her apartment buzzer went off, startling her. Shoving the presents off her lap, Cassie crossed to the window and looked out. A familiar thatch of red hair waited on her steps, quickly getting covered in snow.

"Uh, Mom, I gotta go."

Cassie opened her door, and Logan's green-gold eyes flashed when he caught sight of her. "Cassie. Happy Christmas, lass."

Oh, she'd missed that burr. The throaty purr of his voice was more potent than a hot toddy, warming her insides and making her dizzy. "Logan." She smiled weakly. "This is a . . . surprise. What are you doing here?" He shouldn't be here. He *couldn't* be here. But there he stood, broad shoulders filling her doorway. "*Why* are you here?"

"I've brought you something." He pulled the box he'd been carrying from under his arm and held it out to her.

"What's this?" Cassie eyed the box. *Did he think to win her back with presents?* She thought of the two tiny packages still resting in the toes of her shoes. She hadn't touched his gifts. Hadn't worn that pair of shoes for weeks. His St. Nicholas presents were still exactly where she'd found them, unopened.

"The black bun Mam promised ye."

"Oh, thanks." Cassie took the box, surprised at its weight, it was heavier than the tome she'd bought her dad for Christmas. "Um, why don't you come in?" She closed the door behind him and set the heavy box on her coffee table. "It was sweet of your mother to remember to send this. I suppose she's really missing you right now."

"You know," he said, eyes warm and tender, "I don't think she'll be as bad off as I thought."

"I'm glad to hear it." Cassie recalled how he'd been with his mom and sister at Thanksgiving and considered the pieces of the Logan puzzle Janet had given her. In Lochalsh, she'd had the opportunity to view Logan in a completely different light, the prankster hidden, the ever-present mischievous grin buried under layers of concern for his mother and her happiness. Cassie had seen the burden he carried for abandoning his family's business, the weight of grief for the father he'd lost heavy on his shoulders.

Guilt curdled the suspicion in her gut. It was Christmas Eve, for heaven's sake. The man was thousands of miles away from his home and family, she could cut him a break. "It's good to see you." She smiled at him, only a teensy scared at how true that statement was. "Tell you what, how about we declare a Christmas truce?"

A crooked, hopeful smile lit the corners of his mouth, and Cassie's heart slid sideways.

Logan watched, breath caught in his throat, as Cassie unwrapped the two presents he'd tucked in her shoes what felt like a millennia ago. She peeled away the paper with mcticulous care, going so slowly he thought he was going to expire from impatience. Finally, she gasped and he exhaled.

"They're for your wee bracelet." He'd believed the charms a grand idea at the time, but now he worried they would seem uninspired, or worse, remind her of the other charms he'd bought for her. The ones that had led to her abandoning him in London.

"They're perfect." She held up the bits of jewelry, a tiny silver fairy and a hammered pewter moon.

Like talismans, seeing the charms in her hand transported him back to that night on the hill in Lochalsh, where they'd laughed and kissed under the glow of a full moon. Christ, he'd missed her. He shifted on the couch, his blood running hot and cold. He wanted to kiss her. Wanted to tell her how stupid he'd been, how sorry he was.

He wanted to tell her he loved her.

She clipped the jewelry to her bracelet and held her wrist up. "Thank you," she said, tilting her arm so he could see the two new charms glittering with the rest of her collection.

Now. Do it now. But the words wouldn't come. Instead, he touched the delicate wings of the fairy charm. "You like them?"

"I love them."

Do you love me? Unable to hold back from touching her any longer, he reached for Cassie's hand. "Lass," he said, a catch in his voice, "I want to apologize. I never meant for the video to get out. It was a stupid mistake. I was . . . well, it doesna matter what I was doing. But I was a git, and I'm sorry. And I hope you can forgive me."

Her mouth worked. He held his breath and stroked his fingers over her palm.

"I do forgive you," she mumbled, gaze fixed on their joined hands.

The iron bands around his lungs loosened a wee bit, and he sucked in air. She'd said she forgave him, but that was a far cry from wanting to be with him again.

"I've had a lot of time to think about this over the past two weeks," she continued, her voice gaining strength, "and the truth is, I'd already forgiven you."

"Then why wouldn't you answer my calls? Why keep ignoring me?"

"Because deep down, I was still upset about something else. Something other than the video."

He tensed.

She kissed his cheek and stood. "Be right back." A moment later, Cassie returned and sat next to him, handing him a brightly colored package. "Your turn."

He took the gift, curiosity and pleasure mixing together in a sweet, heady mash. What had she chosen for him? Unlike Cassie, Logan tore his present open in mere seconds, ripping the paper to shreds.

"Bangers?" He stared down at the box, nonplussed. "You got me firecrackers?" He opened the package, checking to make sure she hadn't hidden something different inside.

"Oh God, it was a dumb idea." She groaned, the crimson flush staining her cheeks rivaling that of any ginger. "It's just, the story your family told about your dad. You all seemed so happy remembering it. And New Year's Eve is coming up, so I thought maybe . . ." She shrugged.

"They're perfect," he said, heart squeezing as understanding dawned.

"You're only repeating what I said." She bit her lip, discomfort radiating off her in waves.

"Nay, it's true." He fiddled with the box and winked at

her. "I'll be delighted to stir up some Hogmanay mischief Da would be proud of."

"Promise me one thing."

He stared at her. "What's that?"

"No exploding toilets. With my luck, it'll be my nosy neighbor who ends up with a banger flying up her bum."

"We canna have that." He grinned and pulled her into his arms. "And I'm serious," he said, emotion thickening his burr. "Yer gift *is* perfect. You wanted to give me joy. Thank you, lass."

"You're welcome," she whispered against his chest.

"You should know . . ." He rubbed a hand across her back. Back and forth. Working up the courage to say the next words. "Thinking about my da . . . talking about him. It's hard for me. It's been ten years, but I still miss him, you ken?"

A damp warmth spread across his shirt.

"Lass, are you crying?" He tilted her chin up so he could see her face. "What's amiss?"

"This," she said, wiping the tears from her cheeks before pressing her wet palms to his face. "*This* is what's been missing. I told you I wasn't angry about the video anymore, and I'm not. I'm upset because I wanted you to talk to me, to let me in. I want you to tell me how you feel."

"I doona always know how I'm feeling myself," he admitted ruefully, covering her hands with his, pinpricks of emotion stinging his eyes. "It's all jumbled."

"Well." She pulled their hands down, fingers laced, and placed them over his heart. "What are you feeling now?"

He cleared his throat. "That I love you. That I want to be with you."

"I want that too," she said.

"Oh," he exhaled, "that's good." He settled deeper into

the couch cushions. She curled into him, and as they fell into a comfortable silence, he relished the simple pleasure of the warm weight of her body pressed against him. He threaded his fingers through her mass of chestnut curls. He'd missed touching her, feeling her.

She shifted, looking up at him. "As this is Christmas Eve," she began.

"Aye?" He traced the column of her throat.

"I was wondering if you might have another present for me." She dropped her gaze to his lap, cheek curving in that wicked way he loved so well.

"You're a greedy wench," he teased, a rogue eyebrow quirking.

"I am," she confirmed, tugging on the zipper of his trousers. "Now be still so I can unwrap my present."

Late that night, as Christmas Eve gave way to Christmas Day, Logan stood at Cassie's bedroom window, watching a gentle snowfall blanket the city street below. Behind him, Cassie lay in bed, her deep even breathing providing a rhythmic background to his thoughts. He glanced back, taking in the lovely sight of her dark curls spread across the pillow. She was on her side, facing away from him, the lush slope of her hip and shoulder an erotic landscape beneath the pale sheets.

Bare feet padding silently across the shadowed floor, he got into bed and snuggled under the covers next to her, wrapping his arms tight around her, his body cradling hers, chin resting on her shoulder. "It's Christmas Day," he whispered into her hair.

"Hmm?" she mumbled sleepily.

"Talk to me, lass." He pressed his lips to the soft warm nape of her neck.

"About what?" Cassie yawned.

"About your future. A new year will be dawning soon. What do you want?"

"I want the dream," she murmured.

"Aye?" He nipped her ear lobe. "What's that?"

She rolled over and faced him, eyes still heavy-lidded with sleep. "Two kids, a dog, and a husband."

Logan snorted with laughter.

"What's so funny?" Cassie snapped groggily, punching him.

"Ow!" He rubbed his shoulder. "That's going to leave a mark"

"Good." She scowled at him.

Logan shifted on the mattress, barely missing a second encounter with her fist. "For someone who's half-asleep, you've quite an arm on you." He chuckled.

"Damn it, this is the problem with wanting a serious relationship with a man who doesn't take anything seriously." She struggled with the blankets and tried to sit up, but he stopped her.

"Serious relationship?" he mocked affectionately, throwing a leg over both of hers and pulling her close, so close he could see the ire darkening the molten honey of her sexy, sleepy eyes in the light from the snow-covered streetlamp outside. "You do realize you put the dog before the husband on your list?"

Her body relaxed beneath him. "Okay, that is kind of funny."

"It is," he agreed, placing a soft kiss in the corner of her mouth, tracing his tongue over her lips, following the curve of her blossoming smile, before dipping inside.

CHAPTER 29

THE DAY AFTER Christmas found Cassie sipping mimosas and dishing on all that happened with her best friends. Despite the snow, the five of them had managed to gather for their annual post-Christmas brunch. Even Delaney had made it into the city, though Cassie wondered if she came as much for the giant stack of carrot cake pancakes, the house special, as to see all of them.

"I think it's romantic." Bonnie sighed and stirred her steeping tea.

"That he went to her apartment after she wouldn't answer his calls or texts?" Ana asked. "That's not romantic, that's creepy."

"How is Loony Lorenzo anyway?" Sadie asked, cheeks pink from her second glass.

"Still in Italy, if he knows what's good for him," Ana said, stabbing the sausage on her plate.

"But still, to walk all the way there in this weather?" Bonnie insisted.

"Only from the train station." Delaney smothered a bite

of pancake with cream cheese icing. "That's maybe a mile."

"A mile and a quarter," Cassie amended.

"Must be that hearty Highlander constitution." Ana waggled her eyebrows.

"Wow," Bonnie said, breaking into Cassie's thoughts, "I don't think Gabe would walk a mile for me, even in warm weather."

"Come on, that's not true. Gabe loves you. He'd do anything for you."

Bonnie stared into her cup of tea.

"Bon?" Cassie asked gently.

When her friend didn't answer, Cassie glanced around the table at the others. They all knew Bonnie had been hoping Gabe would finally settle on a wedding date over the winter holidays.

Sadie cleared her throat. "I'm guessing I don't have to go shopping for a bridesmaid dress just yet, huh?"

Bonnie laughed, but Cassie heard an echo of sadness in the sound. Her heart ached for her friend.

"Fucking men." Ana banged her fist on the table, rattling the silverware.

"Keep it down, woman," Delaney cautioned, giving the side eye to a family with young children at a nearby table.

"Sorry." Ana glanced around. "This is why I prefer Disney movies. I mean, is it too much to expect a happy ending?"

Cassie nodded, adding more juice to her champagne glass. "Yep. Why do you think I read romance novels? At least I'm guaranteed that, by the end of the book, two people who love each other are definitely going to end up together. Real life makes no such promises."

"Oh, come on," Bonnie scoffed. "Don't stop believing

in happy endings because of what's happening—or should I say *not* happening—between Gabe and me. What about you and Logan? Look at how you two are working things out."

"Shouldn't that be 'Gabe and I'?"

Bonnie shot Cassie a haughty look over the rim of her teacup. "That's for nominative pronouns, I was using the objective case."

"Nominative?" Sadie wrinkled her pixie nose.

"Means subject." Bonnie waved an impatient hand at Sadie before turning back to Cassie. "And *you*, stop trying to *change* the subject. What's the story with Logan?"

"I'm not sure." Cassie squirmed.

"What do you want it to be?" Ana prodded, waving her hands over her waffle as if it was a crystal ball. "What do you see in your future?"

Cassie stared at Ana's plate. Logan had asked her pretty much the same exact question. In another place or time, she might have been more careful with her answer, but in the velvet darkness of her bed, which finally felt right again with him in it, she'd let her secret hopes spill out across the pillow.

And though he'd laughed at her, even teased her about the whole dog coming first thing, he hadn't argued with her. There were no explosions. No heated denials. No protests that a future for them wasn't possible.

It was possible. Cassie touched her wrist, fingers tracing the charms on the bracelet now sporting four memories she'd made with Logan. She wanted the opportunity to make more memories with him. "What I want," Cassie said, meeting the expectant stares of her friends, "is to get my happily ever after." She reached out and grabbed Bonnie's hand. "I want us *all* to get our happily ever after."

* * *

A few days later, Cassie met Therese in a coffee shop on the Magnificent Mile. Most of the office was out for the holidays, with *ChiChat* running pre-taped shows all week. It was strange seeing her boss somewhere outside of the gleaming office, almost like spying a teacher at the grocery store.

Therese ordered gingerbread lattes for both of them, shaking her head when Cassie started to dig in her purse for her wallet. "My treat."

"Thanks." Cassie sipped her drink, singeing her tongue on a bit of foam.

Therese wrapped an elegant hand around the handle of her mug. "Let's hear what you've got."

"I've jotted down some ideas . . ." Cassie dug her notebook out of her purse and slid it across the café table.

Therese looked over the notes as she took a long pull on her latte, seemingly unaffected by the insane temperature of the drink. Cassie was beginning to wonder if the woman was human.

"Excellent." Her boss nodded as she turned the last page. She flashed Cassie a smile. "And your timing is perfect. The disparity between how men and women are treated in the sporting world is a hot topic."

"I thought so too." Cassie flipped to a new page in her notebook. "I'm planning to start with some local stories." She started to read off the notes she'd taken about her mom's uniform fiasco.

"Cassie, relax," Therese interrupted. "We can discuss those details later. I've been thinking about your 'Coming Out of the Book Closet' feature." Her boss leaned forward, striking cheekbones a perfect blend of light and shadow in the stark glow of winter sunlight spilling in from the café windows.

"How do you feel about extending the segment all the way through January? I want you to line up interviews from the time taping picks up again next week until the start of February sweeps." Therese paused. "And for sweeps, there's a strong chance I can land you an interview with the Big O."

Finally able to handle the heat of her drink, Cassie choked on her first sip. "Wait, *the* Big O? As in the now retired Queen of Chicago Talk Shows?"

"That's the one," Therese confirmed. "You know how she's always championed books, and this new idea of yours is right up her alley. Maybe I'll see about booking the Williams sisters too." Therese tapped her finger against the handle of her mug. "That would make a fabulous segue to the sports exposé."

Cassie was still trying to process the first part of what her boss had said. *She* was going to interview the Big O . . . it was inconceivable. Cassie gripped her mug in both hands.

"Well, I'm off to Key West for a few days. I'll see you in the office next week. Happy New Year!" As if she hadn't just delivered the biggest news of Cassie's professional life, Therese gathered her purse and exited the café, exquisitely tailored Burberry coattails flapping in the brisk wind of a Chicago winter.

CHAPTER 30

"I CAN'T BELIEVE you're hosting the HoB party tonight." Cassie leaned against her kitchen counter on the morning of New Year's Eve, watching him pour a cup of coffee he'd just brewed.

"H-O-B?" Logan echoed, glancing over his shoulder at her.

"The House of Blues," Cassie clarified. "You know, the funny thing is, until this season, I've been the one handling *ChiChat*'s live coverage of that event these past few years."

"It would have been grand if we could have hosted together." He turned, handing her the coffee. It was bonkers how deliriously happy the simple act of making the lass coffee made him. He wondered if it would always be this way. Christ, he hoped so. Heart full, he traced the lines of the small box in his jeans pocket. He'd been walking around with it ever since Christmas Eve. Afraid to lose it. More afraid to do anything with it.

Unaware of his dilemma, she sipped her coffee. "I can still come and enjoy the party. What time do you have to report to the venue?"

"In a few hours, there's a sound check. The main act is a Celtic band." He dumped some sugar in his mug and stirred. She may like her coffee strong as the devil, but he took his a wee sweeter. "I'm thinking that's why I was the man for the job. I've heard a rumor there'll be bagpipes."

"Oooh, does this mean you'll be wearing your kilt?"

"I suppose." He shrugged, more interested in what she was wearing right now. While he was in jeans and bare-chested, she was bare-legged and wearing his shirt, the too-big sleeves falling past her fingertips, the hem grazing her thighs.

"Then I'll definitely be there. I probably should go shopping for a dress," she continued, oblivious to how he was staring at her over the rim of his mug. "But first I need a shower." She set her coffee cup on the counter and began to work the buttons of the shirt loose.

His gaze locked on the movement of her fingers. Maybe she wasn't so oblivious to his interest after all. She finished with the buttons and raised her eyes to his. "I have a suggestion." The amber flecks in her irises sparked with heat and Logan felt an answering warmth spread through him.

"Oh?" he asked, placing his mug next to hers before reaching up to trace the shirt's collar. He slipped a hand inside and pressed his thumb into the sensitive hollow of her throat. She shivered and he grinned, noting how her pulse beat faster beneath the pad of his thumb, how the hard peaks of her nipples poked through the white linen. He could see only a hint of the soft curve of her breasts where the fabric lay open, and a line of smooth skin leading down to the shadow of her belly button, all of it an exotic tease making him hungry for more. He grasped the lapels and widened the gap, revealing the delicate lines of her collarbones, luminous in the morning winter sunlight.

He tugged on the fabric until it slipped off her shoulders.

As the shirt fell to the floor, he breathed in sharply, trying to take everything in at once. He loved the way her hair tumbled down over her naked breasts, chestnut waves against creamy skin. Loved the dip of her waist and swell of her hips. Logan cupped her, the gentle scrape of her taut nipples against his palms making him hard. "What do you suggest?" he asked, voice rough with lust.

"Let's shower together." She slipped out of his grasp and ran bare-arsed toward the loo.

Laughing, he caught up with her and pulled her close, palming her bum, gripping a cheek in each hand and massaging the generous curves. "That's an excellent suggestion." She felt so good. He couldn't get enough of touching her. He never wanted to stop. Never. She moaned and his cock jerked, reminding him that while she was naked, he wasn't—not yet.

"Come on." He moved aside, giving her room to step into the shower stall. She flipped on the taps, providing him with another fabulous glimpse of that sweet rounded bottom he'd just had his hands all over. Water pulsed down, soaking her hair, cascading over her tits. Through the rising steam, he watched as rivulets trailed over her belly and disappeared into the dark curls at the juncture of her thighs.

"Well?" Her voice echoed in the small space. "Are you planning to join me?"

"Aye," Logan croaked, mouth gone dry despite the humid air, "you doona need to ask me twice." He shucked his jeans and joined her under the stream of water. Her body was slick and smooth, and he wanted to touch her everywhere at once. He moved behind her, holding her against him, her back to his chest.

Cassie rested her head against his shoulder, face upturned, eyes closed, water beading in her thick lashes. He bent and kissed her, tongue thrusting deep. She reached out and twined her fingers in his hair, tugging on the wet strands, pulling him closer. Logan skimmed his fingers over the swell of her hips, up to her breasts. He pinched both nipples, and she rocked backward, the curve of her ass teasing his cock. He groaned at the contact and bit her earlobe, trailing kisses down her neck while his hands continued to work her tits.

Her nipples were rock hard, and he rolled them between his fingers, tugging and teasing until she was panting, bucking her hips against him. Water streamed over his hands, and he followed the path down the valley between her breasts. When he reached the edge of her curls, he paused.

She covered his hand with hers, encouraging him to go lower. From his vantage point Logan watched as she guided him into her, their fingers slipping inside her together.

Hot, wet, slick, soft . . . his brain stopped forming words. She continued to control the movement of both their hands, and he let her lead, let her teach him. She was in command of how fast, how hard, how deep. His cock pressed into the cleft of her ass, aching to get a piece of the action. Logan took a step back and leaned against the shower wall. Slipping his free hand into the space between them, he took hold of his dick.

Still directing the action of their fingers inside her, Cassie reached behind her with her other hand and found him, her wee hand curving around him, right above his own. *Christ.* He sucked in a breath and steadied himself, shoulders pressed against the tile. He slid his hand up and down the ridge of his erection, her fingers doing the same, shadowing his movements.

Water continued to stream down over them as they

followed and led each other, her fingers joined with his deep inside her, both their other hands wrapped around him. He tightened his grip on his cock, guiding her, leading her hand from base to tip. In response, she swiveled her hips and pushed her other hand harder against his, forcing the heel of his palm to brush her clit.

"That's good. Oh, that's so good," Cassie gasped and her legs wobbled. He felt her pulse and throb around their fingers. He shut his eyes, head tilting back to rest against the slick tile as he joined her, his cock jerking in both their hands when he came.

She collapsed against him, closing the gap between them as they released their grip on each other. Logan wrapped his arms around her. He wasn't sure how long they stood like that, or how long they would have remained there, letting the water pour over both of them, if the temperature hadn't eventually shifted. When the shower began spraying cold water, Cassie yelped and jumped away from him, reaching for the taps.

She shut the water off and turned, pushing open the glass door. She stepped out of the shower, yanking a towel off the rack and wrapping it around her. "Here," She smiled and tossed him a towel, her gaze straying lower.

"Ye've a wandering eye, lass," he teased, smacking her on her towel-covered bottom. She yelped and ran from the loo, the sound of her giggles echoing down the hall.

He shook his head and pulled on his jeans. After zipping his pants, he checked his pocket to make sure the box was still in place. Mam had said the joy of loving someone was worth the pain of losing them—was worth the risk. He'd always prided himself on being someone who took risks, and hell, asking someone to spend her life with you felt like the ultimate risk. But to know he would have this woman in his life, to wake up to her each day, make her coffee, and then do the things they'd just done together in the shower . . . well.

He'd take whatever risks necessary. Today was New Year's Eve. A time for resolutions. And tonight, as the new year dawned, he'd be ready.

As midnight approached, the crowd gathered to ring in the New Year at the House of Blues grew increasingly wilder . . . and louder. Cassie and Sadie tried to work their way up to the second level to get a better view of the stage, but there were just too many people. "This way," Sadie hollered over the din, adjusting her course and heading for the bar. Her small lithe form bobbed and weaved through the pulsing mass of dancers as she pulled Cassie along behind her. They made it to the counter and Sadie ordered two glasses of champagne. She handed one to Cassie. "Drink up."

"Thanks." Cassie smiled in appreciation. "And thanks for coming with me tonight." Of all her friends, Sadie was the only one who could join her for the party. Ana had a catering gig, Delaney didn't want to deal with getting in and out of the city on New Year's Eve, and Bonnie had plans with Gabe.

"You bet."

The band, a Celtic rock group called The Rebelles— replete with bagpipes, just as Logan had predicted— shifted into another song. The lead singer had wild, curly red hair and reminded Cassie of Bonnie. Thinking of her best friend sent a ripple of worry through her. "I hope Bonnie is having fun tonight."

"Me too," Sadie agreed, knocking back her champagne.

"Maybe Gabe will finally settle on a date, with the new year and all."

"And maybe Bonnie will realize it's never going to happen."

"Sadie!" Cassie glanced down at her friend, not sure she'd heard her correctly in the noisy club.

"What?" Sadie stared into her empty glass. "I'm just saying, things don't always work out the way you want them to. He was her first love, how often does that last? This is real life, not one of your romance novels, Cass."

"Someone is a downer tonight," Cassie chided. "Maybe you should have stayed home."

"I'm sorry," Sadie said. "Let me buy you another round." She got a refill on their glasses, passed the bartender a generous tip, then turned back to Cassie. "May we all find our one true love." She raised her glass in the air. "To happy endings."

Cassie clinked her glass against Sadie's. "To happy endings."

An odd look, Cassie would almost call it wistfulness, crossed Sadie's face, but it was gone in a blink. Sadie tucked a wayward gold curl behind her ear and nodded toward the brightly lit platform of cameras set up across the room, where Tiffany held court opposite from the stage—the queen of the ball, wearing her headset like a crown and wielding her microphone like a scepter. "Do you miss being up there?"

"Not really," Cassie said, sipping her champagne.

Queen Tiffany, smile plastered on her face, lifted her mic to announce, "We're ten minutes away from the New Year and *ChiChat* is ready to count down with you! How about it, Chicago, are you ready?"

The band launched into another tune, bodhrans pounding. As the Celtic stick drums rattled faster and faster, the stage lit up in a technicolor explosion of pyrotechnics. The audience roared, and when the smoke cleared, Logan stood

centerstage. "Aye!" he yelled, brogue rolling. "I'm r-r-eady!"
Cassie watched, breath hitching as he sauntered forward.
"Back home in Scotland, we celebrate Hogmanay with
a'lot of fireworks. What do you say?" He roared, "Let's
start this New Year with a bang!" He ran along the stage's
apron, more pyrotechnics exploding behind him, whipping the crowd into a frenzy as he high-fived the hands
waving from the pit.

"You sure got yourself a hottie," Sadie teased as they
watched more than one tipsy partygoer try to peek up the
Scotsman's kilt.

Cassie kept her smile in place, though her heart was
beating triple time, thumping faster and harder than the
rhythmic pulse of fiddle and pipe pounding through the
speakers. Her thoughts drifted back to this morning, replaying the things she and the man currently strutting
around onstage had done to each other in her shower.

"Hey, party people," Tiffany called, her face popping
up on all the television screens peppered around the bar.
"Only about five minutes 'til midnight, so grab a glass of
champagne and get ready!"

A crowd quickly formed around the bar. Cassie gripped
the stem of her glass as she and Sadie tried to find some
open floor space. She glanced back up at the stage. Logan
had jumped onto a platform and was rising high above the
crowd. She hoped he was wearing something under that
kilt.

She smoothed her hand over the sparkly fabric of the
dress she'd found to wear tonight. It was a simple tank cut,
the color strikingly similar to the pale indigo of the sweater
dress Logan loved so much. She knew he was busy now,
but hopefully he'd have time to see her later. After midnight.

The band wrapped up the number and as the last notes

faded away, Logan raised his mic and shouted, "Is Cassie Crow in the house?"

Or maybe now.

His voice boomed from the speakers, and Cassie choked, sputtering champagne. The guy standing next to her cursed, glaring at her from beneath his man-bun. "Sorry." She began to mumble an explanation, but stopped when Logan's voice thundered through the speakers again.

"I'm looking for a Cassie Crow." Logan stared out into the audience from his bird's-eye view on the raised platform, hand over his eyes in an exaggerated gesture as he searched the crowd. "Cassie Crow, please report to the stage."

Sadie stared at her, her violet eyes going wide, silently asking, *What's that all about?*

Cassie has no idea. She gulped down the rest of round two, heart slamming against her ribcage. *What was the damn Scot up to now?*

Sadie let out a shrill whistle and jumped up on the bar. "She's over here!" Sadie jumped up and down, jostling Man-bun as she waved her arms in the air, then pointed to Cassie's head. A moment later a spotlight swirled in their direction, blinding Cassie and making the sparkles on her dress glitter like a disco ball.

"Ah, there you are, lass." The platform began to lower and Logan nodded at a trio of bouncers standing near the edge of the stage.

Cassie debated hiding behind Man-bun, but before she could take a step, Sadie pushed her toward the triangle of beefcake. Surrounding her, the bouncers moved with military precision, navigating Cassie through the tight crowd, their big, intimidating bodies parting the sea of revelers with ease.

What the hell was going on? If she'd thought her heart was beating fast before, it was nothing compared to what her pulse did now as the security detail escorted her to where Logan stood waiting. The audience cheered while the bouncers hoisted her up on to the stage. Cassie had no choice but to grab Logan's hand as she was deposited next to him.

"Nice dress, lass," he said, pulling her close, putting an arm around her waist to help steady her. As soon as she had her balance back, he lifted his mic and addressed the crowd, his jovial tone turning solemn. "Before the year is over, there's one thing I've got to do."

He gestured to the band, and the pounding beat subsided. When Logan dropped to one knee, a blast of cheers and wolf whistles careened from one side of the theatre to the other. Loud as the crowd was, Cassie could barely hear them above the blood pounding in her own ears. She stood frozen in the spotlight, transfixed as Logan slipped a small velvet box out of his pocket.

If this is another prank, there's going to be one less Scot in the world. Her champagne-buzzed brain couldn't move past that single thought.

Logan flipped the lid of the box open and the crowd, so incredibly vocal moments ago, went silent, the entire room caught up in the moment.

"Cassie Crow, would you do me the honor . . ." Logan paused, clearing his throat.

Oh my God, he's going to do it. He's really going to do it. She had the weird, wild, fleeting thought that now she'd need to get a dog.

"Cassie," he repeated her name, his voice tender, "will you marry me?

She licked lips gone dry—instantly, startlingly sober. In the sudden hush, it was easy to hear the thundering tick of the giant animated clock emblazoned on the floor-to-ceiling projector screen.

Thirty seconds.

She swallowed and shifted her gaze from the clock to the ring, the sparkle almost blinding beneath the blaze of stage lights.

Twenty seconds.

Was he serious? She turned back to Logan, waiting on bended knee. She'd asked him to be serious, and damn, if he didn't look serious. He stared up at her, and as the moment drew out his face tightened, bravado slipping, the cocksure frat-boy grin she knew so well starting to fade.

Fifteen seconds.

Still, she hesitated. She'd said she wanted this, but that had been in the long-term . . . not the immediate future. A happily ever after that started with a happy for now. This was too fast, too soon. Where would the wedding be? Hell, where would they live?

"I'll marry you, handsome!" someone shouted from the mezzanine. The drunken outburst broke the spell, and the crowd erupted in laughter, excitement swelling as the final countdown to midnight began.

"TEN!"

Cassie thought she heard Tiffany leading the chorus of voices booming around them.

"NINE!"

She bent her head, leaning in close to Logan. "Are you for real?"

"EIGHT!"

His eyes sparked, and she knew he remembered the first time she'd asked him that same question. "Aye, lass." His answer was more breath than sound, a puff of air against her cheek. "I'm for real."

"SEVEN!"

Cassie placed a hand on his chest, the rapid beat of his heart thudding against her palm. Despite the waves of heat rolling off him, she caught the shiver that passed through his body when she touched him.

"SIX!"

When he'd opened the lid on that box, it was like he'd opened her heart, her soul. Hope and dreams and love flooded her veins in a rush of emotion. She was Wendy, back in Neverland, and he was her Peter Pan, offering up her fondest wish.

"FIVE!"

Only it wasn't an escape for a night, or a fantasy foreign fling, or even a fun few months Cassie wished for. She wanted forever, and she wanted it with him.

"FOUR!"

She closed her eyes and envisioned their future together, fragments of a million moments, a thousand adventures, flashing by in the space of a single heartbeat.

"THREE!"

Three seconds until forever. Cassie knew her answer, but something impish grabbed hold of her, and she decided to make him sweat a little. Lord knew the man deserved it. Her lashes fluttered open, and she met his gaze.

"TWO!"

His green-gold eyes held hers, one beloved wicked brow arching, more question than challenge.

"ONE!"

In the sliver of time between the old year and the new, Cassie leaned in closer, pressed her lips against Logan's ear, and whispered a single, simple word. "Yes."

"HAPPY NEW YEAR!" The audience exploded in a cacophony of cheers and Logan surged to his feet. He wrapped his arms around Cassie, crushing her to him so tightly she couldn't tell where he ended and she began. He kissed her breathless and then kissed her again.

The flashing lights of camera phones snapping from all directions blinded her. Cassie squeezed her eyes shut and kissed her Scot back, not caring if this was another moment destined to go viral. Some things were worth the risk.

When he finally stepped away long enough to slip the ring on her finger, she laughed in delight. She waved to the crowd, searching for Sadie. Her friend was clapping and cheering with the rest of the audience. Catching Cassie's eyes on her, she gave her a thumbs-up before blowing her a kiss.

All over the theatre, champagne glasses were lifted high in the air, toasts to the happy couple and the New Year shouted in equal measure. The band launched into "Auld Lang Syne," and the sharp, sweet notes of a tin whistle carried the age-old tune across the crowd, who soon joined in the song, voices weaving together with the music. Logan settled Cassie against his chest, hand warm and firm at the small of her back as he began to slow dance with her. "Happy Hogmanay, lass."

"I have my first-footer," she said, snuggling against him, "we're dancing to Burns, and thanks to your mam, I already ate some black bun. It really is like Hogmanay. Only thing missing are the fireworks."

"Och, just wait 'til I get you home," Logan whispered, upping the brogue.

"Who says redheads are unlucky?" Cassie laughed, lifting her head and brushing her lips along his jaw.

The music shifted, the band picking up the beat with a faster paced number, and Logan took Cassie's hand, waving to the cheering crowd as he led her offstage. She'd almost forgotten they'd been dancing in front of hundreds of people. Being with Logan did that to her, made her forget everything else around her. Shrunk the world down to just the two of them.

Backstage, Logan dodged crew members and sound equipment, maneuvering Cassie to a relatively quiet nook. "Come here, lass," he purred, pulling her into is arms.

Again, the outside world contracted as inside, her heart expanded. How could she come to love someone so much so fast? But she did. She loved her sexy Scot. And now, incredibly, she was going to marry him. All the other details—when they would get married, where they would live, how she would manage her job—everything, could wait. They'd figure it out together. She refused to worry about it now.

Instead, Cassie shot Logan a mischievous grin. "Were you nervous?"

"About what?"

"You know what." She raised her hand, wiggling her glittering ring finger. "Admit it, I got you."

He shook his head.

"For a minute," she insisted. "Admit it—I totally got you!"

He grabbed her wrist. "Aye," he said, and pressed her palm to his lips. "I admit it, you got me." He kissed each finger in turn, sending quivers of delight all through her. "But not for a minute." His mouth left her fingers and found her lips. "You got me, lass." He kissed her, breathing the words into her. "You got me forever." He kissed her and kissed her and kissed her. On the tip of her nose, her cheeks, her forehead.

Cassie kissed her sexy Scot back, smiling against his mouth.

Sometimes, the happy endings in romance novels couldn't compare to real life.

Sometimes, real life was even better.

AUTHOR'S NOTE

Like the heroine of this story, I passionately believe in the power of reading. Books are the gateway to endless new worlds . . . a gate that should be open to everyone.

To that end, I encourage you, dear reader, to check out literacy initiatives in your area.

Thank you, and happy reading!
Melonie Johnson

ACKNOWLEDGMENTS

Like any good love story, the road to my happy ending as an author was a long and winding one. I owe many thanks to the many people who have walked this path with me.

My writing crew, Portland Midwest, a group of kick-ass authors and friends who have been with me every step of the way, offering love and advice and drinks in Mason jars. Clara Kensie, Erica O' Rourke, Erin Brambilla, Lynne Hartzer, Melanie Bruce, Ricki Wovsaniker, and Ryann Murphy.

The smart and savvy Sonali Dev and Shannyn Schroeder, whose insightful critiques forced me to dig deeper, unearthing gems that led to a richer story.

My beta readers and dear friends, Amanda Kochenash and Christine Crow. The care and time you took reading my work and sharing your thoughts mean so much.

My Golden Heart© classes, the Mermaids and Rebelles. I don't know what I'd do without all your incredible support and encouragement. Thank you for the endless supply of virtual hand-holding and belly laughs.

The many fabulous members of Windy City, WisRWA, and most especially, Chicago-North. I owe a debt of gratitude for the resources and support I've received and continue to receive from these invaluable romance writer chapters.

My agent, Pamela Harty. Thanks for going with your gut! I'll never forget our first phone call and am so grateful you decided to trust your instincts. Special thanks to Ann Marie Walker—I had to get through the door on my own, but you helped open it.

The most wonderful partner in this process I could ever imagine, my editor, Jennie Conway. Thank you for loving these stories as much as I do. Your endless energy and enthusiasm are everything.

Finally, and most importantly, to my partner in life, my husband, Hugues. Thank you for making me feel beautiful and loved each and every day. For always believing in me, even when I wasn't sure if I believed in myself.

And to my girls, Aishtyn and Gwyn, you are both heroines in your own amazing stories. How very lucky I am to be your mom, to get to be part of your adventure, to see each page as it unfolds.

Thank you all for being a part of my journey. If you are reading this, many thanks to you as well. Sharing the characters who have lived in my head for so long with the world is a dream come true—the happy ending I longed for. But, in the words of one of my favorite tales, *The Last Unicorn,* "There are no happy endings, because nothing ever ends." And it's true, there are more books to be written, many stories yet untold. I look forward to the next curve in the road.

Stay tuned for the next books in the
Sometimes in Love series
by **Melonie Johnson**

SMITTEN BY THE BRIT
&
ONCE UPON A BAD BOY

Available Summer 2019 from St. Martin's Paperbacks